INVASION USA II

THE BATTLE FOR NEW YORK

T. I. WADE

INVASION USA II. Copyright © 2011 by T I Wade.

Second Edition. Re-edited 2014

All Rights Reserved.

Published in the United States of America.

No part of this book may be used or reproduced in any manner whatsoever without written permission except in the case of brief quotations embodied in critical articles or reviews. For information, address: Triple T Productions Inc., 200 Grayson Senters Way, Fuquay Varina, NC 27526.

Please visit our website TIWADE.com to become a friend of the INVASION USA Series and get updates on new releases.

Triple T ProducTions, Inc. books may be purchased for educational, business, or sales promotional use. For information, please write: Triple T Productions Inc., 200 Grayson Senters Way, Fuquay Varina, NC 27526.

ISBN-13: 978-1479150182
ISBN-10: 1479150185

Library of Congress Catalogue-in-Publication Data Wade, T I INVASION USA II / T I Wade.—

Editor – Third Edition – Jim Doak

Proofreader – Kayla West

Cover design – Jack Hillman, Hillman Design Group, Sedona, AZ

Interior design – WriteIntoPrint.com

To our Readers

Thank you all for reading "INVASION USA I – The End of Modern Civilization."

Did you know that half of this story has already turned from fiction to fact?

Check this out:

"To the Author,
 Here is an article on how U.S. weapons are full of "Fake Chinese Parts". A survey found 1,800 fake electronic parts with 70% originating in China. It states this is just the tip of the iceberg. Your new book, Invasion USA, may actually turn into reality!"

To read The Telegraph.co.uk article online, Google: "The Telegraph Weapons full of Fake Chinese Parts".

Preston – Harnett County, North Carolina November 17, 2011.

So hone that hunter's knife of yours—you just might need it!

Strap in and get ready for a sweaty ride!

Dedication

INVASION USA II – The Battle for New York is dedicated to the men and women of the United States Marines.

Thank you for all you do to protect the United States of America, its people and many others around the world.

Note from the Author

This novel is only a story—a very long story of fiction, which could or might come true sometime in the future.

The people in this story are all fictitious, but since the story takes place in our present day, some of the people mentioned could be real.

No names have been given to these people, and there were no thoughts to treat these people as good or bad. They are just people who are living at the time the story is written.

Are you ready to survive a life-changing moment that could turn your life upside down sometime in the near future?

Read on and find out!

 From the U.S. electrical grid and all its backups, engine control-management systems, early warning systems on U.S. satellites, every motor vehicle, aircraft and ship made after 1985, to even simple memory chips inside children's teddy bears—every electronic fuse, resistor, or connector that was "Made in China" became dormant... forever.

At one minute past midnight on January 1st, every modern television broadcast of the U.S. New Year's Eve festivities on the East Coast blacked out. Millions of motor vehicles with an engine-management system or engine-computerized system suddenly died, causing loss of control and thousands of accidents only seconds into the New Year. Traffic lights, directional beacons, communication stations, and all aircraft landing systems blacked out a couple of minutes later, as their modern backups start failing. Children's Christmas presents, nearly forgotten, stopped buzzing, moving, and blinking and went silent. Radios, computers, and all forms of electronic communication devices—even the latest 132 million electronic Christmas presents given only a week earlier (iPhone 5Gs, iPod Nano 4s, iMac Notepads and iPad 3s)—went dead, never to blink on again. Ninety seconds after midnight, the entire electrical grid of North America deactivated itself and went into close-down mode.

The shutdown of the United States of America, and 97% of the entire world, was accomplished by 12:30 am U.S. Eastern time on the first day of the New Year.

It took only 30 minutes to completely dismantle the whole of modern Western civilization as we knew it.

Contents

Prologue		1
Chapter 1	Captain Mike Mallory – Escape from New York	3
Chapter 2	Z-Day +1 – Salt Lake City – Lee Wang – Satellites	20
Chapter 3	North Carolina – Preparations for an Attack	42
Chapter 4	Z-Day +2 – The First Official Meetings of the New World	57
Chapter 5	The First Attack	116
Chapter 6	Z-Day +3 – It's Time to Hit Back	129
Chapter 7	JFK – New York	163
Chapter 8	Where are the Hit Squads?	176
Chapter 9	China	188
Chapter 10	Flight to Alaska	198
Chapter 11	JFK – Major Joe Patterson	204
Chapter 12	The Hit Squads	219
Chapter 13	Z-Day +6 – China Attacked	230
Chapter 14	Z-Day +7 – The Beginning of the Second Week	258
Chapter 15	The Beginning of the End	306
Chapter 16	The Lull before the Storm	322
Chapter 17	Preparation for Invasion USA	339
Chapter 18	Invasion USA	356
To Be Continued in…		403
About the Author		405

Prologue

SOME PEOPLE GOT IT TOGETHER and some people never would.

The worst areas were in the north of the country, although many houses did still have heat—mostly gas. The older houses with gas systems that were purely mechanical-feed units directly from an outside tank to the house worked better. Unfortunately, many of the existing gas lines were controlled through the house's electric heating systems. The gas still was in abundance but the electronics didn't work.

Some houses had electrical house heaters and used gas as a backup, others had gas that could be fed into fireplaces or small gas heaters, and the only systems that still worked were the most simple. In many houses, where four to six people used to live, 30 to 40 people crammed into them. Hundreds of thousands of gas cylinders of all types, as well as simple gas heaters found in the local Home Depot, Lowe's, Wal-Mart or Ace Hardware stores, were cleaned out within hours on the second day.

Whole streets of people moved into one or two houses, brought food with them to barter for heat and warmth, and a new system in America began to grow. People began to live in protective communes where cash was worthless and heat and food was king.

For the people who could never change, they either died very quickly by freezing to death in their beds or were murdered by others who also could not change and were bad in good times and even worse in bad times. These people, mostly young males, organized squads and gangs and started killing for warmth, food, or even something that had no value anymore—money.

An arctic blast hit areas of the Dakotas just after midnight on the second day and moved all the way across the Great Lakes Region by morning, piling up more windswept snow against the houses and freezing thousands by the hour. Wind chill was again the main enemy and the temperatures dropped into the minus thirties in some areas. Anybody who could not find warm shelter was dead by daylight.

With all these people living and keeping warm together, the sanitary systems couldn't handle the new conditions. Nobody was working at the other end of the sewer lines, and the waste cleaning centers and streets began to clog up, toilets couldn't flush, and there was no water and no more room in the outlet pipes the houses used. It was apparent to most that the next crisis could be disease in the northern parts of the country. If the cold didn't kill them, and they didn't succumb to the escalating violence around them, the chances were growing high that unsanitary conditions would begin to impact them.

In densely populated areas of Canada and the U.S. regions just south of the Canadian border, numbers were decreasing so quickly that it was entirely possible that they would experience a 50% loss of human life by the end of the first week. And nobody was coming to save them.

Every vehicle that still worked and the people in them who couldn't find a warm place to stay, started heading south on the major snowbound highways—many with nothing more than the gas in their tank, which gave them about 300 miles at the most with the vehicle's heater on at full power.

With no snowplows to clear the roads, the conditions were treacherous, and many skidded off the icy roads and couldn't get any further. There, the occupants had to find new shelter or perish once their heaters stopped working.

Many of the survivalist-types found farm houses or rural communities where they were accepted and taken into the warmth of the homes, often dealing with frostbite on several parts of their bodies.

Chapter 1

Captain Mike Mallory – Escape from New York

CAPTAIN MALLORY WAS WORKING HARD. It had been exactly twenty-four hours since he had taxied to the end of the runway at La Guardia and waited to be cleared for takeoff. They had been running 30 minutes late on their flight down to Reagan International in Washington, with airport authorities de-icing the aircraft for ice buildup only an hour earlier.

There were well over 100 boxes waiting for what he thought were their customs clearance—either incoming or outgoing. What interested him were the military vehicles and several of the military-looking boxes heading out of the country.

Many of the passengers did not want to take part in the search, several complaining that it was against the law to look inside what did not belong to them. The captain understood and agreed philosophically with the passengers, but what he had seen out of the window had made him certain that there wasn't much chance of being saved by orderly troops or police coming down the street. The passengers hadn't seen the devastation of the aircraft in the skies above New York the way he had witnessed the destruction through the cockpit window. There had been many aircraft with hundreds of passengers each exploding and crashing into each other. His passengers had only seen the world around their flight, and he knew they did not understand what was really happening outside.

An angry passenger shouted to the flight crew helping the captain that he was an important government official and that nothing should be touched—they were breaking the law and they should just sit tight until the government, police or Army came and rescued them. He was adamant that they should just sit down and leave the property alone. It belonged to the U.S. government and he would see that there were repercussions once help arrived.

John, the co-pilot, got angry and asked the man if he would like to go and get help. He would be happy to open the door for him, and he could bring back the U.S. Cavalry anytime he wished. The complaining man grew quiet and blended back into the crowd of passengers.

The cases weren't badly broken, just opened gently with crowbars, and the higher cases were brought down with the fully operational gas-powered forklift and checked for food or weapons. So far, every case had been packed with electrical gadgets. There were large wooden boxes full of toys, iPhones, and every other type of communication tool by the thousands— new and shiny plastics commodities that were now useless to them. One case, however, held red Chinese-made, 5-gallon gas canisters which might come in useful.

Captain Mallory looked at his Rolex. It was ten minutes to midnight when they got back to the military vehicles and the nine cases in that area that had military insignia and markings on them. These cases were uniform in size and were about three feet by nine feet and packed three high on long pallets.

The co-pilot, now qualified enough to 'fly' a forklift, brought the first three military cases down from the top rack. The first wooden case was hard to open. The wood was at least an inch thick and the box was built well.

With considerable pressure on the crowbar, they finally opened it, and the captain moved away light straw packing to find a 9-foot-long missile sleeping peacefully inside. It looked sleek and deadly, and there were at least a dozen just like it in the case. It was certainly not something to be close to if this building went up in flames.

The second and third cases on the top tier were brought down and held the same contents. He thought about leaving the other six alone, when he noticed that the numbers on the cases in the second tier were different. John brought the first case down and the captain found what he was looking for—weapons. They had found the best, a case of brand new M4 carbines with all their fancy attachments. Captain Mallory and his co-pilot had been briefed on these weapons as part of their anti-terrorist training with the airline, and they had completed a 2-day course on firing M16s and M4s—a shorter barreled weapon that might show up in cockpits as protection sometime in the future.

There were five new and complete M4s in separate boxes in the case, on top of hundreds of boxes of ammunition. There were also boxes of night sights and single rifle grenades—just what he wanted to arm his crew with.

The problem was that there were six cases of them, and all he wanted was a few of the weapons. He knew that the bad elements out on the street would have a field day with these if they came across them. This pile of military equipment would certainly go up with a pretty loud bang if fire ever got into this area. The boxes had been destined for Somalia. He found himself wondering why these materials were being sent there, of all places, but he knew it was not up to him to question. Suddenly, however, the hairs on the back of his neck stood up—there could be hundreds of other military supplies in the warehouses around here. His mind was made up. They were definitely leaving in the morning.

Smoke and the smell of fire and burning debris were getting worse outside. The passenger lookout on the second floor came down to give a report. Captain Mallory walked back with the girl, looked out of the second-story window, and saw that the horizon above the buildings on the opposite side of the street to the north was getting brighter and brighter. Was it the sun or was it fire? He couldn't tell, but they could now work better with the brighter light coming through the windows.

Captain Mallory suggested to the couple of dozen faithful helpers around him—his crew and many of the male passengers —that it was time to get the contents of at least one case of guns to the vehicles, then get the fuel through the door and pump as much into the five vehicle's fuel tanks as possible. Any remaining gas in the drums could then be lifted into the SWAT trucks. John the co-pilot reminded the captain that the forklift could not get through the doorway.

"No problem," replied the captain. "I saw a case of green garden hoses back there and there is a manual gas pump in the workshop. We can push a full barrel on its side, get a rope around it, and have a team pull it through the doorway into the other room. Then we can right it and use the manual pump."

It took the first hour to empty the military cases and share the guns and ammo between the five vehicles. It took another hour before all the vehicle fuel tanks were filled and they knew how much fuel was left over—about 40 gallons in one drum on the back of a SWAT vehicle. For another half an hour, the team searched for food and loaded all they could into the vehicles. It was a reasonable amount, including several pounds of cheese, a case of caviar, several dozen cases of frozen sausages and steaks found in the freezer with "Produce of Australia" stamped on them, dozens of 1-gallon bottles of frozen orange juice, frozen carrots from New Zealand, a case of Japanese rice wine, two bags of Indian rice, and several boxes of Swiss chocolates. They also found and stored one of the gas grills with a couple bottles of propane, three large steel turkey cookers, and two working gas heaters with full bottles of propane.

John tasted the water in the fire engine; it was old and had a slight odor to it, but it was good enough for drinking and cooking with. He suggested that they take as much as possible, as there might be nothing out there and they might need supplies for longer than they anticipated.

It was time to rest and the temperature was now several degrees below freezing. A case of Chinese-made children's "The Mechanic" blankets had been found earlier, and there were enough to ration out several to each person. Everybody bedded down to sleep, knowing that departure time would be early.

It was 7:00 am when Captain Mallory awoke. He thought he had slept past dawn, as the warehouse was brightly lit up from outside.

He ran to the second-story window and saw that it was massive flames, and not the sun, that was causing the light. The fires had gotten a lot closer overnight, and the whole horizon around the silhouetted building across the street showed that fires were burning just a couple of blocks away and that they were very big. He could see dense smoke rising, and it was blowing in a gentle breeze over the top of their warehouse. It was time to go—breakfast would have to be on the road.

The captain got the crew up and asked them to wake everyone. Figures were huddled together everywhere for warmth, and as John walked past the broken door with the forklift keeping it closed, he heard someone knocking on the door from outside. He opened the door by a few inches and saw several little faces peeking out from under the same "The Mechanic" blankets they had issued to the passengers to keep them warm several hours earlier. He let in the group of children who looked cold and dirty. Their group included an older teenage girl who looked a complete mess—her filthy blonde hair was covered in mud and dirt.

"Who are you guys?" John asked.

"I'm Sam, he's Paul, my younger brother, and that's Melanie," the first boy said, pointing to a smaller boy about eight next to him and a six-year-old girl. "We found some of these kids running from the fires after we left here with our parents a few hours ago. We were part of a group of twenty who walked out of here to find help. We didn't want to go, but our parents forced us."

"Where are they now?" asked John.

"I don't know," replied Sam. "We got shot at by a group of guys in an old white convertible. We all ran for cover, but I saw a couple of adults get hit. That car and then another old black car, it looked like a Cadillac you see in the movies, chased lots of people and they were shooting at anybody who moved."

"We hid," added Paul. "A couple of these kids found us and took us to an old building where some other kids were hiding."

"The bigger girl over there," Sam continued, "said that she was being held captive in one of the cars and when the excitement started she flung herself out of the back of the convertible and ran for the river. She was hiding in an alley when we found her. She has a few injuries and her teeth keep chattering. I think the men did something to her."

"We returned to this street just before it got light," continued Paul. "As we sneaked around the corner, we found three of the men who had walked out of here with us. They were all dead. They were all shot. We checked in their pockets for a cell phone to call someone for help, but all their wallets and stuff was gone."

"The rest of you are all from around this area?" John queried the kids without the blankets around them, and they all nodded. "Do any of you know how to get out of here and onto any highway going south?" One 10 year old thought that he could guide them.

"Where are we right now?" John asked the boy.

"New Jersey," he replied.

"New Jersey…or New York?" John asked, now confused.

"No, this is the Marine Terminal in Port Newark, New Jersey. Where did you think you were?"

"Next to the Hudson River," John answered.

"That's over towards Manhattan from here. This is Newark Bay," replied the boy. "Do you have anything to eat? We're really hungry."

"He landed in Newark Bay, huh? The captain's going to like that one when I tell him. He beat old Sully!" smiled John, thinking aloud. "Cheese or chocolate?" he asked the kids.

"Chocolate!" was the unanimous reply.

"Guys, go and see Pam, the flight attendant by the refrigerator, and ask her to get you a box of both," he instructed. They moved swiftly in that direction, all hungry except the teenager, who just stood there with her face down and her teeth still chattering. He touched the girl on her shoulder and she pulled away immediately. "What's your name?" he asked. She did not respond. "Can you hear me?" She nodded.

"We are getting out of this place this morning. It's not safe here anymore." He spoke to her soothingly. "The flight attendant can look after you and keep you warm and safe while we're getting ready.

Come, walk with me and I will introduce you to her." He walked over to Jamie, one of the other flight attendants, who was issuing the kids a box of cheese and chocolate each and cautioning them to eat it slowly because there wasn't much to go around. The girl followed John, and when Pam Wallace noticed her shivering, she grabbed another blanket without a word, put it around the chattering girl, and took her into the office.

A meeting was held several minutes later, and the captain spoke. "These kids came in this morning and said that several of the passengers who left yesterday were shot outside last night. This place is getting dangerous. There are large, out-of-control fires coming closer and there is enough ammunition in this warehouse to blow it all to shreds. Is anybody still contemplating staying here and waiting for help?"

Nearly a dozen people put their hands up. Most were older and sitting near the arrogant government official. The captain tried valiantly to convince them to leave.

"We are going to be tight in the five vehicles we have ready and fueled up. Are you sure you want to stay? This government-employed gentleman is operating under a code of justice I don't believe exists anymore. He hasn't been outside and hasn't seen the death and destruction out there." Captain Mallory waited for a change of heart from the people who were obviously in collusion with the government official. "He is certain that you will all be rescued, and I honestly hope he is right and that you will be. This is a democratic country and you can all make your own decisions. When I leave here, however, you are no longer my concern. You will be on your own. Do you understand?"

"This is the United bloody States of America," replied the government official. "Help will come, and you will hear from the authorities about the damage you have done to this building, I can promise you that, Captain. We have food here for weeks, and I'm sure the fires are being put out right now. The Army or National Guard will be in these streets very soon and will take us out of here the RIGHT way!"

"I hope for your sake, sir, that you are right. You can ask the airline for my address when the time comes. My crew and I, however, are leaving this place and trying to get to safety on our own. Anyone who wants to leave with us should get aboard one of the vehicles at this time. If I see the authorities on the way out, I will certainly tell them of your whereabouts. People! We are leaving in 15 minutes." There was a general move for the door to the vehicle room, with many of the people patting the captain on the shoulder as they passed by, all wearing coats, hats, gloves, and "The Mechanic" blankets that they had found in the warehouse. The kids and families were put aboard first, with couples second and single people filling in the empty seats that were left.

The locks on the outside of the garage-type door had already been broken with the torch by a couple of the passengers, and the door was rolled open. Smoke and cold air swept inside as the five vehicles were started up.

Captain Mallory asked for a headcount from each vehicle and put a member of his crew in command of each one. After the news from the boys, the captain and several of the men had packed in a few more M4 carbines and several dozen extra boxes of ammunition and grenades into the front SWAT truck just in case. It would be the lead truck, with the second SWAT truck bringing up the rear of the convoy. Both trucks had a turret-type opening in the roof of the cab, which was a great firing and sniper position.

Captain Mallory went back and counted the people staying— 21 passengers sat there stone-faced, without making eye contact with him. He waited for a moment to see if any of them would change their minds. Not seeing any change of heart, he got into the driver's seat of the lead vehicle with the kid who knew where they were going squashed in between three armed men. One of the men was standing with his upper body through the turret with an M4 in his hands ready to shoot. Without looking at the unhappy people watching them leave, they drove out into the street and then stopped briefly to make sure all five vehicles got through the warehouse door, which was promptly closed behind them.

John was driving the rear vehicle, and they had at least two men who had been in the military and or had combat experience in each cab with the drivers. One M4 with a grenade launcher was fitted in each cab and the other M4s were ready to fire with dozens of magazines filled and waiting.

The final headcount in the convoy was 86 adults and ten children, and there wasn't spare room in any of the vehicles with the drums of gas, food, and everything else they had brought along. They had placed 28 adults and four of the ten kids in the back of each SWAT truck. In the ambulance, there were three in the front and 12 in the back, including the young girl with the flight attendant and the last drum of fuel. There were 12 in the fire truck and six in the police car, which was behind the first SWAT truck with another two M4s ready for action.

In all, they had ten M4s ready, and their owners weren't scared to use them.

Captain Mallory smiled when his co-pilot told him that they had landed in Newark Bay and realized that he had landed the 737 in a much smaller expanse of water than the Hudson. "Like old Sully, I should get a medal for that," he laughed. "If I'm correct, we are right next to Newark Airport, which means that I-95 South is not too far." He looked over at the 10 year old who knew the area. "Okay, kid, which way? You're my navigator. I want I-95 Southbound—we're heading for Florida!"

"Left, Captain," the boy proudly told him. "Then we turn left onto Fleet Street, I think. Fleet Street should be the second or third road to the left, then go all the way up Fleet Street and we should see the on-ramp to the highway." Captain Mallory did as he was told. There were four vehicles behind him, dawn was beginning to break above the smoke, which was getting lighter as they drove away from the fires, and he hoped the vigilantes were still asleep wherever it was that they were sleeping.

The first few blocks were pretty clear, since not many cars would have been in this area at midnight on New Year's Eve, but they still had one turn to the left to make before they would reach the highway.

They ran into a roadblock of bricks a couple of streets earlier than expected due to a burnt-out and collapsed warehouse that blocked the road they were on, and they had to divert south for several blocks before they found an undamaged road that would take them to Fleet Street. They maneuvered slowly through debris as they navigated a route that would get all five vehicles to the highway.

A couple of blocks later, they saw the highway stretching above the streets in front of them, but they could not see the on-ramp. Captain Mallory turned right to go one more block north and then turned left onto Fleet Street and saw the on-ramp right in front of him.

Suddenly a truck drove across their path and stopped 100 feet in front of them, blocking off the street ahead of them. Captain Mallory stopped and looked at the vehicle. It was an old white delivery truck—a freezer meat truck by the look of it—and it had several men lying on top with guns pointing at them. A man in the cab got out and used a bullhorn, shouting at the five trucks in front of him.

"We are not afraid to shoot. All we want is your vehicles. Get out with your hands up and you can all go. We won't shoot you. Leave the keys in your vehicles and get out now, or we will start shooting. You have ten seconds."

"What do you think?" the captain asked the kid, who had his nose pressed up against the inner windshield.

"I've seen that guy before," the kid replied. "He was leading the group who shot at us yesterday. The other kids called him 'The Executioner.' They saw him shoot people in the head, like you see on television."

"I'm giving you one last chance," the "Executioner" ordered into the bullhorn. "We'll kill all of you one by one and rape any sluts you got with you. You now have five seconds."

"I'm going to open the window and take him down," Captain Mallory stated quietly to the group in the cab. The man who had been standing up had already sat down; his name was Jimmy.

"Jimmy, hand me an M4. You take the one with the grenade launcher on it, and after I shoot this noisy asshole, you stand up and aim to take out the men on the top of the truck with the grenade, and then you get out of the way and let Mike here stand up. Mike," he ordered to the man next to Jimmy. "You stand up and spray the back area of the truck once we have these suckers with their heads down. I'll do the same, and, young man," he looked directly at Jimmy, "you pass us magazines when we need them."

"Two!" the man with the bullhorn called out as Captain Mallory locked the M4 into three-round bursts, rolled down the window, opened the driver's door, took aim through the window, and blew the man's head off. Several shots immediately rang out from the truck in front of them, one dinging the side of the SWAT truck next to the captain's head.

Jimmy fired a grenade at the truck and it landed and exploded two feet short of the truck's cab, spraying it with shrapnel so hard that the truck literally jumped back an inch and nearly flipped over. The engine area immediately caught fire as bits and pieces of roadway and metal opened the fuel lines. Captain Mallory emptied his first magazine towards the roof of the vehicle as the truck, which must have been gas-powered, blew up with an almighty roar, dinging his SWAT truck with hundreds of pieces of flying debris.

The shock wave hit them as the captain jumped back into the driver's seat and turned the truck around on the wide road while Mike gave them covering fire from the turret. He headed back in the direction they had come, closely followed by the other four. The captain then slowly and carefully crossed the low concrete center median and drove back around the corner of the next building to get away from the burning vehicle. He turned left at the next road, a one-way street going the other way, and headed along the side of the highway above him.

"Turn right," shouted the boy. "The closest entrance is to the right." Mike looked behind him, saw the four vehicles in their convoy still following, and then knew where he was. The next entrance to the highway was an off-ramp opposite the main entrance into Newark Airport.

He had to turn sharply to get up the off-ramp, as there were several vehicles parked at odd angles in his path. He aimed his truck to drive between them, hitting one out of the way so that the vehicles behind could follow. The top of the off-ramp was blocked with a small car lying on its side, and he slowly pushed it to the side as he went up the wrong way and got onto the northbound side of I-95, driving south.

"That was pretty close back there," Captain Mallory stated to the others in the cab. "I don't suppose we are going to have a moving traffic problem coming the opposite way." He smiled as he saw the four vehicles still following them in his rear-view mirror, but his smile quickly faded when he saw the dozens of crashed vehicles blocking their way in front of them on northbound I-95.

It was hard work driving. The convoy could do no more than a few miles an hour, continually having to veer around blackened and crashed vehicles everywhere. The road was icy and slippery and the snow was a foot thick in some places. Some parts of the asphalt, or concrete, could be seen through the white covering and had only a light dusting as the snow had blown into drifts on the sides of the highway.

For the first mile, they traveled slowly until they had to stop. A tractor-trailer had turned over and was on its side, boxes of what looked like frozen chicken products everywhere, most of them already just mounds under the snow. It had flipped over onto two cars and had crushed them nearly flat. There were dead human and chicken bodies everywhere as the truck had plowed down the highway for quite a ways, piling up cars in front of it.

There was no easy way to get through, so the captain asked the fire engine to pull up close to the rear of the truck. After pulling a couple of frozen bodies out of the way, the fire engine slowly touched the back of the truck, its bigger bulk helping as it pushed the rear of the truck slowly and opened up a space for them to drive through.

"John, get some help and collect those ropes hanging loosely on the side of the trailer. They look strong and we might need them later on," Captain Mallory shouted to his co-pilot as he drove up next to him. "We should pick up several cases of frozen chicken as well. Throw some in your vehicle. We can have a BBQ for dinner. I was thinking of siphoning off some fuel from the truck, but it is a diesel, so it is of no use to us. No worry though. Hey! A light bulb just went off in my head. We have plenty of fuel in all these abandoned vehicles on the highway. We can siphon it out of car tanks, whenever we need it."

They drove on for another hour without having to stop. The smoke was slowly clearing the further they drove away from the city, and the number of stationary vehicles was getting fewer and fewer. At one point they managed 100 yards of highway without passing a single vehicle, and they felt a bit relieved, until they got over the crest of a hill and observed several cars and two trucks in a heap in front of them. For the second time they had to come to a complete stop.

For the first time that day, and two hours into their trip, they saw clear sunlight for the first time. The smoke was gone and there was a slight wind from the south. Everybody was beginning to feel a little more relaxed. The leaders took this time to let everyone out for a quick stretch and a chance to bask in the sunlight —something no one had seen for days, it seemed like.

This crash looked worse than the last one. Again, a tractor-trailer had turned over. The cab had completely ripped off from its trailer and had wedged a smaller truck and a small bus up against the outside crash barrier. The three vehicles were completely black from the fire that must have been out for hours now, and blackened bodies could still be seen sitting in what must have been seats in the bus, the tops of the bodies covered with a dusting of frozen ice. It was not a pretty sight.

On the other side of the trailer was a yellow moving truck—a small Penske Chevy—pinned against three cars, which in turn were pinned to the rear of the trailer. This area of the accident had not been part of the fire.

"Shall I see what's in the trailer?" asked John, and the captain nodded. He watched John climb up over a broken car and suddenly stop. His co-pilot crouched and slowly backed down and ran back to Captain Mallory. "You are not going to believe this, but I just saw a lion and a lioness eating the remains of a human body back there. They are about 100 yards away."

"What?" asked Captain Mallory, not believing what he was hearing.

"Bloody lions, for Christ's sake!" replied John. They were quiet for a couple of seconds.

"Must have escaped from a zoo or something," Captain Mallory replied. "Get everybody back in the vehicles. I'll shoot a few rounds and see if I can scare them off."

He waited until everybody was loaded back in, and he then climbed up the side of the overturned car, looked past the trailer, and there they were—pulling meat off a bloody body in the middle lane of northbound I-95, as if they were in the middle of Africa. He shouted at them and they immediately looked up, spotting him. He shot three rounds close to where they stood, and they bounded away from him, headed south. He watched them go a couple hundred yards before he looked down and straight into the dead and frozen eyes of the driver of the car he was standing on. He jumped in shock and landed in the snow in front of the car, just managing to stay on his feet.

He pulled the door to the trailer open and found it full of garden supplies, fertilizer and topsoil for some hardware store. He checked to see if the lions were returning, couldn't see anything, and returned to the SWAT truck. He instructed John and the guys in his truck to get a hose and some of the empty gas containers they had tied to the back of the fire engine's ladder.

The Chevy's cab was empty and the back of the truck was filled with somebody's now broken furniture, but the large fuel tank positioned under the door to the cab was not dripping, and Captain Mallory opened it. It was close to full and they siphoned 30 gallons out of it. This filled the tanks of the fire engine, the Studebaker, and the ambulance. The SWAT trucks were still half full, so they emptied the 44-gallon drum, filled the two remaining tanks up, and threw the large drum out, keeping all the attachments.

When they were done, the fire engine pushed the car with the dead, frozen driver out of the way. It was the lightest vehicle in their way, and the fire engine made quick work of it. They passed through the gap, all looking out of the windows for lions. It wasn't every day that one could see lions on I-95!

They caught up with the big cats half an hour later. The lions were faster than the vehicles, which were now traveling at a good five to ten miles an hour. They were spooked by the sound of the vehicles and hid behind a car under a bridge as the convoy passed by.

Forty minutes later, and still crawling around hundreds of vehicles on the highway, they reached the 295 bypass and decided to stay on it going south. By this time, they were past Trenton, New Jersey.

A large gas station came up on their left along with a clear feeder road off the highway. Captain Mallory was not comfortable getting off the highway just yet. There could be trouble in the more populated areas, and he felt that they needed to wait for a more rural area to find a gas station that was safer.

Two hours later, they were bypassing Philly, and the dead vehicles in the more densely populated area slowed them down to a snail's pace for quite a while. They drove past the exit to Philadelphia International Airport and were finally able to speed up to nearly 20 miles an hour. They saw no signs of life and no obvious aircraft accidents, but large fires were still burning in and around the cities they passed, and they didn't know if they were the only ones alive.

They had not seen any other moving traffic on their trip since the gang they had dealt with that morning. The snow was clearing on the asphalt as the sun was melting it. Ice might be a factor in the mornings, and Captain Mallory wanted to get as far south as possible before dark.

It was time for a break, however, when they came upon their fifth accident that required moving something. It was just south of Wilmington, Delaware, on the Delaware Turnpike, when they came across three trucks in one big pile and several cars flattened around and under them. One was a Wal-Mart tractor-trailer and the other two were UPS trucks. They must have been all together when they crashed out of control.

The crew helped the passengers disembark the vehicles for a personal and stretch break. With the armed flight attendants as escorts, the ladies and children disappeared into some road brush for a few minutes to relieve themselves, with the men heading off in the opposite direction.

There was just enough room on one side to get the five vehicles through, and the crew drove them slowly past the accident. On the other side of the broken rigs, the captain, while relieving himself behind a crushed Porsche, saw a second, this time a Ryder, truck—a little smaller than the last one. It was next to a big SUV, as well as a second white truck that also looked like it used gas that was just sitting there undamaged several yards further down the road. All three vehicles were empty of people and in perfect shape. The owners had just left them there, and it looked like a good amount of possible fuel might be available. They had ten of the 5-gallon containers with them and were able to fill all the vehicle tanks and still had enough to fill all the containers.

It took an hour to siphon all the gas, while the others enjoyed the warming sun, trying not to look at the odd frozen body in a vehicle here and there.

One hundred gallons of gas later, the captain suggested that they aim for a place he knew—Harford County Airport—just off the highway, about 15 miles away, and hopefully a good place to stay for the night.

They exited the highway for the first time and headed north on US462. The captain had flown in and out of this little airport as a recreational flyer, and he had spent the night in the area a couple of times. It was situated just north of Baltimore.

The area here, although it was still cold and the roads were still icy, was far less inhabited than where they had come from. Deer jumped across the road in front of them, and only a couple of dead motor vehicles were stranded in the road. Again, they didn't see anybody outside, but now they could see people peeking at them from behind curtained windows, and wood smoke wafted in the air. Captain Mallory felt safer around here than in the city, and he wondered if the people they had left behind were still alive and waiting for Uncle Sam to rescue them.

It took time. They drove carefully and slowly at 20 miles an hour and the airport was reached without mishap. The gate was closed but not locked, and they drove in, noticing that no other fresh tire tracks had been there before them. They found the offices locked and the captain didn't want to break the doors down. Instead, they found a relatively new and solid hangar where it was easy to break the outside lock on the door. They opened it, and it was empty of the aircraft that normally resided there. There was a lot of room—enough to get all the vehicles inside. It looked like someone's private hangar. There was a room off to the side with a gas heater on the wall. Captain Mallory asked John to see if it was connected. It was. He found some matches, lit the gas, and it immediately started warming the small room. There was a toilet off to one side and he discovered quickly that it too worked.

"The girls can bed down in this separate room tonight. It should be warm enough. We can set up the gas lamps and burners out here on the concrete, close the door, and be warmer than outside. What does everybody think?"

There was mass approval from the group, and they parked the vehicles inside and closed the door against the cold weather closing in outside. There was no electricity, but they had two gas lamps, and even though it would be dark in a while, the gas in the room and the gas heaters they had brought would make it much warmer than being outside. The grill was brought out and immediately lit so it would also help warm the place. Chicken and sausages were laid out to thaw, and the women and children were asked to cook dinner so the men could use the smaller room to change, use the bathroom, and get ready to spend the night in the larger, more uncomfortable space.

Chapter 2

Z-Day +1 – Salt Lake City – Lee Wang – Satellites

THE WHITE HOUSE LOOKED BACK to normal when the power came on just an hour after dawn on Day 2. The White House was 300 miles south of ten Chinese termination squads—40 armed men driving south on I-95 in a convoy of eight old Ford and Chevy trucks and two smaller cars commandeered from the people who had owned them and who now lay dead in the streets around New York. They were about to leave the New York area and pass Newark Airport on the southbound side of the interstate and didn't see the tracks of Captain Mallory's convoy joining the highway. Fresh tracks marked the separated northbound lanes only an hour ahead of them.

Mo Wang's termination squads had already checked out the first coordinates given to them over their satellite phones. There was nothing there, except a pile of empty five-gallon military fuel containers which they had destroyed. They then set several houses in the area on fire and shot and killed several of the inhabitants as they came out to see what was going on. The fires had spread quickly, destroying house after house.

The termination squads then left, and within a couple of hours, Buck's house no longer stood. It was just a black pile of destroyed timber now that the fire was dying down.

Like the northbound side of the highway, the southbound lanes were also a mass of metal everywhere, and it took their convoy quite some time to wind their way through it. At one point, it took them an hour to move a large truck out of the way. The Chinese men didn't have the pushing power of the heavy fire engine in Captain Mallory's group. The squads were heavily armed, and as the first convoy had learned, they had plastic hoses and canisters to siphon fuel out of the stationery vehicles around them.

They laughed when they came across the two lions, this time on their side of the highway. The previous convoy had scared them and they had jumped the crash barriers and been forced over to the other side. The two semi-tame lions were feeding on another body as the Chinese convoy came over the brow of the hill 100 yards from where they stood. They weren't as hungry anymore, and they were beginning to get pissed off about these humans ruining their meals. The male roared in the direction of the stopped convoy with the lioness looking on.

Its reward for that roar was a dozen bullets peppering its body and the body of its mate at the same time, amid much laughter from inside the vehicles. The convoy moved forward and several more shots took the lives of the dying beasts as each vehicle passed. Sport was sport to the humans, and somebody had to show who the more powerful species was.

* * *

The president was waiting for something to do. His frustration could be seen by the Colombian Ambassador as they ate sandwiches in the Oval Office. Much of the area was finally up and running with the old electrical generator finally patched into the main system. It could push out enough power to light and heat about half of the large building. There was enough fuel in the stationary vehicles on the grounds to keep it going, since the generator was nothing more than an old Ford gasoline engine with a rooftop exhaust vent built into the building structure around it.

The military men guarding the White House were moved into several of the larger rooms on the first floor so they could have the same warmth and light the president now had.

He still had no communication with the outside world, nor could they find more than the two electricians who had been on duty at midnight to look into repairing the communication equipment, of which there was a lot of in the White House. The president had no choice but to wait for General Allen's return.

* * *

Preston's airfield was bustling well before dawn on the morning of the second day. Most were rested after a peaceful night's sleep. The countryside around them was quiet and desolate. The guards had been up all night, however, and Oliver and the puppy were happy to have constant attention and followed the guards around like lapdogs. By dawn, they were back in the kitchen fast asleep and Martie could tell they would be out for a while. It was cute to see Oliver sharing his basket for the first time. Smokey the cat was still hiding somewhere in the house, long forgotten by the two dogs.

Buck, Barbara, Maggie, and the kids ate breakfast at 4:00 am. They left shortly afterwards on their ten-hour non-stop flight to Salt Lake City. This time, the transponder switch was left in the off position, and *Lady Dandy's* tanks and extra drop tanks were absolutely full. Her only freight was the lawnmower generator for Carlos when he got there, fuel for the generator, and 100 gallons of aviation fuel in five-gallon red containers, also for Carlos.

Maggie and the kids were hoping to get a ride to Edwards AFB from Hill AFB in Salt Lake to see Will. Carlos, much faster in the Mustang, was going to leave two hours after them and catch up with them over Denver. His maximum range was about 1,900 miles, and Preston's airfield to Hill AFB was 1,820 miles. If the headwind was too strong, he would have to land in Denver and refuel from the 20 canisters *Lady Dandy* was carrying. If Denver was snowbound, they would have to find a suitable place to meet and refuel. *Lady Dandy* with her drop tanks had a larger 2,000-mile range.

Sally woke up when she heard *Lady Dandy's* engines, and she and Carlos got up, showered and were in the house for breakfast by 6:00.

Sally left at 7:00 am to be at Andrews by 8:00, her aircraft carrying the second of the two fully operational truck generators. Her transponder was also off.

The sun rose at 7:40 am as Carlos, fueled to the top of his tanks, looked around at the weather, climbed in, and took off as soon as the engine was warm enough. He rose quickly through the cold morning air for optimal altitude to use as little fuel as he could. A couple of soldiers had even taken out Carlos' gun ammo to give him less weight and more range. From this point forward, whoever was watching them would not see transponders from this farm.

He climbed high in the morning sunlight, the sun behind him as he reached 15,000 feet, put on his oxygen mask, and then rose up to 38,000 feet for optimum cruising. Carlos' biggest worry when flying without modern electronic direction and communicational aids was the lack of ground-speed, wind flow, and forward weather condition information. He had never pushed his aircraft to its full range, even when he could use all the modern help, but now he needed experience and luck to gauge the distance and speed needed to get to Salt Lake City.

"Hello, Buck, this is Carlos. Can you hear me?" he tried over his radio. A very scratchy voice came back that he did, and that the weather was clear so far. Buck was halfway there and he figured that their refueling meet-up was about three hours away. *"Hallo, darling!"* scratched a second voice, familiar and very faint, over Carlos' radio.

"Hallo, darling, yourself," Carlos replied, happy to hear

Sally's voice. "Where has your radio protocol gone, Sally?"

"Where the rest of the world's protocol has gone—to pot," she smiled back over her radio. *"I'm in descent for my next port of call. I spoke to our old friend Jennifer a few seconds ago on our private frequency and heard she is on her way back to base. I will be losing contact with you in a few seconds and hopefully I will see you tonight. Know of any good hotels...?"* Her voice faded.

"The airwaves are as bad as before with all these amateur radio operators," added Jennifer's voice to the conversation. *"Hi, guys. I'm pretty heavy and on my way home. Weather when I left the snowy mountains two hours ago was clear, temperature 25 degrees. The runway you guys are heading to in*

Mormon country is clear, and I honestly think I have a headwind. I think I'm feeling the jet stream, and it's pushing me in a southwest direction. I'm at Flight Level 24 (24,000 feet) and it looks there are little thin strata further up. Over."

"I'm feeling the same vibes," added Buck, *"and I think I'm making up a bit of time. I reckon, Carlos that you should head slightly north and turn in over our meeting airfield at ceiling, and if you can make it, glide in to our destination from there. I'm at Flight Level 23."*

"Roger that," answered Carlos. "It is sure nice having company up here. I'm at Flight Level 41 and it's absolutely beautiful up here. I'll turn a little north and contact you in an hour. Buck, what's your air speed? Mine's 355, I'm keeping her cruise down a little to conserve fuel and I'm already at ceiling. Over."

"195, and on time, I think. Make sure you call me in an hour. Out."

"What do you have in your stocking, Jennifer, if you are heavy?" asked Carlos, with nothing better to do. It wasn't as if they were taking up too much radio time. They were the only aircraft in the skies that they knew of.

"Oh! Lots of nice presents for Preston," Jennifer replied. *"I have lots of little things that go boom in the night, a couple dozen pilots on board, and lots of this and lots of that. By the way, our leader at your mountain destination has a couple of things he's putting together for you—some little old mountain toy with tracks instead of wheels so you can go and play in the snow. It's quite cute, and I want it after you're done with it. Also, they have left the light on for you. They found a couple of old vehicles and got them working and they have repaired a few things that light up at night when you want to land."*

"Sounds warm to me," stated Carlos.

"Oh boy! Carlos, they needed it pretty quickly and only a few buildings are nice and toasty," she laughed back. *"I'm going in to get some gas and then I'll be heading north. This school bus driving is better than nothing, but I need some action."*

"I've been told to expect some pretty soon. By the way, I assume you are flying quiet?" Carlos asked. Jennifer replied in code that Sally had told her about the transponders earlier. "See you later. Out," Carlos ended.

Three hours later his P-51 flew over Denver International Airport at its maximum altitude of 41,900 feet. He had a slither of both tanks still above the empty line and had told Buck ten minutes earlier that he was now aiming for Salt Lake City. Denver was clear far below him, the runway white as they had expected, and he couldn't tell if he could land there anyway. Buck was already 50 miles behind him and had turned in for a direct flight into Salt Lake City.

He brought the throttle back a touch, put the nose down ten degrees and descended towards Hill Air Force Base at nearly 400 miles an hour, using as little fuel as possible.

An hour later he swept over Hill at 1,500 feet above ground at 425 miles an hour, pulled her up into a vertical climb of 1,000 feet, turned sharp right, and then right again into short finals for the runway running north to south. His fuel gauges were flickering on empty as he landed and taxied to a group of people already waiting for him outside the main offices with a gas truck standing by.

Buck would still be in the air for another hour. Carlos' flight had taken 5 hours, 45 minutes—the longest he had ever done in his P-51— and he was proud of her. He also knew that in strong headwind conditions, he most certainly would not have made it.

He waited as a short ladder was rolled up to his aircraft, and he stood up, stretched his muscles, and looked at the people waiting for him. He got quite a shock at seeing his friend, Lee Wang, with two Chinese ladies waiting for him—most probably Lee's wife and daughter. The base commander was also there with a couple of others.

He climbed down and, as all pilots do, headed off to the bathroom in the main office after saying a quick hello to everyone. He looked at his watch and remembered that he had gained two hours of time. It was Mountain Time here and only just midday.

Lunch was ready for him in the Officers' Club, and they were all steered in that direction while the mechanics refueled his aircraft, checked the oil levels, and gave the Silver Bullet a wipe down. They didn't have much else to do.

"It is very good to see you again, friend Carlos," stated Lee Wang when they sat down with the commander for lunch.

"I'm happy to see you are safe, and your wife and daughter," replied Carlos. "We have much to catch up on, I hear."

"I think we have," Lee Wang agreed.

"Lee and I have had long chats about what's happening," added the base commander. "He wanted to talk to you first about several top secret things. General Allen, I've been told, is coming in later today, after visiting his naval buddy in Norfolk. He's there right now. The general is coming here, refueling, and then he's heading out to Edwards for a meeting. I'm going to go with him. We have a couple of small generators up and running, landing lights, and just enough for a little warmth and basic necessities. I was told that we might get a bigger one—an old truck generator?"

"That's on its way, thanks to the general," replied Carlos. "He's been given four—one for Andrews, one each for you and

Edwards, and one for Seymour Johnson in North Carolina."

"I was told that he will be returning here by nightfall," added the commander, "and then giving all of you a ride back to North Carolina. Captain Watkins and her backup pilots are dropping off gear at Andrews, then Seymour Johnson, then they'll go back to Andrews to pick up some passengers and then you are all meeting for breakfast in North Carolina. So let's have a quick lunch, and then I will show you your ride up the mountain. You will have the pleasure of flying our 1960s base snowplow that we used to clear the runway in the old days," laughed the colonel. "We have it on a trailer behind an old troop carrier that we were able to start in the museum over there. With a dozen troops, you can go and get whatever General Allen wants you to get. Captain Watkins gave me orders from the general when she came in last night and we have worked all night to get prepared for your arrival."

Carlos thanked the colonel. They all looked exhausted.

The food was served and they ate quickly. Carlos couldn't leave until Buck arrived.

"I heard something about F-4s?" Carlos asked.

"General Allen has his semi-secret pet aircraft project stationed here. Mine, too. We have two F-4s rebuilt to flyable conditions, as original as *Tom, Jerry,* and *Mother Goose* are. *Mother Goose* is supposed to fly into your buddy's airfield in North Carolina. She is an HC-130 tanker from the Vietnam era, and the only one flying at the moment. Two more tankers will be operational within the week. Again, she is totally original and was to be stationed here in our museum. She is currently ready to fly and looking good. *Mother Goose* is one of the old in-flight refueling Hercules, and was especially fitted to service F-4 Phantoms in Vietnam. Her engines were increased in power to get up to 330 knots and be able to refuel the jets. She was the general's project for the next Oshkosh fly-in. *Mother Goose* is the only aircraft we have at the moment that can fly coast to coast non-stop and can either refuel helicopters, AC-130 gunships, or F-4s. All our aircraft here are heading out tonight for Andrews and will be stationed there going forward. We have the second and third HC-130 and a third rebuilt F-4 on display at Edwards. All three are fully functional and will be flying within the week. We have tons of munitions for the F-4s, and they will be our primary fighter wing. I hear the DC-3 coming in," added the colonel. "We have a minute or two before you head out of here. There will be two more Hueys and a couple of other bits and pieces. We are getting ourselves together, and I'm interested to know what the Navy has functional, as well as the Coast Guard. They should have a couple of old C-130s on each coast, and they could be our early warning system if there's an attack." He got up, and so did Carlos and Lee Wang.

"I'm coming with you to the observatory," said Lee. Carlos nodded, looking at the janitor in surprise for a second.

Lady Dandy taxied up and stopped where Carlos' Mustang had stood an hour earlier. The P-51 had been pushed back into a warm hangar and was being checked out by several mechanics that had little to do. A tired Buck and crew got out of the plane, and Carlos did the introductions before stating that he and Lee were leaving. The hungry pilots headed off to lunch.

Buck had installed two RV porta-potties in the back of *Lady Dandy*. Both had a curtain on a rail that could be pulled around for privacy and the usage of the stalls made for more comfortable flying.

Therefore, the crew of this plane was not so desperate to relieve themselves. *Lady Dandy* was attacked by several personnel who went about refueling and checking her out for her return flight. Several men unloaded the small generator and lifted it manually into a troop carrier standing by.

Carlos smiled at the small snowplow on the trailer behind a truck. It was about half the size of the usual snowplows found on ski slopes and had an open cab. The plow feature had been removed and a machine gun newly installed in its place above the small windshield. There was room for four—it was about the size of a small car and had a flat rear bed for luggage. He jumped into the cab with the driver and Lee got in with him. They drove into Salt Lake City, one soldier sitting on top of the cab with an M16.

Much like the rest of the country, there were dead cars everywhere. Twice they saw old vehicles driving on smaller side roads but not on the highway. People seemed friendly and waved. The weather was rather warm for January. The temperature had risen above freezing, so the highway was wet and slippery but just passable traveling at 20 miles an hour. They covered the distance to the mountain pass within an hour, and the truck began its steep climb up. The idea was that the troop carrier would go as far as it could and then they would travel with the snowplow.

Parley's Canyon was always a pretty dangerous piece of road at the best of times, with a steep 6% gradient for several miles. The old troop carrier was pretty old, but a powerful piece of machinery. It could be shifted into six-wheel drive if needed, and had been built for tough conditions. It ground its way up the canyon, winding around several crashed vehicles, many of which had dead and frozen bodies in them or lying twisted and broken around them. It would have been disastrous for anybody traveling on this piece of road going downhill and losing control in the middle of the night. A couple of trucks had skidded on the steep slopes and were burnt-out frames draped up against the sides of the canyon walls.

It took half an hour, but the military vehicle slowly made it up Parley's Canyon and all the way to the turnoff to the road that would take them another four miles to the observatory. Here, the road had a steep downhill slope and the entrance to the road was blocked by several feet of snow piled up by the wind, creating a barrier for any road vehicle. It was time to test the snowplow.

The men got out of the troop carrier and set about getting the plow off the trailer. Carlos had no idea how to drive it, but he was told he didn't need to. Within minutes, the driver was ready, the snowplow was started up, and a second man got in behind the machine gun. Carlos and Lee were offered the rear seats. A set of goggles and warm gloves were given to each of them as they took off over the mound of snow at a quick pace. Carlos gave directions, and the snow, now about a foot thick underneath them, crackled as they moved forward at 15 miles an hour.

The four miles were covered in less than 20 minutes. They had to shoot the lock off the main gate and drive over it where it stood, frozen in a couple of feet of snow. Inside the observatory compound, the drifts were more than two feet deep and the snowplow had to move slowly to keep from covering them all with the fine powder.

The parking lot was empty except for Lee's old car still sitting where he had left it and just barely visible under a pile of snow. The whole place was closed down for the holidays. They drove up to the observatory building and found the door locked. Lee brought out keys and within seconds the door squeaked open, still frozen from the icy wind. It was cold inside, very cold. There was no electricity, so Carlos immediately went around to the rear of the building and tried to start the big generator—the observatory's main backup system. The modern generator was also dead to the world. He then helped the men lift the lawn tractor generator they had brought. It was light enough for four men to lift and place the green four-wheeler by the outer door.

One man started it and let it warm up.

Carlos then picked up the long, thick extension cord he had brought with them, and within ten minutes he had it mated into the building's main circuitry. He first made sure to turn off all the unnecessary switches that he knew they wouldn't be using and shouted for the men to connect the power and engage the generator on-switch that Preston had built. He flicked the main electrical switch to "On" and several of the lights blinked to life. He heard the growl of the generator deepen outside as it accepted the added feed.

Once the generator was warmed up and fully operational, Carlos walked over and checked the telescope, hitting the switch to power it up and move it. The large telescope creaked and then hummed as it activated itself very slowly. It worked!

He tried to start his computer, but it was as dead as he knew it would be. He opened the side of the PC and took out several parts— parts he knew were useless. He had modified his own computer over time and it was very different from the average computers sold in stores, since it was tweaked to his needs. He replaced most of the parts he had changed over time, and he knew that by taking out all the modern parts labeled "Made in China," he could make it work.

It took an hour of messing around, but he switched it on and the "On" light lit up. He went through the rest of the observatory's computer system so that they could begin transmitting signals to and from space. The old observatory system was much like the ham radios—30 years old—but had had modifications installed over time. He removed most of the modified parts and replaced them with older parts found in the storage room. Carlos hoped the computers would start on his first try. They didn't, however, and he spent another hour working on the electronics.

Lee brought him a warm cup of water with a tea bag in it.

"Have you changed the communications oscillator from automatic to manual mode and the output and input DOS regulators to manual override?" Lee asked. Carlos looked at him, his mouth gaping open.

"You know about oscillators and DOS regulators?" he asked, his face incredulous. Carlos was shocked. How did this Chinese janitor know about advanced computer electronics? "How do you know that?"

"I have Ph.D.s like you, friend Carlos. Maybe they are 30 years old, but I read to keep up with the modern advancements in electrical engineering and astronomical engineering, and I have often used the telescope when I was alone in here. I can give you a hand, since my old-fashioned knowledge is perfect for what you are trying to modify, and maybe a little more experienced than your younger knowledge. Together we can get this thing working." Carlos stared at the older man, still in shock and with his mouth wide open. Then he moved out of the way to let Lee Wang sit down.

It took Lee only minutes to remove parts and set up the commands of the system. A little work with a soldering iron and he asked Carlos to switch it on.

This time, the observatory's main computer system lit up and the system worked, although it was extremely slow and the only working screen showed DOS characters. The modern screen was back in DOS mode and Carlos looked at Lee again and connected the two computers together. The telescope and its now simplified computerized system suddenly managed to transmit to Carlos' computer. They were in business.

"We need to talk, friend," Carlos said seriously as he looked for his notepad. It took him several pages, but he found the location of Navistar P and typed it into the computer. The whole system took a while to calculate the input with the computer thinking like an old man playing chess, but slowly the transmitter attached to the telescope moved, as it was ordered to by the computer, and then stopped.

Carlos typed in the satellite's call sign code he had written down on his pad and pushed the "Send" button. Nothing happened for several long seconds. The screen's DOS cursor just blinked back at him, but suddenly Navistar P asked him if he wanted it to turn on.

"Nothing four Ph.D.s, an old man, and a young man couldn't handle," smiled Lee Wang. "If I remember my studies over the last three years here, this one might work like the Chinese communication satellites up there."

"How many do they have?" Carlos asked.

"Several, and I have tracked them and also communicated with them," replied Lee. Carlos suddenly felt like he was a student and Lee Wang was his teacher!

"Do you have your information here?" Carlos asked.

"Of course," was Lee's answer. "It is in my head."

"Let's see what Navistar P can do first, and then we can check out the opposition," Carlos said, typing in the command to turn the lost satellite back on. "I've just realized that whatever we do, we won't be able to see the photos the satellite sends us anywhere."

Start-up will commence. Time estimated, three minutes, wrote the cursor on Carlos' screen.

"If it has digital pictures it can send us, how are we going to see them?" Carlos asked. "I don't think this DOS screen is going to give us any color photos."

"I think you are right, but I know what will," Lee Wang answered, and he was gone.

Main directory online, wrote the cursor, and suddenly Carlos knew what this lost satellite was designed to do. There were several sections on the directory:

A. Continuous Feed Photo Display
B. Communication Feed-in
C. Communication Feed Memory Readout
D. Communication Bounce Angle
E. Automated Setup for Bounce Feed
F. Termination Sequence
G. Deactivation

It was something that shocked him to his core. In the 1970s, the Air Force had actually designed a satellite that could send down continuous photos of Earth, as well as act as a communications bounce-off system. A signal could be sent to its memory and the computer in the satellite would find the longitude and latitude coordinates of where the sender wanted the message to be relayed to, and it would then relay the message. Carlos suddenly figured out how he could set up nationwide communications. It was a shock that they had built this system so early and had never used it. The Air Force had just let it get lost and then forgot about it when it went offline.

Lee Wang came back with an old screen and the small computer it sat on. He began to put it together. "This is something that has been forgotten on the other side of the observatory, and I think it is an original data-processing PC and terminal from the telescope from the early 1980s. This old piece of machinery was stored behind several more modern ones, and I was surprised to find it. It is an Amiga PC computer sold by Commodore in 1985, the newer version of the old Commodore 64, and has better graphics. I studied this when I came over to America. This is the first computer I ever owned, and I pulled it apart and put it together several times. Unfortunately, it is not upgradeable."

"That's Steve Crockett's old computer," acknowledged Carlos, "and I think one of the original terminals he must have used when they built this observatory. They must have transferred over to more modern computers and a new mainframe in the 1990s."

"It was, I think, in 1985 when Zedong Electronics started making parts for PC computers," continued Lee Wang. "This model came out just before Zedong Electronics began to build the parts."

"Zedong Electronics?" asked Carlos. "Zedong Electronics makes parts for everything in the world and has ever since I was a kid!" And then realization hit him like a brick and he hit his forehand with his open hand. "Zedong Electronics! It is all of their parts that have malfunctioned. Of course! All their parts have malfunctioned, or have all been directed to close themselves down, possibly through satellite communications!"

"Terminated," corrected Lee Wang.

"And all the backup spare parts, everything, even whole units, everything we use today…are made by the same company!" realized Carlos, sitting back in his chair and looking upwards with his eyes closed. "They have crippled the world, the whole world, and every electronic gadget in the world apart from their own, I'm sure." He sat quiet, his eyes closed and his brain working faster than any computer could ever do.

It took him a minute and then he opened his eyes and stared at the blinking cursor on the screen in front of him. "Lee Wang, you and I need to have that long talk. Tell me now, are you a spy or do you work for Zedong Electronics?"

"Yes, at least until they tried to kill me and my family last week," Lee replied. "It was then that I became a real American citizen and wanted to resign from the company. They were terminating all of their employees, I believe, so that we couldn't tell anybody about the plan.

"I wasn't a spy like James Bond. My job was to find new products they could copy and then manufacture replacement parts for, or obtain a contract to build those parts cheaper than any other company. That was my job. It was more the commercial stealing of blueprints or finding out future ideas. The first device I worked on in China was a new prototype of a Toyota engine-management system in 1982. I had to catalog all the small and important parts so that they could copy and reproduce them for the Japanese manufacturer. They gave me the same model back again a few months later and asked me to dissect it again and see if anything was different. I did, and the electronic parts manufactured by Zedong Electronics were well-made—perfect, but they included a small antenna that you could only see with a microscope. One of these was included on every new part."

"Big enough to receive an electronic impulse?" asked Carlos.

"I would never have seen them if I hadn't used a microscope, and we were not supposed to use microscopes to dissect the new parts, just eyesight. I got curious and wanted to look through the powerful microscope on my desk and saw the antenna sticking out, but I was nearly caught. The miniature part dropped on the floor and broke. I gathered it up, put it in a piece of paper, and looked at it again through my own microscope when I got home."

One of the soldiers came over. They had been patiently waiting by the front door, eating cookies out of the observatory's food dispenser, and had made some tea after Lee had shown them where it was.

"It's time to go," the soldier said.

"We can't go now," replied Carlos. "We are about to get

important feedback. Lee and I need to stay here overnight. We brought enough gas for the generator for at least 12 hours and it is starting to warm up in here. The temperature in here must be at least 40 degrees. I recommend you return to the base and either tell General Allen to come up here or come back and pick us up at dawn tomorrow morning. What does the weather look like?"

"It's getting overcast, but I don't believe it is going to snow tonight, sir. The clouds are high clouds, the ones that show change but not immediate change. I think it will snow tomorrow sometime, but not tonight."

"Good. Go down the mountain and tell General Allen to look for any old military computers at the base. I mean old junk like this Amiga here." Carlos showed the sergeant the computer Lee was pulling apart. "Tell him 'Zedong Electronics'...'Zedong Electronics are to blame for all our woes,' got that?" The man nodded. "Amiga computers pre-1985, and tell him to get over to the local television station. I want him to get one of those mobile television trucks—you know, the ones that have the satellite-feed dishes on top?" The sergeant nodded again. "Somehow get it loaded onto a trailer or whatever. If there are six of the satellite feed trucks, take all of them. Get everyone he can, because I think Lee and I can reroute the electronics to give us a satellite feed from one truck to another somewhere else in the United States. The TV trucks should fit into a C-130 and can be moved around the country."

"Yes, sir," smiled the sergeant, now understanding what Carlos was trying to do.

"We will need to have constant generator power up here, so bring up more fuel in the morning in case we need to stay longer. Lee and I are going to try and work out a permanent connection here and then bounce the feedback to Hill Air Force Base, and then hopefully to any other place in the country that we want. If we can do that, we can use one of the television trucks as a mobile headquarters. But we need these old Amiga computers and the dishes on the television vehicles to work together. Tell the general that I need to move the satellite into position where it is directly over us here and hopefully that will give us simple but viewable pictures of both our coastlines, understand?"

"Yes, sir," and the soldier was gone.

"I have the Amiga operational." Lee spoke up. "It had an ancient burned-out fuse, and I just re-routed the feed past the old fuse. Not a Zedong Electronics fuse—it says 'Made in America.'"

For the next couple of hours, Carlos and Lee worked, downgrading the whole system. It got dark outside and much colder, and they put on extra jackets to keep warm.

By 10:00 pm that night, Carlos pushed the 'A' command for Navistar P and a dark picture of the earth—a very poor-quality picture—flickered on and was displayed on the old Amiga screen. Carlos could just see the dark outline of what looked like the

North Pole, the northern area of Canada and the top of the United States with the sun's rays off to one side and a quarter of the dark planet in the bottom right corner of the computer screen. Carlos typed in new coordinates so that the satellite would reposition itself directly over Salt Lake City.

Navistar P was already moving in a fixed orbit at 241 miles above Earth, but it was rotating a mile a year slower than it was meant to, so it wouldn't keep a constant position. The readout from the computer stated that it would need several hours to perfect its rotation speed and complete the repositioning process, and it asked for permission to move. Carlos gave it the necessary permission, and the latitude and longitude coordinates on the screen slowly started to change.

"That's all we can do for now," Carlos said to Lee. Lee nodded. "Now tell me your story, Lee. I want to know everything."

Lee did. It took two hours, several of cups of tea, and several packages of junk food from the food dispenser the soldiers had broken into. Lee told Carlos about his studies, his degrees, the old man who met him in the corridor one day, and their family's new home on the island that looked like America. Then he told him about his work in America—how he stole plans for new PC computers from Microsoft and sent over many new software programs and motherboards from several companies Microsoft was working with.

Microsoft had themselves stolen parts from IBM, Acer, and all the other major computer manufacturers to make their new programs compatible.

Lee then worked for several smaller companies that were in the forefront of new communication technology. Nokia was a big one. He even worked for Intel, cleaning floors for a year until he got a new job with Apple. With Apple, he became a sales agent for Zedong Electronics.

Until 1998, he had cleaned floors and downloaded plans from computers belonging to directors, designers, and scientists. After 1998, he wore a suit, used his knowledge, and sold several firms on producing everything they needed to be made in China—the whole product, from computer chips to cell phones. He was the one who got the contract for everything Apple was about to design to be made by Zedong Electronics in China.

"I never thought that it was for anything bad," added Lee, over his second cup of tea.

They glanced at the screen. The earth was still there, still very dark, and the center of the planet had moved an inch closer to the middle of the screen. If it had been daylight, they would have been able to make out Salt Lake City's position faintly in the bottom right corner.

"I never thought for a second that something bad was going to come from all our work and selling for Zedong Electronics. The Russians were stealing technology from you. America was blind to it all. Your country was trying to steal technology from the Japanese, and when we came out with the first parts, I'm sure the Japanese then tried to steal it from us. Even a few American spies went over to China. I met a couple of them, and unbeknown to them, they tried to steal their own technology back!

"It was nothing new, just a copy of what was stolen, and at a cheaper price that nobody could refuse. For years I tried to understand the logic of selling parts at cost or even below cost, but once they started making whole units, the profits must have risen quickly. Zedong Electronics must have lost billions of dollars in the first couple of decades and then got it all back and a lot more by the third decade. It was genius, I thought. The only bank that could have loaned them enough for those two decades would have been the Chinese government—or another country's government, like Russia or America—nobody else was big enough."

"Why did you end up here?" asked Carlos. "There's nothing to steal from here, not from this observatory anyway."

"I think that after Microsoft, Acer, Intel, Nokia and Apple, and all the information I had gathered, I was relocated to a place that would hide me from the people in Silicon Valley. I think they were scared that employees from those different companies would remember me and put two and two together. I was getting old, my daughter was about to go to university, and my assistance was not necessary anymore. I was a liability to them," Lee replied bluntly.

"You were paid for all this information?" Carlos asked.

"Yes, 1,000 dollars for each contract, and I got paid 63 times in 25 years. Then they told me to come here. They paid for my little house in Salt Lake City, purchased our small dry cleaners shop in Holladay for my wife, and told me to sweep floors up here and disappear until they contacted me again."

"How did they contact you?" was Carlos' next question.

"Either through a satellite phone we were issued in late 1999, or here by satellite communication."

"Can you find the satellites they used to contact you from here?" Carlos asked.

"Yes. There were three Chinese satellites that belonged solely to a subsidiary company of Zedong Electronics in Shanghai. All the other Chinese equipment is, or was, controlled by the Chinese government. They must have forgotten that I had enough knowledge to trace their contacts back to the source. I was only contacted here once, then I assume I was forgotten until last week when it was time to terminate me and my family. They often checked to make sure I was cleaning floors here that I was living in my house, and that my wife and I were happy. The last time I was contacted was a year ago."

"Where did they contact you from, Shanghai?" Carlos wanted to know.

"No, from their headquarters; it is a large building in Nanjing. I saw the building go up in 1979-80. It took two years to build, was about 30-something stories and the biggest in the area at that time."

"Who tried to terminate you?" was Carlos' next question. Lee told him about the four men in the SUV who looked like special soldiers. His friend from Las Vegas had warned him, explaining that he himself was running away from a Chinese hit squad of four men. He had seen this squad of four set fire to his house and a couple of other Chinese families' houses. Lee explained that a number of families had been killed all over America at the same time, and that it was the work of more than one team of men.

Lee then described the size of the island village north of Shanghai and explained that there could be hundreds of termination, or killer, squads in America, and all the other countries for that matter. Zedong Electronics could have a whole army of them.

General Allen was busy. By lunchtime, he had met with Vice Admiral Martin Rogers in Norfolk. The Navy, he had learned, was in far more disarray than the Air Force. They had zero communications.

The two men went over possible attack scenarios. The general told the admiral that the Air Force was already under wartime conditions with no transponders or lights on during flight. General Allen suggested that all naval shipping use the same secrecy because they were definitely being spied on from space.

The meeting was brief, only an hour, but the general left Norfolk for Salt Lake City knowing that the Navy had two old World War II destroyers in operational status and three old diesel-powered submarines used for training that still had usable torpedoes. Martin Rogers had explained that this was what was left of the whole Atlantic Fleet, and that there were about the same number of operational vessels stationed in San Diego—the remains of the Pacific Fleet. He also disclosed that they still had tons of armaments for these rusty buckets on both sides of the country. They had at least a small chance of sinking a couple of ships, if and when necessary.

Captain Sally Powers was flying the general, and she flew him over to Salt Lake City. They arrived an hour after Carlos had left, had a late lunch with the base commander, and took *Lady Dandy's* crew with him in the C-130 over to Edwards Air Force Base. They all arrived in California around 4:00 in the afternoon. Maggie and the kids were happy to see Will and decided to stay with him until they were needed elsewhere. Will Smart was still not happy about flying across country.

The general met with the Edward's base commander while the troops lifted the fourth generator from Preston out of the belly of the aircraft, and then he took off for the return flight with Buck and Barbara still aboard, back to Hill AFB in Salt Lake City.

It would be dark by the time they landed, and Sally would get a rest while another pilot flew them back to Andrews. On the way, General Allen had told Buck about the developing Air Force they now had. Edwards AFB would have their own C-130 ready in a day or two. There was the F-4 Phantom at Edwards; two pilots would fly her over to Hill AFB tomorrow, once she was ready for flight. Two more Hueys in the museum could be operational within a week, and now that they would have electricity in a few hours, they could work 24/7 on the aircraft. He told Buck about the two flyable F-4s already at Hill and his loan of an HC-130—a Hercules fuel tanker used in Vietnam that he called *Mother Goose*—to Preston in North Carolina. She would be ready at Hill AFB in the morning and could get into Preston's airstrip half loaded with fuel. It could refuel his airfield tanks daily and suck out fuel from anywhere, since it had pre-1980 pumps to suck fuel out of anything, even a commercial airport system or a tractor-trailer.

Then the general told them about *Ghost Rider*, an AC-130A gunship that was already airborne out of Edwards AFB and on its way to Andrews AFB. The gunship was to be delivered to Washington's newly built wing of the Air and Space museum in its original Vietnam colors, and they would see it at Andrews later when they arrived. The general was excited about this one.

They were expecting to pick up Carlos, return to Andrews, and then talk to the president early the next morning. They flew into Hill Air Force Base, its runway briefly lighted, and the general was told that Carlos would not be returning until morning.

The sergeant, who had delivered Carlos and Lee up the mountain, had returned two hours before the general, and the two only troop carriers and trailers that were operational were already in downtown Salt Lake City working on Carlos' orders to acquire as many television trucks as possible. Several dozen soldiers were inspecting the museum and forgotten areas of storage hangars for any old televisions or computers.

Two old 1970-era color televisions had already been located and tested. They worked, and three old computers like the ones Carlos wanted were located on a back shelf of the Repairs and Museum Storage Depot near the base's aircraft museum.

They also had sent word to Andrews and Edwards AFBs using another C-130 that had come in from Nellis Air Force Base in Las Vegas for them to look for the same kind of equipment. They had had radio communications for over thirty minutes now. An old base radio from the Vietnam War was now operational and working with Preston's frequency and solar towers. This gave them a total of four communication stations across the country—Preston's farm, Andrews AFB, Hill AFB, and Edwards AFB. National communications were getting better!

Chapter 3

North Carolina – Preparations for an Attack

PRESTON'S AIRSTRIP WAS BUSY, AND in between flights he checked the asphalt on his runway for damage. It had been well built, him having spent a lot more money than he had needed to strengthen the ground under the asphalt. He had placed three layers of granite rock, stones, and chips on top of each other to allow the asphalt to bed down on a strong base. He and Joe had built it well, but they had never expected it to handle the larger-than-life C-130s that were now coming and going on a daily basis—every arrival heavier than the one before.

Apart from a slight normal crack here and there, however, it seemed to be standing up well. The C-130s, meant for dirt landings, had several tires in their main landing gear wheel-wells, which distributed the weight a little, and up to now all the aircraft had landed and taken off with very little cargo. That was until Jennifer came in from Salt Lake City.

Tom, the C-130, returned a couple of hours after Carlos left that morning. It was 10:00 am on the second day when Preston heard Jennifer call in over the radio in the lounge. He had just set up the powerful speakers from the new "kaput" stereo system to work outside on the roof of the house to broadcast to anybody working that somebody was coming in for a landing. There was much that had already been completed outside. Barbed wire had been installed along the front fence area and around the only gate at the entrance to the property.

The barbed wire was weird stuff, and dangerous, Preston found out when he was helping to stretch it out. Thick protective gloves were needed. The rolls were extremely thick and weighed a couple hundred pounds. The forklift had been needed to transport them to the gate, which was pretty tough for the little guy on an uneven road surface with its small wheels. It had taken most of the morning to string out the first six rolls. Each roll was placed on the ground and the wire end tied to Preston's truck. He pulled it away from the roll, and the round wire formation just elongated out 100 feet and became a twisted length of dangerous wire, three feet high and three feet in diameter. The next one was pulled out next to the first one, and then the third was placed on top of the first two, creating a triangular effect and becoming a six-foot-high wall.

The same was done on the other side of the gate, and then the gate was dressed in cut sections of the wire. It still moved, but was virtually impenetrable when shut. Preston left the men and his truck to complete the next 100 feet and returned to inspect the runway.

"Hi, Jennifer, Preston here." He responded to her call. It was pretty quiet in the house with several members gone and the new arrivals still sleeping.

"Hi, Preston. I'm about 20 minutes out and coming in a little heavier this time. I have some Christmas gifts for you from the Rockies," she replied.

"Wind from the north, five to ten miles an hour, temperature 38 degrees, runway lights are removed, you have the whole field.

Over."

"Roger," she replied. *"Will be coming in from the south, unpacking, and then refueling at your neighbors to the south. They are now up and running and selling gas."*

"Good to hear that. We are heading out anyway to get some extra, just in case, but I'll wait for you," he replied.

She came in, her rear tires hitting hard on the ground several feet before the beginning of the asphalt and using the whole runway this time, her propellers on full reverse, slowing her speed. This time, he did see plumes of blue smoke spew out from the tires as she came to a heavy stop.

He was surprised to see a small, camouflaged bulldozer and a second forklift back out of the rear of the C-130. That was not all. There were another two dozen troops, tents, two porta-potties, boxes of rations, gas cylinders, and another dozen rolls of barbed wire. Then three large mortars, nearly five feet tall, and dozens of cases of mortar bombs on pallets were lifted out. Lastly, bags of what looked like sandbag cases, on plastic wrapped pallets, were forklifted out.

"We are digging-in here," stated Jennifer, standing next to Preston and wiping her face with a cloth. "We are planning to increase your perimeter around the airfield, take down the brush and the trees with our old Vietnam museum-piece mini-dozer here, stolen from Hill's museum, and set up a perimeter of sandbagged mortar and machine-gun placements—especially around the entrance, which should have the barbed wire up ready to repel any unwanted people."

"Yes, we installed the first 200 feet of it this morning. Horrible stuff, that barbed wire," Preston replied. "We are going to need at least 600 yards of the stuff just for the front area, and I worked out another 700 to 800 yards to cover the sides. The rest of the perimeter should be ok with the natural water boundary. We can't do the whole lot."

"I agree," acknowledged Jennifer, "just enough to stop anybody coming in from the farm's frontal boundary. Once we clear the brush around the sides, we can protect it with night vision goggles and infra-red warning devices. I know that the wildlife will cause some issues, but that can't be helped. The troops will have what's left of the wire out front by tonight and the general wants to place tripwires outside the fence to warn us of any human creepy-crawlies crawling around out there. The general thinks that an attack could happen here as soon as tomorrow night and we need to be ready for them. Tomorrow we have a platoon of Marine snipers coming in, and they will be placed up and down the highway to let us know if we are going to get company. They will make sure that nobody leaves the party. I suggest that you have one of your aircraft ready. You might be the air backup and you'll get to use your machine guns. I know Martie is not dying to use them on humans, but she may not have a choice."

Joe radioed in that they were on their way over, and Jennifer was impressed by the loud speakers blaring out the message. The guards at the gate heard it on their radios and replied that they would look out for them. It was time to go and get the other two fuel trailers.

"I saw a couple of little Cessna 172s at the airport and thought of getting someone up there to patrol tomorrow," said Preston, nodding up at the sky. "When some of our fly-in pilots actually return, and we are almost out of flyers right now, it could be an early warning system to get something up there to serve as a spotter plane. A Cessna 172 could stay up there for four hours at a time, and as long as the heater works, it could give some of our fancy Air Force or civilian pilots some very boring flying time."

"No one thinks that anything will happen today," replied Jennifer. "It's only been 36 hours since New Year's Eve, and they couldn't have seen our transponders until we used them eight hours later. If they have troops in the United States, the general thinks that they will have to travel in from around Washington or even further north. It will take them time to decipher their information, contact their troops, who will need to find transportation, and then drive down here. The highways are pretty lousy up around Washington, and they must be worse further north. If they start moving today, most probably later today, they would still only be here by dawn tomorrow at the earliest, and then they will still have to case the joint. That is when our troops will let us know, and of course your 'eye in the sky,' if you get one up during daylight hours. Anyway, I'm headed off to Seymour Johnson to refuel, grab some more men, and wire they are putting together right now, and return here. Then I think I'm going north."

"How much fuel can the Air Force get their hands on right now?" asked Preston.

"They have set up a system hotwiring one tank of jet fuel at Seymour Johnson. It's the smallest one of three tanks, but still holds about a million gallons. The other two are bigger. Andrews AFB has your generator up and running and has access to a fuel tank similar to one at Seymour Johnson. Hill AFB should have one selling gas soon, as well as Edwards AFB, so we have enough jet fuel to start a war, just not enough airplanes to use it all." Jennifer paused to look at her watch and check the weather pattern above her.

"Also, before I forget, there are one or two more C-130s in service as of later today, so expect some new traffic in here. I hear we might have three old F-4s serviceable today or tomorrow as well. They were General Allen's retirement project for the Air Force museums. He told me that he had *Tom* and *Jerry* completed, two F-4s at Hill, and a third one at Edwards. *Mother Goose* is a surprise—one he wouldn't even tell me or Sally. She should be here sometime today, and his 'surprise' to you will hopefully be here by morning. *Mother Goose* is yours, on loan from the Air Force for a while. I was told not to tell you about her, or the surprise—the even bigger surprise."

Preston was left still puzzled as he watched Jennifer in the now-empty C-130 taxi and take off for Seymour Johnson. He stood with Joe, David, and the team of Joe's sons ready to roll back to RDU. This time they had the two armored cars, the Saracen, and the two tractors to pull the fuel trailers back. Both he and Martie, who was taking Little Beth with her, would fly two more Cessna aircraft back.

They left the front gate, which was now looking very secure, and Preston was surprised to see his truck at the end of his driveway with a large green wooden sign on two legs being lifted out of it. They stopped and went over to the men digging the holes in the ground for it with shovels. "Strong Air Force Base," it read in big letters across the top, and there was a picture of a Stealth Bomber in the middle. "Government Area—Do Not Enter" was written underneath in smaller letters.

Preston smiled. "The general has been hard at work," he said to the crew.

They drove down US64 towards the city and the airport. Carlos' three Colombian bodyguards accompanied them this time, as well as the sergeant and four men in the Saracen. They all added firepower and wanted to see the country and the effects of this disaster on the surrounding area. The 'newbies' hadn't seen much except a street or two in New York, or flying over in aircraft from Seymour Johnson. Preston rode in the Saracen with Martie and Little Beth, who would not leave Martie's side. Little Beth had slept well, was full of food, and seemed to have recovered a little from the shock of her harrowing ordeal.

The road was as quiet as the last time. The air smelled like smoke again and he could see the rising of smoke here and there through the trees in the more densely populated areas to the east of them—fires that had not been there yesterday. This time, they turned right down State Road 751—a rural road that would take them to the entrance of the nuclear power station in New Hill.

Three miles later, they turned into the main drive to the power plant. The gates were locked and there was no movement. The main buildings were off the road by 100 yards or so, and the armored car easily tore down the gates so they could drive through. The first building was nothing more than offices and a welcome center, and they continued past it for another mile. This time, they came to a second gate—the same kind as the first—and it was locked, with no guards guarding the small guard house. This time there was a bell to be pressed, and several seconds later a guard came running down the road.

"Are you the Army?" he asked. "We are not allowed to let anybody through unless you are the government. There are two gunners positioned in the woods and they are armed."

"We are on orders from the President of the United States," Preston answered, getting out of the Saracen's side door. "Washington wants to know the condition of all the nuclear reactors immediately and whether they are a severe danger to the country. There are no communications and these troops here are Air Force personnel out of Seymour Johnson. The Air Force is willing to place troops here for protection against any future terrorist threats, but first they want to check to see if the reactor is safe." The guard ran back the way he had come, presumably to report back, and the gate opened several minutes later to allow them through.

Preston went into the main office and control center with the sergeant and two men. The two men were armed, and there was a group of very anxious-looking people waiting for them. Several still wore white coats, and there were three guards around the main door.

For an hour, Preston was shown around the control center. The system had gone into full safe shutdown mode, and nobody could stop it. There was nothing they could do once the shutdown control system had been automated.

"It's a measure we knew was in place, but only for extreme emergencies where nobody was alive in this room and automated procedures were needed," explained the engineer in control. "It went into its automated mode exactly one hour after New Year's Eve and the system, now still several days from complete and safe shutdown, is working perfectly and out of our control. All we can do is watch and monitor," he finished.

"What is still needed for complete shutdown?" asked Preston.

"The rods are closed and dormant, but the reactor's cooling will still take several days to bring temperatures down to a safe level. The electrical turbines are down, but the cooling pumps are still operating, pulling in cold water from Harris Lake. I believe that another week's pumping will be needed until the final phase is complete," the man in the white coat replied.

"Do you need military protection?" the sergeant asked.

"I would assume so, since we do not know what is going on out there. This installation needs constant protection and I would suggest that a team of soldiers stay here until further notice. We have the gas heating system working and a small generator lighting up the control center. We have several days of gas and supplies, but naturally we would like to go home to our families at some point. We've all been on duty since New Year's Eve and don't really know what's happening. What is going on out there?" he asked.

Preston gave him a brief rundown of what he knew, and the Air Force sergeant told him that they would be back in 24 hours with a guard detail and supplies. They also explained that there was no way they could help get the staff home, unless one of the group had an pre-1985 vehicle. Two of the power plant's security guards stated that they did, and Preston explained that any vehicles older than 1985 still worked and that they were priceless at the moment.

The two guards offered to get everyone home. Preston suggested that somebody who knew the workings of the power station should stay at the plant at all times until further notice. They agreed to break into shifts, and there were a couple of dozen other employees that they could go and find.

The armored car convoy left two men to add to the guard detail and helped stand the outside gate back up as good as possible. Then they returned to US64 to drive towards the airport.

As they got closer to RDU, they saw more fires in the suburban areas. Houses were now on fire here and there. They saw the odd movement—people driving around on lawn tractors and such—and Preston thought that this might be the only form of transportation in the United States for the foreseeable future. It was slow, but you could get to the supermarket on lawn tractors and take your loot home!

Several other cars were spotted driving around Apex as the convoy drove north along 55 towards the airport. Several shops were on fire. A supermarket had dozens of people running and one or two vehicles driving around outside of it. They were looked at from all directions, but not a shot was fired.

They got to the turnoff to the main street and found that it was blocked off by a couple of armed men wearing dirty police uniforms and white armbands on their left arms. At the power station, Preston had jumped into the front cab of the front tractor with Joe and sat with a soldier who had an M4 carbine at the ready.

They stopped. "Who are you?" asked one of the men in front of them, feeling a little overpowered by the amount of firepower that had just driven up. He wouldn't have had much of a chance if these were vigilantes. Preston got down from the truck's cab and went over to talk to the policemen. They had crowd barricades up, much like those at a football stadium.

"I'm Preston Strong." He introduced himself. "I live and own a farm in Apex out towards the lake. Are you real cops?"

"Yes," replied the man who had asked them the first question. "There are six of us at three barricades around Apex. We are starting a neighborhood watch until the power gets turned back on again. We all live in the Apex area and are trying to stop the supermarkets from being ransacked here in town, as well as keep away any troublemakers. We have shot three people so far, but they shot at us first. We have our shotguns from our police cruisers to keep the peace."

"Can you show me police identification?" Preston asked.

"First, tell me who you are. Those are armored personnel carriers I've seen at a show. Are they U.S. military?" the man asked.

David got out of the rear armored car and came up to the roadblock. "I know this man," he said. "I've met him a couple of times. He is an Apex policeman, I can verify that."

"Yes, and I remember you—you own these babies. What I would give for one of these at the moment!"

Preston shouted to the sergeant in the Saracen to come out, which he did. The policeman was even more relieved to see real U.S. Air Force clothing, and he put his shotgun down.

"Do we have an extra carbine and a few boxes of ammo for this man?" Preston asked. The two military men swapped IDs and both verified each other.

"What is your mission here?" the sergeant asked the two police officers.

"Trying to keep our town as safe as possible, Sergeant," the first police officer answered. "We have six guys on duty at all three of the major roads onto Main Street—four hours on and eight hours off. We have 18 crew members left in the Apex Police and Fire departments. All are still on duty and trying to keep the crap out of here. We reside in this area and are currently working on getting the people organized to help us with our neighborhood watch program and close every single other road into here permanently. We have several vehicles which still seem to work and are collecting as much food from the supermarkets around here as possible. Our collection trucks have white stars painted on their side doors. I don't know how long we are going to need to survive, but we are planning to survive this. I'm sure the electricity will come on sometime, and we currently have enough room and heat for 1,000 people."

Three M4s were handed over from the military personnel with 100 rounds of ammo per carbine. More was promised for the next day, once the okay was given to arm people with Air Force weapons. Preston told them to get all the new lawn tractors they could find from the local stores and find an electrician in the area to convert them into mobile generators. With 30 horsepower, a lawn tractor engine could light and heat a house. They would return tomorrow, once he had spoken to the commander of operations.

The convoy didn't need to go through the barricade, as their destination wasn't down that way. They continued north, and many of the cars in the middle of the road had already been pushed off the asphalt and into the grass. They went down the hill, next to one of Apex's shopping centers, and saw people scurrying everywhere looting and carrying out handfuls of food, clothing, and blankets. Two vehicles stood in front of the main supermarket and both had white stars painted on their doors.

They continued north up the 55, connected with 540 Ring Road and got onto the beltline highway that would take them the rest of the way to the airport.

"What do we do with all these poor people?" Preston asked Joe. "Do we help them or do we let them die?"

"That sure is a hard question," replied Joe, pulling onto 540 a couple of miles before the site of their last encounter with the guys in the green truck. Apart from the same dead cars, the road was empty except for a family pushing a shopping cart down the side they were traveling on. The small group didn't know what to do and just stood there as the convoy passed. "Someone else would have shot them and taken their looted stuff, I suppose," added Joe. "Hell, we can't feed the world. There are most probably tons—millions of tons, maybe—of food at the military bases, but if we tried to feed 300 million people, it would all be gone in a day, maybe two. I think that we should all sit down with the general. It's his food now, and we need to discuss what can be done for the civilians. Carlos and that crowd will be back tomorrow, and I'm sure they will know a lot more by then. I've been thinking about it, though, and even the modern farm equipment is dead now. How are they going to feed 300 million people with a bunch of old tractors?"

"Good point," Preston replied, as they pulled off the highway and onto the feeder road to the airport.

It was then that they came across a gunfight. Just outside the airport entrance, a blue car was overturned and three men were firing from behind it in the direction of an old U-Haul truck manned by another group in the ditch on the other side of the road. There was a lot of heavy fire being exchanged by the sound of it. As the convoy came out from under an overpass a couple of hundred feet away, both groups saw the newcomers and turned their fire on the convoy. Joe braked hard and did a quick U-turn, and the second tractor driven by one of his sons followed him. The Saracen stopped behind the first armored car and the second one came abreast of the first one. The two tractors retreated under the bridge and stopped in the shadows to watch the fight. There was no reason to get the vehicles damaged.

Preston could hear several bullets ricocheting off the armor as the two Ferrets' .30-caliber machine guns each chose a target and emptied 10 rounds per second into each vehicle. The blue car virtually disintegrated several seconds later and then blew up. The old truck became holey as the machine gunner raked its side. The Saracen then moved into a clear path and all three vehicles concentrated their fire on the old truck, cutting it to pieces with parts thrown everywhere.

It had taken about a minute, and the guns stopped, still smoking from the heavy fire. The Ferrets moved forward and there were gunshots still coming from behind the blazing car.

All three machine guns again blew holes into anybody who moved in the vicinity.

Then everything went quiet as the Ferrets moved forward to the fires on each side of the road to inspect. Nobody got out, a turret was opened and the tractors were told to come through. They passed through the scene, and Preston's face went white when he saw nearly a dozen dead and bloody bodies by the burning truck and several more lying around the car, which was now a mass of flames. They were all young boys, and there were rifles everywhere. Preston asked Joe to stop so he could get out. So did the soldiers and bodyguards in the other vehicles. Martie, and Joe and his boys, stayed away.

It was carnage, with broken bodies everywhere. "I suppose that was necessary?" Preston asked around.

"I believe so," replied David, walking up and standing with him. "I was hoping that they wouldn't shoot, but we would have been pretty dead by the time we opened up with our weapons if we had been in a regular truck or a car. They aimed straight for where we were sitting, with no warning shots at all. Plus, I reckon several of them were hit before we got here. It looked like they had been going at it for some time. Why did you get out?"

"These guys are well-armed," replied Preston. The sergeant and his troops stood guard, making a perimeter. "If we don't take these guns with us, then other groups will find them and pick them up and we will have the same shootout somewhere else tomorrow. I can understand Will Smart's predicament when he had to shoot those kids in California. I assume the rules of engagement have changed and that only the strongest will survive. I think we should pick up all the weapons and ammunition and hand the stuff over to the cops we saw back in

Apex. I'm sure they could put it to better use than these guys."
"They do look like a mean bunch," stated the sergeant.

"I agree," added David. "It didn't take these guys long to go bad. On the way back, and if the vehicles have stopped burning, we should pull what's left of them across the road. It might deter others coming here, and if they are been moved, it could mean that somebody's in the airport."

"Good thinking, David," replied Preston. "It could also serve as a visible warning if we have to fly in here. I'm hoping to fly back, so you guys do what you need to do and we can see from the air if our placement of these vehicles has been moved."

The convoy continued and found the gate still locked and the airport just as they had found it yesterday.

"Let's look for any old vehicles in the long-term parking garages," suggested Preston. "We could grab a lot of food from the terminal and take some supplies back to the cops to feed their people." Everybody agreed, and after they broke the lock, the Ferrets drove into the parking building and began to cruise around.

Martie got out and inspected the aircraft on the ground. They looked in flyable condition but were all locked. It was time to get into the private terminal. As they walked over to the separate private air terminal, they heard a car's engine start up from the parking area, and then a second one did the same.

Preston threw a rock through the window of the door leading from the apron into the terminal and carefully walked in with Manuela and Mannie as protection. He found the flight office where several keys were hanging and kicked the door in. The two Cessna 172s belonged to a small flying school, and both sets of keys hung on the wall with several others.

The two bodyguards followed Preston as he went through the whole terminal. Mannie found a kitchen and walk-in warm refrigerator full of food, along with a small storage pantry to one side. Then they walked outside with the keys.

Joe already was over by the Delta hub hitching up the trailer, and his sons were getting a second trailer attached. David, one of the soldiers, and Dani drove through the gate with an old rusty Suburban, a Mazda truck, and a small Ford half-ton. They stopped in front of Preston.

"These are the biggest we could find," reported David. "I think there are one or two more old ones among the hundreds of new ones. It's like a car dealership up there."

"Get everybody together," ordered Preston. "Let's clean the private terminal out first and put the stuff in the Ford. It should all fit. Then we can get into the Southwest terminal and see what's in there. We can always come back tomorrow and empty out the newer terminal. We'll need Joe and a large trailer for that one."

With everybody working, it took an hour to fill all three vehicles.

Preston found several still-sealed cases of good single-malt whiskey in the bar cupboards under the liquor display and packed these into the Cessna 172 that Martie was going to fly home. He asked Manuela to go with Martie, and they immediately took off in one of the 172s, with Little Beth sitting on Manuela's lap in the right seat, and she waved to the group as they raced down the runway. It was necessary for Martie to get back and monitor the radio.

Preston got into the other 172 with Mannie and told the rest of the guys to deliver the three full trucks to the roadblock and then get the fuel back to base. He started up the plane and taxied around to the newer RDU terminal he had never been to. It had only been built a couple of years earlier and he didn't often fly commercial.

As usual there were over a dozen aircraft at the gates and it wasn't difficult to get inside. The inside was like the other one, semi-cleaned and empty. Security had closed the doors as they had left, and here there were dozens of closed restaurants, shops, and several bars. Now he only had the small Cessna and could take maybe 300 pounds in the rear seat. There were bread and bagels, still semi-fresh, and they packed a couple of boxes into the plane. They weren't heavy, but it could be the last fresh bread for a long, long while. There wasn't much more room, but Preston couldn't resist spending a few minutes to break the lock into the Duty-Free shop. Here, he was amazed. In the back were well over a hundred cases of top quality bottles of everything he loved.

"Let's take a dozen cases, Mannie. I'm sure we can squeeze them in, and this stuff could all be gone by tomorrow." Mannie agreed, and they found a trolley and took the cases back to the doorway where they had come in. He couldn't help but add a bottle of Martie's favorite perfume and a couple of odds and ends to the trolley.

It was difficult, but they removed the big boxes and put the bread and bagels, still in plastic bags, back in. The little Cessna was now full to the roof, and so were its tanks, Preston realized. The poor aircraft was probably at maximum weight. He was right. She took a lot of runway to get airborne for a little 172 and slowly gained height, giving them a low view of the blackened vehicles now pulled onto the road and guarding the airport. David had even draped a few bodies over the vehicles, Preston assumed, to deter any other visitors.

The grisly site would stop him going any further, but he would be flying in with a C-130 on the next trip to clear the complete terminal out. It would require a whole C-130's cargo bay to empty it.

He climbed and headed south at first and then west over Apex, finally making 5,000 feet. Mannie turned the heater to full power and looked for the convoy beneath them, which was just leaving the roadblock. He decided to do a quick inspection of the I-95 corridor and flew east for 15 minutes. He flew up the main north-south artery for a ways through North Carolina, and the road looked like all the others. There were battered vehicles everywhere on the highway, fewer than in Raleigh but still in both directions. Some looked undamaged and others had been in big accidents. Dead tractor-trailers comprised at least half of the vehicles on the highway.

He then flew back along US64 going west and caught up with the convoy as it was about to turn onto his road and off the highway. He radioed in and brought spotter aircraft number 2 down to its new home, full of bread, bagels, and booze.

Chapter 4

Z-Day +2 – The First Official Meetings of the New World

THE HIGHWAYS TO THE SOUTH of the northern U.S. states were beginning to get busy. Since there was nobody to read the local weather reports, very few knew that a new and large storm was currently brewing over Idaho and Wyoming. It was dark in the United States and Canada, and it was 3:30 am when the storm blew into the northern United States from Canada and became what many would call an "arctic blast."

In Yellowstone, the animals sensed and knew what was coming, found shelter, and hunkered down ready for the harsh icy winds that began to lash at them. The humans that were still alive were not as good at predicting future weather conditions, because they were used to the well-dressed guy on a flat screen who told them what they needed to know. In rural areas, farmers and outdoor people gathered and made sure there was going to be enough firewood—the rest of humanity was either in a place of safety or not!

By 7:00 am in Boise, Idaho, the temperature started a rapid descent as the warmer air was pushed south. The temperature plummeted down 15 more degrees by 9:00 am. The sky was clear and blue.

The wind started blowing the dirty air out of the Salt Lake City basin around 10:00 am. The temperature in Park City, Utah, as well as the other side of the main highway to the east where Carlos and Lee had left two hours earlier, dropped from -13 to -27 within two hours.

It got colder and colder as the icy winds shot out from the north, bringing all the freezing arctic air southwards at 30-plus miles an hour. The wind chill dropped to -30 and -40 in some mountainous areas, and people who had no heat perished quickly.

The blast spread out quickly, moving into Washington State and the Dakotas by midday and as far south as the Arizona border. For the folk who loved the heat in Las Vegas, the wind chill dropped quickly from 15 degrees to zero, and then a bitter -5, and these poor folk who had very little to wear for warmth froze in their lightly covered beds in their houses. The blast carried on, mainly in a southern and eastern direction, moving quickly and catching up with the people beginning to head south.

In many areas, the roads were dry and the dozens of old vehicles moving south were okay. It was the people who were trying to walk along the roads, or across the uneven terrain, that felt it. Whole families tried to bundle up and stay alive, but slowly their body warmth ebbed in the face of the raging winds. They slowly stopped moving and the blowing snow began to cover them over.

The northern East Coast was beginning to experience the same downdraft of arctic air coming out of Canada. In some areas, it got as horrible as -40, and anybody outside lasted only minutes. In New York, the cold weather hit at about 11:00 am. The temperature was already cold at 15 degrees and dropped ten by midday. The sky was blue, an icy cold blue that was the last view thousands of people witnessed as their bodies went cold and their eyes became vacant.

Up to this morning, the north had been experiencing the highest numbers of deaths in North America, Europe, Russia and Asia. But on the third day, the population in the southern regions began to panic. There was no power, no open stores, no police, and no fire engines to put out fires, so the southern areas of the world began to turn to violence. For many people, their refrigerators were now empty, the milk gone, the pantry was down to a couple of items and frozen food was thawing—the non-frozen meat having to be consumed before it went rotten.

All the locked stores had products people now needed. There was a new sense of survival—a new sense that nothing was going to happen for a longer amount of time than they had first envisaged. For the first time, neighbors met their neighbors, and people began to form groups, arm themselves, and walk down to their local stores to meet other groups doing the same. Many didn't want to break the law, but hunger and the welfare of their families came first.

Humans were only human; it took one brave soul to walk up to a door and break it open with a crowbar or steel rod, and then there was a stampede for the food that was neatly packed on the shelves inside. Candy and chocolate was fought over first, once any shopping carts had been commandeered. People with guns entered the store, first civil and decent, but once they realized that they had more power than the people without guns, they held the others at bay while their friends and neighbors helped themselves.

It was inevitable, but the first group with guns was confronted by another larger group with guns, and by the third day alliances were being made. Many of the armed people were still sharing their spoils with others. There was still enough for everybody.

An average supermarket in the United States held several million dollars' worth of food and merchandise, and in many areas of the country, including the south, these were half empty by early afternoon. Like piranha, thousands upon thousands of people denuded the shelves.

By late afternoon the food was gone, as were generators, pet food, lawn tractors, wood, gas cylinders and all heating and cooking items and steel fencing. Everything that could be eaten, used to heat or cook, or to protect people was on the move. Pawn shops and gun stores were attacked and opened. The owners were a little more protective of their institutions of business, and dozens of people were shot trying to get inside until the owners and shooters were themselves shot or injured and the invaders free to help themselves—often climbing over the owner's dead bodies to get to what was inside.

The mass of people heading home with piles of merchandise began to push the junk aside and clear the roads so that they could get through. Cars were pushed off the road and fires were lit to burn the remains of trucks and cars for warmth, once their insides were emptied.

Most of the people got supplies for several days of survival. Useless electronics were still taken by many, the people hoping that one day they would work again. Banks were attacked and many tried in vain to open the vaults and the buildings were then torched in frustration. Gas stations were cleaned out of snacks and drinks, the gasoline and diesel sitting safely below ground in tanks. The majority of the people had never hotwired a car in their lives, never mind something more complicated.

As the stores emptied, the late or honest people were left with bare shelves and empty isles staring back at them. It was time to go and buy, barter, beg and then forcibly take things away from the people who had gotten there sooner.

It was time for anarchy, exactly what Chairman Wang Chunqiao in Nanjing thought 30 years ago would be his army of devastation—the American people themselves. A far bigger army than he could ever put together, well-armed and dedicated soldiers who would kill anybody for anything they had.

It was time for Chairman Wang Chunqiao's army to fight in earnest, and they started just before dark on the third day.

* * *

Dawn was breaking when Captain Mallory woke to the smell of freshly brewed coffee. First, he thought the events of the past few days were only a dream and the world was back to normal, but after opening his eyes to the sight of one of his flight attendants standing in front of him with a steaming cup of fresh brew, he sadly realized that it was, in fact, real.

"We heard faint noises outside," Pam Wallace told him. "We couldn't see anything, but I'm sure I heard a tractor or two moving around out there earlier. We let you sleep, Captain. You needed a good night's rest."

"Thank you," he replied, taking the coffee and sitting up. He had slept on the front seat of the SWAT truck, a few blankets had filled the hole between the seats, and he had slept well, exhausted from the previous two days. The captain was still dressed, except for his thick winter coat, and he put that on and unlocked the main door to the hangar. He slid it open just enough to walk outside and was confronted by a dozen men—three sitting on old farm tractors and the rest standing, all armed and interested to see who was in the private hangar owned by a doctor friend of theirs who had gone down to Key West for Christmas and was not yet expected back. Also, there were no wheel tracks of his aircraft landing on the runway.

"I don't believe you own this hangar?" started one of the farmers sitting on his tractor.

"Unfortunately, I don't," agreed the captain. "I'm Captain Mike Mallory, a pilot with Southwest Airlines. When the power went out over New York, I landed my aircraft in the water, managed to survive, rescued my passengers, and I am now taking my crew and what's left of my passengers south to escape the cold. It is bitterly cold up there in New York and very dangerous."

"You mean that this power outage is bigger than just around here?" the same farmer asked.

"I believe it's countrywide," replied the captain. "There are fires in New York as big as some of the buildings. All of I-95 is clogged with dead cars and trucks. We must have seen at least a thousand dead bodies in the cars, frozen to death. We even saw a couple of lions that must have escaped from a local zoo eating a human body in New Jersey. It is pure carnage out there, and I think it's getting even colder."

"You're right," replied the farmer. "Air smells like we going to get an arctic blast sometime today. Why are you here in our friend's hangar? Do you know him?"

"Unfortunately no, but I've flown into this airfield several times on recreational trips and fueled up from those fuel tanks over there.

Mickey Mason was the guy who always refueled me when I landed here."

"We know Mickey! He also flew out of here just before Christmas, down to Macon, Georgia, to visit his folks," added the farmer. A fourth tractor appeared, driving into the airfield as fast as it could with a young boy on top. He pulled to a halt and was excited.

"Pa, I saw a convoy of more old trucks driving south. There was at least nine or ten of them. I saw them through the binoculars. Fords and Dodges they were, and they went past the off-ramp and didn't stop."

"I'm sure there will be thousands coming south to escape the cold up there," continued Captain Mallory. "There must be thousands upon thousands of dead up there already and this cold blast is not going to help anybody stay alive."

John came out and introduced himself, still in his flight uniform, and so did a couple of the flight attendants.

"We have cleaned up our mess, Captain. The trucks are packed and we are ready to go," he reported to Mallory. He then turned to the farmer. "We got a donation from all the passengers and crew and there are a couple of hundred dollars on the owner's desk for what little food and drink we consumed."

"I'll let him know when he comes back," replied the farmer.

"Captain Mallory, what are we supposed to do?" "Can you survive the winter?" the captain asked.

"Sure," the farmer replied. "We have firewood and food. We have enough hay stored for our cattle. We will have to milk the cows by hand since nothing works, but yes, we can last the winter. When are things going to get back to normal?"

"Unfortunately, with what we've seen in New York and on the highway, I don't think things are going to be right again for quite a while. Gentlemen, nothing electrical works, apart from any old mechanical machines and vehicles. It is as if every piece of modern machinery has died, from jumbo jets to I'm sure some of your newer farm equipment." The farmers nodded, agreeing with the captain. "People are going to get hungry and mean. They are going to die, first from the cold, and if not that then hunger will get them. My belief is that the meanest will survive by killing the weak and honest for their food. I'm sure this scenario has been played out many times in Hollywood movies depicting the end of the world since the 1930s."

Everyone nodded, listening to him. They had all seen the movies, even the very latest. "The only major forces to protect us against people with guns are the military bases or police stations, if they are still organized...or even groups of people in communities protecting what they own."

"What can we do to help our country?" another farmer asked.

"I think that you guys must stay alive for one, protect yourselves for two, and start growing edible food as soon as it's time to plant. Corn, vegetables, meat and whatever you can provide to keep people alive. Help your local communities. Get your community numbers up. Barricade the off-ramps to stop people in vehicles coming to attack you. I don't know, I'm a pilot for God's sake. But this country must survive, and for the people to survive, they must be housed and fed."

"But there are hundreds of miles of farmland around here. How can we protect that?" another farmer asked.

"I know that there are other communities of farmers just like you out there. Go and spread the news. Tell them to get ready, both for good people begging for food and bad people who will shoot to steal anything they can. I don't think money has any value anymore. Maybe bartering is the new form of financial system. Staying alive and keeping this country going will have to be the ultimate reason to survive for everybody." Captain Mallory thought for a moment and then asked John to open the hangar door and start the vehicles. "Farmers, go to your local National Guard station or military base. Ask them for help in return for food when they run out. That's bartering. They will also run out of provisions one day and die without guys like you growing new food. I think that a strongly protected community will deter vigilantes and they will go where the pickings are easier. Try and help the poorer citizens if you can. Maybe the Army will give you guards or weapons to defend your farms. The promise of future food I'm sure will help. Send out people on horseback or tractors like the Civil War days and get other communities to do the same—protecting themselves and growing food to bring this country back to strength—and then we will see an end to this whatever it is. Tell them that the cities are dying and to expect the cold and hungry, good and bad. Look after the good and repel the bad."

There was silence until the old engines started up behind him.

"There are a couple of us who would like to stay and help the farmers," said one of the male passengers, "if they will feed us. We can increase their numbers and help protect their community. Some of us are from around here and the surrounding areas and we have nowhere else to go."

The farmers asked how many there were, and a family of three put up their hands, as well as several men and women. One of the flight attendants said that her town was only 20 or 30 miles to the west and she would like to try and get home to her husband. The men on the tractors nodded, inspired by Captain Mallory's speech.

"I think letting people know that they could be in this for the long haul is most important, then community protection, and then food production. Getting that information out as far and wide as we can will help keep this area of the country alive. People not being able to text on their cell phones will certainly be a benefit, in my point of view," smiled the captain, and he turned to the group behind him. "This is still a democratic country. Anybody who is invited to stay may stay. As for the rest of you, we are leaving in five minutes. I want to see if we can catch up to the convoy that passed by several minutes ago." He then turned back to the farmers. "If I don't come back and refuel here again someday, tell Mickey Mason to remember me, and that he still owes me a beer. Tell him Mike Mallory and the white Cessna 210 say 'hello'."

With that, the farmers thanked him, and the people leaving on the convoy made their way to the farm vehicles with their belongings. A count was made of those staying: 15 passengers and one flight attendant.

The trucks moved out, and the captain stopped to say goodbye to the lead farmer. "It's going to take men like you to keep this country alive. The politicians are history. The manufacturers are useless without electricity—nothing works anymore. I don't believe that there are many vehicles working out there anymore either, including ships and planes. We are stranded on this continent and the people who are alive after the winter are going to depend on you to feed them. Spread the word, get others to spread the word, and tell them to get this country running again." And with that he shook several hands, got a goodbye hug and kiss from the flight attendant who was staying and they drove out of the gate towards the main highway.

They found the tracks of the other convoy running north to south in the snow, about six inches deep, as they climbed onto the southbound side of the highway. The captain realized that this convoy would not have seen their previous tracks, since his convoy had stayed on the northbound side, and he decided to follow them on the southbound side. The convoy up front would have to clear the road, which would help Captain Mallory and his vehicles catch up with them. He had no way to know that he did not want to catch up with them—they were Chinese.

For an hour, they drove south as fast as they could, sometimes getting up to 30 miles an hour for short stretches, but the unending dead vehicles continued to be a problem, even though it was slightly easier to follow the tracks of the forward convoy around them. The number of stranded vehicles started increasing the closer they got to Washington, D.C. Their fuel was down to less than half when they came across several parked SUVs together, and the captain decided to call a break and siphon as much gas as they could.

Captain Mallory looked up at the sky as he was resting, eating a large Swiss triangular chocolate bar. Bad weather was coming in and he didn't like it. With his experience, this storm looked ominous. Long wispy high Stratus clouds were nearly pencil thin going south, showing high wind speeds in the atmosphere, and it was only 9:00

am. They needed to get as far south as possible today.

They managed 60 gallons out of four vehicles, not enough for more than a quarter tank per vehicle, but enough for two hours of driving. The next stop 15 minutes later was at an actual gas station just off the highway, deserted and almost hidden amongst thick trees. The small and desolate building was out of view of everybody except those who had seen the signs. He had hoped that the convoy in front might stop at a place like this, but they had continued on.

A window was broken, and he sensed life in the small shop area of the gas station. It did not have a restaurant attached to it, just a small Subway sandwich bar. He gathered a couple of the men together with M4s and carefully went inside.

"Don't shoot, mister!" shouted a young boy's voice from behind the candy aisle. "Don't shoot, sir! It's only me, my mom and my two sisters. We are cold and trying to keep warm in here."

"Anybody else with you?" shouted Captain Mallory.

"No, sir. There was a couple—a man and a woman—a couple of hours ago with a dog. They were from the accident on the highway, but they left to walk south. It's only us here now, mister."

John ordered the boy to come out with his hands up, and a grubby kid about nine or ten years old appeared with chocolate all over his face. He was trying to be brave.

"You're okay, kid, we aren't going to hurt you. We're just stopping to get supplies and head on south. Where are you from?" asked the captain, as they lowered their weapons and the boy let his hands slowly drop.

"We live in Charleston, South Carolina, sir. We were on our way home after visiting our grandparents for Christmas in Philadelphia. My mom has to go back to work. She was driving when the car stopped, skidded on the snow, and then hit another one—belonging to the couple who left a couple of hours ago."

"Where's your father?" John asked.

"I don't know, sir. He left a couple of years ago." The flight attendants went behind the counter to get the rest of the boy's family and brought out a woman and two little girls about six and three. The woman had a severe cut on her head, her clothes were covered with blood and she, or her son, had used a First Aid box to bandage and clean the wound. She looked sick and was cold and shivering, as were the two little girls, who were carrying the blanket they had wrapped themselves in.

It took 30 minutes, but they took everything that remained on the shelves, all the bottles of water and soft drinks, got the new travelers warm and comfy in the back of the truck, and continued on their way.

It was only two miles later that they saw fresh blood on the packed snow in front of them and two bodies lying motionless. A dog was curled up next to the bodies, but it ran for cover when they stopped. The blood was still fresh and freezing as it hit the snow, the captain noticed, as he and John looked down at what used to be a man and a woman, obviously alive only a couple of hours earlier. They had been both shot a dozen times, had fallen backwards, and then been run over by several large vehicles, most likely to make sure that they were dead. Their dog was off on the side of the highway barking at them, and John got the young boy to see if he could identify it. It belonged to the couple that had been with them in the gas station, and the dog remembered the boy, ran up, wagged its tail and was lifted into the back of the truck.

"I don't think we want to meet whoever is driving up ahead of us after all," suggested John, and the captain nodded. "The 495 interchange is a couple of miles ahead. I think it would be better to take the one they don't take, since both of the 495 legs will get us back to I-95 just south of D.C."

"Hopefully we don't arrive together at the south interchange," added the captain. "I think we should fill our tanks before we get there, and if we reach I-95 first, we'll keep going until our tanks are dry and get back on the northbound side to hide our tracks."

Ten minutes later, they arrived at the 495 beltline around Washington, and the weather was getting bitterly cold and the wind increasing from the northwest. The first group's tracks turned right on the beltline towards Fairfax, so they went east.

The stranded vehicles were fewer on the beltline and they made good time, averaging 30 miles an hour. They decided not to take the shortcut using 295 directly south, knowing that traffic could be heavier on that stretch and they could come out behind the other convoy or be very close to them.

An hour later, they found another refueling opportunity— three Chevy Suburbans and a third rental truck all on the same stretch of road a few hundred yards from each other. They separated and began filling their tanks. It took 20 minutes, and when they ran out of gas from those trucks, they switched to any other gas-powered vehicles, draining fuel until they had every tank filled to the brim, including the ten five-gallon canisters.

They were now three miles from the southern interchange and ready for action. All their weapons were checked and a couple of grenade launchers added to each vehicle. There was a lot of tension as they reached the final mile of 495 and saw the end of the other convoy, still in front of them, already on I-95 about a mile or so ahead of where they were. They felt a sense of relief, because if they hadn't filled everything when they did, the two convoys would have reached the interchange at the same time, and ten vehicles was a big army compared to what they had.

Captain Mallory then decided to get off the southbound highway and rejoin it driving south on the northbound lanes. If they came across the people in front of them, they could have a little cover from the crash barriers.

It was 3:30 by the time they had reached the end of the 295 beltline around Richmond, refilled their tanks as much as they could, and reconnected with I-95. They had thought that they would be further behind the other convoy, but there were no tracks on either side of the highway, so they decided to carry on as far as possible on the northbound side hoping that the ten vehicles, now behind them if they were still going south, would stay to the other side.

For an hour they headed south, the skies clearing again and the threat of snow diminishing. The roads were also drier, with patches of ice in the shadows and dead vehicle congestion lighter than around Washington and Richmond.

"We should be coming up to the North Carolina border soon," John stated over the radio from the rear SWAT truck. They had three working radios, in the two SWAT trucks and the fire engine, which was being driven by one of flight attendants.

"About 12 more miles," replied Captain Mallory, still driving the lead truck. They were bunched up as close as possible, making themselves a smaller target for anyone watching. "I used to refuel at a very small airport a few miles from here. The town of Emporia has a small municipal airport and I'm thinking we could stay there tonight. Hopefully those other guys will just carry on and leave us alone."

"I think I hear a small aircraft engine somewhere close by. Do you hear it, Mike?" asked John.

"John, yes, I think I can. The Emporia turnoff is two miles ahead. Let's take it. The airport is to our east, and if we head there, maybe it will follow us, or maybe it's even headed in to land there. Make sure nobody sees us turn off from behind. Use the binoculars. We don't want to be followed."

The five vehicles headed off the highway following the on-ramp and had to push a small car to the side that had turned over. A small Nissan, it moved easily as the SWAT truck pushed it down the ramp and off to one side. It was empty. They then followed SR58 east. A road sign showed that the airport was a couple of miles outside of the deserted town. Here, a couple of the buildings were blackened ruins and one three-story building was still on fire. Damage, the captain figured, that had started after midnight. They were in the eastbound lane of SR58—a two-lane highway—and it was several minutes before the small airport was seen on their left side. They drove into the airport and found it deserted.

The five vehicles stopped in a line in the only aircraft parking lot in front of a couple of buildings and hangars and switched their engines off. For several minutes, the three radios had been tuned to try and find the frequency the aircraft, which could still be heard far off to the north, was using. They tried but did not get any response.

It was 4:30 pm, and Captain Mallory thought that they had about 45 minutes of daylight left. There was no other noise, apart from the flying aircraft, which sounded like it was getting closer.

"Sounds like a Cessna 210," John suggested, now standing next to his captain. Owning one himself, the captain nodded his agreement. It sounded like his own aircraft he kept where he lived just outside Dallas, Texas. The M4s had good sights on them, and it didn't take the captain long to find the aircraft. The Cessna was coming towards the airport, easily silhouetted by the grey northern sky, and dropping rapidly from a high altitude.

"Southwest staff, get your uniforms on!" ordered the captain, going for his uniform jacket and replacing his warm jacket with it. Within seconds, his crew—again dressed as Southwest flight personnel—moved several yards closer to the only northwest/southeast runway to their right. He ordered everybody to hide all weapons and for all the women and children to line up in front of their vehicles to show the incoming pilot that they meant no harm.

The 210 came down to the northern edge of the airfield at well over 200 miles an hour, and they waved as it passed over the runway at full speed less than 100 feet above the asphalt. The aircraft rose into a steep climb, slowed, and dropped its flaps and wheels for a swift landing from the south.

The Southwest pilots knew what the pilot was doing and within a minute the wheels touched down and the Cessna came to a stop very quickly on the runway. It did not take the little feeder road, but turned back on the runway and slowly came forward, stopping about 200 yards from them. As the engine shut off, the pilot got out of the left side with an M16—the older version of the M4 they carried—and aimed at them from beneath the engine cowling of the Cessna.

"You are wearing pilot uniforms. Who are you?" an unexpected woman's voice shouted over to them. "I have enough firepower here to blow you apart before you can get back to your friends. I also have enough company in my plane to help me. You, come closer. Tell me your name, rank and serial number." The captain went forward, and she saw by his insignia that he was the most senior person in the group.

"Captain Mike Mallory. I fly 737-400s for Southwest. We went down in New York, and I'm trying to get my remaining passengers and crew to safety. That is my co-pilot and two of my three flight attendants. We lost one."

"Senior Flight Attendant, please come forward," the lady pilot asked, and Pam Wallace stepped up beside the captain. The young girl from New York went as well, not wanting to leave her side. "Tell the other one to stay where she is," the pilot ordered.

"I can't, she's injured and I'm looking after her. She's a kid, only sixteen," Pam replied. The pilot then ordered both of them to come forward and spoke to Pam for a few seconds. Then she dropped her weapon's barrel and went around to the passenger door of the 210. She leaned in and pulled out a young girl, putting her on one hip, and came forward to the captain, Pam, and the teenager.

"I'm sorry about that, Captain Mallory. I needed to make sure we weren't in any danger. We are expecting it at any moment. I'm Martie Roebels and this is Little Beth. Where are you guys going in such an interesting group of vehicles?"

"South," the captain replied, gladly shaking the hand offered to him. "Pam," he turned to the flight attendant, "tell everybody to relax, and send out a couple of armed men to search the hangars and offices over there for a place to stay while I chat with Ms. Roebels here." He turned his attention back to Martie. " Did you see another convoy on your flight north?"

"Yes, they were less than a couple of miles behind you on the southbound side. You were heading south on the northbound side. By the time I lost sight of them, they had just passed this exit and still heading south. They have ten vehicles—trucks, by the look of it, and not as pretty as yours. Do you want me to tell them where you are?"

"Negative," replied the captain. "We thought they might be okay at first, but we found two recently killed people on the highway north of Washington and we think they did it. They had driven straight over the bodies with every one of those ten vehicles they are driving in. I think they are a bad bunch, whoever they are."

"They must be the people we are expecting," Martie replied.

"They should probably reach us by tomorrow morning."

"Where is that?" asked the captain.

"We are situated off US64 in North Carolina, on the shores of Jordan Lake about 15 to 20 miles west of RDU."

"I know the lake well," replied Captain Mallory. "I fly into RDU a couple of times a month."

"I have about 20 minutes of light left, so I need to keep going," Martie calculated. "If you want to come and use our facility as a home base, I recommend you getting to RDU. It is safe and still locked. We have a dozen Air Force guards on duty there since earlier today. Mention that General Pete Allen sent you. I apologize that we have already cleaned out the Southwest terminal of food, but if you head there in the morning, I will come and find you once we have dealt with this other group."

"How do they know where you are?" John asked.

"Simple, our transponders were coming out of our airfield for a day or so, and the Chinese, or whoever they are, still have their spy satellites up. We are now on high alert and the president should be at our airfield by now."

"The U.S. President?" the captain asked. "Do you have enough firepower?"

Martie laughed. "We have what is left of the entire U.S. Air Force, and we definitely need more pilots!" she chuckled. "Our Air Force is hiring right now, actually. Your passengers will be safe with us and then we can get them to Seymour Johnson Air Force Base, if they prefer more of an official military presence."

"Count us in," the captain and John said at the same time. "We have a badly injured lady with three small kids and the young girl with Pam who we believe was raped in New York. Do you have enough room in the 210 to take them with you? The rest of us can sleep here tonight and get to RDU by midday tomorrow, and then wait for you."

"Get your wounded aboard, Captain. I have four spare seats and a couple of the children can share one. Little Beth here would be glad for the company," Martie replied, saying her goodbyes and walking back to the aircraft.

They hurried, and Pam helped the young girl, the injured mother, and her three kids squeeze into the six-seat aircraft. Martie took off just minutes later, waggled her wings, and disappeared to the north, climbing hard to hide in the sky and sneak a peek at the other convoy further south.

* * *

The White House hadn't changed. The streets were quiet, and people stayed away from the sacred building. Everyone knew that if they got too close, they were likely to get trouble from the guards in return. Nobody in the White House rose early, since there was nothing to do except wait. The president had never been so bored in his life.

A hot breakfast of eggs, bacon, hash browns, and toast was finally delivered to the two men in the Oval Office. The Colombian Ambassador and the president sat on the couch and enjoyed their first decent breakfast since New Year's Eve. The president's family stayed out of the area while their father worked, and things went about as usual except without any modern electrical gadgets. The two kids drew, wrote stories, and did some homework that had not been completed before Christmas. The family had spent Christmas in Hawaii and returned on the last day of the year.

General Allen had promised the president that he would be back as soon as he could, and an anxious president had forced him to say that he would return before lunch. He wasn't able to keep his promise, due to circumstances beyond his control, but it made the president even more edgy. The general was currently taking off from Andrews AFB and heading to the White House with Buck piloting *Baby Huey*; the overnight hours had not gone as he had planned.

At 1:00 am in Salt Lake City, the truck and trailer were sent up the mountain to get Carlos and Lee Wang as Buck was getting ready to take the air in *Lady Dandy*.

Buck also inspected the cargo going into one of the C-130s as he inspected *Lady Dandy* for takeoff. There were three television trucks advertising a local television station. One was being loaded into the C-130 and the other two were by the hangar doors waiting for Carlos to return. Several computers were also being loaded into both the C-130 and *Lady Dandy* with several old television sets. Buck then realized that Carlos must have satellite communication capability and that these were to give them more options than just the ham radios. It was so simple, yet it could work if they could bounce communications between these trucks via satellite.

Buck left the apron for the end of the runway as two more dark aircraft came in to land. The first C-130 looked like *Jerry*, but the second one took his breath away and he immediately wanted to fly it. It was a real AC-130 gunship, and, yes, it did have the 105mm howitzer sticking out of the side. He shouted "Yippee" with excitement and got on the radio.

"Pete, this is Buck. Is that YOU flying the second bird?"

"Now how did you guess that, Buck?" Pete replied. *"I'm too tired to fly, so I'm acting as engineer and I'm half asleep in the back. You get your lady friend home. There's a big storm on its way and we were blown south of our flight plan by 20 miles. It's crappy flying without a GPS. It looks like you will get one hell of a tailwind, because this stuff is cold and coming directly in from the north. How long is your estimated flying time?"*

"Ten hours," replied Buck, turning onto the runway and letting the engines warm up.

"You'll do it in nine. Fly at high cruise. We have a busy day ahead. Yours is the only whirly-bird still operational at the moment and I need it to get up north. Radio Preston when you get close enough and tell him to fuel up Baby Huey *and clear out her insides, I need three or four comfortable chairs in her before we take off, and a nice rug and center table. She will be picking up the boss from you-know-where. Also, keep it a secret. Everything we have is going into the East Coast this morning and I already have a special passenger on board. We are going to need every bit of room around his airstrip. I hope to get there before you do, but I have to wait for our buddy Carlos and fill these babies up. I'll get the base to try*

and give Preston a call as well. Travel safe. It's getting nasty out there." "Roger that," replied Buck.

"What does he mean by 'the boss'?" asked Barbara.

"Our little *Baby Huey* is going to be Air Force One for the 11 miles from The White House to Andrews," replied Buck with a chuckle.

Carlos was still awake, as was Lee, when the men arrived a little before 2:00 am. Both men heard the snowplow arrive, and they were ready. They had worked most of the night and had three large pieces of equipment that had to be handled with care ready to be packed aboard the plow.

"There are two men staying behind to guard," the sergeant told Carlos. "They have just unloaded 20 gallons of gas, and the rest of the guard detail will return on the plow once you guys head down the mountain in the transporter. The 'boss' has ordered you, sir, to be at Hill by 3:00 am at the latest. There is a bad storm coming in and he's flying in from Edwards ahead of it."

The sergeant was quickly shown what to do to keep everything on and as warm as possible. The telescope was set, and Carlos explained that although it was inside the building, it was in its own case and walled in from the working area by thick Perspex. The snow wouldn't do anything to it, and they could stay warm in the observatory. Carlos showed them the heaters and electricity switches, and told the men that the telescope with its antennas must be kept powered up at all costs. They nodded, enjoying the toasty 50-degree inside temperature.

Then it was time to leave. It was bitterly cold on the plow, and Carlos was half frozen by the time they reached the truck—its lights still on, the engine running—and their three large packs were quickly moved into it. They got into the warm cab and the driver pressed his foot on the clutch, slipping it into gear and jerking forward, leaving the rest to take the snowplow back to the observatory.

It was pretty slow and slippery back down the hill, but the driver was good and they made it back to base at exactly 3:00 am. Carlos was surprised to see four C-130s parked on the apron, their engines starting up as he arrived. "Lee, you are coming with me. How long will it take to get your wife and daughter packed up?" Carlos asked.

"It won't take them long to get ready," Lee replied and ran off to tell them they were leaving.

"Good morning, Carlos," greeted Pete Allen, walking up to the tired astronomer. "We can sleep enroute. The men found and packed what you asked for in *Tom*. Sally is back at Andrews resting. We can fly together in *Jerry*, talk, and catch up on the way."

"We need to wait for Lee Wang," Carlos stalled. "It is imperative Lee comes with us, Pete. He and I think that we can find out who is behind this, and he might even be able to deactivate their satellites."

"That's worth waiting for," Pete responded. Only five minutes later Lee and his family returned from a room behind the Officers' Mess and followed Pete's instructions to follow him and get aboard *Jerry*. Carlos and Pete were far too exhausted to even think of flying themselves.

Carlos walked up the ramp into *Jerry* and got a tired hello from Jennifer, who was resting on a foam mattress in the rear. A few familiar faces also looked at the new visitors. Maggie and the kids were there and she seemed to be half asleep next to a man that he assumed was her husband, and who was totally out cold. Carlos had never met him before, but he knew about Will's phobia of flying. He winked at Maggie.

"Hi, Carlos," she smiled sweetly, sitting on the floor of the aircraft holding her husband's head in her lap. "Will is under heavy sedation. I told the doctor at Edwards that if he was conscious he would not get on the plane, so the doc gave him a double dose of whatever it was—a damn hurricane wouldn't wake him up. I hear you have been busy!"

"Yep," he replied. "I need some of that sleep medication Will was given, though. I'm very tired." He introduced the people with him. "This is my buddy, Lee Wang, his wife Lin, and their daughter Ling." The newcomers were quickly acquainted and they all opened side seats next to Jennifer to sit down for takeoff.

"You also look done in, Jennifer," Carlos remarked as he strapped himself in next to her.

"Lots of hours, Carlos," she replied.

The pilots weren't messing around. They taxied to the end of the runway at an alarming speed, completed their final checks on the way, and went straight into their takeoff runs as each one reached the end of the runway. These guys were certainly in a hurry.

All four C-130s climbed into the dark, cold sky—dawn still many hours away—and General Allen came back to see everybody.

"Do we have a satellite connection, Carlos?" he asked.

"Yes, we have a simple connection. Navistar P will soon be stationary over Utah. For how long, I don't know. It depends on how good you guys made her, but she's flying well up there. The repositioning will still take a couple of days, and it is still dark, but with dawn an hour out over the eastern seaboard, I believe that our U.S. visual on screen is both coastlines plus 300 miles of ocean either side in a day or two. I could have made her go further out, but it would have taken weeks to align her even further, and I didn't think it was necessary. With any shipping, 300 miles is at least a full 24-hour warning." Pete looked at Carlos.

"We have a television truck on board *Tom*, and several of the computers you wanted and a couple of old television sets in storage. Are we going to see the satellite broadcast on them?"

"I believe so," Carlos replied tiredly. "I also think we can set up a communication feed to the other bases. Lee and I are working on trying to mate the radio feed into the television trucks. Or I was actually thinking we could use the old simple commercial Hughes Satellite Internet systems around the country to communicate to every base and the White House. It will take a few weeks to get that far, but I need your guys all over the country to go out and find the Hughes two-way satellite systems and we can go from there."

Carlos then changed the subject, hardly taking a breath. "Two of those other C-130s flying with us look very different from the others."

"Good eyes, as usual," replied the general. "This is my secret project for my favorite air base museum at Hill AFB. The first one is one of the original Vietnam-era AC-130 gunships. I have had people working on her for over a year now at Edwards. She is the same model as *Tom* and *Jerry*, but over the years has been made as original as she was back in 'Nam. I reckon she has cost as much as an F-22, but she still has her added 105mm howitzer, fuel drop tanks and air-refueling intact. We were going to take them off next year. Most importantly, however, she has been refitted with all her original electrical gauges and flight systems. That's why she can still fly but also still has the latest firepower—the same as the more modern 130 gunships that are now all grounded permanently."

"*Ghost Rider* and one other, *Easy Girl*, have the only 105mm howitzers still flying, as well as the full load of 20mm and 40mm cannons. *Ghost Rider* actually went down twice in 'Nam, but was repaired and survived. Her older sister had the call sign '*First Lady*' and was put out to pasture years ago in one of our museums. This gal has upgraded engines, and no modern electronics, or she wouldn't be flying. Her underbelly is thin armor and that 105 mm howitzer makes your teeth rattle when it goes off. *Ghost Rider* is my real baby, and she is the only one of three old, secret gunships still flying. I lovingly put her back together, and later today she will serve as Air Force One—a real promotion for this old girl!"

"The president is moving?" Carlos asked.

"He wants to come and visit you guys," the general continued. "The guy just wants to get out of Dodge and see the world, and I don't blame him. Now let's get some sleep. It looks like we all need it, and Will Smart will be wide awake later when he realizes that he has flown across country and missed it all. I'm dying to see his face!" He smiled, grabbing a foam mattress from a pile and a few blankets, and lay down. He was asleep in seconds, and the rest weren't far behind him.

* * *

Preston was up early, about an hour after everyone got to sleep in *Jerry* almost 1,300 miles to his west. Oliver and his new pal, Spot the puppy, were by his side. Preston couldn't sleep and was beginning to worry about the possible incoming attack. They had such sketchy news about everything. It was a clear, but still dark morning. The temperature was 32 degrees and he wanted to walk. The Air Force guys had worked all night on the perimeter fence and it wouldn't be long before the runway would be receiving visitors.

He had heard over the radio, from Edwards and now Hill, that aircraft were coming his way. He knew that *Lady Dandy* was airborne out of Salt Lake City, and that C-130s were headed into Salt Lake to refuel. They were all expected around lunchtime. A radio operator had answered when Preston had called and spoken for the first time to Hill Air Force Base and relayed the weird instructions from the general. Pretty interesting instructions, but he felt something exciting was about to happen.

Baby Huey was predictably parked behind the fuel tanks, out of the way of the fixed-wing aircraft. She couldn't just taxi forward and get fueled up, so Buck had lifted her up and landed her on the dirt where the fuel line could easily reach her. Preston hotwired the pump and began to fill her tanks. She was off to Washington as soon as Buck got in. The poor man would be having a very long day. It took nearly 15 minutes as the slow pumps, not made for large deliveries of fuel, pumped just under 200 gallons into the helicopter—she was thirsty.

After turning off the pump, Preston went to look for a rug to place on the floor of *Baby Huey*'s belly along with a couple of easy chairs. He went to the lounge and moved the wooden coffee table and the round rug underneath it out to the helicopter. The rug had been a present from Martie's grandfather and was an oval copy of the American flag. Preston placed both in the rear of the helicopter. The six-foot rug fit well and covered much of the metal floor. He walked into the hangar and took the new set of EZ-Boys from the downstairs room. Nobody was upstairs. Carlos, Buck, and Barbara were on their way from Salt Lake City, both Sally and Jennifer were still flying, and the Smarts were in California.

The previous evening, Martie had washed all the bedding in their 20-year-old washing machine, which, along with the old gas dryer, was the only electrical machine still working at the farm. The new washing machine he had purchased a couple of years ago was dead, and he was thankful that he had just put the old one out in the barn.

Preston moved each chair on a small four-wheeled trailer he often pulled around the farm behind his green lawn tractor, and then went back to get the two-seater couch—the smallest of three Martie had purchased for the party. The other two were double the size and wouldn't fit. The radio operator had stated that they would need a minimum of three chairs.

When he was done, the inside rear of the helicopter looked like a small, comfortable lounge. He locked the side door behind the couch from the outside so nobody could get in or fall out of that side since the people on the couch would have no parachutes if the door was opened in flight. She was ready.

Then he thought about drinks. He went back and unplugged the small bar refrigerator he had used before Martie shopped for the fly-in. It was still cold, and would be colder still if he left it outside for a couple of hours. He placed it in the rear of *Baby Huey*, and filled it with cans of soda, Gatorade, and beer from the stocks purchased from the closed-down gas station. He placed a tray of potato chip bags on a rubber mat on top of the fridge, but then he took the bags out and refilled the black wooden tray with dozens of small packets of Southwest peanuts and pretzels. He hoped their guests would see the humor in it. He put a box of Jerky on top of the bags and, now finished, was quite impressed with his accomplishments.

"Looks like a mini Oval Office," laughed Martie, sneaking up behind him and giving him a good morning hug. "Pete Allen will think he's the president sitting in here."

"Just following orders, love," Preston replied. "Buck is flying her out later this morning."

"I just got off the radio with Jennifer," Martie reported. "Actually, she relayed our conversation through Hill's new radio. She said that both *Tom* and *Jerry* are coming in with a few others. A surprise, they have Will Smart on board with Maggie and the kids. Will has been completely sedated since Edwards, is sleeping like a baby, and doesn't even know that he is flying across the country."

"That will certainly screw up his internal time clock," laughed

Preston. "He's going to suffer badly from jetlag, poor guy. It will be fun to see his reaction when he wakes up."

"I'll do up the beds before they get here, in case they need to let him sleep," Martie answered. "Let's go walk around and see what the soldiers have done."

With Oliver and the happy puppy in tow, and with Little Beth still asleep, they walked down the runway towards the guard tower.

"Good morning, sir," came a voice from 30 feet up. "We have been working all night and I think we are about done."

Preston and Martie said good morning back and continued down the driveway and around the corner, their progress being forwarded by radio. The gate was now a mass of barbed wire, and nobody could get through it without armor.

"Good morning, sir…ma'am." The tired sergeant in charge nodded to them as they walked up. "Those dogs never stop playing. I wish I had as much energy."

"Good morning, Sergeant," replied the couple in unison. "It looks like we are now secure from the road. Is that true?"

"Yes, sir! We have put down over 300 yards of triple-lined wire, and the whole stretch can be seen from the fire tower. We wanted to put some tripwires down, but then thought that the dogs could walk into them, so we wanted to ask your permission first. Then, I had an idea last night about the possible attack we might be getting. If we lure the attack away from the perimeter—say on the dirt road just as you turn off the highway—and put up a barrier across the dirt road about 200 yards in from the asphalt, we can stop them before they reach the gate of the property."

"Sounds good," replied Preston. "A sort of ambush zone?"

"Correct, sir, basic military tactics," replied the sergeant. "I was going to ask Mr. David if we could place his armored cars several yards into the forest on the other side of the road. They could be camouflaged under brush and act to cut off the escape route once the attackers realize it's a trap."

"It sounds good. I'm sure David would enjoy the action. Those machine guns will rip anything civilian to shreds in seconds. I've seen them in operation," replied Preston.

"There is enough brush along where your fence goes and we can position a dozen or so men down the road to ambush whoever arrives and help the guards at the barrier and the tower," the sergeant added. "We currently have 32 fully operational soldiers on site, and that should be enough."

"Unfortunately, I need a couple of your soldiers to set up a guard post at RDU Airport this morning," added Preston. "There is a ton of stuff there—food, and gasoline in the large fuel tanks—and I think we are going to need everything we can get our hands on. I will ask General Allen to set up a permanent 24/7 guard at the main gates and I was even going to ask Joe for the use of one of his jeeps to patrol the airport's perimeter."

"Not a problem, sir," the sergeant replied. "I'm sure a C-130 will fly into a base later today, and they can always bring back more troops. The general said that there was little chance of an attack today. It will take at least a day for them to find us and ready themselves, but from tonight, midnight, we should be prepared for action. We are nearly done here, the men are going to rest this morning, get six hours of sleep and then we will get back at it. I will forward my ideas about the ambush to the general when he arrives. It will only take a couple of hours to take fresh troops into RDU from Seymour Johnson, and I don't need to send any men from here. They already know the layout of the land, and that is real valuable right now." Preston agreed, and he and Martie said their goodbyes and walked back to the house.

"It's a pretty good plan," Preston stated to Martie. "I think it is going to work. We don't know how many are coming, but I'm sure it's not thousands of fighters—most probably less than 100, if any come at all, and they won't be expecting our fancy armored reception."

"I want to help," replied Martie. "I think I could spend some time in the 210 cruising up the north/south or west/east highways looking for movement. These bad guys will have to drive from the north, wherever they are. I'm sure they will come south from Washington,

I-95, or east along US64 or possibly I-40. I can't see why they would come north from Florida or Georgia. There isn't any reason for them to be there. Also, I-40 must be closed around Asheville. I'm sure that winter weather is making for potentially dangerous driving over the Blue Ridge Mountains."

"They could already be here, but I don't think so," added Preston, throwing a stick for Oliver. "It's only been a day since our transponders could have been noticed, and since they are all now silent, the enemy can't see any new activity from here. They might not even come at all. But I think you're right. If they do come, I think the I-95 corridor is the best bet. We are short on pilots until everybody gets back, and I want to secure RDU as soon as possible today. So you might as well take your new toy up and cruise around. But don't you want to take your Mustang?"

"I was thinking about that, but she's far too fast and noisy. I was thinking about refueling one of the 172s, but then I realized that it would take me too long to get back in a 172 if I saw something. I can power down the 210 to minimum cruise altitude, say around 130 miles an hour, stay up for five hours with the fuel reduction, and then scream back to get help if I see something," Martie explained. "Little Beth is falling in love with flying and I can take her with me. It's keeping her mind off her mother. I know you miss me, but with Maggie's kids coming in, they'll be able to take her under their wing and keep her occupied." She snuggled up to him as they reached the house, and he told her to make breakfast and he'd refuel the 210 for her.

Most of the troops slept in that morning and were only awakened by *Lady Dandy* coming in. Several minutes earlier, Buck had gotten on the radio to Preston to get landing details. The temperature had risen to 45 degrees. Buck already knew that with the powerful tailwind they had enjoyed for the first several hours of the flight, he would need to come in from the south. He also reported that *Tom* and *Jerry* were now only 50 minutes behind him and were also planning to land at Preston's airfield. Buck needed *Lady Dandy* to be well out of the way, so he would park her on the other side of the hangar next to *Baby Huey*.

That prompted a question, but Preston kept silent and just gave *Lady Dandy* the wind speed and temperature. "Why are you parking her so far away?" he finally asked as Buck and Barbara jumped out after landing and positioning *Lady Dandy* off the runway.

"A few surprises are coming in," smiled Buck. "Carlos has some old gear with them. Can you order up some help to unload? Our cargo is a few antiquated computers and television sets. I need to freshen up because Barbara and I are heading straight out to Andrews in *Baby Huey*. Thank God it's only an hour each way! Barbara flew most of the trip and I slept for five hours to stay fresh for the next leg. I'll be taking off before midday and hope to be back by dark, Preston."

While the DC-3 was unloaded, Martie fixed everybody a brunch of slightly old sandwiches and bagels full of ham and cream cheese, all commandeered from the deli at the airport the day before. "I hope we can get fresh stuff like this every day," she smiled at Preston, knowing that it would all be gone soon. She had a couple of bread makers in the kitchen—one worked and one didn't—but she would need bread-making ingredients pretty soon or she would run out. A couple of loaves of bread would certainly not go far with the increasing crowd at the Strong Ranch.

Buck and Barbara took off for Andrews after brunch, and Barbara was hoping to get some sleep on the way to the city. She got out as Buck was about to start *Baby Huey* and retrieved a foam mattress from the hangar, putting it in the plane. The two had just disappeared over the horizon to the north when Jennifer came over the intercom, and Preston gave her the wind speed and temperature. She could be heard faintly talking to other pilots, describing the landing techniques for the airfield. Preston could hear several voices he didn't recognize and knew there were a lot more arriving than he had expected.

"Be gentle with my little runway, guys," pleaded Preston into the radio. "And Jennifer, the lights are removed, the trees have been sort of flattened by the dozer on the south end for 40 or so more yards, and you can come in about 30 feet lower and begin your flare-out earlier."

"Roger that," replied Jennifer.

The drone of several heavy aircraft engines could be heard off to the west as they flew further south of the runway to turn in northeast for the landing. Then he saw them—a line of four C-130s—stretching on the horizon for what seemed like miles. Jennifer came in first, followed by what looked like *Tom* or *Jerry*—it was hard to tell the difference. They each landed and taxied onto the apron area to get out of the way. The third one came in and looked a little different, but the fourth one took his breath away. It was a gunship—an old 130, just like the other three—but as a pilot he knew about these super birds and recognized that this one had all three of the modern guns sticking out of the side. The engines had a much deeper rumble to them, and it took the whole runway to get her down once the third airplane had moved onto the dirt at the end of the runway, giving the gunship enough room to use the whole field. They all taxied back, and the third C-130 parked over the fuel tanks while the gunship sat on the runway idling.

General Allen was already out, the troops standing in a line at attention for the occasion. The sergeant spoke about his ideas, the general nodded to him, and Preston got to them as they finished.

"The sergeant here told us about your need to place a guard detachment at RDU, and I think it's a good idea. Actually, one of the 130s is going to head down to Seymour Johnson. They can pick up a guard detachment and gear, and fly into RDU in about two hours. Which gate do you think would be best to set up a guard base?"

"I would recommend the gate by the private terminal," replied Preston, raising his voice over the noise of the engines. "I think we need to make our presence very obvious to anybody spying on the airport. I'll go up there earlier with one of Joe's jeeps, or even the Saracen, so your men can use it to patrol the perimeter."

"Sounds good," agreed the general. "I like the sergeant's idea of creating an ambush zone on the road outside your entrance. I've given him the go-ahead to set it up and there will be two more companies of 100 men each ferried in here this afternoon. Captain Watkins will do two trips in from Pope to get them here. The extra troops will only be here for a day or so before they need to head up to the White House, but while they're here they can set up and dig the mortar positions around the tarmac as well as sandbag machine-gun placements. I want sandbags on the insides of your gate, and they can sandbag an area on the road as protection from any attack. We will put up a professional and defensible barrier to stop traffic if need be. It's a surprise, but we need to have this place under lockdown until this threat is over."

"I agree," replied Preston. "Martie is going up in the 210 in an hour to be our spotter plane. She's going south for 50 miles and then north for a hundred miles to see if anything is moving on the I-95 corridor. I'm going up in my FedEx special and head out on US64 for 100 miles, and then I'm going to meet Joe and David, who are driving to the airport. I can show your guys the lay of the land when they get there."

"I'll be back by 4:30 at the latest. Like *Ghost Rider*?" Pete Allen winked at Preston as he turned and pointed to the gunship. Preston nodded with a grin of his own. Martie returned and gave the general a cooler full of lunches for he and his crew.

"Everybody has their orders." The general began to wrap things up. "By the way, that is an HC-130 sitting over your fuel tanks. She is an in-flight fuel tanker—your fuel tanker for the time being, along with a full crew at your disposal until I need her. That represents a big 'thank you' from me. She can pump fuel in and out of rocks if you need her to, and she can siphon all the fuel out of the RDU's main tanks and pump yours full. She can fly across the country non-stop. Her range is 4,250 miles. Her crew of three is directly under your command and her military call sign is '*Mother Goose*.' It's still painted on her side from Vietnam."

The general ran back to the idling AC-130 gunship and it immediately began its way to the southern end of the runway for takeoff. Preston turned to the other arrivals and watched in amazement as the medics took Will Smart off, looking dead to the world and asleep on a stretcher. The two Smart kids ran up and gave Preston a hug, with Maggie close behind, before she followed her husband into the new medical tent from Seymour Johnson erected only an hour earlier. Carlos disembarked next with a short Chinese gentleman behind him and two Chinese ladies. The group walked up to greet Preston as Jennifer hopped out of the forward door and ran to give him a hug.

"I've got to shower and get out of here. I'll be ferrying in troops for the rest of the day," she gasped and ran off toward the hangar as *Ghost Rider* raced by, lifted off the runway and headed north. Within seconds the gunship was a speck in the sky, chasing after Buck.

"Preston, this is my Chinese friend, Lee Wang, his wife Lin, and his daughter Ling," Carlos introduced everyone. Preston shook hands with his new guests and suggested that since Martie had cleaned all the sheets, they could sleep in Jennifer and Sally's room. "We are exhausted," shared Carlos. "I was told that the soldiers will unload our gear? Ask them to put all the stuff in the hangar out of the way. Lee and I have been awake all night and I need at least another six hours of sleep. There is a single bed downstairs. Shall we get it up to the third room for Ling?"

"Good idea," nodded Preston. "I don't know if Buck and Barbara are coming back this evening, so I guess I'll have to give their room to the Smarts. We ran out of sleeping places several sets of visitors ago, so it's going to be cramped tonight." Carlos suggested that he would sleep in his old room for the time being and then downstairs if it was needed. Preston concurred.

Preston helped the soldiers unload all of Carlos' equipment out of both *Tom* and *Jerry*. He quickly recognized what Carlos was up to when he saw what was being taken out of the aircraft. While they were unloading, a freshly showered Jennifer returned, and with her crew from the house, she took off for Seymour Johnson.

Preston silently hoped that nobody else would appear who needed lodging. He had asked Jennifer to see if the base had any forms of room dividers—walls, doors, partitions—and at least a dozen new beds. They were running out of room.

***

The chairman was in the boardroom—he had hardly left it since he had pressed the red buttons three days ago—and he was being briefed by his team from downstairs.

"We have not had one transponder out of the airfield in North Carolina for 24 hours now, Comrade Chairman," reported one of the engineers.

"And why do you think this is so?" The chairman turned to an advisor who was dressed in a Chinese Air Force uniform with the rank of colonel on his shoulders.

"We have seen no flights out of this airfield, Comrade Chairman," the man explained, "but we have seen single flights showing transponder activity over other areas, mostly heading from the north in a southerly direction, I assume to get away from the cold weather. This current storm is looking very bad for the American people and very good for us."

"We know our satellites are picking up aircraft transponder signals correctly, Comrade Chairman," the colonel responded, still standing at attention. "We have destroyed three aircraft and their pilots in Europe. There was one terminated in Australia early this morning. The other two reports are far out in the western desert and our termination squads are preparing for desert travel. There can only be one of two reasons why we are not picking up transponders in the United States. Either they have run out of fuel and have no way of refueling their aircraft, or they have turned their transponders off."

"Why would they do that?" the chairman asked.

"All military aircraft use their transponders over friendly territory and turn them off during battle conditions, or over foreign soil if needed. All small propeller-driven aircraft can do the same. It is part of their pre-flight checks and mandatory internationally to have their transponders transmitting,

Comrade Chairman."

"Why would they suddenly go to battle conditions, Colonel?"

"If they aren't transmitting for that reason, and we have no evidence to suggest that, it could be that they have realized that an attack might be imminent, or they have found out about our plans and termination squads," the colonel responded.

"Impossible," replied the chairman, snarling at the man. "My plans are 30 years in the making and our termination squads will die before they surrender any information, of which they have little. There is no way the Americans can know who is behind this 'situation.' It was made to look like a natural disaster—to them anyway—and with no communications, nobody should be able to organize anything. They should all be running around like chickens with no heads."

"Yes, Comrade Chairman," the colonel responded. The chairman ordered someone to fetch Comrade Wang. Several minutes later Lee Wang's old boss appeared, looking tired.

"You wanted to see me, Comrade Chairman?" he asked.

"What is the latest information from our people in America?" the chairman asked.

"The ten squads on the East Coast are currently moving south and should be in a position to check out the airfield in North Carolina within 24 hours. There has been much more movement on the East Coast than on the West Coast. We really thought that the warmer weather would produce more work for our men, but may I suggest that we transfer the West Coast teams to the eastern seaboard, Comrade Chairman? We are going to be there two weeks earlier than on the West Coast, and this move will make our teams more successful at eliminating trouble and help the food ships arrive. Once everything is under our power, they will have two weeks to return to the West Coast and organize the food ships there."

"I also have a feeling that something is wrong on the East Coast," the chairman agreed. "Something is not right. Send all the squads in the continental United States in the direction of Washington, D.C. They will take at least three days to get there. Make sure they travel on different roads and in convoys of no more than five or ten vehicles. Travel during the day only, and do not terminate anybody in the farming regions. We are going to need those American farmers to produce food for our new country. I want a complete report as soon as the squads have terminated everybody at this airfield, or whatever it is. It could even be empty of people at this point. Why would anybody stay if there is no fuel to fly anything? Destroy it anyway. Tell the squads to go in fast and terminate everything they see, and then report back immediately. Understand, Comrade Wang?"

"Yes, Comrade Chairman." Mo Wang left, noticing that the old man was getting tired and irritable. He needed to come back with good news.

* * *

The president was waiting, as patient as a man could be with his country in the middle of a meltdown. It was with a sense of satisfaction that they finally heard the rotors of the Huey coming to get them. "About time," he grumbled to the ambassador as they got up to leave. The president had a small overnight bag packed, and his wife and kids came downstairs to say goodbye. He gave them all a big hug and headed out to the garden.

"I don't think you should be leaving the White House, Mr. President," his chief bodyguard commented, worried about losing his control of the protection of the president.

"I understand your concern and I take full responsibility for my actions. I have a letter on my desk relieving you of your responsibility to me, but I want you to protect my wife and children in my place. I will be back here as soon as possible and then you are back in control, understand?" The man nodded. A direct order from the president was an order he couldn't refuse.

General Allen came out to meet him and guided the president and the Colombian Ambassador to the stairs the marines had placed next to the door of the Huey. It wasn't a perfect set of stairs, but it did its job. Buck rose vertically, turned the helicopter around and slowly climbed out of the White House garden as gently as possible. "It's pretty neat in here," the president remarked at the Huey's interior.

"Thank Preston Strong when you get in tonight, Mr. President," laughed the general. "Has Philippe been driving you crazy?"

"Not really. It's been better to have someone around to help me keep what little sanity I have left. What's the game plan, Pete?"

"I have your new bird ready and refueled at Andrews as we speak. We are changing planes and heading straight to North Carolina in about an hour. I'm leaving the helicopter at Andrews for your return flight. We should arrive in North Carolina just before dark. It's time to introduce you to what we have, and then I have arranged for the best room at the Officers' Mess at Seymour Johnson for you to sleep tonight. Unfortunately, we are anticipating some trouble in North Carolina tomorrow and do not want you there when or if it happens. I want to have you back at the White House by midday."

The arriving storm was getting fiercer, and Buck had to concentrate to put *Baby Huey* and its valuable cargo down close to the gunship. After the president and his group departed, a dozen Air Force personnel grabbed everything out of the Huey—chairs and carpet, small fridge, and snacks—and moved them into the rear area of the AC-130, turning it into a more cozy area while the president had a hot cup of coffee in the Officers' Mess.

A half hour later, they all strapped themselves into the uncomfortable side-seats for takeoff, as it was going to be bumpy until they reached cruising altitude. Once the ride smoothed out, however, the three older men moved out into the more comfortable chairs.

* * *

Preston was about to leave RDU. They had had a busy afternoon. As soon as the three C-130s left, he had organized Joe and David to take both armored cars and a jeep over to the airport for the guard unit to use for patrols.

He flew in with the FedEx Cargomaster and did a sweep of the entire area, including flying over the two burnt-out vehicles from the day before. They hadn't moved, but when he saw three vehicles driving around to the east of the airport on the 540 beltline, he flew low to inspect. What he saw was potential trouble-makers—several men aiming their rifles at him as he flew over at 500 feet. He radioed the information to Joe and warned him. Joe and David returned that they were spoiling for a fight but that currently it was all quiet and they were just getting onto the beltline.

Preston flew in to land, and after disembarking, he inspected the gate they had used for their entrances. It was still locked. He listened to see if he could hear any aircraft engines, and all he heard was the odd rifle shot here and there. The wind was picking up, and he smelled a storm on the way. Preston waited a couple of minutes and then heard engines from different directions at the same time. A C-130 cruised overhead, and he radioed Jennifer to come in from the east. He hadn't heard the aircraft in advance because of the noisy armored car engine that arrived with the tractor-trailer, and he unlocked the gate.

Joe reported that they saw several cars headed away from the airport once the C-130 came overhead, and that they had had clear passage all the way in. Preston told Joe and his boys to take the emptied truck around to the other terminal and start loading anything they thought would be needed at the farm, and that they had 90 minutes.

The C-130 came in and parked on the apron close to the gate and shut its engines down. At least 30 soldiers exited and immediately started unloading their gear. A lieutenant came up to greet Preston, who asked if half a dozen men could get in the back of the Cargomaster and help them pack up some stuff. The lieutenant whistled when he saw the armored Saracen that his troops would be using.

"Nice," he smiled at Preston. "It looks like a pretty cool ride. I hope we see some action with her!" Preston grinned back as he took the lieutenant on a brief tour of the area.

"So, this is the main gate?" the lieutenant asked as they checked the lock again. Preston explained that the terminal must be protected, as well as the fuel tanks, and if needed, he and his troops could move to a better location if they found one. He also suggested that the troops try to talk to visitors before engaging them physically, since there could be friendly people driving around looking for food. He spent five minutes with the lieutenant explaining what they had seen on the streets, and that he himself was under the direct orders of General Allen.

By that time, Jennifer walked up and told him that *Mother Goose* was on her way and that the crew was requested to test the civilian tanks here. "Also, Martie says 'Hi'," she added. "She called in to say she is currently flying south at 9,000 feet down I-95 and is doing just fine."

Preston got back in the Cargomaster and started her up before taking six men around to the tractor-trailer's location by the door into the second terminal. Joe, David, and all Joe's boys were already carrying cases to the rear of the trailer. With 14 strong men, they filled the trailer up with case upon case of stuff—two whole pallets of still-frozen bread rolls out of a large walk-in freezer, hot dog buns and sausages, hamburgers, and steaks by the case. They filled the trailer with case upon case of ketchup, mustard, salt and pepper, boxes of frozen vegetables, and cases of mashed potatoes. They also found a complete mobile bar with three beer taps and several dozen kegs.

As a team, they used the gas-powered forklift which Jennifer had flown in from the farm to move the entire unit down an empty walkway into the truck, and then packed two dozen full beer kegs and every case of alcohol out of the restaurant.

It took 30 minutes and all 14 men sweating, but the area was finally cleaned out and empty. Preston even took the bar stools and dining tables to place in his hangar area as a cafeteria. One of the soldiers asked if he wanted a gas oven and grill top, and Preston replied that if he could undo everything, he would take the whole kitchen. Three of the soldiers got to work and had everything on the truck in 15 minutes.

The next restaurant had even more stuff, and again, anything that moved in the airport terminal was used to transport goods to the walkway Joe had backed the truck up to. At each location, a two-week supply of food products was left for the soldiers. A second bar area was emptied of anything to sit on and tables to eat from. The bar itself was emptied of alcohol, as well more bread, pizza dough, and anything that looked like it would last longer than a couple of days.

Within 90 minutes, the trailer was full and the kitchen equipment, parts of it ready for transportation, were being moved and loaded with the forklift. Preston remembered that Jennifer had an empty aircraft and asked one of the men to tell her to taxi it over.

It took another 20 minutes, but a second gas grill and dozens of 100-pound propane tanks were stacked into the C-130. Joe and his team were already leaving, with the full tractor-trailer truck sandwiched between the two armored cars. Jennifer came running over to Preston.

"Martie just called back," she stated, breathing hard. "She has a few injured people aboard, about 30 minutes out. She found a convoy of survivors and told me to tell the guards that two Southwest pilots, their crew, and about 60 passengers will be arriving here tomorrow around midday via ground vehicle. We are to let them in. They will use General Allen's name. And Preston, it's time to leave." With that, she told one of the men to run over to the lieutenant, who was still erecting his tents, and give him the new information.

The few remaining men closed everything down and Preston and Jennifer climbed aboard their respective aircraft, noticing that *Mother Goose* was also starting up.

Within 15 minutes, RDU was cleared of all visiting aircraft.

Martie was still several minutes out when Jennifer arrived at the Strong airport, followed by *Mother Goose*, with Preston a mile or two out, circling above Joe and waiting for Martie. She was already in view and came straight in from the south as Preston closed in and began to circle his farm. He saw that sandbags and a barrier were already in place and that the tractor-trailer could just squeeze through the defensive wall that closed off the dirt road south of his entrance gate. The whole farm was starting to look like a military installation.

While they were away, Sally had returned from Andrews with more troops and equipment from facilities along the East Coast. There were new sandbagged mortar placements around the perimeter protecting the area nearer the lake. A second hospital tent was up next to the old barn and the whole airfield looked like something out of M.A.S.H.

Then he heard General Allen's voice say over the radio that Alpha Foxtrot One was ten minutes out and needed landing conditions.

"Pete, this is Preston. I'm above our airfield and it's busy down there right now. Don't rush. I need to get down first. The wind looks like 15 to 20 knots from the northeast and straight down the runway, temperature about 40 degrees. Did you say

Alpha Foxtrot One?"

"Roger, Preston. You get down there and organize a place for Ghost Rider on the apron by the hangar. Get a red carpet if you have one. All Air Force pilots, get your birds off the apron area and park on the other side of the runway in a line next to the barn," Preston heard the general say.

Preston went down like a rocket and landed quickly in the growing storm and parked in the first available empty space where *Baby Huey* was normally stationed. He quickly turned off the aircraft and jumped out to organize a reception squad from the remaining troops on the tarmac—the president was incoming. They quickly ran to find the parts of their uniforms that were missing and Preston changed direction and crossed the runway just behind Sally's third C-130 that was taxiing off onto the grass. He got blown about, but was more interested in checking on Martie. He found her helping dress the wound of an older lady with a new woman Preston hadn't seen before helping her. This extremely good-looking new arrival was dressed in a dirty flight attendant's uniform and she had a young girl, a teenager, sitting very close to her. Little Beth was trying to talk to the teenager, who looked scared and very unsure of herself.

"Martie, I need you in the hangar. We have a VIP coming in," Preston said.

"Preston, this is Pam. Pam, I'd like you to meet Preston," Martie said quickly as she finished the bandaging.

"Pam Wallace, Preston," the newcomer replied, shaking his hand. "Martie, you go on. I want the girls to get to know each other better and this injured lady here has offered to look after them. She's a school teacher and our younger additions will be better off with her for the time being. I think we have serious work to do. I'll catch up with you in a few minutes, okay?"

Martie gave Little Beth a hug and told her to make friends with the older girl and that the older lady would look after them while she was at work. Beth seemed to understand, and left Martie's side for the first time since she had arrived, allowing Martie to follow Preston. Preston noted that the first medical tent was already quite warm with heat generated by several gas heaters.

They had already connected the hospital electricity to his generator, but he didn't have time to check it right now. He and Martie ran across the tarmac just in time to see the fourth C-130, about three or four miles out over the lake, just a few moments away from turning into its final approach. The sergeant was also preparing himself for the reception. He was the senior military person on base, apart from the new doctor.

"Do we have a red carpet?" Preston asked Martie.

"No," she replied. "The only moveable carpet we own you already sent somewhere into Washington this morning. By the way, I saw what we were looking for. There are ten trucks with about 30 to 40 guys, and they should be turning off I-95 in about 30 minutes to an hour."

"You did?" He suddenly stopped and looked at her. They were right in the middle of the runway, but the news floored him for a second. The roar of the incoming plane shook him out of his surprise. "Let's get off here! You tell the general that as soon as you can!"

They ran off the runway in the direction of the house as a groggy looking Will Smart came out of the back door, moaning to Maggie about foul play. "Get yourselves together. Maggie, get inside and tell everybody that the President of the United States is less than a minute out. Go!" Preston shouted to them, and Maggie looked at him in surprise. Preston looked at Will and laughed. "Will, buddy, you are an experienced pilot, I've heard. Martie is willing to give you flying lessons any time you want. Ever meet the president?"

"No," replied Will, still groggy.

"Well, I'll take you over. You look a mess, but then we all do," he said, and he helped Will over to Sergeant Perry, who was now standing with 30 or so men in three lines ready to welcome the president.

There were sudden exits from all doors as people came running, Michael pushing Grandpa Roebels in the wheelchair from the direction of the house. Carlos and the whole Wang family came out from the hangar's side door. Joe, David, and their team were just pulling into an area by the house, and several dozen soldiers were running in all directions to man their guns and secure the main gate.

Preston beckoned over to Joe and his group as they came to a dusty halt, and he smiled as he looked over everyone. Martie stood at his side and the rest of the Air Force pilots ran over to join them. Everybody was grubby and most of the troops were missing bits of uniform here and there, but they were as ready as they would ever be. Joe and his group ran over and asked what was going on.

"Joe, get your boys lined up, and you, David, stand by Martie and me. All civilians, listen up! Please get into an orderly group, like our troops over there. We are about to welcome the President of the United States!" Preston turned just in time to see the tires of Air Force One touchdown on his little runway in North Carolina.

The troops stood to attention as the aircraft passed them, and it turned in at the end of the runway, turned in front of the gas tanks and came to a halt facing north before the pilot let its engines go quiet and opened the side door.

General Allen was the first to disembark, giving the President of the United States a hand with the small jump to the ground. An older man was helped out next, then Carlos' father and three Colombian-looking bodyguards. Finally Buck and Barbara came out. In his head, Preston was just hoping that there were enough beds in the hangar for all the people spilling out of the airplane!

There were shouted orders from Sergeant Perry, and the troops did what troops do when the president arrives. The president smiled at everyone and he and the older man walked over with General Allen to be introduced to the civilians.

Preston and Martie were first. "Mr. President, I'd like to introduce you to the owners of the farm, Mr. Preston Strong and Ms. Martie Roebels," the general said. All parties shook hands.

"I've heard you guys are having more action down here than I'm seeing at the White House, so I hope you don't mind my visit," the president said with his world-famous smile.

"If I'd known you were coming, sir, I would have built a Presidential Suite for you," replied Preston, grinning.

"It would have only taken us a week, Mr. President. General Allen could have given us a little more notice," added Martie, also smiling at the president and winking at the general. "General, I need to speak to you about our now-confirmed incoming visitors as soon as possible."

"Okay, let's get the introductions done," the general replied. "Preston, you know everybody here. Could you please introduce the president and his friends to all these fine folk while I have a conversation with your lady here? Preston, Martie, this is Carlos' uncle, Uncle Philippe, the Colombian Ambassador to the United States, and Carlos' father, Manuel." They all shook hands.

"I've heard many good things about you, Preston and Martie" the ambassador said as he greeted them. "Carlos really appreciates your friendship. These are my bodyguards—actually, family—Manuela, Mannie, and Dani." The bodyguards quickly moved and stood with Carlos.

It was now up to Preston to introduce the president and ambassador to the rest of those in attendance. General Allen, anxious about the president's safety, took Martie by the arm and led her away to talk.

The introductions were first made to all the civilians, and the president was extremely interested in his introduction to Lee Wang and family. Once the president had met everyone, Preston took him over to meet the troops while Carlos explained to his uncle and father who Lee and his family were. Preston introduced the president to Captains Powers and Watkins, who introduced him to the other pilots. The pilots spoke with their Commander-in-Chief for a few minutes and then Captain Powers introduced him to First Sergeant Perry, who in turn introduced him to each of the troops at attention.

By this time, the general was back and asked all personnel to move into the hangar where it was warm. It was time for a meeting. He asked First Sergeant Perry to attend and for volunteers to find snacks and drinks—it was going to be a long meeting. Joe enlisted some soldiers to follow him and his boys to the trailer and get several tables and chairs out of the back.

"Quite a setup you have here, Preston," the president stated, walking down the runway with its owner, a totally free man for the first time since he had become president four years earlier. He was without his bodyguards hounding him every step of the way. The perimeter was now secure, the defenses on the road nearly complete, and he wanted some fresh air while everybody was getting ready for the meeting. Both men spent a few minutes inspecting the old aircraft. Preston walked with the president, as did Oliver and the puppy. "It took a bit of money to get all this together."

"It did, Mr. President," Preston replied. "My father was the co-pilot on the flight that went down over Lockerbie, Scotland, and the settlement money helped fund my airport."

They quickly went over each aircraft. The two remaining Mustangs were parked next to the hospital tents on the south side of the old barn facing the runway, and the P-38 was next to them. The president was impressed. The FedEx Cargomaster was the last one on that side.

"You are doing FedEx deliveries these days?" the president queried.

"I'm thinking a little forward with this one and those Cessna aircraft we commandeered from Raleigh-Durham International Airport, Mr. President." Preston explained his idea. "I'm thinking about food distribution to the hungry in the area, and I know that the bases around here have well over five million meal rations in storage that were destined for our troops overseas. Since there is no way we can get them over there, I was hoping to use them to feed as many people on this side as we could." The president was quiet when the mention of the overseas troops came up. He shook his head and looked down at the ground.

They completed the tour at the last aircraft, which was the gunship he had arrived in. It was being refueled to fly high for protection while the president was on the ground. The president was unfamiliar with the AC-130, so Preston asked the aircraft's armaments officer to explain the weaponry pointing out of its left side.

"This is a 20mm Vulcan Cannon, sir—the same fitted to most Air Force aircraft since Vietnam, such as F-15s, F-4s, etc. It's a Gatling gun that can fire up to 100 rounds a second and normally is used for the destruction of ground troops and small vehicles. We hold 3,000 rounds in *Ghost Rider* and normally use the cannon for short bursts of 300 to 400 rounds. The Bofors 40mm light anti-aircraft gun is for protection from the air. We carry 240 rounds. This baby saved *Ghost Rider* a couple times in Vietnam. The last gun, the big one, is the 105mm Howitzer. We carry 100 rounds for her, sir, and she is mainly used for larger ground vehicles like tanks or any buildings we need to flatten. We are currently carrying 60 rounds that can penetrate most armor on tanks and or many naval ships, as well as 40 rounds that are HE, or 'high explosive.' If anybody comes sniffing around tonight, we will see them miles away with our original and working infra-red and heat scopes. We can see the movement of a mouse at 5,000 feet. She is one of two Air Force C-130s that were heavily modified during Vietnam. Like all of these older C-130s we have flying, she can be refueled in the air."

Preston and the president thanked the man and walked back to the hangar. They entered the side door as the gunship began her whine. Preston noticed the two armored cars disappearing down the driveway towards the gate. In the hangar, they found that chairs of all sorts had been placed in rows for the meeting, the most comfortable ones in the front. Preston also noticed that three new rooms had appeared on the southern wall of the hangar with movable partitions, and he could see wooden army beds inside them. He figured there were about a dozen beds per room.

The general was waiting, and Preston was surprised to see Joe and David still in the room. They must have allowed the Air Force personnel to drive their valuable toys out to the ambush zone.

"Mr. President, you are seated next to the ambassador and Mr. Rodriquez, please. We need to get started," instructed General Allen. "Preston, your seat is next to Martie, naturally." Preston noticed that he was also sitting next to the president.

Everybody was in attendance. Next to Martie was Pam Wallace, the extremely pretty flight attendant, and next to her was Grandpa Roebels with Michael next to him. The second row was the 'complete' Smart family, Carlos, the three Colombian bodyguards, Sally, Buck, and Barbara. In the third row were Jennifer, David, and Joe and all his sons. The fourth row was the Air Force doctor, his chief nurse, First Sergeant Perry, and the technical sergeants. The fifth and sixth rows were assorted Air Force personnel who were not currently on duty at the entrance or in the fire tower.

"Good evening, y'all," the general smiled, using his best southern drawl. "We have two hours before *Ghost Rider*—the AC-130 gunship—lands and the president leaves. Hopefully, we will not be attacked during our meeting, but I want Martie and her new friend to come up and tell us what they saw today and what we can expect. Martie, Pam, you have five minutes." The two women got up and walked to the front of the room.

"This is Pam Wallace," started Martie. "Pam is a senior flight attendant with Southwest Airlines, and she was on a flight that took off from La Guardia four minutes before midnight on New Year's Eve. Her pilot, Captain Mike Mallory, managed to put his dysfunctional aircraft down in the water around New York with no loss of life. The captain, his crew, and many of his passengers drove south with a very interesting group of vehicles that I got a chance to see today, just north of the North Carolina state line." Martie continued and gave her report on the Southwest crew and passengers she had met, as well as the convoy of ten vehicles she had seen from the air—mostly old Chevy Suburbans and Ford trucks she had seen a couple miles behind the Southwest convoy on the southbound side of the highway.

"Hi, everyone! It's so nice to see civilization again," Pam started as Martie gave her the floor. "The rest of our group will be arriving at RDU tomorrow, thanks to Martie. I know that our two pilots will be itching to help you guys, if you can loan them some wings. They are out of a job at the moment. I also am a private pilot and can help you as a spotter pilot, if you need me."

Pam grinned at the murmur of laughter she heard. "On a more serious note, the other convoy coming south has roughly ten vehicles with what looks like three to six people per vehicle. We never really got close enough to see for sure, but they killed two innocent people for no reason. They passed us during our first night. We had driven down the northbound lane only because it was the only lane we could get onto in New York, and we never bothered to change. The other convoy was driving in the southbound lane, so we do not think they ever knew we were in the vicinity. We tried to catch up with them at one point, until we came across the two freshly dead bodies. They had been shot several times and every vehicle in the convoy had run over the bodies, flattening them into the snow. This led us to believe that they were people to be avoided, and we transferred back to the other side of the highway and stayed away from them until we turned off for our second night's stay at a small airport just north of the North Carolina state line."

At this point, Pam paused as if she was trying to figure out how to word what she wanted to say. "There is something I think we need to deal with pretty quickly, and that is how to feed and provide good drinking water to the U.S. civilians. Mr. President, General Allen, Captain Mallory spoke about this at our last overnight stop, and I think our Southwest team would like to take it further. We had a long talk with some farmers up in Maryland, and the captain told them to start farming and breeding animals as soon as the weather allows, and he asked them to spread the word across the country, telling people to hold on and start finding ways to become self-sufficient. The farmers must produce food for the hungry as quickly as possible, protect themselves from attackers, and help people coming south from colder areas." She got resounding applause from the group, and the president gave her a nod of approval. "To conclude, our trip south on the highway was horrible. We must have seen thousands of people dead in their vehicles or around them. It's very cold out there and there must be millions of people dead or dying from being exposed to these horrible weather conditions. The snow on the highway south of New York was up to six inches deep and icy conditions just before New Year's Eve must have been the cause of many of the accidents. Many of the big fatal accidents happened near tractor-trailers going out of control, and the carnage—just on the piece of highway south of Newark—was terrible. Thank you."

Martie stepped back in to continue. "I had my binoculars fixed on the other convoy while I was in the air, and it looked like the vehicles were full of people, as Pam said. If they are coming our way, they most likely turned off I-95 about an hour ago and should be on the outskirts of Raleigh by now. The dead vehicles on the incoming roadways will slow them down for the last 20 miles or so, but if they are coming here, they should be in our area within the next couple of hours."

The general thanked the two ladies for their reports and asked First Sergeant Perry to give his situation report on the defense structure for this potential attack scenario.

"Mr. President, Mr. Ambassador, General Allen," Sergeant Perry began, "we have set up a perimeter around this field that is ready to hold off an ambitious attack. We have completed our ambush scenario along the 300-foot dirt road leading to the asphalt feeder road, and have changed it slightly since our initial ideas this morning. The men have made and painted a simple wooden airport sign with an arrow pointing to the entrance of the airport—the way we want them to come in. This is to make sure they drive into our ambush. We have a wall of sandbags across the dirt road 50 feet before the gate entrance to this property. This is to make sure that any incoming vehicles will have to stop. There are no vehicles allowed in or out except Mr. Joe and Mr. David. They turn left anyway and one of David's two armored cars has been placed further down the road, 250 feet behind the barrier. Our latest scenario takes the entrance gate out of the ambush. The armored Ferret is behind a double wall of sandbags to protect it from any shoulder-operated missiles. It is positioned where the lights of any incoming vehicles will light up the barricade, but leave the armored car in the darkness behind the barricade, if they decide to attack before dawn. After dawn, we will review the ambush zone and make the barricade across the road the main focal point. If they open fire at the barricade, we will know that they aren't friendly and fire back. The barricade is 3 feet high and made of a triple line of sandbags behind the turned-over dining tables we brought from Seymour Johnson."

Sergeant Perry paused to fish some notes out of his pocket to make sure he had the information listed correctly. "The barrier will be manned by 20 soldiers with M4s and a machine gun on either side in the shallow drainage ditches, again protected by sandbags and camouflaged with heavy brush. There is no way around the barricade, and the 200 feet of road where any enemy vehicles would need to stop is fully visible from the fire tower. A third and fourth machine gun has been placed on the fire tower, which will be invisible before dawn, but unfortunately very visible in the daylight. Two small 2-inch mortars have been placed 200 yards inside the wired perimeter and are ready to fire into the ambush point. My plan is that there will be three to four men in civilian clothes with hunting rifles 'guarding' the barricade. I want it to look like a bunch of farmers protecting their road from visitors, so we have hidden any forms of military presence as best we can. As soon as the men see the lights of vehicles, they will get behind the sandbags and shout to anyone to stop. That is when we expect action. The men will be surrounded by Air Force troops along the barricade with automatic carbines.

"Last, we cannot allow the ambushers to retreat. Carlos has explained that the first items we must find are the communications devices they are using. He thinks that they are small satellite cell phones. So, we have set up a first retreat kill zone in the trees on the other side of the entrance on the feeder road. Thanks to Mr. Joe and Mr. David, we have enough mobile radios for all groups and the commanders of each section to be in radio contact throughout the fight. The attack armament for the retreating ambushes is the second Rat Patrol jeep facing down the short piece of road from the trees on the other side of the feeder road. Again, we have placed sandbags around it for protection. The two machine guns will wreak havoc on any retreating enemy.

"A mile north and south on the feeder road, I have placed a platoon of 30 men who are to stay hidden in the forest until any convoy passes, and then they will close down the road and shoot anybody who runs into them with two mortars and machine guns. In the forest to the east of the feeder road, and dug in to protect themselves from friendly fire, is another dozen troops, spaced out every 100 feet with night goggles. Their job is to bring down anybody escaping through the forest. My last ambush position is one flanking ambush squad of 12 men who are behind sandbags, and are facing towards the ambush road area, and inside the perimeter fence. The perimeter fence is 20 yards from the road—a little closer than I would like if the mortars land short, but their job is to kill the ambushers from the side and to make sure our perimeter is not breached. That ends my report."

"How strong is your barrier at the front of the road?" David asked.

"We have considered what the worse armaments are that potential ambushers can carry in small vehicles," replied the first sergeant. "The worse they could have are shoulder rocket launchers like an RPG, then rifle grenades, and lastly machine guns. If they have anything more, then we could consider them a suicide squad. Our men have been issued with gas masks if the attackers are wearing them upon entry, Mr. David. We are hoping that our forward troops on the feeder road using night binoculars and infra-red scopes can tell us their exact numbers and whether they are wearing any protective equipment. That should tell us their intentions."

"And this is complete and all the men are in position?" asked the general.

"Yes, sir. The men have camouflage gear, there is no snow at the moment, and they have rations to last 24 hours. Apart from

Mr. Joe, Mr. David, and me, we are ready for action."

"Could they have mortars and decide to shell us from outside the one-mile radius?" asked Preston.

"They could, sir, but anything that big couldn't fit in a Suburban or Explorer," Sergeant Perry answered. "The attackers might have small mortars, but I believe that our troops, from three angles, will be fast enough to keep them from setting up any mortars or tripod machine guns. I think that shoulder rocket launchers, however, are the best bet. We have several troops at the front barricade and on the sides of the ambush zone ready with flares. The flares are quick-action, low-level flares that will light up the scene within seconds. The men in the forest have sniper rifles with night scopes, as well as the men on both sides of the feeder road. I believe nobody can escape, sir."

The general nodded and thanked Sergeant Perry, who then asked to leave to complete final checks.

Preston noticed that one of David's mobile radios had been placed to one side of the podium and it suddenly squawked a message calling Pete.

"*Ghost Rider to Pete!*"

"What's up, *Ghost Rider?*" Pete Allen replied, walking over to the radio and picking up the microphone.

"*We have a visual of the ten vehicles moving through the middle of downtown Raleigh. We have seen several civilians go out to meet them, and it looks like the men in the vehicles shoot to kill. There are several dead bodies on the streets they have been traveling. There is heavy civilian population in this area.*

Do you want us to take them out?"

"Negative," the general replied. "We are prepared for their arrival."

"*They seem to have disappeared into…I think an underground parking* area…no, they have come out the other side. They are still all together in a convoy. Another person has been shot and several civilians are running for cover. They have gone into another building and we have lost sight of them. I don't believe they can hear us—the wind is gusting down the streets about 20 to 25 miles an hour from the north and we are south of them. We are in a holding pattern and will keep watching. Over."

"Let us know if you get visual again. Out," replied the general. "We still have time. I would like Carlos' friend Lee Wang to come up and tell us his complete story. Mr. Wang, you have 20 minutes. Mr. President, this is going to blow you away!"

For the full 20 minutes, Lee told them his whole story, from his degrees obtained in China, to the first day he met the cleaner, to Zedong Electronics in Nanjing and its new building. He described the special private island belonging to Zedong Electronics across the river from Shanghai where they lived and were taught how to be Americans, and then how he dissected the small electronic part for a Toyota engine's computer system. He explained his job in America and how he got into private companies to steal, copy or describe new inventions about to go to market. It was necessary for Zedong Electronics to get this information so they could produce cheaper parts for the world to buy. He then explained how Zedong Electronics had so many different departments and virtually took over the world's manufacturing of every electronic part and or unit. He explained his duty to Zedong Electronics for his daughter's education. He had worked at Microsoft, Qualcomm, Intel, Acer, IBM and Apple—twenty-five years of work. He thought that he was doing good work, so that the electronics giant would be successful for China and its people and bring China into the forefront of the world, and that his work would mean a better life for all Chinese.

He never realized, until the termination squads started killing all the operatives like him, that something was wrong.

Lee Wang finally explained about meeting Carlos, hearing from friends about the danger they were all in, and the attack on him and his family. He said that he and his family were lucky to be alive, and then he sat down.

General Allen asked Carlos to come up and explain what he and Lee Wang had completed in Salt Lake City. Carlos introduced himself and his qualifications and got straight down to business.

"Lee Wang did not tell you that Zedong Electronics has the only three still-working satellites covering the globe for communications. These hit squads, or whatever you want to call them, are being ordered around through the use of these satellites. Lee and I sourced communications going both ways from the United States and Western Europe into the area around Nanjing, China. If we still had an Air Force, the headquarters of Zedong Electronics would be the first building to be taken out. If we could do so, it would destroy their whole communication setup. But we cannot do it from space."

For the next several minutes, Carlos told the audience about the Navistar P—a secret project spearheaded by the Air Force in the 1980s. Because it was sent into space such a long time ago, as well as being subject to simpler computer communications using DOS, he and Lee found older computers to communicate with it. Carlos explained how it had been lost and that he had found it by mistake. "Through the satellite, we can now see the United States, as well as a sea boundary. I will be working to increase our range out to a 500-mile boundary, but remember, the digital footage is antiquated and the screens we can use are also antiquated. The zoom on the camera lenses is only treble magnification, which means the further we send her out, the less detail we can see. Currently, we could see a large ship enter the viewing area 200 miles out to sea. One thing I did see, moments before we packed up to come down the mountain, was a large storm over Canada and the northern areas. It's a bad one, and it is flowing south out of the Arctic. We rode in on it, and these winds are the result of the arctic blast, as the weather men used to call it. I would hate to be north of here. It's getting very cold up there."

Carlos paused for a moment and looked over at the man he now called friend. "To continue, Lee Wang should be complimented on his willingness and ability to help us in our time of need. Through the satellite communication relays from Navistar P, we have found three areas of space where communications are being transmitted to and from. Unfortunately, Navistar P was not armed with lasers, and or else we could, like in a James Bond movie, blast their communications satellites out of the sky. In the 1970s when this thing was being designed, lasers were only just being researched."

"So, with television trucks and their satellite-feed systems juiced into simple television screens, again from the 70s, we think we can set up a range of communication tools across the country. A large national system will take several weeks, and that is not most important yet. The current pictures from space will be our first alert of any attacks on the United States—any long-range aircraft headed our way, etc. We need every television truck, every Hughes two-way communication dishes that are placed on homes or businesses, every working pre-1985 computer, every two-way radio that works, and every old television set we can find to carry out this project. Lastly, any old civilian camcorders or film cameras will give you visual as well as audio communications. Within a week, we hope to have communications with several military bases in the country and might have some troops ready for repelling insurgents."

"Great work, guys," applauded the president. "It seems that we are going forward after all, and it was well worth my visit."

"Thank you, Mr. President. And thanks to all these guys who have worked non-stop since the beginning of this year—three days ago," stated General Allen, getting up to stand next to Carlos, and there was applause. Once it died down, the general continued.

"I know that for most of us, it already feels like a month, but let me conclude this meeting with MY report. So far, thanks to these guys here, we have radio communication with Andrews AFB, Edwards AFB, Hill AFB, and our own Strong Air Force

Base right here, pun intended. We will not install our temporary Air Force sign at the front entrance on the main road until our soon-to-arrive visitors have been dealt with. So far, we have four C-130s flying and three fully operational F-4s now at Andrews. We will have several more C-130s operational in a day or two, most stationed at Hill in Salt Lake City and Edwards in California. Another HC-130 tanker should be operational in Yuma, and I'm heading down there tomorrow. As far as more flyable aircraft, two Hueys that have been in museums until now are being made operational at Andrews. A lot of you know that we have over 50 Air Force bases here in the United States. Several of the bases on what we would call the front line have only the most modern equipment, so I will visit them last. Tomorrow, I'm dropping the president back in Washington, and then I will be spending three days continuously visiting bases to find anything I can that is flyable."

The general looked over at Sally and Jennifer. "Captains Powers and Watkins will be coming north with me tomorrow. We will fly in formation back to Andrews. Once we repel this attack that I believe will happen tomorrow morning, I can concentrate on getting a big defense force together. Since I know all my bases and museums well, I believe that we could end up with a dozen C-130s, of which three are fuel tankers. I know there are another dozen or so helicopters around. I must find them as well as several other types of aircraft. As Carlos reported, our current aircraft could give us a long arm into Asia to take out the enemy's headquarters. Now whether or not all of China is involved, I don't know. If it is, and their Air Force is operational, the boys and I would not return from such a mission. If only Zedong Electronics is the enemy, and the Chinese Air Force is grounded, then we'll have a chance to blow their headquarters apart, and the HC-130 tankers can refuel us and get us back to friendly soil. This mission should take about a week.

"Here on U.S. soil, we have the three F-4s as our first line of defense or attack. They can still be refueled in-flight with one of our Vietnam-era HC-130 fuel tankers. Our second line of attack or defense will be the three P-51 Mustangs and the P-38 Lightning. All four of these aircraft can be fitted with 500-pound bombs, and their .50-caliber machine guns are fully operational. The P-38 can carry two 1,000 pounders—she has pylons that we can modify and fit two Sidewinder missiles on each wing, and all her cannon and machine guns are operational. Behind the second line are the three Huey helicopters, which we can arm with four air-to-ground rockets and a 20mm Minigun each, if needed. It is not a lot, but it's a start.

"I will be meeting with the Army and Navy this week, as well. I believe the best we can expect from the Navy is six operational submarines and four destroyers—all World War II era. The Army has a lot more potential with artillery than the Navy. The only army weapons, apart from the men and their carbines, will be manually controlled artillery pieces, which are still a powerful force to be reckoned with for sea and harbor defense. They will hopefully have dozens of older trucks or troop carriers to drag these old howitzers by the dozens to defend against any sea attack. The range of some of these weapons is as good as five miles out to sea, and any Chinese ship's intricate missile systems could be blocked by hundreds of ingoing artillery rounds from bridges, beaches, and even the tops of buildings. We can lift these howitzers anywhere with the larger lifting helicopters that I must still locate. I saw them in operation less than a year ago, in San Diego, I believe. The Coast Guard has a couple of old C-130s. In total, our potential to drop paratroopers at a moment's notice in a dozen C-130s will be a maximum of 900 troops, and I will be preparing for this."

"The last thing I want to get to is what Ms. Wallace mentioned—civilian aid. We have been primed for a year now to send maximum numbers of supplies overseas. Our now defunct C-17s have been working around the clock to take food supplies and ammunition to the vast numbers of troops over there. Our bases, especially on the East and West Coasts, are full to overflowing with rations and could potentially keep a large number of our American population alive. We must set up distribution centers at Bragg and Seymour Johnson to deliver quantities of food on a regular basis in this area. We can use all of our aircraft which aren't needed for troop movement and firepower in this endeavor.

"Can we help the whole country? No, not for a few months, it's not possible, but we must help as many people as we can. Survivors from the north will logically head south over the next couple of weeks, and we must help people in rural areas with military supplies we will also fly in on a regular basis. I'm thinking that we should deliver to an area of the country that is below a specific line across the country, say from Washington, D.C. to Salt Lake City and then down to Edwards in California. Under this line there will be a greater chance of survival than further north."

"We cannot go and get the people—they must first migrate south, where we can hopefully provide some food and use large buildings for shelter. If the remaining American population can hold out until spring, then I believe the United States of America has a chance of survival. Any questions?"

"What are the chances of our current Air Force going up against the best of the Chinese fighters, if they are flying?" Preston asked.

"Suicide if we attack China, since about 80% of their military is for defense and not offense," answered the general. "The Chinese have a very small Blue-Water navy, which means they have the ability to travel over any ocean and attack a foreign country. I believe that they only have five to seven ships that can legitimately be called 'Blue-Water' capable. Our understanding is that the Chinese military was never expected to cover global action until 2009 when more ambitious programs went into build mode, and as far as we know everything is still in build mode except for their one aircraft carrier purchased from the Ukraine. We were told last year that this carrier was nearly operational.

"In other words, they have very few aircraft or naval ships that can travel over the Pacific and attack the United States and then fly all the way back again. Actually, no aircraft in the world can do that. All aircraft must either refuel in the air, or refuel on land for their return flights, or land on an aircraft carrier. Our only real defense is non-guided rockets or missiles, and I believe we still have a lot of those that are still operational. I'm hoping that the Army can come up with enough old rockets to fire from batteries on shore to keep the Chinese anti-missile machines busy long enough for us to either drop bombs on them or sneak up and attack. I will let you know about that tomorrow."

The general stopped for a moment. There was so much information to present and review that he was worried that the mixed crowd in the room might be on overload.

"Now I believe everybody in this room is as prepped for war as the president. Our main question is where they will attack first. Of course, the West Coast or Hawaii would be the closest, but Washington, D.C. will be the real prize. I'm sure that they think we are already on our knees and on the verge of begging for mercy, but this country will not go down without a fight. Everyone knows that. This weather rules out any attack from the north or around our northern cities. The attacking force would need to bring in too much gear.

"Maybe they will attack in the spring, after more of us have starved or frozen to death. They don't want us—more likely they just want our land. The Russians and the Chinese have enough people to transfer over and start a new life. Americans will just get in the way. Hence, I don't expect a full-scale attack during the coldest time of the year. The weather will do more damage than they ever could.

"I would like to get tomorrow's hostilities over with first, hopefully capture a few of their satellite telephones, and then we can get Carlos and Mr. Wang to tap into their communications and figure out their future plans. Then I want to destroy their building in Nanjing. It will show them that we still have guts. *Ghost Rider*, *Easy Girl* and the tankers are the only aircraft that could make the trip at this moment, but I believe a third gunship is operational. I have just got to find her. *Ghost Rider*, two other gunships and several normal C-130s were especially prepared to be refueled in flight during the later days in Vietnam. These aircraft have the same refueling nozzles as the Vietnam Hueys and F-4s have, and I'm lucky we planned to keep a few around.

"The United States needs to get every ship we can over to the Middle East and bring as many troops back here as possible, much like the retreat of Dunkirk during World War II. Then, I want to destroy the people who have caused the deaths of millions—and maybe billions of the world's population—even if we have to declare war on China, Mr. President. A declaration of war would be our last resort, and only upon your orders."

The room was deathly silent as General Allen then walked over to the radio and called up *Ghost Rider* to return for a sitrep. Nothing had changed. The enemy convoy seemed to be holed up in the city for the time being and *Ghost Rider* would be landing at the Strong AFB in 15 minutes. Preston automatically went over and turned on the runway lights already repositioned for maximum runway length.

"I would like Mr. Wang and family, the newcomers, all non-American citizens, and all Air Force personnel to leave the room for a few minutes, if you don't mind," the general instructed. "I believe that what I'm about to say is not for your ears yet." Many people, including the ambassador, got up and shook the hand of the president. Pam Wallace escorted them into the house and Martie suggested they make fresh coffee while they waited. The soldiers left to go back to their duties, guards were placed outside the side and front doors, and the general continued. "The reason for talking with you separately is that if we are able to break into communications in China, Carlos, Mr. Wang might need to interpret on our behalf and I don't want him to know all our details. Also, this would normally be just between the president and me, but in these circumstances, I need you to be aware of more than you would normally be authorized to know. What I'm about to say cannot go further than the walls of this hangar!" Everyone in the room nodded affirmatively.

"If we find out that all of China is planning to attack us—in other words, if this situation is directly attributable to the Chinese Ruling Party—we have an old set of Bay of Pigs/Vietnam War-era active nuclear missile silos in the Dakotas. If I am right, they are still active, purposely forgotten through all the disarmament treaties with the old Soviet Union. Much like Japan and the Second World War in the Pacific, a couple of these dropped on Moscow, Nanjing, and Beijing could end this attack on us and the rest of the world.

"If I do not return from our trip to China, we will initiate this last scenario. If Carlos can get us in touch with the Russian or Chinese governments first, then we can introduce them to the fact that we are still a country with a mean bite and if we are going to go down we will make sure that we take as much of them as we can. We have a total of six nuclear weapons on quality missiles that I believe can still reach any targets we provide for them, without any modern satellite guidance."

There was silence as the truth dawned on them that there was little chance that the world would ever be the same again, and that Armageddon might still be possible. Unfortunately, nobody had much to lose here anymore, and being Mr. Nice Guy was not going to be part of the procedure.

"Thank you for your time," the general wrapped up. "You are as up to date as the president, and by the way, I like Ms. Wallace's idea. Preston, get with the Southwest captain when you can, and commandeer any private aircraft you wish to, to begin organizing the distribution of food under direct orders from the President of the United States."

The president stood and faced Preston and the group. "I completely support the ideas stated here in this room and I give all of you the authority of my position as Commander-in-Chief to commandeer anything you need from the military, National Guard, and civilian organizations to assist the American people in any way you deem fit. I will get a letter drawn up for you as soon as I get back to my office."

There were many words of thanks and best wishes as everybody rose and the departing president got ready to leave.

Twenty minutes later, Preston watched as the AC-130 left the airfield, with Sally flying, a full crew, and Buck aboard as a passenger, to fly the president back to the White House, if need be, from the air base. The ambassador, Manuel, and the three bodyguards were also aboard, since the ambassador wanted to get back to his staff at the Embassy to sort out their safe passage south for the remainder of the winter. Preston felt that the president actually wanted to stay and be part of the action here, and he was pretty sure that the Commander-in Chief would be back pretty quickly. The president was that kind of a leader.

Preston turned off the runway lights and switched his focus to preparing for the incoming attack.

Chapter 5

The First Attack

AS DETAILED IN ALL MILITARY TEXTBOOKS, just before dawn is the best time of day to attack an enemy camp. In the book *The Art of War*, Sun Tzu describes how attacking at that hour has an immediate benefit for the attackers. The writing also states that surprise is a key element and, unfortunately, you cannot tell if surprise has been achieved until you actually attack the enemy camp.

Surprise was not to be on this cold morning in North Carolina. The convoy of Chinese men from New York, with no lights and traveling under blackout conditions, passed the outer point of the Air Force troops at 5:30 am. They had driven slowly and quietly, undetected by anybody, and with the airfield's coordinates on their maps, they followed US64 west.

The Air Force troops on guard were cold, frustrated with the weather, and ready for anything to happen. Better to be in a hot fight than lying around under cold, damp plastic bivouacs trying to get some sleep while others were on guard.

"Highway Vanguard to base, we have incoming," whispered the dozens of radios around the airstrip. Everyone moved, stretched, and prepared themselves for their part in the drama.

"Ten vehicles, one man standing up through the sunroof with shoulder unit in each of the first four vehicles, no gas masks, around 40 enemy, looks like four to a vehicle, traveling west at about 10 miles an hour. ETA to the turnoff, three minutes. We are about to move towards the feeder road. Have fun. Out."

"*Forest Checkpoint here. Ten vehicles about to turn into the farm road, but have stopped,*" whispered the guard post on the other side of the road in the trees to the private road entrance off the feeder road several minutes later. "*They are discussing something, it sounds foreign from here. They are grouped together and I think planning their next move. One has a flashlight and they have a map out on a hood. I can see automatic weapons and shoulder rocket launchers in each vehicle. It looks like one man in each vehicle has a rocket launcher, modern RPGs by their silhouettes, and all the other men seem to be armed with AK47s. They have 30 round 'banana' magazines strapped back to back. They are ready to fight. Boy, these night goggles are good! Now they are pointing a flashlight down the dirt road and they have a second flashlight directly lighting up our fancy new private airport sign. The one who looks like the commander just got into the front vehicle and is standing through the sunroof. He has the shoulder rocket launcher ready. I confirm now that they all look Chinese or Asian at least. A second car is moving into position next to the first one. It looks like they are planning to come down the farm road two by two. Now, eight vehicles have moved into position two abreast and the last two are positioning themselves to block off the road in front of us. They have turned around 180 degrees and are facing us. Over.*"

There was silence as everyone waited. The winter night was pretty dark at 5:30 am in the Carolinas. "*They are rolling slowly, eight vehicles in pairs coming your way, about to turn the corner. You should have them visual in a second. First four vehicles have shoulder units at the ready on men standing out of the sunroofs. They have just put the lights on the two forward vehicles. They are now out of sight. We are ready to terminate the last two vehicles once you guys get things started. Out.*"

"*Roger, Forest Checkpoint. We have the visual. You can go ahead once we have daylight from the flares. Out,*" stated Sergeant Perry, who was in charge of the ambush. Preston recognized his voice.

Preston had climbed up the stairs of his fire tower to join the two machine gunners up there. He was handed bits of cotton wool and showed via hand movements how to plug his ears. He was handed an M4 and directed to stand back in the corner where he could see everything. Preston also had a radio on his back. He had taken the one from the house, since everybody had been moved into the hangar.

He saw faint lights approaching on the road and knew the convoy would come into view in about 100 feet.

"Snipers, look for and bead on four men standing up through the roof of the first four cabs," whispered Sergeant Perry. *"You will have two seconds from my command to take out the four men holding the shoulder units before the flares ruin your night vision. I will give commands for snipers to fire and then for flares. Listen to my commands, men, we need prompt action here. All men behind the forward barricade with me crawl to the edges to get out of a potential blast, slow and silent now. Do you have sights on the four men, snipers?"*

"We have sights on three, the fourth is down very low and we can't get a good shot. The vehicle in front of his is in the way. Over."

"Those on left side of barricade and those on left side of tower, I want both of you to aim into the second vehicles and terminate them once the flares light up. We have ten seconds until they see our barricade. Get ready," whispered the sergeant. Time began to slow down as the truck lights closed in on the barricade in the dark.

Preston watched as the black shapes of the vehicles came into view a couple of hundred feet away.

Very slowly, the eight vehicles came into the ambush zone, and their lights suddenly flickered onto high beam as they lit up the wooden tables facing the attackers. In the glow of the headlamps, it really did look like a make-shift civilian barricade.

Orders barked out from the lead truck as engines revved and the first two trucks began to accelerate to rush the tables. Preston could see the men's silhouettes standing waist high out of the cabs as raised their rocket launchers to fire at the tables. They were 40 feet from the barricade with all eight vehicles in view when the radios came alive.

"Snipers, fire!" ordered the sergeant. *"Flares, fire! Rear team, fire at the last two vehicles facing you, now!"*

The snipers opened fire, hitting the two front men as the targets fired their rockets. One rocket went straight into the middle of the tables, disintegrating the middle table, blowing the remains several feet into the air, and opening a hole in the three rows of sandbags, which flew in all directions. The second rocket angled off into the air over the barricade as the man was hit by sniper fire a split second before he pulled the trigger. The rocket flew into a bush further down the road and harmlessly blew up.

The flares suddenly lit up the sky, and several machine guns immediately opened up, deafening Preston's protected ears and opening the third and fourth trucks like cans of sardines as a steady line of tracer rounds from two directions rocked both trucks up and down. The man standing in the sunroof of the third vehicle and his rocket launcher quickly disappeared back into the cab.

All the vehicle doors opened as the flares illuminated the dark roadway like daylight. Men flew out in all directions, hitting the ground as hundreds of rounds poured into the ambush area from three directions, mowing down everything in their path.

Within seconds, the eight trucks began to look like twisted pieces of metal. *"Armored car, fire down the middle space in between the vehicles—now! Men are hiding in between the vehicles,"* shouted Sergeant Perry into his handset. *"Ambush squad—aim low, aim for the tires and anybody hiding underneath the eight vehicles."*

The second truck in the second row blew up. The blast enveloped the truck in front of it and it blew up as well. The area turned lighter than day as continuous fire poured into the kill zone. Several of the enemy succeeded in getting into the forest on the other side of the road before the rest of them went down. A couple of men disappeared into the trees.

"Ambush area, ambush area—cease fire, cease fire!" shouted the sergeant. Apart from the two trucks on fire, and machine-gun fire from the armored car at the end of the farm road, the area went silent.

In less than 30 seconds the attack was over.

"Team behind the barricade, keep low, move forward slowly and in a line. There could be wounded. Secure the area."

Preston watched as a dozen men slid forward over the sandbags and tables. Two shots rang out and the shooter was immediately silenced. Silence once more reigned down the road as the radio squawked again.

"*Check all bodies. Need number count. Pull them out and away from the vehicles in case they blow. Snipers in the forest —I believe you have two or three coming your way. I want clean kills. Await my orders to move. Forest Checkpoint, what's cooking?*"

"*Forest Checkpoint here—both trucks immobile, no moving bodies. We believe two Charlies still alive and heading towards Highway Vanguard group. Over.*"

"*Highway Vanguard here. We roger that—we are ready for them. The road to the highway is secure and we will clear it from our end. Over.*"

"*Forest Checkpoint,*" continued Sergeant Patterson. "*Stay put in case we have more issues coming your way. To all parties—we have friendlies in the kill zone. Do not fire! They will be clearing the road towards you. Forest Checkpoint—I repeat, hold your fire.*"

"*Forest Checkpoint, we copy that.*"

"*Highway Vanguard, did you copy last message? A couple of possible Charlies coming your way. Over,*" continued the sergeant as they heard more shooting from the burning trucks.

"*Highway Vanguard, we copied that and our guys with night sights are searching for them now.*"

"*All forest snipers—try and keep your shots high. I'm going in to secure the ambush zone and then work towards the main road. Medic section, we have wounded. I need stretchers immediately,*" continued the sergeant over the radio.

The firing had stopped, and Preston climbed down from the fire tower and headed for the entrance gate to his farm. Several soldiers and the doctor ran past carrying stretchers. He ran with them to the gate, and then around the corner down the dirt road towards the barrier.

It was a mess. The fires from three vehicles glowed behind silhouettes of soldiers pulling bodies away from them. He got to the barrier, where he was halted by a soldier.

"Their tanks are going to go up at any second, sir. The sergeant said nobody past this point."

The medics had already picked up two American soldiers and one of the Chinese men, who had an arm missing and several bullet wounds in his legs. Two more stretchers arrived as gunshots were heard deep in the forest.

Carlos arrived a few seconds later, and they both watched as bodies and body parts were pulled out of the surrounding undergrowth. The troops moved forward as another flare lit up the sky, and they saw half a dozen soldiers with Sergeant Perry halfway down the road. They were on each side of the road, bent over, running a couple of yards and then stopping in a crouch, slowly cleaning and checking the area for enemy.

Automatic fire suddenly erupted from the forest several yards in front of them, and the men dove into the ditches as a firefight ensued. The first vehicle's tank blew up as the men were still scrambling to pull bodies away from the rear vehicles, and one man went down. There were soldiers searching through the trucks at the back as the front truck went up with a loud boom, and they scurried away from the fourth row as the whole line of mutilated trucks began to catch fire.

"Preston, get us all your fire extinguishers and all the water containers you have! We need to stop the brush from catching fire. All soldiers not clearing and still in the ambush zone must go and help bring water," shouted Sergeant Perry, running back to the barricade. There was a mass run towards the airport. Preston had 600 feet of garden hose he used to wash down the runway when it got dusty, and it was still connected to the nearest faucet to the road. The pipe would make it about halfway to the gate, if it went straight through the brush.

It took a couple of minutes to get the garden hose into position as close to the fire as possible with water gushing out of the end. Several men ran forward with fire extinguishers and plastic buckets collected from the medic tent and elsewhere.

A human chain was made from the end of the hose, and full buckets of water started moving from man to man and then were carried by more men down the farm road to the burning trucks.

For the next 20 minutes, they worked hard pouring water into the wooded areas that had several fires blazing. The fire extinguishers had dealt with the vehicles, smothering the flames pretty quickly as several men aimed their extinguishers onto the fires from several directions.

The heavy effort managed to stop five of the vehicles from going up in flames. As dawn broke an hour later, troops were still walking in from the outer areas dragging a body here and there to add to the row of bodies by the barricade.

As the sun broke over the trees to the east, dense smoke still filled the surrounding area and a slight breeze started pushing it southward. Preston and Carlos, as well as the rest of the water team, were tired and finally sitting around the barricade, eyeing the dead bodies of the enemy. The road was soaked with a mixture of foam from the extinguishers and the hundreds of gallons of water they had poured onto the immediate area. Both sides of the dirt road had puddles of water that was tinged a reddish color from all the blood.

"Carlos, Preston," a dirty-faced and hatless Sergeant Perry began as he walked up to them. "We have everything that we've taken from the attackers piled up further back on the road. We have pieced together 39 bodies plus the one injured in the medical tent. We have two dead of our own and three wounded, and the medical staff is taking care of them. Would you like to come and inspect the equipment we found in the vehicles and see what is important?"

They walked past the bodies and body parts the soldiers were already placing in black trash bags for disposal.

"I don't think their mothers would recognize any of them. Maybe Lee Wang might?" suggested Carlos. "Sergeant, could you send a radio message to the hangar and have Lee Wang escorted down here?"

Lee arrived five minutes later. By that time, they had concluded that all 39 bodies were Chinese. The rear of the last two trucks still facing the opposite way were full of food and water, and one truck—an old Ford V8—had obviously served as an armory. It housed several rockets for the shoulder units, six cases of hand grenades, and several boxes of 7.62-cal, AK47 ammunition protected in a steel, coffin-like box. They had been lucky that it hadn't exploded, or there would have been far more casualties and fire damage.

"Lee," Carlos asked, "do these men look like Chinese soldiers? Do you recognize any of them?"

Slowly Lee looked at the bloody and bloodless remains of every man. He stopped at one of the first ones.

"This is Bo Lee Tang, I think. Bo Lee Tang was an American-dressed Chinese policeman on the island where I studied.. Bo was only about 18 when I saw him last, but it looks like him. He was part of the security detail on the island that kept the discipline and who told us to go home once we had had too much to drink in the American bars. I liked him because when he was off duty he was one of the worst drinkers, and he tried to introduce me to American whiskey. He liked it so much that he had a small bottle of American whiskey tattooed on his right shoulder."

Several soldiers stripped off the sweater and shirt from the body, and a small tattoo of Jack Daniels stared back at them. "The other man, that one about 50 years old next to him, was Mi Jo. He was head of the guard detachment for the block we lived in. He rang the bell at 4:00 am in the courtyard every morning for us to get up. He has certainly aged since I last saw him."

"I believe he was the commander," the sergeant added.

They continued on, and Lee did not recognize anymore. Many were much younger and would have been babies when he left China, he explained to the men around him.

Then they got to the weapons and other items the men had carried with them. "We searched every pocket in their clothing and every corner of every vehicle we could, including the two on the main road," continued the sergeant. "Our men have secured the whole area. The forest snipers killed three and the last two enemies were taken out by the highway snipers. Once the sun is up, we will do a sweep of the entire area as far out as the forest snipers. Two groups will walk out in both directions along the feeder road searching for any dead or injured. But I don't believe we have missed any."

They all looked down at the mass of equipment. Many of the shoulder rocket launchers, and there were eight of them, were twisted broken metal.

"There are three in good working order," observed one of the soldiers looking over them. Many of the AK47s were also bits of twisted metal. "We have five usable AK47s, sir," he added. "They are very modern, no more than two years old, and have the skeleton-steel shoulder butt versus the old solid-steel and wooden ones. Here are their personal electronic gadgets."

Carlos and Lee found what they were looking for in the pile of equipment—satellite telephones.

"These are American satellite phones," Carlos identified as he picked one up. "I have the civilian version of these, the Iridium 9505a. These phones are the 9505c military version. Do you recognize this phone, Sergeant?" Carlos asked, and it didn't take long for the man to recognize it.

"I was issued one of these two months ago on a training mission when we were down in Georgia," the sergeant replied. "Before we left Seymour Johnson three days ago, we tried to activate all the units we have in our supply closet, but every one of them was dead. How come this one works?"

"It doesn't," Carlos replied. "A bullet has broken off its antennas, but we can fix that." Carlos bent down and found one that seemed intact, and Lee found a second one. Carlos switched his to its "On" position, and it lit up and went into start-up mode. So did Lee's.

"Switch yours off, Lee, in case they see someone operating it and try to communicate with us. I'll do the same. We need to prepare for any response to them. Preston, they must be working on a very simple communications satellite system. There were over 70 communication satellites around the world before December 31st, but I did a check when I was in the observatory and found only three operational satellites on perfect stationary points for very slow and limited two-way communications. If I'm right—and Lee checked me on my results—then Zedong Electronics has terminated the rest of the satellites up there, including ours—even those belonging to the

Chinese government and all their military communications satellites. I'll bet that Zedong Electronics are the only people communicating around the world right now. Maybe the Chinese military are as useless as our own."

"Can we start filling the bags, Preston?" the first sergeant asked.

"Of course! Sorry, guys," replied Preston. "Let's collect everything in these equipment piles and get it into the hangar for inspection. Carlos, find a dry bucket and take the phones and parts separately. Maybe you can cannibalize them into more working units."

"Good idea. Sergeant, let's check the last two trucks at the end of the road before we head back," suggested Carlos, placing the small pile of phones into a bucket as they moved on. Lee stayed with the bodies, looking them over and searching for anything he might have missed. He asked a soldier to place all their personal papers, mostly bloody, into another bucket.

The sun was over the trees by the time they got to the road, and a light mist, or smoke by the way it smelled, was clearing. Here, there were no bodies, since they had been carried to the ambush zone. There were just two guards watching over the vehicles. The first sergeant walked up to the machine-gun peppered vehicles as the Rat Patrol jeep made its way out of the forest on the other side, bouncing through the shallow ditch. Joe was driving next to a soldier who was still behind the front gun with three more soldiers standing on the back as the jeep came up to them and stopped.

Preston also noticed a line of half a dozen soldiers walking away from them in both directions, slowly checking both sides of the road, already a couple hundred yards away.

"Did you leave the sandbags in position?" asked Sergeant Perry.

"Yes," replied the soldier in the front seat of the jeep.

"Good. We might need them again for the next attack," Perry said, looking into the first vehicle. It had a couple hundred holes on its right-hand side, and there was drying blood all over the leather seats of the old Ford. It had been cleaned of bodies, as well as anything small. The rear, enclosed bed of the truck was still full of equipment, and the first sergeant pulled away a canvas cover to show food, water, and what Carlos was looking for—two satellite phones, brand new and still in their cases, a backup satellite receiver dish, and a two-way communications box on the front arm of the dish.

The small dish was connected to a tripod and was lying on top of three large marine deep-cycle batteries, a small military field generator, a laptop computer, and a couple of red gas cans. There were also several cases of ammunition, all being protected by a coffin-like box of quarter-inch-thick heavy steel three feet wide, a couple feet high and six feet long. The frame had been placed in the middle of the bed and they had stored the food and water around it as added protection.

All the food and water containers were completely ruined and their contents had drained out or lay in piles from the damage, but the communications gear had been protected. Not one round got through the steel. The second truck was also an old long-bed Ford with a roof extension and had the same setup, again with the same communications equipment protected.

"I wonder why these two trucks have more gear than the others," Preston wondered.

"I assume that these guys were two groups from separate areas and had backup communications between themselves as well as with their headquarters," suggested Sergeant Perry. "It would be nice to get more of this stuff. Can we ask the rest to come and visit? I'm sure they have more guys out there—maybe thousands of them!"

They returned to the hospital tent to find the doctor working hard on a wounded American soldier. "I need to get him back to Seymour Johnson quickly," he said to the first sergeant. "He is losing blood. I need to amputate his arm. Unfortunately, the other two men were DOAs."

"Sergeant Perry, get some men to carry the bodies and the wounded aboard the FedEx Cargomaster," suggested Preston. "There will be room for you, Doc, and a nurse. We can be at Seymour in 15 minutes. I'll go and get her started and I'll swing her by the front of the tent."

It was ten that morning when Preston returned from Seymour

Johnson with a fresh medical crew. He saw as he came in that the bulldozer had forced a route through the blackened enemy vehicles. Preston went over to check out the road damage, and he agreed to Sergeant Perry's suggestion that the bulldozer should dig a large hole a couple of hundred yards into the forest on the other side of the road and place the bags of the 40 Chinese bodies in it. The last one had died on the operating table at Seymour Johnson due to loss of blood. The bulldozer moved out into the forest just in time for a late breakfast prepared by the ladies. Nobody was really hungry.

After breakfast, Preston called a meeting. Martie had already told him that the general had been briefed on the attack and wanted to congratulate the team when he returned. Will Smart had stayed in the hangar with two soldiers to protect the civilians as a last resort. He was still not feeling well from the "drug overdose" he kept complaining about, so he went back to bed.

Carlos stated that he and Lee would be busy for the rest of day, and asked Martie and Maggie to help them disassemble the radios once the meeting was over. A tired First Sergeant Perry was asked to give a report on the happenings and he told everybody about the success of thwarting their first enemy attack. He got a standing ovation from the group, was thanked profusely by everybody and told, once the meeting was finished, to get himself and his troops some rest.

"Well done, guys. We have succeeded in winning our first attack against the enemy," said Preston, "thanks to First Sergeant Perry and his men. I watched everything from the fire tower, and the other guys never had a chance. It was better organized than a ballet. You were fantastic and I'm happy to be working with you guys.

"Ok, Carlos, we need to meet and figure out what is the best way to reply once they communicate with us. My thoughts are that I would like Lee to respond, saying that the attack went well. He should say that we were a base of ex-military pilots and put up a good fight. Lee tells us that their commander, or the guy they usually communicated with, was killed. Lee, you could put a cloth over your mouth and pretend that you are that young man. What was his name?"

"Bo Lee Tang," replied Lee. "I could say that my commander is dead and we need a new commander for the group. I could ask for future orders?"

"Carlos, you and Lee work out a perfect act and prepare for communications. Say that several of the men are wounded and ask what you should do with them. Tell them that you have killed twenty-odd pilots and damaged a dozen or so small and large aircraft, all old propeller machines. Tell them there was lots of fire—they might have seen our explosions out there on their satellite feed. I think the fire was big enough, especially the two explosions, to verify your story. You guys head out and I will continue with the rest of today's plans."

"Will you be around today?" Carlos asked Preston.

"Yes, in and out. I want to bring in the Southwest group; they are expected at midday, now that the road is cleared. Pam, you will fly a 172 into RDU, I'll fly in the Cargomaster, and Barbara can fly in *Lady Dandy*. We also need to take in fresh troops for the guard post and bring a couple of them back for rest."

Preston looked around at the tired but satisfied faces. "Once we get the Southwest group back here, I want Seymour Johnson to house the passengers and anybody else who is not a pilot. Only working pilots and crew will stay here. Other than that, we need to know what Carlos and Lee can find out, and then, guys, we must start work on a food-delivery plan."

Chapter 6

Z-Day +3 – It's Time to Hit Back

THE FAST-MOVING ARCTIC BLAST was a big one, freezing everything in its path as far south as Washington, D.C. The icy wind blew at over 40 miles an hour and snow fell thick and fast. The northern cities were already ghost towns. Tall buildings and single houses were cold and dark places. Many people had retreated to basements to escape the bitter cold wind-chilled temperatures.

There were now millions of frozen people throughout Canada and North America. People were dying by the thousands every hour, and the chance of survival was now only halfway decent for the very few who had enough power, heat, and food to keep them alive. For one long day, this fast-moving storm battered the northern areas. Cities that had once been home to millions of people now had only pockets of cold and hungry people here and there. The storm came and went, leaving piles of windswept snow behind it.

The southern states were a little easier to stay alive in, but even most of Texas had temperatures in the teens and people there were even less prepared for cold weather. The death toll was nearly as high as further north. In the warmer areas by the coasts like Florida, gangs of starving people shot each other for food and warm shelter. Many gangs would form one day, just to be knocked off by a bigger gang the next. Any food stockpiles were now exhausted in many well-populated cities. Supermarkets and stores were empty and not much more than blackened ruins by the end of the first week.

Food looted from neighborhood stores in other areas would normally last many thousands of people several weeks, but having the food meant that everybody who saw you steal the food was keen to take it away from you. Large gangs of 30 to 40 men roamed in stolen vehicles, running into houses, killing the families inside, and running out with any spoils they found.

By the beginning of the fifth day, and by the time warmer air fed into the north, a third of the U.S. population was dead.

* * *

Captain Mallory and his group had found another clean hangar in which to spend the night. It was not as comfortable as the one the previous night, but with the gas heaters on, it soon became so. The group bedded down once they had the standard fare of hamburgers and hot dogs followed by cheese and chocolate.

The weather got close to freezing outside. They decided to leave early, find their way to Raleigh's airport, and then have breakfast. The fuel in their tanks would just make it. After leaving a few dollar bills for the hangar owner from their now-empty wallets, they left just after dawn with hot cups of black coffee and tea in hand. Two hours later, without seeing anyone else in moving vehicles, they reached the US64 off-ramp and turned west towards Raleigh, their southern migration over for the time being.

Again, they noticed a slight increase in stranded vehicles as they got closer and closer to the city. A car sped by on the other side of the road and the occupants waved as they went past, driving towards the coast. Another car appeared in John's rear-view mirror, tailing them a half a mile behind. It shadowed them for several miles before it turned off the highway and disappeared.

They knew they were close when they entered the 440 beltline around the state's capital. Here, there were many more dead vehicles, but luckily a path had already been pushed through the pile of metal by other vehicles that had come before them—the Chinese convoy, for one.

An old black Cadillac suddenly appeared on the other side of the highway coming towards them with a second car close behind it, both driving through the wrecked traffic pretty fast. Captain Mallory could hear gunshots coming from them as he rolled down his window. The two cars seemed to be engaged in a gun battle with each other and ignored the convoy as they passed 20 yards away on the other side of the highway.

The group drove onto I-40 as the signposts to the airport directed them to. The cemetery of stranded cars and trucks was much heavier here, as this part of the road was the direct connection between Raleigh and Durham and there must have been many people traveling around midnight four days ago. There were blackened wrecks everywhere, and for the first time since Washington, the SWAT truck had to carefully force its way through tangled wreckage.

Captain Mallory thought he heard aircraft engines as they neared the off-ramp to the airport, and then three small, black dots flew over the gap in the trees a couple of miles in front of them. One of them, he recognized, was an old DC-3 going into the airport.

By now, his fuel gauge was on empty and he radioed back to John to find out that his was the same. They slowly crept up the highway off-ramp and turned right towards the airport. It took several more twists and turns before they came across the two blackened cars close to the underpass that Martie had told him to look out for. The cars had already been moved to one side, and the convoy continued into the airport itself.

The captain headed for the private terminal entrance and found the gate he had been told to look for, guarded in plain sight by U.S. Air Force guards. He also saw a FedEx Cargomaster taxiing towards the guard tent as he stopped in front of the gate and switched off the faithful truck's engine. They had reached their first official destination.

* * *

Breakfast was being served in the White House. The president had left Seymour Johnson at 7:00 am and arrived at Andrews at 8:30. Buck had fired up the Huey and the general was already getting *Ghost Rider* refueled to continue on his base tour. Buck had taken off with the president, the ambassador, Manuel, their three bodyguards, and cases of food supplies for the Colombian Embassy.

Everyone apart from Buck and the president was getting off at the Embassy. Helpful hands, shocked at seeing the U.S. President aboard the chopper, unloaded the several cases once they had landed inside the embassy grounds.

Once everyone had said their goodbyes and the president had shaken hands with many of the Embassy staff, Buck rose off the grounds with the president and flew on to the White House. Both Buck and the president had a good chance to view the blackened mess that the capital city had become.

"I count about a dozen large areas where aircraft must have gone down," Buck stated as he flew over the damaged Pentagon and the untouched Capital building.

"*I think that we need to discuss when you can pick me up again,*" answered the president, over the intercom. "*I want to get the official letters printed for Preston, Manuel, and you as my private pilot, and you might as well have breakfast with me while they are typed up. I'm sure we must have a typewriter somewhere at the White House.*"

"Picking you up, Mr. President, is not a problem. It will take me about 90 minutes to get to the White House from Preston's airfield and 90 minutes to get back. I can do it without having to refuel. I'm sure you will get permanent communications soon, as the general is getting a military radio sent in with an old jeep later today. They are also looking for other vehicles to commandeer. You will be patched into Andrews and then you will be able to communicate to Raleigh, Hill, and Edwards."

There was an inch of new snow on the White House lawn when Buck readied to land, and an icy wind howled out of the northwest, making it pretty tough to get the Huey down in a gentle and disciplined way. The Secret Service was happy to have the president back, but the bodyguards stared in disbelief when they saw him exit the Huey with no security detail.

By this time, the kitchen was running, a large section of the downstairs had electricity, and the rooms were warm. It was good to sit down in a hospitable White House and have breakfast.

They chatted for a couple of hours. Buck was introduced to the first lady and the children, while the president was making some decisions about his next moves.

"I would like to go down and help with the food distribution project, and I'm sure my wife and girls would enjoy getting out of here," he explained. His family nodded in agreement. "Will and Maggie Smart's kids would give them other children to mix with, and I know my wife would love to get involved. There is no reason for me to sit here and do nothing, it will drive me crazy," he added.

The president called for one of the office staff and gave dictation for the necessary letters he wanted, and he asked if they could be typed out on official White House letterhead. The man replied that a Commodore computer had been located with a working printer, and they were working on refilling it with ink. He would have the paperwork within the hour.

"You know what, Buck, it's time I became a real leader again and gave orders myself. What is the weather like?"

"Certainly a bad storm to our north," replied Buck. "I would say that going further that way in the next few hours is not good. Washington seems to be on the edge of the more severe conditions."

"Do you think you can fly into Dover Air Force Base in Delaware?"

"It's about 100 miles due east of Andrews. I would think that the weather is no worse than here," answered Buck.

"Good, get on your helicopter radio and find out where General Allen is. I believe he will be headed into Dover pretty soon. If he is, tell him to wait for us and organize some fuel. I want to talk to him." Buck did as he was told and picked up a faint *Ghost Rider* transmission on the radio. The general was on his way from Langley Air Force Base in Virginia and confirmed that he would be available for the president.

The letters were going to take some time, so Buck, the president and two Secret Service agents climbed into *Baby Huey*. It took several minutes to get her airborne. With the president in the left seat again and the agents sitting in the comfortable chairs in the back, they aimed for Dover.

Thirty minutes later, with a strong tailwind, *Baby Huey* landed close to *Ghost Rider*, which was already being refueled by a small, antiquated 3,000-gallon fuel tanker truck. It would take a long time to refuel the larger aircraft.

The general gave orders to refuel the helicopter first, and Buck was invited into the meeting with General Allen, the president and the base commander, General Ward.

General Allen introduced everybody. "Mr. President, you wanted a meeting?" he asked.

They sat down, and cokes and fruit juice were brought in.

"I want to get involved with the food program and see what I can do out there. I'm not going to sit in the White House like a scared cat and do nothing. While you are organizing the country through our air bases, I would like to work with the guys down in North Carolina and get a distribution network operational."

"I was hoping you would say that, sir," the general responded with a smile on his face. "It would get rid of the need for protocol and you having to authorize everything I do, plus it would solve the need for that extra radio or satellite-phone system."

"Yes, I was thinking about that, too," the president responded. "If we are expecting a full-scale invasion in the near future, it doesn't make sense to have the Commander-in-Chief sitting virtually unprotected in the White House like a sitting duck. They should have to work very hard to find me, don't you think?"

"Totally agree," answered General Allen. "Mike Ward, what do we have operational here? I'm hoping your oldest C-130, a C model I believe, could still be flyable, and I'm sure you must have a helicopter or two in storage?"

"We are checking through the older models now, Pete," the other general responded. "Every older aircraft is currently undergoing tests.

We lost 17 aircraft on flight missions over New Year's Eve, and I did not think to check the old stock until yesterday when we received your C-130 and the pilot's message from Andrews. We are servicing one C-130C's engines. She's flyable, but several of her electronic components are toast. We have servicemen currently working on bypassing them. We have another C-130A that is flyable, Pete—an old HC-130 tanker which could be operational by tomorrow—and we are working on two Vietnam-era Bell helicopters right now."

"I want the HC-130's tanker engines fully inspected within 12 hours," Pete Allen ordered. "Get all the maintenance men on her you can and get her to Hill AFB in Salt Lake in 18 hours. Get the helicopters and the other C-130 flown down to Andrews as soon as possible. I'm leaving ASAP and need the tanker. I'm flying to Japan with *Ghost Rider*. Also, Mike, please check the refueling rigs and make sure that her refueling line is compatible with *Ghost Rider*. I'm going to need the tanker to pump fuel into *Ghost Rider* over the Bering Sea."

"You are taking these old birds over to Asia?" asked General Ward in shock.

"That's right, Mike. I want two of the best and most experienced crews in that tanker and two more of your most experienced crews in *Ghost Rider*. I've done my homework. *Ghost Rider* has a range of 2,200 miles. I'm going into Hill to refuel, then I'm heading up to McChord Air Force Base in Tacoma, Washington. I believe they have a couple of old C-130s over there as well. Then I'll fly into Elmendorf Air Force Base in Anchorage—that's well within range from McChord. McChord might have a couple of old operational helicopters as well, but I haven't been up there for a while. Elmendorf in Alaska should have cleared runways—they usually clear them 24/7 since they have so much snow."

"So will Misawa Air Force Base in Japan where they should have bulldozers still working and something flyable. It's a 3,200-mile flight into Misawa from Elmendorf. From Misawa, I plan to refuel and fly into our bases at either Osan or Kunsan in South Korea. The distance is only 900 miles from Misawa. The HC-130 tanker has a 4,500-mile range. If you take out 1,000 miles of fuel for *Ghost Rider*, that will give her 3,500 miles, and if I put a soft 1,000-gallon fuel bladder into *Ghost Rider*, and there are several bladders at Elmendorf, both aircraft should make it into Japan. I believe that there is a still-operational AC-130 gunship at either Kunsan or Osan. By the way, Buck, I want to take Mr. Lee Wang with me on my mission. He needs to be at Hill AFB in 36 hours. Somebody will have to get him there by then."

"Why the rush to Asia, Pete?" asked the president.

"Carlos believes that if we take out their satellite communication station on the other side, we could take over complete control of all their operational satellite hardware. If we capture or kill their mercenary squads over here and relieve them of their cell phones, we could be in control of global communications again, plus I will get the chance to blow their headquarters off the face of the earth. I want to take one of the captured cell phones with me, since I heard from Carlos on my way in that they have captured several American satellite phones. That could give me direct satellite contact with you, Mr. President. Carlos is going to get as many of the systems working as he can. I will take one with me on my flight, since he thinks that by using the aircraft's transponder for short intervals and using the aircraft as a massive antenna for the satellite phone, he can satellite-guide me across the Bering Strait into Japan, and then on to my target. I can also warn you, Mr. President, about any attack on our aircraft by Chinese fighters when I get there. If that happens, you can act accordingly with a missile strike."

"How many cell phones did they capture?" asked Buck.

"They have three fully operational and three broken ones. Carlos said that he and Lee Wang can repair the three broken ones. There were ten in total and they have four for spare parts," the general replied. "Why?"

"Any extra spare parts could be built into the dead ones you Air Force guys use," suggested Buck. "I know Carlos has a satellite phone. I bet he hasn't thought of replacing the electronic parts in his phone. I'll tell him when I get down there later today."

"Good point, Buck," smiled the general. "My plan is still in the making, but if I survive over Nanjing, Mr. President, I want to fly into Beijing and find out the truth—whether or not the Chinese government has anything to do with this catastrophe. Then I want to fly up to Moscow. I'm sure I can refuel in both cities, and if the Chinese government is friendly, they can fuel us up and get me to the Russian border. Or I can go via India since there must be tons of unused jet fuel at all the world's commercial airports. If I take my own tanker, I can refuel anywhere. If I come up against opposition forces, I can relay the information back to you."

"That's one hell of a trip in old C-130s," stated General Ward, not so optimistic. "You are going to need a lot of luck to find little Japan in the middle of nowhere, on low fuel reserves and without modern navigation. How long are you expecting to fly around the world, Pete?"

"Only ten days, Mike," laughed General Allen. "I want to get from Moscow, through to our base in Turkey. My biggest challenge at the moment is getting our troops back to the States—a million men and women. Lady Luck is going to have to show her face. I believe that we must try and thwart any attack on our mainland by the opposition as soon as we can—by either Zedong Electronics or the Chinese or Russian governments. I don't know how they plan to do it, but they will need fully working naval ships and aircraft carriers to get to us, and when they do, we must try and capture what we can, fill them up with gas, and send them over to the Middle East to bring back our troops."

"South Korea should be okay, and our troops should survive in Europe, but with no backup vehicles or protection in the Middle East and Africa, those guys have only a few weeks or months at most. I can't do much here against the weather at the moment. You guys can start a food distribution system with a civilian air force and workforce, but over there I must find massive ships to bring back our men and women. First, I want to know who we are dealing with. I believe that any attack on the United States will be caught by Carlos and Navistar P in time to prepare. I'm hoping I can get back in time to see the action—I will be returning via our base on the Azores, just within range of Andrews."

* * *

The boardroom on the 30th floor was busy. On Day 4, the full membership of 16 men was in their seats. Once again, it was time for reports. The room had only one other man waiting to speak—the chief technical officer from the satellite communications department one floor below. The chairman rose and gestured for silence.

"Before I get into my latest report, Comrades, I would like our specialist from downstairs as well as Comrade Wang to give their reports on our first major attack on foreign soil." He pointed to the technical officer.

"Comrades," the gentleman started, "Comrade Wang and I have been in contact with our termination squads in America. It took a couple of hours, as it seems the battle was long and hard. We lost communications with them for over three hours. From the communications side, we are now up and running again and I will let you know of any news. Comrade Wang has the rest of the report." He bowed and left the room.

"Comrade Chairman and fellow Comrades, I have excellent news from America," Comrade Mo Wang smiled to the room, even though his gut was signaling to him that something wasn't quite right. "We had a two-hour battle with Americans at the small airport in North Carolina. It was an unimportant and small air base, and it seems that there was a platoon of 30 American soldiers guarding the propeller-driven aircraft. This caused our comrades a bit of a problem and we unfortunately lost half of our brave men. On the positive side, our men killed everybody there, including all the American soldiers, as well as 20 pilots, several civilians and their families—a remarkable feat. Our squad commanders were brave and fought well, but many lost their lives in the attack."

"If our commanders are dead, Comrade Wang, who are we communicating with?" asked the chairman.

"A man I know well," replied the stressed Wang. "A man I

personally recruited, and even though I haven't spoken to him for 30 years, I recognized his voice. I have given him command of the remaining troops and told him to stay at the base until I get authorization from you to send more troops to take over command from him. He stated that they are still seeing several small civilian aircraft around Raleigh and believe that the city's international airport could be another place that has a group of aircraft. I have ordered him to go and take a look and told him that we would send in more squads to deal with any enemy problems before they are needed in New York and Washington.

"And this man is dependable?" asked the chairman. "I want him to remain close by that Raleigh airport until we get more squads in. It sounds like this area is full of civilian aircraft. I believe it may be due to the massive storm over the northern states. I will assume that these aircraft flew south and are congregating at this airport south of the storm. It is in our favor, as we could potentially destroy all of the remaining aircraft in one battle and then move our squads north to meet us in New York. Comrade Wang, send the 50 termination squads from the southern American border area to this Raleigh airport, and check with our technical staff downstairs to see if there has been any transponder movement around this city. They must destroy everything they see in this area! Once this problem is dealt with, order our squads to move north."

"We only have two and a half weeks before our arrival and we need all three major airports ready for our airborne troops and, with American aviation fuel flowing, to get our 30 747-400ERs and five Airbus 380s back to China. Thank you and well done, Comrade Wang. I knew America wouldn't be easy to invade and I'm sure we are going to deal with more problems before we can call North America our own. Wang, I want the rest of our East Coast termination squads in New York to get to the JFK airport on time. They will inspect and start up the six bulldozers we have hidden in the rented warehouse. The squads must be there 24 hours ahead of our aircraft as planned. They must first clear the main runway at JFK and meet our incoming men and troops at the airport. Remind them,

Comrade, they have a ton of salt and the six bulldozers to do the job."

Comrade Mo Wang sat down, his mind spinning. He had recognized that voice on the satellite radio, but something was telling him that it sounded different. Maybe his memory was vague, but he had a notion that the voice didn't belong to the man who had said it belonged to.

"We will now hear the latest report on troop readiness, food ships, and aircraft. Comrade Rhu, please," ordered the chairman.

"Thank you, Comrade Chairman," started Rhu. "All plans are ready for our invasion, Comrades. You are all to be ready to depart here in three days. We will sail out of Shanghai Harbor with five of our container cargo ships. Each of the five of our most modern container ships owned by our shipping company, China Shipping Lines, holds 9,600 containers of food. Each container has been packed with 1,800 meal packs and each meal pack holds enough basic food to feed one person for a week. Our first shipment will be 60 million food packs, and is expected to supply the northern area of the East Coast of America for three months. We have new, red Chinese passports printed for 15 million women and children. They are to be handed to male children under ten years old only. Any male children over that age will be terminated. Each new Communist citizen will be given four weeks of food, which should get them through the middle of the winter, or at least to when our container ships return. Our Boeing 747-400 aircraft is due to leave Shanghai for America tomorrow. The 747 will be taking 100 electrical engineers into New York's John F. Kennedy Airport. They will be protected by our Special Forces flying with them—over 200 of them—as well as our squads already there. The engineers' first job is to get the airport's fuel tanks back online and get road transport from our termination squads into the La Guardia and Newark airports. They will get these two airports ready for our arrival.

"After the airports are operational, they will move into New York Harbor and work on getting the large harbor cranes around the New York Global Terminal operational so we can unload the five container ships when they arrive. A second Boeing 747 aircraft is full of the needed electrical parts to get the American machinery working again. This aircraft, a transporter, does not have the extended range of the first aircraft and is currently in a secret location much closer to New York than the others and will join the first aircraft once it gets into U.S. airspace. The 747 transporter will operate in and out from that secret location. The transporter will also have four large generators on board to help with fuel delivery, and the aircraft has been modified to unload itself without ground assistance. Our termination squads have been given orders to get enough vehicles for the transportation of these 300 men around the three airports and harbor areas, which hopefully have little or no damage. Both 747s will be emptied and refueled as quickly as possible, and then return to their bases. Any questions so far?" There were none.

"Twenty-four hours before our arrival, our entire fleet of 35 commercial aircraft will fly 20,000 Red Army troops into New York. These troops are to take control of the airports, the entire area between the three airports and then the harbor to protect our entrance from any American forces still hiding in the New York area. Our flotilla of five naval and five container ships will reach and grandly enter New York Harbor. Gentlemen, great news, we will be sailing through the Panama Canal, which has been captured and is currently fully operational and guarded by our forces. Again, any questions?" Again, there were none.

"One week after we have captured New York, our second armada of five container ships will leave Shanghai Harbor and take seven days to sail to Los Angeles. Before they arrive, the same engineers will be flown across America from New York to Los Angeles to set up the airports and harbor area there. Everything is working according to plan, and we have ten days to take control of the East Coast before our invasion of the West Coast begins. We will reside on our new aircraft carrier, and she will be protected by our two attack cruisers and two destroyers. We will not be backed up by submarines, as had been planned. Unfortunately, our own government purchased the submarine satellite-communications electronic parts we produced for the rest of the world without our knowledge, and the entire Chinese fleet of submarines is now useless. Unfortunately, they were too stupid to listen to our warnings. We have tested our six warships, our fleet of ten container ships, the thirty 747s, and the five Airbuses, and they are all fully operational." He sat down.

After the meeting ended, Comrade Wang was in the communications room trying to raise his new squad leader in North Carolina. He had already spoken to the commander of the 50 termination squads currently in Arizona, New Mexico, and Texas, and they were getting ready to move east. He could not get hold of the new man, and his sixth sense was eating at him as the engineer was finally successful and got a very bad connection.

"Is that you, Bo Lee Tang?" the engineer called over the radio telephone in front of him.

"I can't hear you well, we have bad connection. This is Bo Lee Tang," said the faint voice on the other side. "We are burying our comrades."

"Tell him to hurry up and get to the Raleigh airport," Comrade Wang told the engineer in front of him. "Tell him he has Comrade Deng's 50 squads coming in. They should be there in two days." The message was relayed.

"We need many squads?" asked the man at the other end.

"Fifty squads are coming. Comrade Deng will take command when he gets there, Bo Lee Tang," stated Comrade Wang, taking over the microphone from the engineer. "Once Comrade Deng has destroyed the Raleigh airport, you are all to go north. I have told Deng that he will take you with him. You need to be at the airport and harbor area within one week to prepare for our arrival."

"Which harbor you want my men? I can't hear you well. What happens if I don't see Comrade Deng?" the voice asked.

"Something is not right, Bo Lee Tang. You should know the operation," Wang said, worried.

"My dead commander did not tell us anything," was the reply. "We left the north, came south. He did not tell us anything, and now

I am commander." Comrade Wang was worried. He could understand a need-to-know basis, and he racked his brains to remember what the men in the termination squads were actually told. It was quite normal that the men knew very little, and he now needed to check to see if he was talking to the man he knew—after all, he had recruited him all those years ago. In those days Bo Lee Tang was a good boxer and Mo Wang had won a good amount of money on his achievements in Shanghai.

"Bo Lee Tang, what do you have on your shoulder?" asked Wang.

"A tattoo," was the reply.

"What is the tattoo?" Wang asked.

"You know, Comrade. A bottle of Jack Daniels. You often must have seen it when I was boxing in Shanghai?"

"Of course! Comrade Bo, I needed to check because your voice is not the voice I remember," continued Mo Wang.

"I have small injury and have bandage on my face. I have a small piece of metal in my cheek, have lost a little blood, and I can't talk too good." The telephone crackled back at Wang. This seemed to satisfy most of his worries. Of course! Bo could have been injured.

"Your orders, Bo Lee, are to destroy the Raleigh airport with Deng. Then, go north to your original position. We have engineers and troops flying in on two aircraft tomorrow night to reconstruct the three airports and harbor before our aircraft and ship arrivals. You are to report to our troops at the biggest airport. You need to be there in one week. It will be under our control. I will be there several days after you arrive, and I will communicate to you and Deng once you get to New York, not before. Good luck!" said Wang, still feeling in his hollow and empty stomach that something was wrong.

* * *

Carlos and Lee had been working hard since they had received the equipment from the dead Chinese. They had studied each piece and found all the equipment to be simple satellite communicating electronics. Thousands of Americans had the same quality two-way systems with Hughes Internet.

"I think we are ready for communication," said Carlos to a worried-looking Lee Wang. "Remember to keep the cloth of the towel over the phone. It will hide most of your voice tone. Tell them that a platoon of 30 military troops killed your commander and many of the others. Ask for orders. Remember to state that you are in control. You can be nervous, you haven't been a commander and you are only told stuff on a need-to-know basis. Remember, there were 30 troops, 20-odd pilots with guns, and a lot of small airplanes. Other than that, buddy, just wing it. You need to get information from whoever is at the other end. Don't be scared to ask and act stupid, Lee. It always works."

They turned on one telephone and waited. It wasn't 30 seconds before the phone rang—a sound they hadn't heard in days! Lee Wang made sure that the cloth was covering the mouthpiece, and he looked at Carlos. Carlos smiled, gave him the thumbs up, and Lee Wang answered the call.

"Control, this is Bo Lee Tang. Mi Lee is dead. This is Bo Lee Tang, Mi Lee's number two in command," answered Lee Wang.

There was silence at the other end.

"Bo Lee Tang, you said your commander is dead?"

"Correct, Control. It was a bad fight, but we won," Lee Wang continued. Then he heard a voice he recognized from his days in China. It was the floor sweeper—the man who had recruited him. He looked up at Carlos, who was dialing another number on the second phone. Then Carlos remembered that he was holding a telephone and not a radio, and his brain suddenly clicked into gear. Anybody could use the system, and he wondered if the control center in China would notice a second phone being used at the same time. He scrambled through the pile of phone components and found one with a number written on the backside so that the owner wouldn't forget it. He then found a second one and saw Lee looking at him. Carlos told him to keep going, but he could see that Lee Wang was in shock for some reason. Then Carlos heard a voice on the other end fire off in rapid Chinese.

"Bo Lee Tang, this is Comrade Mo. Get one of the other commanders on the telephone to give me a full report." Lee Wang looked at Carlos, and his face told Carlos that he knew the man on the other end. Carlos whispered for him not to worry, that the cloth should hide his voice.

"All commanders are dead. We have 23 dead men, Comrade Wang," Lee Wang replied nervously.

"Don't ever mention my name again! Or use my first name, understand Bo Lee Tang?" replied the man in Nanjing venomously.

"Sorry, but I need to know who is to be in control here. I will give you my report," continued Lee, with Carlos showing numbers on his fingers. "We killed 30 American soldiers, 20 American pilots with guns, and all women and children are dead. We had 12 airplanes on fire, but the fires are now over. Two of the airplanes were American Air Force—not jets, but they had propellers, very old airplanes. We have 23 dead, three wounded. End of report."

"Yes, I saw the small flickering of fires on our satellite screens. Good job, Bo Lee Tang. Wait five minutes and I will call back," replied Comrade Wang in Nanjing, he and hung up. Lee put the phone down on the table in front of him and Carlos congratulated him for a job well done.

"I'm sure he has to go and get orders for you," Carlos explained, looking at the back of Lee's phone. There was its own number printed in black ink on the back side as well as a second number printed in red ink. He checked the others; they all had it, one black number, different on every phone, and the same red number on each phone, and Carlos sighed with relief. Then he told Lee that he was going to dial a number while they were on the line to see if they got a response.

"I know Comrade Wang," replied Lee. "He is the man who recruited me right at the very beginning. Remember the floor sweeper I told you about? That is him!"

"Don't worry," reassured Carlos. "Remember to act stupid, like you have a head wound or something. He must have recruited hundreds of people. Just don't panic. We need all the information we can get. Remember, this guy hired you and then was prepared to kill you and your family. I'm going to see if they respond when I call one of these other phones. I will cover it up so that they can't hear the ring if it goes off." Lee's phone rang again.

"Bo Lee Tang, this is Control. Bo Lee Tang, Control," stated the first voice over the telephone, and Lee tried to sound breathless.

"I can't hear you well, we have bad connection. This is Bo Lee Tang. We are burying our comrades."

Carlos phoned the third working phone from the second working phone, and he could hear the ring under the cloth. He switched the third phone on and spoke a few words of gibberish into it. He made funny sounds for several seconds and then turned both phones off. Lee Wang indicated that he had not received any notification about the phone being used.

Lee Wang ended his call and Carlos grabbed the second phone and dialed the red number. "Ask them if you should continue to bury the dead men and if it matters which phone you use," added Carlos. The call was answered and Carlos listened to Lee speaking Chinese rapidly into the cell phone. Then Carlos ended his call.

"Control said not to phone them again, and that all the phones ring to him with the red number. I asked him if I could phone Deng, and he gave me his number. I asked if Control wanted to hear my conversation, and he said that they couldn't and did not have full control of who was using the telephones, so it wasn't necessary."

"Great!" replied Carlos.

"Carlos, I know Comrade Wang had reservations about my voice." Carlos was looking for a clean piece of paper to write the information down.

"He asked me, or Bo Lee Tang, about the tattoo. He knew Bo was a boxer, and he was a good boxer before Mo Wang recruited him. I watched him fight often. I think we have won the war of hiding who I am, so far," said Lee, now very relieved.

"Lee, call me on your phone and talk stupid so that nobody can understand you. I want to see if they come back and complain about you using the phone. Say 'Zedong Electronics will lose' in English, or something stupid." Lee did, and they spoke stupid talk for two minutes, sounding like a bunch of monkeys.

"Okay, let's write down the information we've collected," stated Carlos, after they hung up. "First, we have 50 squads coming in from somewhere—where, your friend did not say—but after destroying RDU Airport you are to head north, so I think that this Comrade Deng is coming from the south or west. Does that sound correct?"

Lee Wang nodded. "I think a squad is four men in one vehicle. That is what I saw in the SUV when they passed me in Salt Lake City. That means that there are 200 men coming here in about two days and the next fight will be at the Raleigh airport," replied Lee. "Then I, Bo Lee Tang, must go north in one week, under the command of Comrade Deng, who will take over from me if he survives the fight at the airport. Also, Wang said that engineers and troops were flying into somewhere tomorrow night and that I must report to the airport with Deng and my men. So I am expected somewhere in one week at an airport that is under their control. That is what I understand."

"So they have airborne troops flying into the United States, but they can't land without landing lights, and the airports need to be cleared of snow. So they must be leaving China tomorrow, flying overnight, and I'm sure landing at dawn. The runways up north will have a lot of snow on them, so somebody has to clear them before any aircraft can go in. That means that other squads must be heading into this airport. I think it can only be one or two northern city airports, since you have been instructed to meet them somewhere big. We need to speak to General Allen immediately!"

Carlos switched on the radio. "We can easily have lookouts in Washington, and if they are flying in directly from China, they will either have real big military jets, or real big civilian jets. That's a 7,000-mile flight," said Carlos, waiting for the radio to warm up. "Anything else we can put together?"

"Yes," added Lee. "Comrade Wang said that he was coming several days after we supposedly arrive there. If he is coming, then so are many others, I think. He said that he would see me and Deng there. And he said the engineers were fixing three airports and a harbor area for their arrival by air and sea."

"To bring in more troops," added Carlos. "I think we know part of their plans now. They are getting three airports and a harbor ready. So that must be a big city with more than one airport. It could only be New York or Washington. All are on the coast...with a harbor...with a harbor," Carlos thought aloud. "Washington doesn't have a harbor! Only New York has three airports. Boston doesn't, but both have large harbors for shipping. Yes, they must be coming into New York—JFK Airport, Lee! Timeframe—they are leaving China tomorrow, also two days before Deng gets here, then one week later you must be in New York, then Wang is coming in several days after that—two days plus about two weeks' time!"

Carlos got responses from all three of the other bases within five seconds. The radio operator knew where the general was, but he didn't want to say. Carlos told the man that he needed to speak to the general immediately—or as soon as he was within radio range. The radio operator understood.

* * *

Preston drew the Cargomaster up by the airport gate and saw the most interesting group of vehicles—even more interesting than the ones they had at the airstrip. He closed the engine down and got out as *Lady Dandy* switched off, also on the apron. A dozen troops got out, and Pam Wallace brought the slower 172 to a halt next to Preston's. She jumped out and waved at the onlookers as the gates opened to let them in.

Pam ran up and hugged Captain Mallory and brought him over to meet Preston. They were introduced, as was Barbara as she walked over to meet the newcomers.

"Old Michael Mallory—I believe we went to flight school together. Dallas...1992?"

"Barbara Mclean. Yes, I remember you. You were the hot redhead all the guys were after. Still hot, I see. Where were you flying before all this crap hit the fan?"

"Learjets for a private company out of Phoenix," she replied.

"Funny how all pilots seem to know one other," remarked

Preston. "Okay, Captain Mallory. Your escorts, Joe and David, are about three minutes out. They are going to take you guys back to our airfield. We are loading up supplies here and will be back in about an hour. My hangar is off limits for the moment, as we have a couple of guys who don't want interference until they have sorted out the communication hopefully making some Chinese satellite phones work. The men you saw in that convoy on I-95 are not a threat anymore."

At that moment, the two armored cars pulled up to the airport gate and stopped. Joe and David got out and came over to meet the newcomers.

"Captain, I'm planning to transfer your civilians to Seymour Johnson Air Force Base in Goldsboro after you arrive at my place," continued Preston. "They can use the empty housing there. There is lots of it due to so many troops being overseas, and the Air Force has plenty of rations for them. Anybody who can fly a plane will stay at my airfield. Joe, David, get these interesting vehicles back to base. We sure could have used that fire engine this morning!" he laughed.

Preston and the soldiers stationed at the airport helped load *Lady Dandy* with over 100 boxes of food supplies. There were still dozens upon dozens of food and booze cases left after she headed out onto the runway with Barbara in the cockpit. They filled the Cargomaster with more boxes, and a dozen were placed in the rear seat of the 172. Then it was time to look at the few remaining aircraft. Preston took a quick look around. Anything worthwhile was too new or too small. They now needed aircraft to carry supplies, and an old 172 was not much good.

He headed for the Cargomaster. Six of the soldiers had gone with *Lady Dandy*, so he told the remaining six to get in with him and Pam.

His radio squawked to life as he came in for final approach at his airfield. The hangar door was being opened on Carlos' orders while Carlos was on the radio desperately trying to reach General Allen.

Preston heard the other bases come online, and Jennifer reported that she was an hour out, arriving from Texas, and would land first at Preston's field. He noticed the convoy pulling onto the dirt road and driving through the attack zone as he came in low from the southeast. He landed and parked close to Barbara and Pam, whom he had followed in. The 172 had landed first. Pam was a pretty good pilot for a flight attendant.

It was quite a sight once all the vehicles were parked in a line. It looked like they were waiting for Noah's Ark to arrive: two Rat Patrol jeeps, two armored cars, two old SWAT team vehicles, one ambulance, the fire engine and an odd-looking Studebaker police car at the end. On the other side were the three Mustangs and a plethora of working and non-working aircraft. There were a lot of people getting out and looking around in amazement. It looked like Disney World.

"Welcome, Captain Mallory! Welcome to my Air Force," Preston exclaimed, shaking the pilot's hand.

"Preston, we need a meeting right now," shouted Carlos as several of the aircraft radios started chattering at once. Preston went over to the Cargomaster and picked up the microphone.

"Preston, this is Buck… Preston, this is Buck… Do you read?"

"You are very faint, Buck. I can just hear you," replied Preston, with Carlos coming over to listen.

"I overheard Carlos' message 20 minutes ago while I was in the air over the White Cliffs of Dover. I went back down and told Pete that Carlos was having a nervous breakdown, and I suggested that we head straight back to you since it's not very often Carlos gets a bee in his bonnet. Ghost Rider *needs to be refueled and* Baby Huey *has a fresh tank, so Pete is onboard with me. We are an hour and ten minutes out from your airfield and I have* Baby Huey *at maximum cruise. By the way, I'm Alpha Fox-trotting around the world again, so be prepared. I told Alpha Foxtrot One that there could be a spare room in the house. If not, he's happy staying at his ranch to the south. Over."*

"Roger that," replied Preston. "Jennifer is also 55 minutes out, so keep a visual for her."

"Will do," replied Buck.

"What was that all about?" Captain Mallory asked. "And call me Mike—everybody else does."

Preston and Carlos both laughed.

"New in-flight radio procedures, Mike, not approved by the FAA," replied Carlos, shaking the captain's hand. "We talk in a kind of code in case we are being listened to, and we know we are closely monitored. It is now against the law to fly with transponders because the enemy satellites pick them up. That goon squad that passed you was coming here to take us out. Buck McKinnon, who was just on the radio, has an old Huey helicopter that we call Air Force One when the president is on board—yep, that's right, the president. *Ghost Rider* is an AC-130 gunship that belongs to a friend of ours, General Pete Allen, who you will meet soon. Jennifer is Air Force Captain Watkins and she is bringing in a C-130 transporter."

"And the 'White Cliffs of Dover,' I assume, is Dover Air Force Base in Delaware," added Preston. "Any aircraft built before 1980 still flies, and General Allen is trying to bring all the older military aircraft together that he can. Most of the stuff is from the Vietnam era, but so far we have three F-4s, eight C-130s, and three helicopters. One of the 130s is a gunship and one or two are in-flight tankers, and we are growing by the day. We also have our own private civilian Air Force here. The P-38 is now fully equipped with air-to-ground rockets and or 1,000-pound bombs, and the three Mustangs' rocket additions will be finished tomorrow. The only piece of junk here is unfortunately the general's private aircraft—the King Air 200—the rest are ready for action."

"John," laughed Mike, "it looks like our best flying days are still to come. From now on can I assume my call sign is Mike and he is John? What happens if we have more than one Mike or John?"

"Mike One and Mike Two, I guess. Shit, who cares!" laughed Preston. "Let's help unload the aircraft and wait for our meeting. If I know my good buddy Carlos, this is going to be a good one. I've never seen him so excited!" He patted Carlos on the back. "I hear I owe you $500, you naughty boy!" Carlos grinned back but said nothing.

An hour later, *Baby Huey* came in directly from the north, turned in over the hangar, and came in to land from the south. Captain Jennifer Watkins had arrived five minutes earlier and the majority of the passengers from Captain Mallory's convoy were getting ready to depart for Seymour Johnson.

This time, there was no honor guard as *Baby Huey* landed, but a lot more civilians were totally shocked to see the president. The general and Secret Service men exited the plane first and then the president. He shook as many hands as he could, especially the children's hands. Little Beth gave him a kiss on the cheek and shyly introduced him to her new teenaged "big sister" and all her other friends from New York—especially the ones who also had a puppy like she did.

The president was then ushered into the hangar where Carlos and Lee had already set up a meeting room, and the hangar door was closed.

All goodbyes and kisses and thanks had been shared with Mike Mallory, John, and Pam, who were staying behind while all the others from New York were transferred to Seymour Johnson. The other remaining flight attendant was going along to look after the passengers. Jennifer started up and taxied out to the runway for takeoff as the growing team sat down for the next meeting. Martie was the last inside after hugging Little Beth, who was also leaving for Seymour Johnson with her new sister, new friends and the retired teacher as her chaperones. It looked to Preston as if he had Martie to himself once again, and he smiled.

She is going to make a good mother one day when this mess is over, he thought to himself.

"Please, we have little time. I must call this meeting to order," started Carlos, a little agitated. "Mr. President, General Allen, we believe that we have about 24 hours before New York is the victim of an invasion of sorts." THAT got everybody's attention and they all immediately sat down.

There was silence for 20 minutes as Carlos explained what he and Lee had achieved over the satellite link to China. He also showed an old television screen on a table on which was a real live picture of the United States showing the massive winter storm heading northwest and currently over New York and New England. It looked like a Lego-made view of the earth, but he explained that they could now see only very large ships coming in from 300 miles out and the map stretched down to northern South America.

"I believe that within another 24 hours, Lee and I can patch ourselves into the three Chinese satellites and get their digital pictures bounced through our Navistar P. I don't believe they ever thought to scramble their pictures, because who else would be watching if they terminated the electronics of all the other satellites? This is an important factor, General Allen. If we can see what they are seeing, then we can view China and Russia and see if they have their cities lit up. If they do, then they are the enemy. Whoever the real enemy is out there will light up the night sky. So please do not touch our stolen Salt Lake City, Utah, television truck out there. We are getting live feed from across the United States and will continue to do so. The pictures are just good enough to see any extremely large ships approaching within 300 miles of either coast, but not Hawaii or Alaska, I'm afraid.

"Pilots, important! This picture is your only source of weather information, and once other television trucks are set up, they can also view the same picture for weather patterns. Hill is already up, so is Edwards, and I believe Andrews will be online by late this evening. General, tell your men at the bases to find the same electronics we found at Hill and they will be able to see the same picture. An unlimited amount of people can view a satellite feed—it's like satellite television was last year."

"Okay, back to the situation in New York. I have taken the liberty to warn all your bases through our radio link so they can prepare troops for battle. Jennifer—Captain Watkins—is dropping off the civilians at Seymour Johnson and picking up a company of readied troops—92 soldiers plus gear—and transporting them to Andrews. Captain Powers is currently heading to Andrews with another 92 fresh troops from Hill. I believe the Edwards-based C-130 is in the air with her and is loaded with two small bulldozers that can be lifted in by helicopter. They were put aboard by the commander at Hill to help clear the snow off the New York runways. I took the liberty, General Allen, to get things started since you were not in radio contact. I will now hand the operation over to you."

"Thank you, Carlos," replied the general. "I appreciate your quick thinking. I would have mobilized what I could if I were in the same position. So, Mr. President, pilots…thanks to Carlos and Mr. Wang, we have a little knowledge about our future. At this point we are transitioning into express mode. Everything has to be done yesterday. I now have six C-130s available to ferry troops into New York starting at midnight tonight, but the runways are blocked with snow. As Carlos explained, they must have men in or near New York who are going in to clear a runway for something big straight out of Shanghai. If that is the case, they must have bulldozers stashed away somewhere. We might as well let them clear the runway for us, but I want troops into JFK in the next couple of hours, before any incoming enemy army soldiers or Chinese termination squads get there." He walked over to the radio.

"Andrew, this is Pete. Do you copy? Over."

"One moment, Pete, I'll get him for you," came the response.

The base commander arrived a few seconds later.

"Hi, Pete."

"How are those two whirly-birds, Bud?" the general asked.

"Ready for service, Pete. We had two more units come in five minutes ago from our buddy Mr. Dover. That makes four. Ghost Rider *will be taking off in an hour and she has Cousin Seymour's address down yonder."*

"When you get her in the air, tell her to go and see Grandpa Pope (Fort Bragg) instead. He's waiting to fill her up with men and she must return to Mr. McGuire's (McGuire AFB) house."

"Roger that," the base commander replied.

"I want your four whirly-birds full of bad boys, a radio, and lots of firepower ASAP and sent up to Mr. McGuire's. Get gassed up at old McGuire's and then drop them into Juliet Foxtrot Kilo (JFK) by midnight. We are expecting visitors. Tell them to hide and monitor for any incoming. Let any visitors clear the footpaths and then watch for a few more buddies who will fly in and join them. They need to be up in the hunting lodge by the main airstrip before dawn to see the big boys arrive. The friends of the visitors are expected to fly in.

'Allen Key' is the code exchange for friendly conversation. Over."

"*Copy that, Pete. Confirm Juliet Foxtrot Kilo, our civilian neighbor to the north?*"

"You got it, buddy. We are expecting visitors sometime tomorrow, but they could arrive early. I recommend a silent entrance into Juliet Foxtrot Kilo from the water; you know the game. Out." The general put down the microphone and thought out his next problem.

"The only aircraft I know of with a range to get here from China are the numerous civilian Boeing 747-400 long distance models, or the new Airbuses China has purchased in the last five or six years," he continued, facing the people in the room. "I could not fly into McGuire Air Force Base in Trenton, New Jersey, today. They were still struggling to clear the runway with two old snowplows, but I managed to get the base commander, General Billy Johnson, on the radio. Luckily, they had an idea to try everything in the storage depots.

"They have zero operational aircraft, since they were equipped with only the latest C-17s and Stratotankers, but they have a gazillion tons of fuel and he told me that C-130s could get in there by about 8:00 tonight. I'm going to use McGuire Air Force Base as my headquarters for this New York operation. Are there any questions up to this point?" There were none.

"Okay, next, Captain Powers completed a tour of four bases today on my behalf—Yuma, Tucson, Phoenix, and Vandenberg in California—and found a couple things I was searching for. I had forgotten where they were. Captain Powers is returning from Hill at this moment and two of our Vietnam-era, fully restored and operational Jolly Green Giants—Sikorsky S-61R helicopters—are an hour or two behind her and will be going in to Hill for refueling in about an hour. I will order them into McGuire once I'm up in the air, and they will have to refuel one more time before they get to the East Coast. Once they arrive, we can airlift the bulldozers into any location where we want to clear the airstrips. They also have 30 soldiers on board—some of our specially trained Air Force anti-terrorist troops from the West Coast. That now gives us seven helicopters in total."

The general went over to the radio and called the commander at Andrews AFB. "How many companies of soldiers do you have ready for battle?" he asked.

"I can give you five companies—500 men. They are ready to go at a moment's notice, Pete. That will leave me two companies to defend the base," was the reply.

"As soon as you have delivered my first order, start transferring your men up to old McGuire's place with the choppers and then the bigger girls once they land. Your chopper pilots can report back to you as soon as it's clear for runway use. I'm sending up everything we have down here to go to Mr. McGuire's as well. I need 24/7 action. I will get back to you once we have worked out the next plan. Out."

The general came back to the bar table podium and looked at several world maps he had brought with him. He then looked at Carlos' television set and thought for a minute while everybody, including the president, looked on.

"The commander of McGuire, Billy Johnson, will take over command of the New York operation once I'm finished at this meeting. He has tons of military experience—worked with the Army and Marines as a liaison fighting officer for several years—and he will attack and sterilize any foreign troops arriving on our soil. We are going to base all our military aircraft at McGuire starting tomorrow. Right now, we need to thwart this incoming attack in Raleigh in 48 hours, right, Carlos? Lee?" They both confirmed 48 hours.

"They seem to like another potential dawn attack at RDU this time," Carlos commented.

"We need to get a couple radios or communication stations on the incoming highways—I believe I-40 from the west and a site north and south of I-95. David, what range do we have for these radios of yours?" the general asked.

"Thirty to fifty miles," stated David.

"If they transfer transmissions into my Chapel Hill tower, I'm sure that range could be extended," added Preston.

"Fifty miles is a good distance," suggested Pete Allen. "Carlos, back to you."

"Based on what Lee suggested in his conversation earlier today," Carlos continued, trying to prioritize the most immediate problems, "it sounds like a group of engineers are being flown into JFK tomorrow, or the next day, also around dawn. I'm sure that they will be bringing in supplies and troops to protect these engineers. We should expect another couple of hundred people in New York to clear the runways and help prepare before these guys fly in. So, I believe that a maximum force of 500 troops will be enough to overpower our 'visitors'."

"Sounds good to me, Carlos," stated General Allen.

"That means the troops with Sally and Jennifer could come in here, we could fly in another crowd from Pope 30 minutes away, and then have 300 men on the ground ready to fight the battle that will start tomorrow. Plus, we have the new firepower of our aircraft. Immediately after the confrontation, we can send the troops up to McGuire. We clean up here, you get the guys up there, try and capture the engineers and supplies, kill the troops…" he thought for a few seconds. "…and capture the aircraft, if possible. Yes! They could help bring our troops home faster. Then we transfer all the soldiers, howitzers, tanks, aircraft and naval vessels we have to New York, and we will have two whole weeks to do that."

"How many men can fit in our smaller civilian aircraft, Preston?" the general asked.

"We can get about 30 in *Lady Dandy*, 15 in the Cargomaster, 12 in the Pilatus, and six in the 210. That's over 60 we can put down anywhere we want on any cleared highway and return to get more."

"Good. That will help, since you guys can put them down anywhere. Once we see them on a clear piece of road, perhaps just after the brow of a hill on the highway would be a good ambush point. You guys can fly in tomorrow and pick up men from Pope and Fort Bragg. You might invite the president to go with you, since he is Commander-in-Chief," directed the general, looking at the president.

The president smiled and nodded his head in approval, excited.

"Preston, Carlos, you have First Sergeant Perry here," the general said, nodding at the first sergeant. "He has shown great leadership and experience in ambushing the first group of insurgents. This time, Perry, do the same type of attack. It could be daylight when they arrive, so set up positions a mile in front of them, and then have our civilian air force blow them to bits. Then take your soldiers in, charge the position, and take no prisoners. Remember, Perry, we need those cell phones, so go for head shots from snipers on prominent positions."

First Sergeant Perry nodded. "Yes, sir," he replied eagerly.

"Captain Mallory, good to have you with us. You will take over command of the civilian food supplies once the fight is over and Preston gives you all the non-fighting aircraft. It looks like you will have the FedEx Cargomaster, a 210, and two 172s to work with. I've thought about this for a few hours, and I suggest that you take supplies into a local rural airport, find someone to take control of that airport, or use Air Force troops if you think it necessary to guard the position of the supply—a machine-gun post with sandbags, if necessary. I will let you have one C-130 to ferry in pallets of food and troops as soon as I can. I suggest you search out the pilots in and around that airfield and get the local pilots to distribute the food further—maybe into even smaller, more rural airfields. I'm going to borrow your tanker, Preston, and fly into Hill after we are finished here. I will take off in the first C-130 that gets here and meet up with *Ghost Rider* and the other tanker from Dover, send yours back to McGuire and then, Preston, you will take over command of this area until further notice. I want Captain Watkins and Powers to work for me for the next 24 hours moving troops out of Seymour Johnson and Pope into McGuire." Again he walked back to the radio.

"Jennifer, this is Pete, do you copy?"

"Jennifer here, just off-loading."

"Is the boss there?" continued the general.

"Boss here, Pete," answered the base commander at Seymour Johnson.

"How many battle-experienced guys can you find me?"

"You've taken a company already. I reckon I can give you another 300. They could be kitted out by midnight."

"Roger that. Get them ready," continued the general. "I need Jennifer to refuel and bring a company of 100 men back here ASAP. I need to get to Hill. Get a jeep, or some transport, over to Pope's place. I know they have tons more men. Tell the boss there what we're up to. I need maximum fighting numbers ASAP. I need to get as many as possible up to Mr. McGuire's place in the next 24 hours."

"How many are you looking for?" the base commander asked.

"I need 180 for a party here and then as many as we can carry in over seven days with four of our big girls working 24/7. I think about 10,000 will do. Go and visit with our Marine buddies at Camp Lejeune and get numbers. Billy Johnson will be in charge. He must be in radio contact with you by tomorrow. Also, get two sets of crew aboard each 130. I want non-stop action for a week. Out." The general went back to the front of the room and thought before he spoke.

"Okay. My plan of action is this: I'm leaving for China tonight," he explained. "I'm taking *Mother Goose* and *Ghost Rider*. *Mother Goose* will refuel *Ghost Rider* over the Bering Strait from Anchorage into northern Japan. Carlos, will the phone you have for me work?"

"You and I will be able to talk as well as if you were on your old cell phone," replied Carlos. "If you activate your transponder for three minutes, I believe I can view it through their system and patch it into our system. It will take Lee and me all night tonight to work on our satellite, but I think it will work. Remember, the enemy in Nanjing will see you as much as we can, but they will scratch their heads trying to figure out what type of aircraft is flying in the middle of nowhere for three minutes at a time. I think you should turn on your transponder only once or twice. I have a repaired cell phone for General Johnson and a fourth one will be repaired by morning. I will give you all the direct numbers. Who shall I give the fourth one to?"

"I want to take all you have," answered the general. "I am going to need at least six working units to distribute around the world. Carlos, can you fix your own and make it work? Buck said you could. That will give me three and yours could be your base's communications from now on when I need to talk to you." The general turned back to the group.

"Let me continue. My mission is to flatten their headquarters. Then I'm going into Beijing. If they respond with fighters and shoot us down, I will disappear from view. But I believe I will be able to use my transponder once the Zedong Electronics building or headquarters is history, because that should cancel out their global communications worldwide.

"I want to see if I can talk to the leader of China—hopefully by radio before I go in. I must make sure that they are in the same position as us. Then, and with help from their airports and fuel, I want to get to Moscow. If the Chinese are friendly, they will help me. I want to do the same in Moscow, and I will carry all their military radio frequencies with me on board. If I survive through Russia and they are friendly, I want to stop at our base in Turkey. From there I can see what condition our troops are in and where they are situated. From Turkey, I'm heading to Baghdad and then into Ramstein to see if our European troops are okay. From Ramstein, I'm heading over to our base in the Azores and with a bit of luck will get back into McGuire before I miss the Super Bowl.

"I've worked it out that a week's non-stop flying will get me around the world, and I hope that you guys are not communists by the time I get back. *Mother Goose* can get fuel out of a rock, and we will have transponders on and communications to keep me informed throughout the journey.

"Everyone, I want it known to all active personnel that if the insurgents arrive in this country on civilian aircraft, I want every jet they fly in on commandeered without damage. Those jets can be turned around in hours and we have dozens of out-of-work Stratotanker and Galaxy pilots at McGuire that can fly these birds into Turkey, Korea, Iraq, and hopefully Kabul to get our troops out—800 per aircraft. I'm hoping we can get them safely back on U.S. soil, or at the least, into Europe and then shipped back to the

United States. The attackers can only come in on big aircraft and big ships. We know that some aircraft are incoming from somewhere tomorrow. My plan is to have our attack forces closer to New York's JFK, but where?" he thought out loud.

"Teterboro Airport in New Jersey," suggested both Buck and Mike Mallory, who both knew the area well.

"Of course," nodded the general. "Thanks, guys. What are the distances?"

Buck nodded to the Southwest captain to continue.

"La Guardia is the closest, about 12 miles. I'd say Newark is about the same but to the south, and JFK is the furthest at about 20 miles."

"Let's set up our main base of attack there, then. I want at least 10,000 men in the area within two weeks, which we understand is when their big attack will commence. Many soldiers can walk in from McGuire if necessary. It would only take them a day, but we must do it undercover. I don't want them to get wind of our movements. I'll try and get relayed from Andrews into McGuire when I leave here and give Billy Johnson his orders."

The general looked back over at the communications team. "Carlos, work on scrambling their communications, and get Lee Wang's help to figure out their plan of action. I'm going to assume any electronic parts will be coming in with their engineers to repair the airports and harbors, and our own Air Force engineers can wear their clothes if necessary, and even go undercover and complete the Chinese mission. I believe that we must keep control of our three airports, have troops in the surrounding terminals, and be ready for the big one. If they want to repair the harbor cranes, then they are bringing in troops by sea.

"On my way out of here, I will send a plane into Norfolk and tell Vice Admiral Rogers to get whatever he has floating up to New York Harbor, stay in the Long Island Sound, and prepare for an attack. Questions?" There were none.

"Ok, recap. Captain Mallory, John, Pam, Barbara, Maggie and Will Smart—commandeer whatever you need to start supplying the local population with food after the attack. I'll get you a C-130 down here as soon as I can. Remember, *Lady Dandy* can carry some weight. Move outwards as fast as you can and send word to civilians in the surrounding states. Go as far north as those farmers you met in Maryland and then work across. I'll leave the planning up to you."

"Preston, Carlos, Martie, Buck, and Lee—you are all heading up to McGuire once the fight here is finished. We need your firepower. Lee, does your wife know the building in Nanjing?"

"Yes, very well," Lee replied.

"Will she be able to show it to me from the air, maybe at night?" The general rephrased his question.

"If the lights of Nanjing are on, then she can point out the building by looking for the bridge across the river."

"Good. Lee, I'm sorry to tell you this, but I must take her with me. Carlos needs you here. At least as the military always promises, she will see the world and arrive back safely, I hope, in one week."

"I will tell her to go and prepare for a long journey," Lee replied, and he headed over to the house.

"Mr. President, I think McGuire Air Force Base or down here at Preston's airstrip will be your best places to work," the general advised.

"I would like to stay here," replied the president, "as long as I'm free to go out on flights and help with logistics. I would like my family brought down as well, if you don't mind, General."

"I can get them over to Andrews and then down here on one of the 130s coming south," replied General Allen. "It might take a day or two.

"Good luck, everybody! Stay in radio contact with no transponder usage unless you want them to see it. I'll sort out their headquarters, and, Preston, I will tell General Billy Johnson that as far as I'm concerned each one of you is a general in the Air Force, same as him, and that he must listen to you and your plans until I get back. Carlos, keep me posted. I'm out of here."

Pete saluted the president, smiled at the team in front of them as they heard incoming aircraft engines, and walked out of the hangar to see where Mrs. Wang was.

Chapter 7

JFK – New York

THE SNOW WAS DONE. It finally disappeared off the New England coast and the sun rose at dawn on the sixth day and stayed like that—icy cold but sunny. The sun could not warm the frozen air, which in some very northern places was as low as minus 40, but it did lift the temperature several degrees. Cities were quiet, their streets under several feet of snow. The central United States was the worst hit—some towns nearly buried up to their rain gutters. Most of Canada was a frozen blanket of snow, and the only places where any movement could be seen were along the warmer West Coast. The only movement in the northern United States was ravens, crows and small animals scurrying about without any human interference and digging for any meat that was not yet frozen solid.

New York was a barren land of white, with frozen skyscrapers heavily laden with snow. The streets had banks of snow as high as second story windows, in some areas, and there was little or no movement. There was movement at JFK on the morning of the sixth day, however, and there had been for several hours.

Nine hours earlier, and just before midnight on January 5th, four U.S. helicopters had come in low over the icy waters of the Atlantic, and in nearly white-out conditions, they carefully touched down on the roof of the nearest terminal building to Runway 31 Left—the longest runway at JFK.

They had unloaded men and gear and had taken off immediately, hugging the ground and disappearing out to sea the way they had come in, over Rockaway Community Park, frozen under three feet of snow. They returned three more times, every two hours, until a very late dawn slowly breathed light into the dispersing storm clouds, and for the fourth and last time, the helicopters dipped down close to the ground and with a strong tailwind dove out to sea to be lost from sight over the dark grey waters of the Atlantic.

By then, the storm was gone and the sun's rays began to light up the sky. A total of 180 Special Forces soldiers from Andrews, via McGuire, had landed on the terminal roof. In total, they had four shoulder rocket launchers with a dozen rounds for each, four heavy machine guns, cases of grenades, and hundreds of rounds of ammunition, and they now owned the desolate airport terminal. The men had quickly found entry into the terminal via a walkway entrance. The inside of the terminal was as cold as the outside, just without the wind chill, and they took out maps and searched for places to hide.

Their orders were to lay low, expect activity, and monitor it. They had four radios between them. This gave them radio communications into McGuire, which now had direct communication by cell phone to General Allen, who was now in Tacoma, Washington.

One group of men planned to have ringside seats for Runway 31 Left, and they took up residence in a small stranded commuter jet, parked right next to the runway. They had an excellent view of the surrounding area. With 40 seats, a toilet in the back, the windows drawn, and a couple of small gas heaters warming up the inside, it became a home away from home for 30 of the troops. They locked the aircraft's doors and made sure that there was no light peeking out from inside, opened the flight attendant areas to access food, checked their own rations, and waited.

A second aircraft, a slightly larger McDonald Douglas M-90 commercial airliner parked at the closest gate overlooking the runway, became home for another 40 troops. With two toilets and a fully readied snack service waiting for passengers who would never arrive, the men closed it down, took watches, heated the interior of the aircraft, locked the doors, and waited.

A third group of 60 not so lucky troops got the cold terminal closest to the Van Wyck Expressway—the direction in which the visitors were expected to arrive.

An empty Boeing 777 stood right in the middle of the taxiway. It had been turning out of the terminal to reach the taxiway when its engines and electronics must have shut down. A single ladder was standing by the front door to the aircraft, and when troops walked up it and tried to open the door, the door easily opened. Inside, the aircraft was empty, and it looked like the passengers had left in a disciplined exit. All hand luggage was gone and the overhead bins empty and open. The aircraft was in a perfect place to view the surrounding area, especially from the cockpit. It had several toilets, lots of snacks and drinks, and the window blinds were already drawn.

The inside warmed up and an interesting "in flight meal" was served.

The last group was the most unlucky and took turns nearly freezing to death on the roof of the terminal for an hour at a time, after finding a storage room close to a restaurant and a bar where they could warm up between shifts. They closed down the area so that they wouldn't be seen if someone walked through the terminal, and radioed in to report that they were in position.

It didn't take long for the visitors to arrive. The cold meal was just about over in the Boeing 777 when the lookout in the cockpit stated that he saw several vehicles approaching—a couple of old Suburbans behind an even older Ford 4x4 truck working hard to get down the Van Wyck Expressway. The truck had to be pushed and manhandled until it finally got down the exit ramp closest to the terminals. The invaders cut a hole in a hedge, then the high security fence, and drove through the holes onto the aircraft area.

"We have visitors." The troop manning the radio from the 777 quietly sent the message. *"Seven vehicles and a couple dozen armed men have gotten out and are waiting for something. They are Chinese or Asian, mean-looking critters, and have carbines and shoulder launchers. I can see three of the shoulder launchers. Over."*

"Keep them visual," whispered Air Force Major Joe Patterson, the commander of the group in the terminal, into the radio in response.

"I see some bulldozers coming into view from the airport warehouse area. There are three at the moment. One is beginning to clear the expressway and the other two are heading out towards the runway and clearing the area in front of the men. It looks like they are preparing for aircraft to arrive. It will take the Charlies most of the day and tonight to clear that runway out there," reported a lieutenant in the 777.

For three hours they watched as the bulldozers cleared an area right next to them. A couple of men were clearing the fuel openings in the apron cement right next to the 777. An electrical generator on wheels was being pulled into sight behind one of the trucks and they could hear the motor starting up and then shutting down. It was a big one—the type of generator used to pump fuel into large aircraft. It had "Air China" written all over it. Pipes and connections were off-loaded from a fuel truck and stacked neatly by the building out of the way. The third bulldozer slowly came back into view followed by a dozen other vehicles, mostly an assortment of 30-year-old trucks and cars. One white Cadillac had what looked like red blood down the side of it. The road was now passable and the radio squawked on.

"How many men are out there?" the major asked.

"I see about 30 so far," answered the lieutenant in the 777. *"The new vehicles are being parked in a line, and three or four more are coming into view. Each is being driven by one man. A fourth bulldozer has come into view pulling a second "Air China" generator, and the man is being given orders. It looks like he is being told to start clearing a second parking area. The first area is complete by the looks of it, as a road is now being made out to the runway itself. The finished clearing could fit a large 747."*

"Roger that. It looks like you guys have the front row seats. We are going to move to the closest terminal next to you guys and will let you know when we are ready. The incoming aircraft are going to have to use stairs if they are parking over there. I want to see if we can find some more and bring them forward so that they leave yours alone. Check out a bottom exit to your aircraft in case they move your stairs, and don't drink the first-class liquor, boys," the major said with a smile on his face. "Pack it up and we'll take it back to base. We must not be seen until we have their aircraft in the hands of our pilots, who are waiting here with me. Their incoming pilots might want to freshen up, powder their noses and use these bathrooms, and we will take them out in here. We are going to collect their clothes for the use of. Hopefully our guys are short enough to fit into their clothing.

"The way they are clearing all that snow, we will have enough packed snow to use for defensive positions. They are obviously not considering that anyone will attack them and are walking around as if they own the place. I'm sure they won't miss a couple of their guys. And remember, men, the brass reckons the aircraft are not due in until dawn tomorrow morning. Out."

Over the rest of the day, the major worked out what the visitors would do if they had access to the terminal. First, he made sure the door was ready to be opened, and then he studied the closest store, one full of warm clothing.

Yes, he thought to himself. *The pilots going back won't resist getting a few presents for themselves and their girlfriends.* He formed a plan of action and broke the lock of the door. There was no electricity, and the concourse was dark, but they would come in here for warmth. He saw the bar on the other side. He broke that lock, too, opened the steel mesh doors on top of the counter, and then arranged cases of beer in a pile so that they couldn't miss them—what man could resist a mountain of cold beers ready for them? He opened a couple of cases and put six cold bottles on the table and poured three down a sink to make it look like somebody had already been there when the airport closed down. He then lay one on its side and let one break on the floor.

The action on the runway went on and on throughout the day. It was one of the longest civilian runways in the United States. They only had three bulldozers working on the runway itself, and the snow was a couple of feet deep. It took each dozer about an hour to clear a narrow line from one end of the runway to the other.

Another old truck came out, and men started throwing salt onto the parking areas. They even got an aircraft weather-spray truck pulled in close by the fourth dozer. It didn't work, but they were obviously expecting whoever was coming in by air to have everything they needed, and they might need a spraydown before takeoff if bad weather came in again.

Night fell, and the lights on the bulldozers showed that they were still working out there. They were halfway done, and it was going to be a very cold night. The salt truck had gone out several times and they had done a good job. One of the major's men in white snow gear had snuck out and inspected the runway. It was quite dry, and they had about three hours of work left to go.

The major had allowed many of his men to sleep part of the day, and he had talked with two of his Chinese-American Air Force pilots who spoke fluent Mandarin and together they had worked out a plan. Quite a few of the Chinese had come into the terminal a couple of hours earlier and helped themselves to food and the beer placed for them. The major and his guys had gone on high alert when they heard voices in the terminal for the first time. They were over 100 feet away from the door and a couple of soldiers had crawled down the dark terminal floor and found two men sitting at the main table of the bar drinking cold bottles of beer.

They hadn't finished their brews before their necks were broken and they were dragged back to the storage area where Major Patterson and his team of pilots were holed up.

An hour later, six more men came in looking for the other two, whispering their names, an interpreter told the major. Two came down to the dark area where the troops were waiting. One American soldier made a grunt on the opposite side of the concourse, and the two flashlights held by the Chinese men quickly swung around towards the sound. That was their last move before being terminated from behind by strong hands. The other four had found the beer, the demise of many men, and bottles were opened.

It wasn't long, however, before the first two were missed. The crew in the store shouted for them, and one of the Chinese-American pilots impersonated them with a cloth over his face to hide his voice and told them that they had found some good chocolate and American candy. One of the four men, carrying a shoulder missile launcher, swaggered over to the dark area of the concourse shouting that beer was better than chocolate, and then he, too, went eerily quiet.

It took several more minutes, but the last three went the same way as the rest, sitting around the darkened terminal with flashlights and the moon, their only source of light. The eight dead men were relieved of their clothing and it was given to the shortest soldiers in the group. The two Chinese-American pilots were now as mean-looking as the guys outside.

Going through the pockets and jackets, they had found two satellite phones as well as lots of small things, and now they had communications with the outside world. The major had been told to update the general whenever a phone became available, so he called the general and was connected just like he would have been on his regular cell phone a few weeks earlier. There was no answer on the other side until the major stated "Allen Key" into the phone.

"Name and location?" General Allen requested curtly.

"Patterson. Juliet, Foxtrot, Kilo," Major Patterson replied.

"Well done, Patterson. I assume you have terminated some visitors to get this?" the general asked, now well on his way to Elmendorf Air Force Base in Alaska.

"Roger that, Allen Key."

"Give me a quick sitrep, Mr. Patterson," the general continued.

"We have 180 friendlies in four separate locations. We were visited by 40 guests in trucks a little earlier, now down to 32. We have two new cell phones and hope to have several more by tonight. So far today, two areas were cleared by four bulldozers. Area 31-Lima (left) is about 120 minutes from being totally cleared. Salt has been laid. I have a plan in place. Two friendly Charlie-American pilots are ready and prepared to get into any arriving empty birds and take them to Mr. McGuire. Then we bring in reinforcements and terminate the uprising ASAP. We have one friendly Charlie ready on a cell phone to tell any aircraft that everything is okay. Any suggestions? Over." The major gave his brief report into the cell phone as more visitors suddenly entered the terminal shouting for their friends.

"I have a situation. Our next cell phone has just entered the building. Out." And he hung up on the general.

Four more cold Chinese men found the beer and were momentarily distracted. It took several minutes for them each to drink one and open another. Another group of eight joined them, and then another four men came in out of the cold. Two more cases were ripped open and bottles hissed as their tops were twisted.

"Bring six men with silencers forward and place them in positions where they can take them out if need be," the major ordered his first sergeant in a whisper. He also had an automatic pistol with a silencer and watched through its night sights as six men crept forward and got into position on the floor in a line where they could hit the men without breaking the large windows around the concourse.

Suddenly the satellite phone rang in his hand. "Shit!" he whispered, trying to find and hit the kill button to turn it off. The men drinking beer immediately shouted to see whose phone it was. Major Patterson immediately whispered to the Chinese-American pilot next to him to answer as if he was drunk. The man did as he was told and several men laughed and hooted from the bar area. He swore, telling them to leave him alone, and told the "person" on the phone to call him later when he woke up, which prompted raucous laughter from the bar crowd.

Three men, laughing, came to find him, and they were quickly laid to rest without bullets. One made a grunt as his neck was broken, and the men in the bar suddenly went silent. The major prodded the other Chinese pilot and told them to shout at each other and make drunken laughter. They did a good enough job that another two came over to see what all the fun was about. They also didn't make the party, and this time the two Chinese-American pilots got really rowdy. They started getting angry at each other and swore in rapid Mandarin to each other about being left to sleep. This time the rest at the bar went silent, one drew a pistol, and they all came forward flashing their torches into the darkness.

Their clothing couldn't be saved, as the major shot first and the six silencers followed suit firing several shots and killing all ten men without a sound, and with no broken windows. Immediately, the major told the troops behind him to drag the bodies back, far down the concourse and out of the way, clean up any blood, make sure the prisoners were dead and strip any clothing off that did not have blood on it. This was completed in seconds with the men still wearing night goggles.

Major Patterson immediately sent two men to cover the door to the outside to watch for any more Chinese, and he sent another two men to set up the bar tables again with fresh bottles, just in case.

Within three minutes the concourse was quiet, with the bar area looking like a lot of drinking had been accomplished, and with the odd jacket and hat lying around.

"Allen Key," he spoke into another, new phone, and he waited for a response from the general.

"Busy night, Patterson?" the general asked.

"Busy bar night, Allen Key, just like any Friday night. All these guys are drinking and we now have 24 of them hidden in the broom closet, all as dead as Do-Dos. They are down to the five guys on the dozers and seven others somewhere playing in the salt pit. We have clothing for 14 and six fancy phones."

"Don't answer any cell phone unprepared," cautioned General Allen. *"If the red number comes up when your phone rings, that's a no-no for at least two more days. You will see the number on the back of the phone. Turn off all phones, and if the red number crops up and you need to say hi to Uncle Charlie, use a guy who can talk the lingo. Get my drift?"*

"Roger that, Allen Key."

"And this is your number from now on, Patterson. Let me know how your plans go tomorrow. Tell me immediately what comes in. You will have to play this drama out in the spur of the moment. Hopefully I can hand you an Oscar when we meet. Mr. McGuire will have the four choppers full and three big 130 mama's ready to take off by dawn. As soon as you have pilots aboard the aircraft and they are about to take off, tell me and Mr. McGuire and he will release the hounds

into the attack. They will take 20 minutes to get there and will be below 500 feet to stay out of any aircraft radar contact. That's 300 guys and what you have there to terminate the guests. Call me when you are about to attack—a buddy of mine believes that he can jam all their communications for a while. Well done, Patterson, and good luck. Your plan sounds positive, and we want those big aircraft undamaged. Out."

Major Patterson got back on the radio to all his men and explained the plan to them.

"Team Four," he stated to the 40 men based in one of the outside aircraft, the M-90. "Go through your exit in the bottom of your aircraft and find the salt pit. There are seven or more Charlies working with a truck. Try and take them out without bloodshed. We need their clothes and cell phones. I say again, we need undamaged cell phones and clothing. Use silencers."

"Roger that. On our way," the commander of Team Four replied.

"Team Two in the commuter jet," Patterson continued. "I believe they will park the dozers close to the area where they want the aircraft to land and refuel. It looks like two aircraft will be incoming. Once the dozers are back from the runway, take the drivers out and we should be clear of bad boys until the next lot comes in."

"Roger. We are getting on white gear and heading out. What about the line of vehicles? Shall we leave them alone? Over." The commander of Team Two needed to cover all the bases.

"Take the keys out of the ignition and put them under the seat of the front passenger, not the driver's seats. Confirm!"

"Copy that, the right passenger seats," the commander replied, and within five minutes Major Patterson could see dim white shapes leaving the express jet and crawling over to the large mounds of snow between the arrival area and the runway.

It was a clear sparkling night, and it took three more hours before the dozers returned and parked, and the tired drivers were relieved of their lives, cell phones, and clothing. The salt team had also been terminated, and the airport was finally clear of unfriendly visitors. It was time to get into action. The Chinese pilots were given two of the captured radios, and the vehicles were inspected and relieved of two more radios and a lot of ammunition. The major worked out that the incoming aircraft would need to use the radios to ask for landing instructions and prepared his Chinese guys, both C-17 pilots, to call the shots.

It was midnight by the time they were finished. The terminal was cleaned and the pile of dead bodies was moved to another stranded aircraft, the blood and remains cleared away and the bar made to look like a party had taken place. The major's men opened the clothing store and pulled several tables into the hallway, piling all the expensive coats, hats, and other winter items onto the tables as if the visitors had made a presentation for the incoming dignitaries.

He and his men also piled up a mountain of chairs and tables in front of where they had set up base as a wall against any incoming fire. He did the same on the other side of the bar area and called in the squad from the M-90. Patterson placed 30 of the soldiers on the other side of the mountain of furniture with sniper rifles, automatic rifles, and grenades. They were hidden behind the large assortment of steel and wooden furniture 50 yards from the bar area. The major wanted to have 60 of his troops inside the terminal on both sides of the entrance door and an attack zone 100 yards wide.

He ordered 20 of his men in the 777 to exit and put on the confiscated clothing. This group would be led by one of his Chinese-American pilots, Captain Chong, who would form a guard with all their captured shoulder rocket launchers.

Four of the Air Force personnel, including Major Patterson, as well as the two Chinese-American pilots, could fly anything Air China flew into JFK on the now cleared runway. He allowed all his men to come into the warmer concourse and gave his orders.

"Ok guys, we believe we have two jets incoming just after dawn from Beijing or Shanghai. We need to get our pilots aboard each jet, hidden hopefully where they can take over the jet once takeoff is underway. Pilots, I think that the only people expected on board will be the flight crews on the way back. Also, there will be no fighting until both aircraft are at least halfway down the runway or already airborne. I'm hoping that most of the troops will be in here, in the middle of our ambush. If anybody gets over our wall of chairs and tables before our attack, take them out silently. I will place a lookout on the Van Wyck Expressway in case they have more men incoming with motor vehicles. The worst scenario is two jets with a maximum of 700 to 1,000 troops, but I've heard that there will be engineers included in the group. Do not—I say again—do not attempt to take out the engineers, unless they are a direct threat to your life or you see them talking on a cell phone. We have to play this by ear, and until the aircraft are out of here, we only kill by hand, understand?" Every soldier nodded.

"You all have your orders. I want three of our best hand-to-hand killers behind our terminal. Kill any enemy soldiers by hand who go for a piss or walk around the building to smoke. The worst case, if there are more than one or two, gentlemen, use your silencers, understand?"

Again everybody nodded.

"I want every short man possible dressed in the semi-decent-smelling civilian Chinese clothes we have taken off them. Hide your eyes and faces with new scarves from the store, look Chinese, and everybody, do not kill any person dressed in civilian clothing! It could be one of our guys. Password if you have to question somebody is 'Allen Key.' Repeat after me, 'Allen Key'."

"Allen Key," the crowd in front of him repeated.

"If you are about to get your throat slit by one of your own guys, say the code words 'Allen Key' quickly," instructed the major. "Okay, everybody, get into a warm place and get five hours of sleep. We will head outside just before dawn."

Thirty minutes before dawn, Major Patterson went outside with the remainder of his troops, now all dressed in white Arctic gear, and began to place them in sniper positions around the cleared areas where the two aircraft were expected to unload. They dug into the snow and disappeared from view. By dawn, he had 60 men with every sort of weapon at their fingertips around the area, as well as 20 men dug in on the roof of the terminal with sniper rifles at the ready. The rest were in the confiscated clothing as well as new clothing from the store, all had thick hats and bandanas across their faces, and apart from their eyes, they were indistinguishable from the 42 men who had arrived at the airport 24 hours earlier.

As the sun rose over the horizon, the radio crackled on and a voice in Chinese asked for conditions for landing. A few minutes later they could see two minute black aircraft shapes over the eastern horizon coming in to land. Major Patterson radioed McGuire and told them that they had incoming and would call again once they were ten minutes from takeoff.

Chapter 8

Where are the Hit Squads?

BACK AT THE NORTH CAROLINA FARM, the dawn on the sixth day found aircraft and another group of soldiers getting ready for action. Preston had fueled every working aircraft to the brim the evening before, and the plan was to first go out as far as the two 172 spotter planes could, at least 200 miles out along I-40 and north along I-95 at 10,000 feet, and search for any movements on the two major incoming highways. With the snow and icy roads, the travel into North Carolina would be slow for anybody coming from the north and northwest, and Preston had a gut feeling that anybody using his brains would stay as far south as possible.

John and Pam were planning to fly out along I-40 and Maggie and Barbara were flying north. Martie, in the faster 210, was to fly south first down I-95 as far as South Carolina, and then west across country to pick up the US64 highway in case they were not using major roadways.

A plan of action had been put together the previous day. All the fighter aircraft had been checked and their guns and Sidewinder rockets deemed ready for action. A fresh group of 100 well-trained and hardened marines had been brought in from Camp Lejeune in Jacksonville via a C-130 that had returned from McGuire at dawn and picked them up. Carlos was happy to see that Sally was the pilot, and the president, now comfortable in the house, was happy to see the first family exit first out of the cargo door. They rushed up to greet him and he introduced them to the whole team.

Carlos and Lee had worked for 24 hours solid on the electrical equipment, and they figured that they could scramble the whole system if need be. Unfortunately, as he explained to General Allen over his own cell phone that he now had working, everyone would lose communication while they scrambled the satellite feeds. The general told him that every available aircraft in the United States would be up and running by the end of the sixth day and that they would all be sent to McGuire, apart from Sally and her aircraft, which was the transport for the southern attack.

"Preston, John. Do you copy? Over," came the first midday radio call from the spotter aircraft.

"John, this is Preston."

"Preston, we are at our limit, about 220 miles west of you. We are currently over the Ashville airport at 16,000 feet. We have binoculars on the highway over the mountains. Pam tells me there is no group of vehicles and she can just about see the Tennessee border. She confirms no convoy. In the last two hours we have seen three vehicles, and more could be hidden by the mountains, but I must return, my tanks show half full. Over."

"Roger that," replied Preston, "Martie can head over that way a little later. Out."

"Preston, this is Mike. Do you copy? Over."

"Mike, this is Preston."

"We are well into Virginia and have seen a couple of vehicles on I-95 North, but no convoy. I'm returning to base."

"Roger that, Mike," Preston replied.

The hangar was full of soldiers waiting to board *Tom*, the C-130 patiently sitting on the runway. They carried a lot of gear and were ready for anything.

Baby Huey had arrived back from Andrews where Buck had flown the president's family to meet up with the C-130 for the trip to North Carolina. Now it was time to change into *Lady Dandy* and do some convoy spotting in comfort. The president and family were going along and were excited about it. The Secret Service agents would be in attendance and the furniture, snacks, and drinks from *Baby Huey* had been transferred into the DC-3.

Preston was planning to take the FedEx Cargomaster up in an hour and head out along US64 and back over the I-40 landing before dark. He had suggested to Buck to go south to South Carolina for an hour and then head northwards to the Virginia border. Preston was going to do a full western sweep of North Carolina. Earlier, *Tom* was flown into RDU by fresh pilots, packed what was left in the food and drink department at the terminal, and returned, leaving all the troops stationed there in case the convoy got through and decided to attack the Raleigh airport unannounced during the night. Two hundred enemy soldiers was a force to be reckoned with, and a plan had been arranged in case the incoming death squads didn't arrive where the civilian air force personnel were setting up an ambush scenario like the one before. Everybody was keen to find the convoy and get the fight away from the farm. *"Preston, this is Martie. Do you copy me? Over."*

"Martie, it's Preston," he replied.

"Preston, I went as far as Charleston. I'm currently at 15,000 feet and have turned northwest, following the 77 north, and am about to fly over Columbia, South Carolina. I have seen several vehicles going in different directions, but nobody within ten miles of each other. I plan to fly over Charlotte and then turn northeast over Mount Pleasant and follow US64 home."

"Roger that, Martie," replied Preston. "Carlos has just come in and said that we should take the Mustangs for a ride around the block. He said that he's sick of radio work and needs some fresh air. His buddy can look after things while he is away."

"Preston, that's not fair!" retorted Martie with everybody listening in. *"You send me out in a 210 to do your dirty work and then the boys go out and play with their toys!"*

"You tell him, girl!" crowed Maggie through her radio.

"Well, if you see those bad boys," added Mike on his radio, *"stop their forward movement and blow their transportation to bits. Then we can all have a good night's sleep while they are fixing their engines and flat tires!"*

"See?" replied Preston. "Martie, there is a method to my madness. I promise you will be flying with us tomorrow, okay?"

"Bloody load of old codswallop, or whatever those weird English say! I'm going

to complain to the Equal Rights Commission!"

"There isn't one left, love," added Barbara. *"It's now us against them again. Us against the men, I mean. From now on and in our next civilization, I'll be the one carrying the wooden club...and you'd better be listening, Buck!"* she finished.

Preston mentioned to Carlos that they should take off before Martie got back, and Carlos readily agreed, prompting a grim look from Sally in sympathy for her friend.

An hour later, and after the final reports from all three pilots, Preston and Carlos both took off in formation ten minutes after *Lady Dandy* headed north. Their tanks, guns, and rockets were full, and heavily loaded, they headed west to meet up with Martie, who was currently over Siler City 30 miles west of the farm. She was flying high at 12,000 feet, and they rose to meet her five minutes later and got into formation on each side of her.

"Want two good-looking men to escort you home, darling?" joked Preston, and he got one finger pointing upwards from the right window of her 210 in response.

"Go out and play, little boys," she said, trying to be cross. *"And you'd better get take-out on the way home, because after a hard day at the office, I'm cooking corned beef hash. The first family said that they were looking forward to some good home cooking, and we are all going to eat corned beef just to piss you off, General Preston."* And with that she pushed the joystick down and pushed the 210 in a dive for home, leaving the two Mustangs flying by themselves.

"Come on, Carlos. Let's go get the bounty on some bad guys." Preston turned his aircraft to the right and headed in formation west towards Charlotte at 5,000 feet with Carlos just behind him.

They flew over Charlotte 15 minutes later at 320 miles an hour. That was as far as Martie had come, and Preston decided to check out several of the roads leading in from the west. They stayed above I-85 and cruised down to Atlanta, arriving over Atlanta 40 minutes later. They had only seen one old truck, and the highway looked pretty empty of dead cars.

"If they are staying out of the weather and coming from the west, I reckon they would use I-20, wouldn't they?" suggested

Carlos. "How's your fuel, Preston?"

"Three quarters full, and I agree," replied Preston. "Let's continue along I-20 to Birmingham, and then turn north up 59 to Chattanooga. If we haven't seen anybody by then, we can turn for home. If they are further out, they won't get to us until morning. I suggest we climb up to 15,000 so we can see more.

The weather is so clear out there."

At 15,000 feet, they were just under the requirements for oxygen masks, and from that altitude they could see for 30 to 40 miles in either direction.

"There looks like a long convoy of moving vehicles coming towards us, about 12 miles west of us on the highway," stated Carlos a few minutes later. "On my map, they are passing a highway exit to a town called Helfin or Heflin, a mile to the north of the highway. Do you see them?"

"Roger, I have visual. Do you think they can hear us at this altitude?" asked Preston.

"If they were not driving in vehicles, I would think so, but stuck in cold weather, and in moving trucks and cars with the windows tight, I don't."

"Okay," replied Preston. "It looks like they are doing about 40 miles an hour and there is an area of open highway about three or four miles in front of them. I want to go down low and buzz the convoy right over the top of them. You stay off to the side, Carlos, and tell me if they shoot at me with anything. If they do, we then come in from the east, in front of them, and hit them hard."

"Roger that. I'll be your wing-man, Mr. Vader," replied Carlos, and they went down fast, the convoy still several miles in front of them. Carlos peeled off to the right side and Preston screamed down and flew over the top of the vehicles at 100 feet and 400 miles an hour with Carlos a quarter of a mile out.

"I see them trying to get out of the car roofs and windows," stated Carlos. "One guy has a shoulder rocket launcher and is trying to fire at you. A couple of others are standing up through the sunroofs and trying to fire at us with carbines. I don't think they are friendly and they definitely are firing first."

They carried on a couple of miles past the convoy and then turned left and returned east several miles south of the highway at 500 feet. There was no way that the convoy could see them.

"I think we should fly a pass with machine guns all the way down the convoy and then turn back and use the Sidewinders," Preston called to Carlos. "The convoy is about half a mile long. I'll take the second half at 500 feet and you come in and gun the first half at about 700 feet. Just look out for any explosions. With the Sidewinders, we should be at least above 1,000 feet altitude or more, as those babies pack a punch. Then we come in again with the guns until they are empty, use up our rockets, and survey the damage. What do you think, Carlos?"

"I think that by the third run the riders will be in the nearest ditch and the vehicles empty. I should probably fire down the ditch instead of the vehicles," Carlos suggested. Preston agreed as he flipped off the safety on his never-used .50-caliber machine guns, which packed a total of 1,250 rounds per aircraft and would give them about six seconds of firing, Preston estimated. It would take about three seconds to strafe half of the 50 vehicles below them.

"Testing guns," Preston stated, he and fired a very short burst. The Mustang shuddered slightly and Preston told Carlos to keep his sights on the convoy and to expect a slight decrease in speed. They climbed higher and decided to go in at full throttle, 430 miles an hour, and gently dive in from about 2,500 feet to pepper every vehicle. They turned sharply westwards at 3,000 feet and the convoy came over a brow five or so miles in front of them.

It looked like the men in the convoy were not expecting an attack, as they stayed in one long line, kept moving forward, and several vehicles had men sticking out of every orifice. Preston got ready, set his sights, and pushed the throttle forward as far as it would go. The engine began to scream as the Mustang went down in a shallow dive. *"I'm a couple of hundred yards behind you,"* stated Carlos. *"Don't put on the brakes for any reason. You turn out left and I'll turn out right and then we can regroup for Round Two."*

The first vehicle, a truck much like Preston's own Ford, quickly came into his sights, and he waited until he thought that he had passed over at least 20 before pressing the firing button on his joystick. The first vehicle stopped immediately and literally blew up. He kept his eye through the gun sight and felt the blast from underneath. He managed to keep firing until the last vehicle and took his finger off the button as he turned left to get out of the area. He rose to 2,000 feet and turned.

"Are you ok, Carlos?"

"I took a little damage, but everything is holding together. It was that first blast of yours that got me."

"I want to go straight back in from the west before they scatter," continued Preston. "I don't know what damage these rockets do, but let's climb up to 5,000 and then swoop down to 2,000 and, Carlos, no closer."

"Roger," replied Carlos, and they rose and turned towards the heavily smoking convoy, still in the middle of the road, and both armed their rockets. They had two triggers for these, and each trigger released two rockets at the same time.

"Carlos, we have two shots at this. I'm going to do the last half again and you fire at the forward half just before we go over."

Preston went in first, lined his sights up on the third car from the rear and pressed the first trigger. Two rockets flew away from him and went into the rear of the fourth and fifth vehicles from the end of the convoy. It was a little off, he thought to himself as he pressed the second button and the second set went even further along the convoy and blew a truck up and onto the one in front of it. Even at 2,000 feet, the blasts were felt. He turned left as he had done the time before. "Are you okay, Carlos?"

"I'm fine, the second two rockets went off late and hit the second car instead of about five down."

"Let's get rid of what we have left and survey the scene. As you said, let's go in together and you spray the closest hedges, or whatever is on the side of the highway nearest the area our vehicles are on, and I will make sure as many trucks as possible don't work."

They started on the first non-burning vehicle this time. Preston nearly got to the end of the convoy before the chambers rattled empty, and he knew their attack was over.

For the first time, they really looked at the damage from 5,000 feet. It was a mess down there. At least a dozen of the vehicles were burning brightly; another large explosion blew a couple of men into the air and bodies lay everywhere. It looked like the convoy had come to a halt.

"My oil pressure is a little low," reported Carlos. *"Let's head home. As soon as we are in radio range we can get Sally and her military guys out here to set up a roadblock for the night."*

"Good idea," replied Preston, and they climbed for height and headed straight home.

Thirty minutes later they scrambled Sally on the radio and told her about the incident on I-20 about ten miles before Heflin, Alabama, and to get her boys down to set up a roadblock at the Alabama-Georgia border. There were about 200 men in 50 vehicles, minus dead and wounded, and the convoy was about three miles from the Georgia border. She acknowledged, and both Mustangs rose to 16,000 feet and saw other aircraft heading out 15 minutes before they arrived at the farm. Martie was getting her moment in the sun and came over the radio to say that she was flying fighter escort for her friend Sally.

"Don't get too close, Martie," warned Preston. "They have shoulder rockets, and you will not have much time before dusk. If you use your guns, don't get closer than 1,000 feet. Sally, tell your passengers that we will be coming back just after dawn with backup and we will be in radio contact before we arrive. The current situation report is that we used everything we had, and about a dozen or more vehicles are on fire out of about 50. There are many dead, and I'm hoping they can't move forward. Aim for the smoke, it is easy to see. We messed them up pretty bad. Over."

"As Martie says, you boys have all the fun. I'll keep an eye on her and make sure she comes home. And leave the light on for us, we are going to need it," replied Sally.

They got a landing report from Maggie and came in from the

south and pulled up next to *Lady Dandy* on the apron. The president and first family were stretching and waved as they arrived. The mechanics dashed out to inspect the aircraft, and both pilots jumped down and shook hands with each other and then told the president about the attack. A few minutes later, Tech Sergeant Matheson came up and told Carlos that he had two small holes in one wing and a tiny piece of metal had done a little damage in the engine. They could have it repaired in about 24 hours.

Meanwhile, Sally and Martie headed out at 5,000 feet—Sally with a full load of soldiers, and Martie with full tanks and a full load of weapons. It was only 50 minutes of flying before they saw the plumes of smoke rising ahead of them, and they decided to first take a look from a higher altitude and see what was moving. They climbed up to 7,000 feet and flew about a mile north of the highway. Sally had her co-pilot take over the flying as she trained powerful binoculars onto the road below them.

"I see about 50 vehicles," she reported. "There are a dozen or so who have left the road and are under trees about 100 yards to the southeast of the convoy. I think I counted 12 vehicles still burning, another three that are destroyed, and about 14 vehicles about a mile in front of the burning vehicles and slowly heading east. I've found what looks like about 800 yards of open road five miles ahead of them and I'm going east and will come in low for a couple of miles and get the ground troops in. Martie, stay up here and tell me if they are getting close to me."

Sally switched to her internal intercom. "Gentlemen, prepare for ground evacuation in five minutes. Over." She then switched back to the radio. "Martie, I'm landing, turning around, lowering the ramp, and then I'm out of there!"

"Roger that," replied Martie. *"I think you have about ten minutes of daylight left, and I want to hit those vehicles on the move and then see if I can shoot a couple of these rocket things into the group under the trees. Then the boys can clean up for us, right, boys?"* There was an acknowledgement from the troop commander in the rear of the 130.

"And don't be nice guys, boys," added Sally. "They have most probably killed a lot of innocent civilians getting those vehicles. When you come upon bodies, check them for everything—we need their cell phones."

"*Roger,*" answered the major in command.

She guided down on low power for several miles behind the landing area, her co-pilot taking fixes of landmarks so that he could tell her the distance from the landing point, and she turned in for final approach at 1,000 feet, then dropped down to 500 feet to stay higher than any electrical lines or cell phone towers.

"I'd say three miles," her co-pilot stated as she brought the speed back to about 20 miles an hour above landing speed and began her landing checks. "Two miles to target," he continued. Sally was struggling with the sun off to the left of the road, which was affecting her vision.

"The enemy is about three miles in front of your landing area, and they seem to have men lying on the vehicle roofs. I'm going in from the west and will start my run when you tell me you are airborne, Sal."

"Roger that," Sally replied. "Just remember we have our own troops down there when you go in. Out."

"Half a mile to touchdown," added her co-pilot.

"I have it on visual," she replied, and she took *Tom* in on the westbound side of the highway, skimming a few feet over a couple of dead cars standing in the middle of the road.

"I'd say about 1,000 yards of clear road ahead of us," her co-pilot added. The wheels touched, and Sally worked on slowing the fast-moving aircraft as silently as possible. She used up the whole space and hit the brakes hard as she closed to within 50 feet of an upside-down burnt-out Volkswagen beetle, next to a low-slung sports car, also burnt to the ground and with dead bodies still sitting in it. She turned off the highway as far as she dared, her co-pilot giving her distances to anything the wings could touch, and slowly turned the large aircraft about, and as she got back onto the asphalt, the co-pilot pushed the rear door release.

Immediately, Sally began her takeoff checks as the door slowly opened and the full load of troops ran onto the road and around the aircraft to cover her takeoff.

"The convoy is about a mile behind you, Sal," stated Martie. "You'd better get moving so that they don't see you, and stay as low as possible. I'm at 1,000 feet to the south and going to come in from the west, guys. Keep your men off the road."

Sally slowly pushed the throttles forward as the door came up and tip-toed the now-empty aircraft out of there as quietly as possible, clearing two stationary cars by a few feet and following the contours of the road as she brought her landing gear up and kept the power settings as low revs as possible.

"I'm clear," Sally stated into the radio. "Martie, fire a short burst to get the feel of the guns. They will slow you down slightly and screw up your aim." Now that the sun was behind her, Sally could see clearly in front of her, and she kept the aircraft as low as possible until the ground fell away as the road went over a brow. She gained a safe height and kept the revs down for another five miles before pushing in the power slowly, pulling the aircraft up and turning to the north and then to the west to see what was going on behind her.

"I'm going in with the guns on the moving vehicles. I'm about a mile out at 1,000 feet and diving in from the sun," Martie stated, her excitement coming through the radio and making Sally smile.

"I got some, I got some!" Martie shouted over the radio several seconds later. "Two trucks are burning and several are trying to get off the road in all directions. I'm coming back in from the north." There was another bout of silence before she came back on again. "I got another one! It just blew up in front of me! I'm turning in at 1,000 feet and going in from the south."

"Roger that," replied Sally. "Martie, you should have about six seconds of ammo before they start clicking. When they click, leave the firing button alone—you'll be out of ammo. You can then arm your rockets."

"I got the two I was shooting at!" Martie shouted over the radio another 20 seconds later. "One exploded and made the other one catch on fire. I'm heading back west to hit the stationary group hiding under the trees with my rockets. Thanks, Sal, I heard the clicking. Over."

"Ground troops—'Martie the Terrible' is finished in your area. I see two to three vehicles still driving around trying to hide. They are about a mile in front of you and I'd set up a road ambush if I were you, plus a couple of side ambushes in case they try to rough it, but the trees look pretty dense and I don't think they can get far off the road. I see eight burning vehicles, three sitting still on the highway, and three mobile—and a couple of those have smoke coming out of them. We'll be in bright and early tomorrow, guys. The sunset is beautiful. As they say, 'red sky at night, trooper's delight.' Out."

"Thanks for the lift, ma'am. We can see that that girl can shoot, so we'll see if we can leave a couple of bad guys for you to deal with tomorrow. Out," replied the major on the ground.

Martie went in from the north since they were hiding in the trees on the south side of the road. She watched as her first two rockets landed 20 or so yards short and blew up in the verge, not causing any damage. She flew over and around, and on her second attempt, her two rockets went straight into the group of five trucks, and she watched as the middle truck literally lifted off the ground and exploded about ten feet in the air, spewing the other trucks with fire. She screamed the Mustang upwards as the sun went down over the horizon.

Apart from the several fires burning up and down I-20, the area was getting dark beneath her.

"Come on, girl, let's go home," advised Sally. "I don't think they're going anywhere tonight, and if they are, I believe they are in for a nasty surprise. The boys are heavily loaded with everything they could carry. I have you on visual about a mile to my south."

They moved into formation and flew home silently, Sally letting Martie alone as she worked through the ramifications of her action. Men had died down there, even if they were the enemy. Either she was made for this type of work, or she wasn't.

Sally knew her friend well and believed that Martie was a fighter—a good person to have around in times of need—but left her alone to her own realizations. The end of the fifth day of the new world looked like there could be hope.

Chapter 9

China

THE BOARDROOM ON THE 30th floor of Zedong Electronics in Nanjing was busy, and there was mixed feelings of excitement, apprehension, and dread. The 16 men were getting ready to tour Shanghai's international airport and then go on to the harbor. They had just finished an early breakfast and their transportation was ready for them downstairs. It was 5:00 am, early on the morning of the seventh day in Shanghai and thirteen hours ahead of East Coast Time in the United States. The first of the Boeing 747ERs would be taking off for its non-stop flight into John F. Kennedy Airport later that morning, which in a few weeks would be renamed Guomindang International Airport.

Chairman Wang Chunqiao raised his hands, and everyone took their seats. The room was cleared except for the 16 men sitting around the boardroom.

"Comrades, we have achieved something nobody in the world has ever achieved—the control of every living man, women and child in the western world!" The men in the room applauded this statement.

"To remember the words of our great leader Mao Zedong, 'If the worst came to the worst and half of mankind died, the other half would remain, while imperialism would be razed to the ground, and the whole world would become socialist: in a number of years there would be 2.7 billion people again and definitely more.' Comrades, I believe we are carrying out and completing his legacy, and whoever must die in this transfer of power from world capitalism to world communism will be replaced by our own breed of people. The most powerful influence in my life was my training, and much of your training, by our leader's great wife, Jiang Qing. As you know, our success will be the ideas of controlling the world that I learned from her teachings for 15 years. Her vision was a world full of people where everybody was equal and worked for the state. Now, the remaining 2.7 billion people will work for us. They will work for her, and they will work for the world's greatest leader, Mao Zedong, and the original Guomindang Communist Party. We are its 16 leaders. We are the Politburo of the future. Tomorrow, we leave our country of birth and, with 4,000 of our Red Guards, go forth and carry on 'The Great Leap Forward' and multiply and complete the Cultural Revolution our beloved leader began over 50 years ago. As my father, Zhang Chunqiao, believed, this revolution, created in 1966, was designed as a necessity for world maintenance and the survival of our species on this planet. The capitalistic system of greed followed by every person in the western world does not work. Human freedom does not work, could never work, and will only lead to the end of human civilization. Now it is our turn, and we will rule every man, woman, and child in a state of perfection, where they are the worker bees of life, all equal, and they will live and die to make our world the greatest in history."

He was given a standing ovation as he finished. It had taken him 40 years of work to start his crusade to cure humanity of greed and place everyone in their rightful position, and he knew that nothing could stop them now. He had three close allies—family members on the board from the most powerful force in China a half century ago—and his father's wish to him was to keep "The Gang of Four" alive, take over China and the world, and prove that they were the rightful leaders of the modern world.

They were leaving Headquarters for the beginning of their two-week journey to New York Harbor. This was the last time they would see their boardroom for a couple of years, maybe even longer.

The 15 men were asked to stand up, each wearing the same uniform of the new Politburo—the same clothes Mao Zedong wore most of his life. They were asked to stand in a line facing their chairman, and each member was presented with two gold-encrusted red books, each the size of a postage stamp, to wear on their lapels to show their status in the world as a member of the new Zedong Politburo. They left the boardroom for the last time for their departure transfer from the Zedong Electronics building to their final destination—Shanghai Harbor 170 miles away.

The chairman returned to his private office, which took up the entire 20th floor of the second building next door. As usual, the 12 security guards and the engineer carrying the special packet and equipment, the console with the five special red buttons, followed behind him. He looked around for the last time. It was totally empty. All the furniture and priceless Chinese artifacts worth millions of dollars had been packed and placed aboard one of the container ships, taking up a whole, specially made armored steel container to be unloaded in his new space in the White House—the Oval Office.

Each board member had been given a set of two red leather suitcases of travel luggage, and these, along with their silver suitcases, were already placed in the lower hold of an extremely modern bus, fully armored-plated, with 16 rich, thick, reclining leather chairs.

Once all were aboard, the bus left the Zedong Electronics buildings with every one of the men looking at the two largest buildings in the area—one 30 stories high and the second newer addition in 2005 20 stories high where they had their suites of offices on the top 16 floors. It was the last they would see their old place of work for a long time. Their new offices would be in the Capitol Building in Washington, D.C.

The trip to the Shanghai airport from Nanjing took three hours. A dozen Red Guard motorcycles, the riders dressed in their red parade uniforms, rode in front and behind. It was a sight to see as the bus, still with its motorcade, drove into the airport. The airport road was thronged with Red Army Guards waving little red Mao Zedong flags. They drove into the airport and saw in front of them the fleet of 30 shining new Air China 747s standing in three rows, and then off to one side were five of the biggest passenger aircraft in the world—Air China Airbus A380s—which had been recently delivered over the last two years. The chairman had done his math well. The first payments to Airbus Industries were due to begin on February 1st.

Zedong Electronics had not paid one Yuan for more than 10 billion Yuan worth of aircraft. Twenty-five of the newest Boeing 747-400ERs had been delivered over the last five years, and less than 100 million Yuan, less than the cost of just one aircraft, had been paid for them.

A large wooden seating platform had been placed with a grand view of all the aircraft for the occasion. The chairman climbed up the stairs of the platform to face the beautiful birds.

"Comrades, I stand between our two brave pilot teams who will take off in one hour and lead our first attack on mainland America," he began, standing between two groups of three men each who had been the lucky ones to get the job. All six pilots stood at attention and looked straight ahead. They never looked at the chairman once, since they were too low in rank to even be seen looking at the chairman.

"The first aircraft in our front line is the one that will invade American airspace first. Over a certain country outside of the United States, the position of which only I know, she will meet up with her sister aircraft, the 747 transporter. At this moment the transporter, which is at another location, is ready and holds the five million working electronic parts and spares ready to get New York's airports and harbor infrastructure up and running. We will start by bringing the three New York airports and the complete harbor facilities back online with generator power so that we can take control of New York and start distributing food to our new citizens."

"Down there," he pointed to a group wearing white coats, "are 100 of our best Zedong electrical engineers. They are ready for the task of electrifying our new country and working hard to make her come alive again. To the right of them are 200 of our elite Mao Red Guards, who will protect our engineers from any old-world

Americans who try to upset our plans."

"Once these personnel have been deposited in New York, the aircraft will return here and all of our aircraft will leave 36 hours before our planned arrival in New York. The 20,000 troops they carry in will be placed into position around the harbor and on the bridges, greeting our arrival into New York Harbor. They have 24 hours to terminate any opposition and then give us ground protection against any form of resistance from American military. Our aircraft will be refueled by our engineers and again return here to Shanghai to collect our second load of 20,000 Red Guards, who will arrive as we arrive under the Verrazano Narrows Bridge into New York Harbor. With another 4,000 Red Guards aboard our naval and container ships, we will have a mighty force of over 40,000 soldiers to extinguish any capitalistic flames in America." He paused for the applause.

"Five days after we arrive, a third flight of 20,000 Red Guard marines will land in Washington D.C. and be met by us personally at Ronald Reagan International Airport." Again applause interrupted his speech.

"Two weeks from then, two more flights of 20,000 troops will be flown into Los Angeles International Airport, as well as another 4,000 troops on our naval vessels and container ships. Gentlemen, within a month, we will have a glorious Red Guard Army of over 110,000 men on American soil, all ready to populate the country with children from the remaining women of our new country." There was another enthusiastic round of applause from the massive audience of 15,000 men listening.

"It now gives me great honor to rename this airport in the name of my father, who was one of the most prominent people in China. Comrades, I dedicate this airport, which will henceforth be called Comrade Zhaung Chunqiao International Airport."

Again, there was a loud ovation from the thousands of men who applauded the new name. The chairman shook hands with the six pilots as the men below in long rows began to board the first aircraft through tall mobile stairs, each engineer waving to the platform as they entered through one of the three doors. Then, the 200 soldiers walked up the stairs, and 20 minutes later, the stairs were pulled away and the whine of Rolls Royce aircraft engines could be heard. Nobody moved. A tractor pulled the large aircraft around and out to the taxiway, making sure that the blast of the engines did not hit the platform.

The large aircraft taxied around to the main runway, and with its engines screaming, the large 747 began to move faster and faster. It took a long time, but finally the aircraft could be seen a mile out climbing into the air for its long trip to John F. Kennedy Airport 7,370 miles away. The 16 dignitaries walked back to the bus, got in, and were driven to the harbor area.

Shanghai Harbor was a massive metropolis of cranes and ships, but it was dwarfed by the collection of shipping that had congregated from different ports along the Chinese coast just the night before. There again, thousands of the new and officially dressed Red Guards were everywhere, in red with gold-edged military uniforms designed for parades. They were armed and all male. The bus swept into the main harbor area, and there were gasps of surprise from the men in the bus at their first sight of the new Zedong Navy.

The pride and joy of the new Navy was berthed in the most central location—its new aircraft carrier, the 'Shi Lang,' with the number 83 on both sides of its hull and on the conning tower. Next to her were two modern destroyers, and next to them were two recently completed long-range frigates. On the other side of the harbor were five massive container ships, the biggest in the world, laden down with cargo and with smoke already rising from their stacks.

A second observation platform had been especially built for the occasion on the edge of the harbor, and the 16 men mounted it. The platform was again surrounded by thousands of parade-dressed guards, and a podium had been placed in the middle where the speaker would have his back to the awesome sight of the naval power of Zedong Electronics. The chairman headed towards the podium as the other men took their seats.

Comrade Mo Wang was shaken away from the awe of the view by his cell phone buzzing in his pocket. "Yes, Fung," he stated abruptly into the satellite phone.

"Comrade, I have the latest reports for you," stated the head of communications on the 29th floor of the building they had just left. *"Report from the American airport: our men are at the airport and halfway to completing the clearance of the runway. They report no problems. The airport is totally empty of Americans. There are no American troops anywhere to be seen and they said that they have the two fuel pumpers and necessary equipment ready for a refueling operation. The engineers are needed to start up the electrical systems, and the two aircraft should be back in the air to Shanghai once the engineers have replaced the electrical fuel pump's components.*

They believe there will be 33 plug-in electrical replacements."

"Yes, yes, I know that, Fung. The two aircraft are on their way. It should take the engineers an hour to get the fuel pumps to activate the flow of fuel to the aircraft once they land. What else? I'm busy."

"Report from Comrade Deng. They have arrived in the state of Alabama and are proceeding two hours ahead of schedule. They are expecting to meet up with Comrade Bo Lee Tang within 24 hours and complete their attack on the Raleigh airport, and then they will immediately travel north. Do you have any orders for the other squads? You told me to remind you about moving everyone towards New York."

"I remember, Fung," Wang replied. "Tell all squads to begin moving towards the New York airport called JFK and to report in at Headquarters. They must not arrive until the morning of Day Eight. That will allow our Red Army troops to set up their control base and prepare for our squads to arrive."

Comrade Wang suddenly realized that the chairman, the admiral of the Zedong fleet, another five high-ranking naval officers, and every one of the 14 other men were staring at him. The chairman looked rather angry at Mo Wang for ruining his special moment.

"Comrade Wang, your conversation was important enough to hold up our Navy's christening occasion?" he asked sarcastically.

"My humble apologies, Comrade Chairman," replied Comrade Wang, bravely. He was nervous enough to let his phone slip through his fingers, and it bounced onto the hard wooden platform. He left it there, hoping nobody had noticed the drop. "Unfortunately, I must be in contact with the operations in America at all times, Comrade Chairman. Without our satellite global positioning systems or our satellite communications and directional aids working on our aircraft, I must be informed about weather and runway conditions at all times. Once our aircraft take off and reach a certain point, there is no returning, Comrade Chairman. Good news though, the weather is decent and the runway is half cleared, perfectly on schedule."

"Relax, Comrade Wang, you are worrying too much. Nobody can thwart our attack. Look at what we have to fight with against anything they could possibly find to fly or shoot," he stated, lifting his right hand into the air and turning towards the magnificent scene in the harbor.

Mo Wang's insulting action was quickly forgotten by the rest, and he quickly picked up the phone and put it in his pocket without checking it.

"Comrades," began the chairman. "I give you Admiral Hun, the commander of our Navy. He will explain each ship to you.

Admiral Hun, please."

"Comrade Chairman, glorious members of the Zedong Politburo, fellow naval personnel, I am honored today to present you the most powerful Navy in the world—the Zedong Navy." This was greeted by standing and enthusiastic applause from everybody on the platform.

"May I introduce to you our greatest naval asset, the Shi Lang, the only operating aircraft carrier in the world!" The applause continued. "The Shi Lang has a crew of 2,500 and 30 J-10 fighter aircraft especially adapted for her. She is the largest military vessel which can actually pass through the Panama Canal with inches to spare. The aircraft landed on the Shi Lang for the first time yesterday, and our pilots will practice while we are sailing toward the Panama Canal and then into New York. Naturally, without our global positioning systems and satellite directional radar infrastructure, many of our weapons are not as accurate and their success ranges are limited, but against the United States of America, who has nothing, we are a very potent force."

"Next are our two ultramodern Type 052C destroyers—numbers 170 and 171. They are the best the world offers, fully armed for air and sea attacks, and our main defense for the Shi Lang. Third, our two modern Type 054 frigates—numbers 572 and 573. Both were launched less than six months ago and are the most modern frigates in the world. They have the same capabilities as the destroyers and are completely invincible against sea or air attacks. Here are our captains from each vessel, who are directly under my command," the admiral introduced, pointing to the five men standing behind him.

"May I finally introduce you to five of the largest and most modern container ships in the world? We own ten of these new ships, and these five are named 'Xin New York I' to 'Xin New York V,' and all are destined for New York Harbor. The other five super ships, still being loaded in other harbors, are 'Xin Los Angeles I' to 'V' and will leave two weeks after us and head for Los Angeles. Two weeks will be adequate time for our naval fleet to escort the container ships into New York, and then return through our Panama Canal to meet up with the next five ships in the middle of the Pacific and escort them into the western capital of our new country. We have two military resupply ships already a day out from Shanghai, and they will be ready to refuel our military ships once they get through the Panama Canal. Comrades, I thank you for listening."

The chairman regained the podium as the admiral received loud applause. He finished by giving a short speech on how he was looking forward to the start of the journey and each of the Politburo members would have a specially built stateroom aboard the Shi Lang. He then nodded to the band, which started with the Zedong Electronics National Anthem—the Chinese National Anthem from the days of Mao Zedong.

There was silence as they gazed upon the view.

It was a beautiful sight. They would be staying aboard the Shi Lang that very night, but first it was off to a restaurant for lunch and then a tour of the docks on a tugboat to view all ten ships. The suitcases were already on their way to the ship, and the bus had already left to return to Zedong Electronics Headquarters.

Chapter 10

Flight to Alaska

SEVERAL HOURS BEFORE THE MEN of the Politburo were getting ready for breakfast on Day 6, in U.S. time General Allen was snoozing in *Ghost Rider* at 29,000 feet and cruising at 275 miles an hour. The light was going to fade pretty soon and he needed help, and Carlos would need daylight to get a fix on the whereabouts of Anchorage compared to *Ghost Rider*'s current position. Apart from the two pilots in control, the large crew on both 130s was also trying to catch some shut-eye.

The HC-130 tanker was off their starboard wing, about 800 yards away, and they were over the ocean and about 200 miles offshore of Juneau when Pete Allen called Carlos. The phone rang three times before Carlos answered.

"Carlos? Pete here. I need to get a fix on where we are in relation to our destination."

"I'm in front of the screen," replied Carlos. *"Let me just look at my map of your area and I'll be ready... Okay... Pete, turn on your transponder."* The two C-130s both turned on their transponders and Carlos saw a small flicker of light plus a number 1 and 2 next to it. *"It looks like you are about 60 miles east-southeast of a vertical line south of your destination. I'm getting out my compass and protractor. Hold on a second, and I'll give you an angle."*

"We must have easterly winds at about 20 then, as we have been on this course now for three hours," Pete told the crew with him, as they were doing the same as Carlos was—looking over maps with calculators and protractors getting angles. They waited for Carlos to give them a basic longitude and latitude, as well as a flight angle to head towards Anchorage.

"*Ok, turn your transponders off,*" instructed Carlos, giving them longitude and latitude. "*Your angle into Anchorage allowing for a 20-knot easterly wind is 319 degrees.*"

"Thank you, Carlos. We are about 500 miles from our destination. Two hours of flying and we'll be on the ground. We will call you again on our way into Japan in about 14 hours. Out."

They were about 400 miles out from Elmendorf Air Base when the radio operator managed to get into contact with the base.

"Elmendorf, this is *Ghost Rider*. Do you copy? Over."

"*You are who?*" was the confused reply over the radio. "*Are you allowed on this frequency, whoever you are?*"

"Roger that," replied Pete. "We are incoming from McChord, two aircraft, name is Allen Key. Get your base commander on the radio. Over."

"*He's gone fishing,*" was the reply.

"How do you have a working radio?" asked General Allen.

"*We borrowed one from a local trucking company and have kept it on the Air Force emergency signal,*" was the reply. "*Who are you anyway?*"

"Have you got fuel and a clear runway for two Charlie-130s?" the general asked.

"*I'm not telling you that, whoever you are, until you give me some ID, Mr. Allen Key. You could be a logger aircraft for all I know.*"

"Do you have the blue Air Force book of personnel call signs, radio operator?"

"*Roger that, Allen Key, pulling it off the shelf now. What page are you on?*"

"Page 1, and look for Allen Key," replied the general, smiling. Alaska was a different world.

"*Shit! Shit! Roger, Allen Key. The only aircraft we have operational here is an old 130,* Blue Moon, *and a couple of helicopters from before I was born, sir,*" the radio operator replied.

"Why is *Blue Moon* with you?"

"She was incoming from Osan via Misawa with a tanker about six months ago when her outer-right engine went down. It's taken a year to get her reconditioned engine up here and fitted. They finished just before Christmas and she's waiting for orders."

"Confirm she is still fully equipped. Over," stated the general.

"Affirmative, she's bristling with whatever you want, Allen Key."

"How is your heating situation on base?" was Allen's next question.

"We have a dozen logging companies around here, enough gas for our gas heaters for about a month, and enough wood for the indoor fireplaces for forever. MRE food stocks are down to three to four months, there are tons of salmon, and we are doing okay, Allen Key."

"How are the locals doing?"

"I'd hate to see what's happening stateside, but we are ready for such emergencies up here," the radio operator replied. *"All civilian houses have some form of wood-burning backup, we can never run out of wood, and we can always eat the polar bears when we get hungry. Hell, I've had grilled salmon five nights in a row and would love a burger right now. We have about a ton of frozen salmon on base if you want some."*

"Please give orders to fuel up *Blue Moon* for me," continued the general. "Make sure her tanks are filled to the extreme max. She will be coming with me. Also make sure there are two sets of pilots ready to fly her. We are about an hour out and need fuel ourselves."

"Roger. Runway 34 clear and dry, wind from the north five to ten, temperature minus 21. Radio me and I'll get the lights on for you. Do you want a welcoming committee, Allen Key?"

"I'll radio in for high flares when we are closer. Actually, young man, get about two dozen salmon on that grill of yours and I'll swap you for a couple of cases of frozen burgers, rolls, and cheese so that you can have your cheeseburgers. Out."

They went in directly from the south onto Runway 34. They were still 20 miles off course to the east when the flares went off and could be faintly seen on the dark horizon through the left cockpit windows.

The weather was cold and brittle as the door opened, and they were surrounded by thick-coated personnel to refuel both aircraft.

Blue Moon, three months younger than *Ghost Rider*, was in the same shape, with the same guns. She was expected to be on show at Andrews and hopefully at the Washington Aerospace Museum, if the funding for the new Air Force museum building complex ever went through.

At least five of the aircraft he had currently flying had been destined for this new complex—to have a display of still-operational Vietnam War-era aircraft. General Allen had been waiting for government funding for three years, but it had never been granted. The display would have been great. He had designed a showing of two F-4s attacking ground units, a third F-4 on the ground being rearmed and refueled, two Hueys being refueled by the HC-130 tanker, which was now flying with him, and *Ghost Rider* and *Blue Moon* being air refueled by *Mother Goose* also at the same time.

A squad of 30 soldiers was in formation as a welcoming guard, and he introduced himself to them as well as the radio operator—a young airman that was six foot ten inches tall and weighed in at a muscular 300 pounds.

"You say the base commander has gone fishing?" the general asked the airman.

"We are looking at all possible ways to feed the 1,200 personnel on base, sir," the airman replied. "We have food supplies for a couple of months, or until we are resupplied, but it looks like this outage is everywhere. We've had no traffic in or out for six days, sir. Is this problem countrywide, sir?"

"Worldwide, son," replied the general. "You guys are on your own until we can get supplies up to you, which will be closer to spring. So tell the colonel that he may go fishing as much as he wants, but he needs to have this base on lockdown until further notice. We believe the Chinese are to blame for this electrical meltdown, and I will know more in a couple of days. I have a satellite cell phone for you with the number for Colonel Mondale at Edwards AFB, who will be your only contact until further notice. You are to call into him with a sitrep every 24 hours starting two days from now. Unfortunately, Edwards hasn't received their cell phone yet. I'll give you my number in case you need to contact someone before then, and if you see the red number that is listed on the back of the phone come up on the screen, do not answer it under any conditions. That number is the enemy, and they are going to want to speak Chinese and ask you where you got the phone from, understand?" The airman nodded.

"Does *Blue Moon* still have her fuel bladder?" General Allen asked the tech sergeant who had come up to give him a report.

"Yes, sir. She has both her 1,250-gallon bladders from her flight in here," he replied, saluting. "We have filled her tanks and both bladders for you. She cannot take any cargo or ammo, she would be overweight, and her bladders will give you 1,000 miles at low cruise each. With your tanker being refueled now, General, she has a range of over 4,400 miles and can deliver 3,000 gallons of fuel. You will need 2,500 gallons to get *Ghost Rider* into Misawa, and you'll have 500 gallons spare, or 45 minutes of extra flying time. Since both aircraft can be refueled at the same time, your engineer can also pump out another 500 gallons from the tanker's own tanks into yours and increase your fuel reserves to 1,000 gallons."

"You are exactly correct with your numbers, Sergeant, well done, and we need that extra fuel. We must allow an extra degree or two for wind diversion during our flight," replied the general. "We will fully arm ourselves once we reach Osan or Kunsan in Korea tomorrow afternoon."

"One more thing, General," said the sergeant. "If you don't have GPS or any modern directional systems aboard, how are you going to find land?"

"We have the infra-red locators in the gunships to view islands below us, and as long as the weather is clear, we have a friend back stateside who can give us limited directions. Other than that, Sergeant, we are going to need a lot of flying expertise, and maybe every gallon of gas you pump into us."

General Allen handed the phone and battery charger to the airman and asked for his dinner of grilled salmon. They ate large portions of salmon and mashed potatoes in the Officers' Mess while the aircraft were still being refueled. He also told the ground crew to unload the pallet in the rear of *Ghost Rider* that contained the hamburgers and frozen rolls and ordered the personnel to load up a pallet of frozen salmon in case the Air Force personnel in Japan needed supplies.

Two hours later, the three aircraft, heavily laden with fuel, took off on their 3,100-mile non-stop trip to Misawa Air Force Base in northern Japan, 12 hours away.

Chapter 11

JFK – Major Joe Patterson

THE SUN WAS JUST RISING off the East Coast of the United States as the two specks in the distance on the horizon slowly grew larger and larger. The first aircraft came in, and Major Patterson saw that it was a modern 747-400ER. It came in slowly, and the Chinese-American pilot, Captain Wong, gave the incoming pilot the information he needed to land. As it touched down, 20 Air Force men and the two Chinese-American pilots all wearing the recently acquired clothing and radios went out to show that they had control of the landing area.

Captain Chong, the second Chinese-American Air Force pilot, had found ground control aircraft-directional batons and guided the big jet to its parking position, while Captain Wong talked the second 747 down onto the runway. The first big jet parked, facing outwards, and its engines began to wind down. The second one completed its landing and came around towards the terminal. There were only two ladders on the terminal waiting for the aircraft. The others had been hidden by the U.S. troops to control the newcomers getting on and off without being noticed.

A ladder was pushed out to the aircraft and the aircraft's door opened, guns pointing out from the door in every direction. The major could see communication from between his men and the visitors, and Captain Wong asked for the second ladder to be placed on a rear door of the first aircraft as well. The major couldn't understand why until he watched the second aircraft close its engines down and the large jumbo jet nose of a 747 transporter began to open.

It seemed that everything was in order to the men inside the aircraft. Captains Wong and Chong stated they had everything under control and started being arrogant, even issuing orders to the men coming down the ladders. The American soldiers hidden everywhere watched as about 200 armed soldiers wearing green camouflage uniforms, which were certainly not correct for the snowy, white conditions, exited the aircraft.

That was definitely a bad call on the part of the incoming soldiers, the major thought to himself. The Chinese soldiers took several minutes to exit, walking down the two sets of stairs and forming up underneath the left wing of the first aircraft. To those watching, it looked like there were two companies of 100 men, each with a commander. Then the engineers, all in civilian dress and some in white overalls, began descending the stairs. The two Chinese-American pilots, Wong and Chong, issued orders to the civilians telling them where to find the equipment to refuel both aircraft.

A couple walked up to Captain Wong and asked him something. He shrugged his shoulders and pointed to a dozen large 9,000-gallon jet fuel tanker trailers that the now dead men had pulled closer with the bulldozers earlier. Then Captain Wong, making his Chinese-made rocket launcher more comfortable on his shoulder, looked around and showed the man the skyline for some reason. The major expected that the engineers had asked for the fuel storage tanks. There were none of the noticeable fuel tanks at this airport. The closest million-gallon tanks were in New Jersey.

Fortunately, being Air Force personnel, the American pilots knew what these guys would need to refuel a jet and had tested everything. The men then went over to an underground fuel outlet connection and a discussion ensued. Captain Wong shrugged his shoulders again and pointed at the fuel truck.

Several engineers walked over to the second 747, using an elaborate system to lower two good-sized forklifts to the ground.

Major Patterson was worried, he wasn't so small. At 5 feet 9 inches tall he had dressed in the dead men's clothing so that he could also be mobile. It was time for him to take a look outside. Two of his men made sure that nothing showed apart from his civilian clothing, and he walked up to the entrance and descended the stairs down to the aircraft area.

As he neared the troops, there was an order screamed by Captain Wong and every one of the 200 men stood at attention and saluted. He very nearly saluted back with an American salute, but thought the best of it and waved a reply to the salute as if he was a civilian head of state, and continued walking to the engineers.

The engineers saw his approach, and immediately all stood still and bowed as he arrived. The major, totally puzzled at what his men must have told these people, pointed to Captain Wong and signaled to him to come and talk to him. They moved away as the entire 300-person invading Chinese force stood at attention.

"What the hell did you tell these Charlies?" the major asked.

"I was a little lost as to what to say to these guys, but thought of something that would really scare these Chinese soldiers to make them totally under my control. I told their commanders and their chief engineer as they exited that you, the Supreme Commander, flew in an hour ago straight from China to see how the landing was going to be handled. I told them that your special jet has been hidden from view in one of the far hangars in case we are attacked, and that you are going to return to China once the two aircraft have taken off. That made all the pilots jittery, and I told them to clean up their aircraft and expect company. All became as scared as rats, and then suddenly I was in total control."

"Sir, just act out the scene and I believe we will have these guys refueled and out of here within a couple of hours. I showed him that there were no large fuel tanks anywhere around JFK, which the engineers seemed worried about, but I told them we should have enough fuel out of the mobile tankers my men have pushed forward with the bulldozers. I'm going to get more men to see if there are any more fuel tankers stationed at the other terminals. These birds need about 60,000 gallons each, and we are pretty close right now."

"Tell their soldiers to create a defensive position by the entrance to the Van Wyck Expressway, and let them freeze to death for an hour," replied the major. "Also ask if they have brought the supply of extra cell phones with them. They need to bring them into the terminal building to keep warm, as well as any electrical parts, which can't handle cold conditions. I will go back and watch from the terminal windows. Give me two men in the captured clothing to act as my bodyguard and then tell all the engineers that if they do a good job I will give them some gifts before I leave for China. And don't salute me, soldier, now bow and go!"

"May I suggest you inspect the guard, sir? It might look a little more real," Captain Wong replied, bowing and running off to the engineers. He quickly spoke to them and then shouted to the engineers in Chinese to pull the tanker trucks up one at a time to both aircraft.

The major then acted like he was God. He walked around the aircraft as two men ran up to protect him. He whispered the plan to them and they acted like they were protecting the president. He got to the troops and they all saluted. The commanders did not look at him, but stared over his head, as did all the troops. He did a quick look at the front row of both groups and then walked back to the terminal as the two small forklifts each brought a pallet of products.

An unoccupied exit door was opened by two other plainclothes men in the terminal, and the pallets were lifted into the terminal and pushed into the building as far as the forklifts could reach. They went back and returned with two more pallets, the major noticing that the troops were now being deployed between the vehicles and the entrance to the Expressway and out of the way. Captain Wong returned to say that the troops had no more communication devices, apart from small military communication radios, and that they were beginning to ask questions.

For an hour, the fueling went on using both electrical generators and pumps underneath the aircraft wings as one by one the trucks were pushed into position by the bulldozers and the large generators pumped in 500 gallons a minute. It would take them at least two hours to pump more than 60,000 gallons into each aircraft.

Another ten pallets of equipment arrived on the two forklifts and were placed in the terminal, soldiers moving the pallets out of the way once the driver's backs were turned. They made a hole in the furniture mountain and placed the pallets in a secure place away from the ambush zone. Pallet after pallet was dropped onto the runway area, and the forklifts moved them into a second, unused terminal next to theirs. Meanwhile, another six tankers had been located and were being driven and pushed into place by the dozers.

One of the army commanders walked up to Captain Wong and started gesturing with his hands. Wong angrily gestured back, whispered in the man's ear, and then the man smiled and walked back to his troops happily.

The major inside the terminal called General Allen. "Allen Key," he stated on the phone.

"Well, Patterson, how are things going?" asked the general.

"You wouldn't believe it, sir, but Captain Wong, one of our Chinese-American pilots, told the visitors that the Zedong Electronics Supreme Commander had secretly flown in an hour ago, and I went out in captured clothes and a fancy long coat I had picked up in the shop here with my face covered and inspected their flipping guard."

"Sounds like your man needs a commendation, Patterson. What is the scoop on the aircraft?"

"Two 747-400ERs, and one is a transporter. Shall we take her? My assumption is that she could return again with a belly full of electrical goods that we could desperately need on her next trip. They have off-loaded 62 pallets of electrical parts and goods so far, sir."

"A hard decision," replied the general. *"If we just take one, we have to make it look like it had an accident out at sea. If we take both of them, then we just commandeer them and fly them into McGuire once we have released some of the fuel load. I'm three hours out of Elmendorf and bound for Misawa in Northern Japan. I think your idea is best. Hopefully, we can get another load out of her when she returns."*

"Is that your final decision, Allen Key?" The major asked. "They are about to complete refueling."

"Yes, let the transporter go, but don't get on the aircraft yourself. I don't want the crew to think their Supreme Commander just went down into the drink. Good luck, lad. Call me when you are done and I will call up McGuire for you and get the troops airborne. A couple hundred soldiers, you say? Their flight time is about 20 minutes and I'll tell them to go into your location low, three minutes after the second jumbo jet is airborne."

The major quickly got his men together and told them what he was going to do with the engineers—they would take them prisoner as they walked through the closed black curtain on the walkway into the terminal. He told two of the men to make sure that a distance was put between each man somehow. He got one group of three of his pilots together and told them to follow him out to the aircraft.

The last tankers were in place and the major walked towards the aircraft with the American pilots, dressed in captured clothing, in tow. Captain Wong had headed out a minute or so earlier and was waiting for the major's move. He signaled his accomplice, Captain Chong, to come over to him, and they both ran over and bowed to the "Supreme Commander". The American troops, who were dressed in the captured clothing of the termination squads, and were standing around guarding the engineers working the refueling, immediately stood at attention while carefully watching for problems, their guns at the ready. The three men at the bottom of the stairs stopped and talked.

"Captain Chong, you are taking over this baby," Patterson explained, pointing at the passenger 747. "We will get you in control. Your plan is to complain about some sort of minor fuel problem about an hour out from the coast. Lose height, and tell the transporter to carry on. After an hour of messing around at low altitude, fake a sea accident—scream or something. Once you are out of radar sight of the second aircraft and their pilots who think you have ditched, head for McGuire at below 500 feet and put her down there as soon as your fuel is down to a safe landing weight. Captain Wong, you will be with me. Tell the engineers when the aircraft engines start up to get ready to meet me. Tell them I've decided not to go on this aircraft but will fly back in my own jet. I want to separate the engineers from the troops before our guys arrive."

Captain Wong bowed to him, and then the "Supreme Commander" arrogantly walked straight up the aft stairs of the aircraft, and the two Chinese air crews, six men, bowed as he entered. The major bowed slightly back, and with a lot of waving his hand, he motioned them to return to the front of the aircraft in front of him. Four of the American pilots, fully armed, followed him to the beginning of the first class compartment where they were told to wait. The "Supreme Commander" walked with Captain Wong to the flight deck to inspect it. Captain Wong ordered the co-pilot and flight engineer to get out the commander's way—he wanted to sit in the right co-pilot's seat. He asked them to follow him, and together they walked back to the rear curtain of the first class compartment where both were hit over the head and bound with the rope brought for the occasion.

In the meantime, Captain Wong doubled back to the cockpit for the two pilots of the second crew—the crew captain and the backup pilot—and they too were asked to follow him and ended up in the same toilet, all bound and out for at least a couple of hours.

The aircraft's new crew, in the recently exchanged uniforms of the Chinese crew, took their seats once the remaining Chinese pilots were dealt with.

"Remember, a good disappearing act, guys," Patterson warned. "They don't have enough fuel to come and look for you for too long, and don't let them see you go down. Maybe go out for an hour or even more, get fuel trouble, disappear towards the sea and get back into McGuire or even Andrews. We need this aircraft, boys. Good luck, and remember to check on the bad guys in the back every few minutes."

The "Supreme Commander" walked out of the massive aircraft as the fuel lines were being disconnected from the wings, and now it was up to him to secure the area. He walked back and straight up to the steps of the terminal they had been using. Captain Wong told the engineers to start making their way to the stairs when their jobs were done, as there were gifts and a big surprise for them.

Many were already waiting around, and one by one they slowly each picked up a suitcase unloaded shortly after they had landed and made their way to the "Supreme Commander", who was waiting for them with a couple of guards as well as Captain Wong at the bottom of the entrance to the walkway.

"Ask for their names and degrees one at a time," the major suggested to Wong as he heard the first engines of both jets begin to whine. One by one, the engineers came up the short flight of stairs, bowed and introduced themselves, received a "grunt" from the "Supreme Commander", and then walked up the walkway and inside the terminal through the black curtain.

By the time the first aircraft was moving away and everybody turned around to protect themselves from the blowing debris behind it, 40 engineers had been dealt with. The "Supreme Commander" went in through the curtain and with his radio called up the incoming American troops, still several miles out, while the others were being blown around by the engines outside.

"Patterson, Juliet Foxtrot Kilo. Aircraft are about five minutes from takeoff. Wind is from the west at ten miles an hour and they are heading out in a westerly direction. You guys can get in here as soon as the second one is off the ground. All their troops are at the entrance to the Van Wyck Expressway, on the west side, and we will have all the engineers separated and safe here in the terminal. Our guys are dressed in white snow gear and on the snow mounds around the staging area and will open fire once you guys come in. We are in the first front terminal from the east. The enemy is wearing green camouflage. I repeat, our men are in white gear and Charlies are in green camouflage. Did you copy? Over."

"Roger that," repeated a lone voice. *"Friendlies in white, Charlies in green. We are about nine minutes out and will have the airport visual in three. We will land choppers in close and you guys can give us covering fire while the big mama's come in from the east and unload on the runway in front of you. Our troops will join your guys on the snow mounds. Out."*

The "Supreme Commander" handed the radio over to his lieutenant, who would call in any changes, and he returned outside to greet the rest of the engineers.

It took until both aircraft reached the end of the runway and the first one was beginning its takeoff run before he thought he could see black, minute shapes low over the sea and a couple of miles out—right behind the two 747s. He wasn't certain, but he continued with the last of the engineers. The commandeered aircraft thundered past 100 yards away and thirty seconds later slowly climbed into the air a mile to the west. He looked towards the east, and this time the black shapes were very visible to a sharp eye, several feet above the horizon.

He had only seven or eight men to go when he heard the second aircraft's engines go into a scream, and he continued to bow to each man without looking towards the noise. It was working out perfectly, and he only had three men to go, when the aircraft passed them. There were gunshots from the soldiers in the two formation groups by the Expressway, and everyone looked up. The second 747 left the ground as Captain Wong pushed the last three Chinese engineers and the major into the terminal, screaming in Chinese to take cover as all hell broke loose outside. The last of the engineers were all pushed through the curtain and out of sight of the altercation outside. "Okay, guys, are we secure in here?" Patterson shouted as he got out of his clothes and allowed the last Chinese engineers who had not been knocked unconscious yet to see who he really was. Those three engineers had 60 weapons trained on them, and nobody moved.

Then Major Patterson heard the rotors of the first chopper as it came in just behind the edge of the terminal and out of the line of a potential firefight with the enemy. They unloaded fast as Major Patterson, with his lieutenant and radio, headed for the roof via a ladder on the opposite side of the terminal.

He climbed up onto the snowy roof, with the ensuing firefight in view below him, just in time to see the second C-130 touch down and pull up behind the first one to empty its troops. The Chinese soldiers, professional and battle-hardened, were spanning out trying to get around the gunfire from the snow mounds. The major noticed a third C-130 at about 700 feet and half a mile away circling over the ocean—either directing the attack, or ready with medics, or both.

The second helicopter came in behind the terminal to block off any possible enemy retreat, and any further advancement into the airport area, and 180 soldiers raced out of the back of the two C-130s, charging forward and firing heavily into the opposition's area to protect the 130s as they continued down the runway.

Both aircraft nearly went vertical as they took off seconds later, exactly
where the second 747 had left the ground and out of range of any deadly fire.

The other two helicopters circled around and dropped a platoon of thirty men along the Van Wyck Expressway to cut off any retreat. A rocket flew close by one of the helicopters as it rose into the air, but the rocket missed and went on its way, exploding in a building several hundred yards away. The second chopper hugged the ground as they left the scene empty.

The Chinese soldiers were cornered, but fought back bravely. They were well-armed and had several different types of weapons, but they were not prepared for this sudden attack. Hand grenades flew from both sides and ground missiles flew out from the line of trucks they had set up as protection. Several of the charging men from the runway went down as they ran for the mounds of snow, with the stationary vehicles only a hundred yards away.

For several minutes, the firing was intense from both sides, with over 400 carbines firing at each other and several hand grenades and rockets going in both directions. Suddenly, three small mortars could be heard from behind the snow mounds as mortar bombs flew into the air and started to blow the cars to pieces. Nine rounds went in, as well as dozens of hand grenades, and several shoulder rockets began to blow the rest of the vehicles, and the opposition's cover, to pieces.

Then silence began to envelop the area as the American troops were told to hold their fire by their commanders. A white piece of material became viewable waving above the middle truck that was about to burst into flames. Slowly, several men climbed out of the vehicles, moved forward, and dropped their weapons. The major headed off the roof, told Captain Wong to get all the engineers together, unconscious or not, and frisk them for weapons or phones while he went outside.

The air was full of smoke as he left the terminal. Using his radio, he told his men to stand down, stay on the mounds, and keep the surrendering soldiers covered. The third C-130 came in landing well down the runway and stayed at a safe distance, ready to be called forward.

Dozens of American troops were moving into the attack area, with several of them ready to fire at the growing crowd of injured and bloody men who 15 minutes earlier had stood in formation not knowing that their lives were held in the balance for the battle.

A truck's gas tank suddenly exploded, spewing bodies in all directions, and flames engulfed the two trucks on either side. Orders were given by Major Patterson, and several of his men ran for the bulldozers to make sure that the trucks were separated and pushed further away from the terminals.

After a couple of minutes, Captain Wong shouted to the Chinese soldiers to go back and pull any wounded out of the mess of vehicles, and several men went back and began shouting for survivors. Another five bodies were pulled out, and Major Patterson counted only 37 Chinese soldiers alive and or wounded out of the 200 which had arrived. A U.S. Air Force senior master sergeant who had been coordinating the attack from the C-130s radioed Major Patterson and asked for orders.

"Tell your men to keep the enemy under guard; pull them to one side, check them for weapons, and be careful. Can I assume that the C-130 has medics?"

"Roger that," was the reply.

"Get the medics in here. I want an injury count in ten minutes once we have the area safe and the men checked for weapons. Our injured go into the aircraft first, followed by theirs. I want a report from the Expressway and behind the terminals. Did we lose any?"

"Negative on the Expressway," was the reply over the radio. *"We were charged by about 20 Charlies, but none made it. We are clearing the area and coming towards you. Over."*

"I want 202 bodies or injured men in Charlie camouflage. I counted them before the fight and we are not leaving here until we have 202 accounted for," ordered Patterson.

"We had several try and make it around the building, but they are dead, and we are checking every hole anybody can climb into for any Charlie. Over," added another soldier.

They started with their own men, and there were three dead Americans and 29 wounded—several seriously. The C-130 had over 20 medical personnel ready, and the wounded were quickly transferred to the aircraft. The second C-130 was empty and ready to take on more wounded. There were only three lucky Chinese soldiers who did not have a wound of any sort, and they were frisked and put to work carrying their own wounded into the aircraft as the first 130 made its way down the taxiway.

"Get all the wounded and dead back to McGuire," Major Patterson ordered the flight personnel. He could not speak over the radio to McGuire from the ground, since the base was too far away, but the aircraft's radio operators could from the air.

"C-130s—return ASAP for the engineers and the pallets of electronics we have here. It's going to take at least ten flights in and out to carry the pallets, and we need this airport on lockdown by sunset. Also, ask the base commanders at McGuire and Andrews to wake up all their engineering personnel. We need all the help we can to audit the inventory when the equipment arrives at McGuire. My troops will keep the airport under control until every Charlie is accounted for."

The task was gruesome. A group of medics, under the control of two doctors, tried to piece bits of body to other bits of body. Many of the bodies were whole—the ones who had died from gunfire—but the unfortunates who had a mortar or shoulder rocket land close, or even hit by them, were nothing more than a pair of smoking boots.

Empty boots were placed in a line, some with parts in them and some without, and counted.

A complete search of the surrounding area was underway. A couple of hiding Chinese soldiers had been found, ferreted out, and marched over to help carry the wounded.

Twenty minutes later, the second C-130 took off with the first 30 wounded Chinese lying on stretchers. The third C-130 took off half an hour later with 90 dead bodies.

The first C-130 was already coming in again to land several minutes after the third one had departed, and several more medical personnel exited with stretchers to carry the rest of the dead. This time, a forklift came out with a pallet of body bags, and the soldiers began to place a dead body, sometimes in several pieces, into each bag.

Within two hours of the beginning of the attack, 202 pairs of boots on and not on bodies were counted. The piles of unrecognizable parts were placed in body bags and loaded in the C-130.

The airport was safe, the battle was over, and all that remained was for the engineers and pallets to be flown out.

Major Patterson called General Allen. It had been three hours since his last call. He described the success of the mission to the general and that he thought that they had acquired a smaller pallet of around 120 boxes of satellite phones.

"Get a cell phone into the hands of as many Air Force base commanders in the country as you can, Patterson. This is your next mission. Use all available flying aircraft, from jets to helicopters, for the next 48 hours only. You must have as many bases covered as possible by midnight on January 7th. Spread the aircraft usage around the country wisely. Double the air crews on all aircraft which can get into the southern areas like Texas. Remember, Elmendorf in Alaska and Edwards in

California already have phone contact. Start at McGuire, Andrews, and Bolling Air Force Bases, and work outwards, giving only one phone to base commanders. I want a unit each at Seymour Johnson and Pope ASAP. Give one to the commanders at Fort Bragg and Camp Lejeune. I need one ASAP to Vice

Admiral Rogers at the naval base in Norfolk. Get one to the president in North Carolina. I have two spare units and will leave one in Japan and one at Osan in Korea.

"Patterson, I want to know exactly how many satellite phones we have within four hours. Get the information from the Chinese engineers. Then get a company of men to guard the Chinese engineers while we pair each one up with one of our own engineers. Treat them like gold dust, get them everything they need, and then fly or drive them where they were meant to go and allow them to do the jobs they were flown in for. Try and borrow a couple of them to start repairing some of our fighters at Andrews and see if we can get a few of our aircraft operational again.

"We have two weeks to defend our country. We believe the attack will be there in New York. I want every Air Force base commander that gets a radio to go to their closest Army, Marine and naval bases and get an inventory list of fighting equipment that is operational now. I'm looking for trucks—any trucks—to drag howitzers up to New York. I'm looking for anything that can blow a high-explosive or armor-piercing shell through ship's armor. I want 50,000 troops readied to move into New York in the next two weeks. Are you taking notes, Patterson?"

"Yes, sir, I have you on speaker phone and two men writing your orders down," the major replied.

"I want your five bulldozers to move across to La Guardia Airport and clean that runway, then get them into Teterboro and Newark. I want aircraft to be able to go in there within 24 to 36 hours. Get those Charlie engineers to turn on the lights and get heat into the terminals, or at least get one generator, or even truck engines, generating power in all four airports.

"Patterson, I suggest you fuel up the only long-range aircraft we have left, the second HC-130 tanker, and get two sets of flying crew aboard and at least 24 operational satellite phones, as well as half a dozen of the Chinese engineers who speak English and a varied selection of spare electrical parts. Not enough to deplete reserves needed on the East Coast, but important parts to repair electrical components for getting heat and power into the bases, or hopefully getting some of our aircraft flying. Send the HC-130 out with somebody you can trust and start distributing the equipment. Leave one engineer, spare parts, and a phone with the commander at Hill, then give Vandenberg one engineer, parts, and three phones—two phones are for their neighbor bases. Deliver two phones to Travis,

then *fuel up and head over to Hawaii and deliver an engineer, spare parts, and one phone. Get that baby full of fuel there and head over to Anderson in Guam to deliver another few parts and a phone. Refuel and head to Yakota Air Force Base in Japan to deliver the same. Then, get two phones, one engineer, and parts into Kunsan in South Korea, one engineer and parts into Baghdad, and the same into Turkey. Fuel up and fly to Ramstein and then the Azores, leave a phone at each, and tell the pilots to get back to McGuire ASAP.*

"*The number I'm giving you now is one that can help them find their locations during daylight hours only. The code word is 'Carlos Lee.' Tell the pilots to follow orders from Carlos Lee and they will get a pretty accurate location. Tell them never to answer the phone if the red number, which I assume will be on all the phones, calls them—that is the enemy. Remember, daylight only, so tell them not to get into a bad situation at night. The HC-130 has a 4,500-mile range, but remind the pilots to use their fuel wisely. I want another situation report from you in 24 hours, Patterson. You have all Air Force personnel at your beck and call. I will need a copy of all the numbers, once you have set up which phone is going where. If you have any problems, call me on this number, but right now I need some sleep; we are six hours out in the middle of nowhere and I need to get to Misawa. Good luck!*" And the general hung up.

Chapter 12

The Hit Squads

STRONG AIR FORCE BASE WAS up early the next morning, three hours before dawn. It was cold outside. The temperature was 24 degrees out, which was normal for January. Carlos and Lee had taken turns monitoring the cell phones and the feed coming off the satellites.

General Allen was on his way to Japan, an hour from Alaska, when the airport woke up. The technical guys had refueled and rearmed the aircraft throughout the night. Carlos' P-51 was still being worked on and would not fly that day. General Allen called and asked that the food distribution be put off for 48 hours, as he needed civilian help communicating with Fort Bragg, Seymour Johnson and Camp Lejeune. He wanted exact numbers of vehicles and available troops, and, if necessary, they needed to start walking to New York.

Preston asked Maggie and Staff Sergeant Perry to fly into Pope AFB in one of the 172s and find out what the largest Army base in the country could supply as defensive protection. John and Technical Sergeant Matheson were to fly the Cessna 210 into Seymour Johnson, and Pam Wallace and another sergeant were to fly the second 172 into McClutcheon Field—the main Marine airfield in Jacksonville, North Carolina.

Martie had been pretty quiet that night after she arrived home. Preston congratulated her on a good job, and she began to get back to normal. Sally had been relieved by a new group of pilots, and they had taken off for McGuire as soon as she landed. Sally had been living in her aircraft for five solid days and needed a bath and some sleep.

Lady Dandy was now the main troop transporter and, with the FedEx Cargomaster, was ready to help the ground troops near Heflin, Alabama, just after dawn. Preston decided to fly the P-38 this time; its Hispano cannon was able to put a lot more power down on the enemy if need be. Carlos was totally exhausted, unable to fly, and needed sleep. They had tried to control incoming and outgoing communication all night, but had been unable to do so. The satellites were not, and they realized would never be, able to be controlled by anybody other than their Chinese controllers. Carlos hoped that they were in the headquarters building, hopefully about to be destroyed by the AC-130 gunships under the command of General Allen in about 24 hours' time.

Preston's airstrip was busy two hours before dawn. First, Buck and Barbara flying *Lady Dandy* climbed into the dark sky, then Mike Mallory in the turboprop Cargomaster ten minutes later. The 172s took off an hour after *Lady Dandy* to arrive at their closer destinations at dawn, and then the 210. Lastly, Martie in her Mustang and finally Preston in his P-38 took off 70 minutes behind *Lady Dandy*.

Martie and Preston climbed quickly and reached a cruising altitude of 15,000 feet within 15 minutes. At a fast cruise of 370 miles an hour, they covered ground rapidly and arrived over Atlanta as the sun was coming over the horizon.

"Good morning, ground gentlemen. Your flying backup is ten minutes out. What do you need from us? Over."

"Good morning, flyboys," was the reply from the ground troops. *"We had a skirmish with some guys wanting to continue east just after midnight and hit three more of their vehicles coming along the highway. Since then, we have seen nothing. Our guys inspected the three vehicles—they will not move again—and found two of those fancy cell phones you guys so desperately want. There were nine dead or nearly-dead Charlies, and I think you should land about two to three miles behind the first road attack you guys did yesterday, form a sweep line along the road, and work your way inwards, towards us. We can do the same and you*

can coordinate us from the air. I suggest that you guys head west for 20 miles and see if any Charlie are retreating in that direction. Over."

"Roger that," replied Preston. "Buck, Mike, do you copy?"

"We copy," replied Buck. *"I suggest one of you check the road and look for 800 yards of open space so that our aircraft can get down, and you circle above the spot while we go in. Over."*

"Okay," replied Preston. "Martie, follow me and let's find a suitable landing strip," and they headed over the battle ground.

There were still wisps of black smoke rising here and there since there had been no wind the previous night. The smoke hung in the low-lying areas, making it difficult to see. They found a big enough flat piece of clear road just east of the exit to Heflin on the southern strip of road. The landing area was out of view from the bridge, between the bridge and the first attack, and the only piece of straight road around. It would be safe for a landing, and there were only a couple of vehicles and a rolled-over tractor-trailer on the eastbound side. The clearing had at least 800 yards of clean asphalt before it started curving slightly, and any pilot with a slowing aircraft could negotiate the slight bend if need be. They would have to fly in from the west to make it work, however.

"Mike, do you see the bridge underneath where I am? Over." Preston asked.

"Roger, I have the bridge visual," Mike Mallory replied from the Cargomaster, now over the area.

"I suggest that with your shorter landing distance, you go in on the southern side of the highway just before the bend to the bridge and get your guys out. I'm worried that there might be trouble under the bridge. The bend will cover you, and then *Lady Dandy* can go in. Mike, *Lady Dandy* will need all the available space, and pilots, stay on the ground if it looks safe. I recommend you guys go in and clear the bridge first. Martie, you are backup if need be."

Mike went in while Preston flew off along the highway further to the west, searching for any vehicles moving ahead. He heard the Cargomaster go in over the radio and then *Lady Dandy*, and both aircraft stayed on the ground, saving fuel.

Ground fire erupted from under the bridge several seconds later as Preston turned to fly back. It was only two guys with one vehicle, he heard over the radio, and the men on the ground soon had the situation secure with a machine gun taking out the enemy from an easy 400 yards. Martie hadn't needed to get involved, but she circled at 5,000 feet just in case.

Preston turned again and flew for another ten minutes, not seeing a single vehicle moving. He decided that 50 miles was far enough and returned at low cruise to the two aircraft on the ground.

The men who had just gone in were already in a line across both highways and across the fences and into the woods on the southern side and working their way eastwards and towards the first attack area. Preston spoke into his radio.

"We have a line up and walking along both highways westwards of you and heading in your direction, ground control. They cleared a bridge, and found two injured guys and a broken vehicle. Over."

"Roger that. We have a line up and will do the same, walking towards them," came the reply. *"We see a straight piece of road for about 100 yards and then it curves to the right. What is ahead of us? Over."*

"You have 100 yards before the road curves to the right for another 400 yards, then it curves to the left, and the main attack was in the middle of this straight piece, which is about 1,800 yards long and full of smoking vehicles. By the time you get to this stretch, you should be able see our guys coming the other way. One of us will stay up here until you meet up. Then we need to… Hold on. Martie, is that a tractor coming up to the highway bridge from Heflin?"

"Roger, he's being stopped by our troops," she replied, now lower and circling at 2,000 feet.

"He's a farmer from the area, asking if he can help," the troop leader reported over their radio.

"Get a situation report from him and ask him if he has any friends with aircraft in the area. They could fly into their local Air Force base and get supplies."

He also told Martie to go in and land and conserve fuel but be ready for takeoff.

For an hour, Preston flew over the two lines of men slowly converging on each other. The eastern group had just arrived on the final straight part when they got fired upon from the south side woods, a mile to the west of where the aircraft were waiting. He noticed three vehicles in the trees as far in as they could go, and he relayed a message to the ground troops. He pulled his P-38 away and went north at full power, climbing rapidly to 8,000 feet. Preston turned, fired several rounds with the cannon, and swept back into the area where he had seen the vehicles. He let go with the Hispano cannon a mile out and watched as the large cannon rounds danced across the grass and into the area where the vehicles were hidden. A massive explosion rose up to meet him as he straightened out and radioed the guys on the ground to go in.

He watched as the line of marines ran into the smoking area, began a firefight, and dispatched the last of the Chinese hit squads.

That was the end of Mr. Deng and his group. Preston flew around for another 15 minutes and saw that the second group of soldiers had already reached the site and were searching for anybody alive in the carnage.

Just before he went in to land where the other three aircraft were waiting for him, he counted 43 stationary vehicles that he could see, and one under the bridge that made 44.

It was weird standing in the middle of a U.S. interstate, with two World War II aircraft, a FedEx aircraft, and a DC-3, while chatting with a farmer sitting on a tractor older than the aircraft themselves. The farmer was about 70, born during the Second World War, and had been given the 1930s tractor by his father. It was the only thing left on his farm which still worked, and he explained to Martie, Buck, Mike, and Preston that he could run his farm with it for the next century, or at least his sons could. Preston asked him about airports and military bases, and the farmer told him that the closest Army base was Anniston Army Depot due west. It had a lot of ammunition dumps and supplies. As far as airports, he thought the town with the same name would have the closest one.

Mike Mallory suggested to the farmer that he should drive over to the base and get food if need be, and Preston stated he would fly in to see what was going on there.

"Martie, why don't you fly into Moody Air Force Base," and he showed her on the map where it was, about 30 miles north of the Georgia-Florida border. "Tell them about General Allen and 'Allen Key' and see if they have anything flyable. If they do, tell them on behalf of General Allen to fly it up to Seymour Johnson. If they can't refuel you, go straight into Robins Air Force Base in Macon, Georgia—it's on your way home—and tell them the same thing. Hopefully they will give you fuel, but you should still have enough to get home. I'll go into the Army base here and find out what the Army has in the area and try to get it moving up north."

By this time, half of the ground troops were filing aboard the two aircraft, and Mike and Buck took off to get the men back home. They would only have time for one more flight in and out during daylight and might have to get the last troops out the next morning.

Preston asked the farmer on the tractor if he could pull a few vehicles off the highway—three would be enough—so that anybody could land closer to the burned-out wrecks on the other side of the bridge, and the farmer went about his mission with excitement.

An hour later Preston was sitting in the Army post commander's office telling him the whole story. He had seen a straight piece of road inside the barracks. The 800 yards of two-lane tarmac road was clear, with no electrical wires, and he had gingerly put the P-38 down with several yards to spare on both sides.

The Army was pretty worried about an old aircraft landing in their private area, but it did have U.S. Air Force markings on it. For an hour, Preston told Colonel Peter Grady everything that had happened and that they were expecting an attack by the enemy in New York in about two weeks. The president was currently in North Carolina and was expected to start a food distribution program in a couple of days.

"What do you have that's operational, Colonel?" Preston asked.

"We have 12 old transporters, and another ten loaned to the area's National Guard that we can go and pick up," he replied. "Apart from three old jeeps we use around here and a couple of fuel tankers from the 1980s, we have tried to start everything, and that's all that works."

"What sort of weapons and troops do you have?" was Preston's next question.

"We have five old artillery pieces operational, training equipment from the 1970s. They are big boys, the older M198 155mm howitzers. They can fire two rounds per minute sustained, and we have 75 HE extended-range 155mm projectiles in our armory. They have a range of up to 18 miles, and the HE can put a good dent in anything out there that's made of steel. Then, Mr. Strong, we have ten of the older 105mm howitzers, and those have a range of seven miles. We have 500 armor-piercing projectiles stored for those. We have eight operational 5-ton howitzer transporters from the 1960s that still work and can pull those 155mm howitzers. We have another three flatbed trucks, which can carry the 100-pound projectiles. Since we only have 75, we can fill the flatbeds up with the lighter 105mm projectiles that weigh just less than 50 pounds. As far as troops are concerned, we have 1,500 on alert and we need several companies of them to guard our base here. If we got a platoon of 30 troops into our 22 usable troop transporters each that would be 660 men with ten of the trucks pulling the 105mm howitzers. We could fill one of the jeeps with rations for a couple of days and head over to our nearest base just outside Atlanta for more rations. I know for sure that the colonel there has one or two more howitzers and I'm sure a couple of old trucks to pull them with."

"Could your fuel tankers get you to each Army base between here and New York?" Preston asked.

"I think so. We might need the Air Force to drop us a bit of fuel, but if I stopped and picked up troops at each Army base between here and Fort Bragg, I reckon I would have three times as many vehicles, howitzers, and projectiles and we could have a convoy miles long by the time we reached New York."

"Well, on behalf of the President of the United States of America, I have a letter enabling me to commandeer anything I think will help us defend this country," stated Preston, pulling the letter out of his flight jacket.

"And what is your rank, Mr. Strong, if I may ask?" replied Colonel Grady, checking the letter that was direct from the White House.

"I'm of equal rank to General Allen, head of the U.S. Air Force, so that makes me a four-star general, Colonel."

"Well, General Strong, that's good enough for me, sir. I can have my soldiers ready and out of our gates in six to eight hours. I aim to make four stops at other Army bases close to our route to increase our convoy before we reach Fort Bragg. I think that I can reach Fort Bragg in 48 to 60 hours, depending on how long the bases take to get their men ready."

"Tell them to head north up I-95. You can clear the way, and with less traffic, they should catch up with you. Also, remember, Colonel, it is cold up there. Take every luxury you can to keep warm and all the food you can carry. You can stay at my place on your way up. The address is on the piece of paper.

"I will give you this letter dated four days ago from the president. This is your authority to commandeer everything you can on your way to my location. Once you get close to Fort Bragg, use our frequency. I've also written it on this letter, and if you need supplies I will try and get a C-130 to land close to you. I suggest that you move a bulldozer or two out right now to start clearing a route for your men. The highways are congested with overturned tractor-trailers."

"I forgot that we have an old tractor-trailer carrying a bulldozer," added the colonel. "The tractor itself has an armored front and steel fender to clear a pathway, and the dozer can be pulled off to clear larger trucks. I'll get them kitted up and out within the hour."

After a few more minutes of discussion, Preston walked outside and hitched a ride with the colonel in one of the old jeeps back to his P-38, which was being guarded by a couple of armed soldiers. They shook hands, and Preston started the aircraft, much to the delight of the dozen military onlookers. He taxied as far down the road as he could, turned around, and completed his final checks. It was a well-paved piece of asphalt about 200 feet shorter than his airfield.

Luckily, there were no buildings to get over at the end, only a 4-foot-high fence surrounding a sports field.

Just to make sure, he gunned both engines before releasing the brakes and sped down the road, past the onlookers halfway down, and left the road 100 feet before the fence. He pulled the stick back hard and went high and fast to get out of the building area before turning his aircraft back towards I-20 East and bringing his engine revs down a notch.

He landed back on the road 20 minutes later where the farmer had cleared enough space to get pretty close to the burned-out vehicles. He had only been away two hours, and already the fires were out and there were several soldiers carrying dead bodies and equipment as he turned the aircraft around and closed down the engines. He got a situation report from a Marine lieutenant and was handed three unharmed satellite cell phones.

The lieutenant went through the list of injured. They had one dead soldier and three slightly wounded men. On the enemy's side there were nine injured. The two medics had done their best, but seven of them had already died. Two were still alive, but they were not sure they would make it through the rest of the day.

So, his final count was two still alive, 143 bodies and 51 sets of Chinese boots. His men had done a full sweep and had found several more dead bodies, but nobody alive. There were 50 vehicles, of which two still worked but had flat tires. Thirty-three were blackened remains, and 17 had given up a little merchandise here and there. There was very little equipment that wasn't damaged. The farmer on the tractor came up and smiled, his job done. Preston was about to thank him when he heard the unmistakable sound of a C-130 coming in.

It came from the east at 500 feet and very low. Preston asked for a radio and called up to the aircraft as it flew overhead.

"Hi, Preston, Jennifer here. I've come to take some boys up north. Buck and Mike are two hours behind me and I have a doctor and three medics on board. I've got to head up north to help with a big fight up there."

"There is enough room to land here. A kind farmer has cleared

700 yards on both sides of the highway for us, and I suggest you come in on the other side of the P-38. Over."

She did, and let the engines shut down before getting out and coming over. She was introduced to the excited old farmer and then the tired marines, who were excited that they were going with her to New York. Tired or not, they certainly didn't want to miss any action. They would need every soldier up there.

There was a problem with the dead enemy bodies though. The farmer spoke up and told them that he and the townsfolk had enough old equipment to dig a mass grave and that a communal grave just off the road was as good a place as any.

Preston told Jennifer about his luck with the Army base and the movement of troops beginning in a few hours from Anniston. He asked the farmer if he could give the two confiscated phones to Colonel Grady, who would be coming through in seven to ten hours, if he left written instructions for how the phone should be used. The farmer replied that they would dig the communal hole and then wait for the Army to show up.

A quick note was written including Preston's new cell phone number and General Allen's, which he got from Jennifer. He then wrote down the instructions on how to use the phone, to always state the two words 'Allen Key' when starting to speak, and explaining why not to answer if the red number called. Both phones were from the batch the lieutenant had given him and still had full battery life. A charger had been found unharmed in one of the trucks, and Preston also left that for the Army commander. It had a vehicle-lighter attachment and the phone could be charged while driving. He wrote for the colonel to call General Allen when he got it and provide him with a sitrep. The men were piling up all the workable weapons in the C-130. The two injured Chinese were also loaded, the new medics looking after them as well as the injured Americans. The dead American soldier was lifted into the C-130 with the remaining troops.

Jennifer took off to the west 15 minutes later and Preston waited for her to climb away. He waved goodbye to the nice old farmer, who saluted him as he gunned the engines for departure.

With Americans like that, this country will certainly survive, he thought to himself, and as he flew over the bridge spanning the highway, he felt good and had hope for the future for the first time in several days.

He beat Jennifer in by 30 minutes after telling Buck and Mike to turn back. They were half an hour out from the farm when they did as told and reached the airstrip together. Preston had radioed Martie earlier, and she was just taking off from Robins Air Force Base and on her way home—she was an hour out and had enough fuel.

It was 4:00 pm and an hour before dark when Martie came in and Jennifer went out, saying "Hi" as they passed each other in flight. The wind was coming from the south, and Preston noticed that landing was from the north for the first time this year. He hoped the winds were the winds of change. Somehow, he knew that this day had been a real victory for the United States. Now it was all up to General Allen. Hopefully he would cut off the head of the "serpent" in the next 24 hours. America had certainly just cut off the tail.

Chapter 13

Z-Day +6 – China Attacked

AT THE EXACT MOMENT THAT Preston was thinking about General Allen, the general had been in Japan for 20 minutes. Carlos, before he packed up to leave, had guided General Patterson and his aircraft into an overcast Japan. Luckily, the overcast conditions were only ranging about 20 miles offshore, but during the night, Carlos had changed the three aircraft's course three times as they flew over the ocean for the second half of their 12-hour flight. Carlos and Lee needed to be set up at McGuire within four hours to help guide General Allen and Lee's wife into mainland China.

The first half of the trip had been easy. They had followed the Alaskan islands in a southwest direction from Anchorage, with the Bering Sea on the left and the Pacific Ocean on the right. They had passed over Atukan and Unalaska four hours into the flight, the infra-red scanners and the antiquated but working 100-mile radar systems onboard the gunships giving them eerie views of the islands 29,000 feet below them. After five hours, they needed to head away from the land as it began to stretch in a west-northwest direction and towards Russia. For the next several hours, they needed Carlos to guide them.

All the way through the flight, General Allen, with his cell phone permanently on charge from the flight deck, made and received calls. For the first few hours, it was Major Patterson giving him sitreps, and by the time they left the last islands on their radar and infra-red scanners behind, the fight was over and it sounded like they had their first prize—an intercontinental aircraft to ferry troops back to the States. He had given orders to get it checked out, refueled, and ready to meet him either in Ramstein, Germany, or at their main Air Force base in Turkey. General Allen wanted to move troops away from all front lines immediately and get them into safer areas.

He managed a couple of hours of sleep before they were scheduled to call Carlos again and get their latest position in relation to a line they had drawn on a map. He called Carlos at the appointed time, got all the aircraft's transponders switched on for several seconds, and within minutes Carlos was telling them that they were over 100 miles off their line to the south. They changed flight direction, and everyone not doing anything went back to sleep.

It was weird, flying over pure blackness and having only one person in the world to talk to, several thousand miles away, who could give them accurate information on where they were.

Two hours later, they did the same, and this time they were only 20 miles off course. The winds from the north must have lessened. At this point, seven hours into the flight, they decided to add 1,500 gallons into each gunship from the tanker. It took nearly an hour to get both aircraft refueled, and half the fuel was used during this period, but it got them 275 miles closer to their targets. Once this fuel was used up, they started small electrical gravity-feed pump motors that pumped the stored fuel from the soft bladders in their holds into the fuselage fuel tanks, which in turn pumped any excess up and into the wing tanks. That took another hour, and by the time they were finished, they expected to land in just three more hours.

Two hours later, they phoned Carlos and got a third location report. This time it looked like they were 40 miles north of their line into Misawa Air Force Base and 400 miles away from Japan. The area around the base was also overcast, and it could be snowing. They were 100 miles behind schedule and it was going to be tight on fuel.

Then General Allen got a call. It was not from the red number, but an American voice with a southern drawl said, *"Allen Key."*

"Name and location?" asked the general.

"*Grady, Army, State-Alpha Lima (AL),*" was the reply.

"Nice to hear from you, Mr. Grady. What can I do for you this cold winter evening?" the general asked.

"*Got this phone from a Mr. Strong, sir,*" Grady answered. "*He told me to contact you when I got it and give you a sitrep.*"

"Well, get on with it, Mr. Grady. I assume you know who you are talking to. I don't, yet."

"*Allen Key, we are heading due east on I-20 in the direction of Bragg. I have 700 men in 22 trucks. We are towing five 155mm howitzers and ten 105mm howitzers, tons of ammo, and I estimate we will find more men and materials at four more Alpha-Lima bases on our way to November-Charlie (NC), where Preston lives. Did you copy?*" asked the colonel.

"Roger that, Grady. Best news I've heard all day. What is your end station?"

"*November-Yankee (NY) in hopefully six days,*" was the reply.

"We are going to need you Army guys. You've seen what the Alpha-Foxtrot (Air Force) boys are working with. The November (Navy) boys are even worse off than us, with four or five boats that can't even catch fish. Anyway, I'm heading to the other side of the world. When you get to Preston's, I want at least 100 big guns, 10,000 buddies, and I don't care if they have to walk to November-Yankee, just get them there. I hope to be there a day or two after you and I'll buy you a beer, Mr. Grady. Good luck. Out." He signed off as he heard his radio operator trying to contact the Air Force base 350 miles in front of them.

It took several minutes, but every person aboard the three aircraft was very relieved to finally hear a voice respond from somewhere in front of them. After several codes and two-way communication was exchanged, information was received. The weather wasn't bad. Cloud height was at 3,000 feet above ground with a very light snow. Wind was from the northwest at five to ten and the temperature was 32 degrees. The runway was clear. They had had no traffic for a week, but they did have flares to help the general land. The landing lights were operational with several generators and the runway slightly slippery, but it would be checked out and cleared with their one working bulldozer by the time they got there.

General Allen called Carlos, thanked him for saving all of their lives, and for providing radio communications, and told him that he was free to head up to McGuire. There was already a C-130 flying down to get him, and he had four hours to get there and set up his equipment in case the general needed help flying into South Korea.

Twenty minutes later, the three 130s lowered themselves to 3,000 feet and began to pass under the cloud layer. Visibility was about ten miles, and they hoped to see the flares or at least be heard from the ground. Ten miles out, they saw flares through the infra-red scanning systems, and they quickly brought the three aircraft to the correct course and began their landing checks. The two gunships would go in first, and then the tanker, who could still get to Korea without refueling.

The bright and welcome landing lights formed into two lines in front of them, and with less than 30 minutes of flying time left in their tanks, they went in and touched ground for the first time in 12.5 hours.

Four hours later, fully fueled and totally out of the salmon they had brought with them, they took off and headed on their 3-hour trip to Osan, South Korea, 840 miles away. It had taken an extra two hours for the tanker to suck the fuel out of the dead tanker trucks, transfer the fuel to the gunships, and then take on her full load. While they were being refueled, the men stationed there had emptied the Misawa Air Force Base's armored bunker of all the 105mm HE rounds, which amounted to 120 projectiles per gunship. General Allen knew that there would be more in South Korea, but he wanted to go in with twice the ammunition he would normally have on board.

Fresh pilots had taken over the flying duties. The relieved pilots got a couple of hours of sleep, and the general started thinking about these old birds. They had been flying for nearly 40 years, had gone through several wars, and still they just flew and flew and flew. A third gunship was expected to be located at Osan, and the Japanese bases, now behind them, had absolutely nothing flying. At least they had used their clean and readied runway for a few landings and takeoffs.

Three hours later, the radio operator got into contact with Osan. They were flying low, at less than 1,000 feet to stay out of any North Korean coastal radar systems, and again they were guided in with flares, before their infra-red scanners found the operating runway lights.

There were heavy, pulsating bursts of light through the thin snow on the horizon to the north, and it looked like there was military conflict around Seoul, 40 miles north of the Air Force base they were flying into. The pilots could very faintly see large lights, which meant that large buildings must be on fire.

They landed in an inch of snow, and the weather was beginning to close in around this part of Asia. They couldn't waste any time getting over to China.

Osan was a large base that included the 51st Fighter Wing and the 7th Air Force. The base had two generals and five colonels who were waiting for him with fuel tanker and generators as they drew up to the hangar. Refueling would only take 30 minutes, due to the short haul from Misawa, and the general asked about *Easy Girl*. To his relief, she was ready and operational, had a full crew and just needed to be topped off and armed. She was in a hangar, and the brass gave orders to have her brought out and for her crew to get ready. General Allen asked for two backup pilots, and they were found. The only working jeep and one old troop transporter were started up, and his armaments crew drove out to the underground bunker to load all the ammunition they needed.

"Gentlemen," Pete Allen spoke to a two-star general, a one-star general, three colonels and seven majors as they all stood about the aircraft. "I need a sitrep about the fighting to the north, and in return I can fill you in on our worldwide problems. I will need some coffee and whatever you have to eat, as will my men. We have been flying now for 24 hours. I want to get out of here within two—my AC-130 weapons chief will fill your guys in on what we need."

They went into a large and relatively warm conference room.

Several men had obviously been sleeping in here, and the room was immediately cleared for the meeting.

"Okay, so tell me what happened here at Osan," the general asked Base Commander General Hal Whitelaw.

"I assume you know everything went dark here at 1400 hours on January 1st," replied General Whitelaw.

"Actually, midnight East Coast time was what the perpetrators were aiming for," General Allen stated. "It was dark, freezing and we believe that at least 10 million North Americans are already dead or dying." The men around the table looked at him, many with their mouths open and their faces white.

"We had the usual 20 defense fighters and five armed bombers up, as well as eight C-17s on their way to Misawa," continued General Whitelaw. "We had three Stratotankers about 300 miles out in different directions, and we lost the lot. Not one aircraft made it back to base. Even the two Apache helicopters patrolling 30 miles north of here just disappeared as the radar went down and all of our millions of electrical components just stopped working. We are sitting here with 400 pieces of junk that used to be called aircraft, and one Vietnam-era AC-130 gunship, two old operational F-4 Phantoms, and three Vietnam-era Bell helicopters. How did this happen, Pete, and when is somebody going to turn the power on again?"

"Never, guys...not for a long time. All the Chinese-made electronic gadgets and parts worldwide—billions of them, trillions of them, I don't know how many—were all built to fail, and there are no spares or replacements until we set up new manufacturing facilities. These parts were made by the same company—Zedong Electronics."

For half an hour the general told them everything he knew. He was tired, unshaven, and had bags under his eyes, but after tonight he would have a little more time to sleep.

"So you all now know as much as I do. My next stop is to attack the Zedong headquarters. Hopefully my actions will turn off their lights, too. We don't believe the Chinese or Russian governments are involved, since Beijing is as dark as the United States is, as well as all of Russia. I'm hoping to get to both capitals in the next 24 hours and let both governments know that it wasn't us.

"To see for myself, we traveled as far west as we dared on the way down here from Misawa. There were lights visible on the coast of North Korea. We have seen them on our screens back in the United States. On the simple screens that we have gotten operational again, we have seen lights in Shanghai, Pakistan, north of Kabul, parts of North Africa, Syria and all of Iran. Everybody who we are in a conflict with has lights on, and we don't. The engineers traveling with me are showing your techs how to set up satellite communications by bouncing off the same satellites the enemy is using. They don't know we are doing it, however, and I'm just hoping that when I blow their headquarters into little pieces around midnight tonight that we all don't lose communications.

"Hal, since you are so close to the fighting, I will give you the cell phone I had reserved for Ramstein. I left the other one I had in Misawa, so you guys now have worldwide communications, even with the president, who got one just like it several hours ago. Here is a list of numbers to call, which will be updated and phoned through to you every 12 hours as new phones are handed out. We have just short of 200 phones, and these are our entire world communications until further notice. Just remember, these might all become useless in a few hours when we hit their building in downtown Nanjing."

General Whitelaw explained Osan's current situation. Apart from several 105mm howitzers, a hundred or so rocket launchers, a dozen machine guns, and 4,000 fully armed men, there was little they could do against a full-on attack on the base by North Korea. The enemy outgunned the base by far, if all their modern equipment was still working.

"My mission tonight, gentlemen," continued General Allen once General Whitelaw was finished, "is to take out their headquarters and show them that we, the United States of America, are not defeated. I believe the whole Chinese Air Force could be grounded, just like ours. Maybe they are in control of sections of it, but I'm 100% sure that they do not expect a blue-water attack from us. I'm going in to flatten Zedong Electronics Headquarters and then fly on to Beijing to try and land at the international airport there. *Easy Girl* still has the old flare system we used in Vietnam, the one which lights up landing zones for the Hueys so they can take in troops. The other two don't have the flare system, but they do have their infra-red fire control systems still operational, so each gunship has a definite purpose in my operation. I believe that with the flares we can pinpoint Beijing International Airport and get in if there is not too much snow.

"Since the weather report you gave me earlier said it has been sunny but cold since December 30th, the runway in Beijing should be clear enough for our 130s to get in. I will also communicate with the president as soon as we are over Chinese soil, and if I'm attacked and our aircraft are destroyed, three older but fully operational nuclear missiles will be launched from our only working site in South Dakota. One is for the capital of North Korea, one for Shanghai, and one for Beijing. Three more are ready to defend the United States, or can be directed into Iran if need be. Pakistan, we believe, can still retaliate, and we don't expect trouble from their government."

An hour later, the meeting was done and it was time to leave. During the meeting, the loading of ammunition was underway with every available man filling the magazines of all three gunships. They had 400 rounds of 40mm for the three rapid-fire Bofors guns—their only protection from enemy aircraft.

Since *Easy Girl* had been in Asia for several years and mostly used as air cover for naval exercises, she had not received the 105mm howitzer modification. She did, however, have the older gunship gun installation—two sets of twin 20mm Gatling guns. These could put out a heavy fire, and with the 105mm's installed on *Ghost Rider* and *Blue Moon*, they had enough firepower to flatten a building, any building!

The Korean tally was 300 projectiles, which were loaded into the aircraft for the two howitzers—200 HE projectiles and 100 concrete-piercing projectiles.

The gunships usually carried 100 105mm rounds each, but the

grand total of 200 rounds per gunship, or 20 minutes of non-stop firing, was a lot of explosive power for one building. It had to be enough, and General Allen chose the firing setup command to be one concrete-piercing round followed by two HE rounds, each filled with 5 pounds of TNT. His idea was to blow the building down from the roof, floor by floor, blowing holes through the concrete. The concrete-piercing rounds would make craters through the floors of the buildings one by one, and then they could send in the HE after that.

Twenty-thousand rounds for the four 20mm Gatling guns were loaded into *Easy Girl*—four times more than usual—as well as 100 rounds for her 40mm Bofors anti-aircraft cannon. Ten thousand rounds were placed in the other two gunships, and 150 Bofors rounds were loaded into each for aircraft protection.

It had been dark for an hour when General Allen called Carlos. Carlos had just finished setting up the satellite equipment at McGuire. He had flown in and gotten four hours of sleep while Lee Wang got the equipment organized and started placing all the computers and the one satellite dish into their perfect configuration, which took a couple of hours. Lee then worked on connecting everything together and woke Carlos to continue. They were an hour from receiving their first new digital world photos when the general phoned.

"Carlos? Allen Key."

"*Hi, Pete,*" replied Carlos. "*We need another hour before I can get a picture. We have our picture of the United States on screen now, but I need time to set up the codes to reach into their satellite feed and receive their pictures. What is the weather like where you are?*"

"Not good, Carlos. Light snow and it's getting worse. Visibility is about 2,000 feet and closing in. I need to know if this storm is big enough to affect the area I need to get to, and from there I want to go north into their capital city, or might I have to return to Japan or my last port of call? I'd hate to be lost up there without a place to go, but I must leave now and I want to attack as close to their midnight as possible. That will represent one week and 13 hours since their attack on us. I'm in trouble if this is a full-scale storm, but we have *Mother Goose* filled to the brim with fuel, and at worst she can give us 600 extra miles of flying time.

"Carlos, we have grown to three gunships, so we now have four transponders. I have no option but to leave here ASAP and I want to try and get into the attack zone without transponders. We have Mrs. Wang, who has enjoyed her trip so far, and I intend to get her back safely. I have a new phone number for you. The call sign is Whitelaw-base Osan-South Korea," and the general gave the number to Carlos to redistribute.

"I'm leaving our meeting here and will call you again in 30 minutes once I get into *Ghost Rider*." He did, and they talked again as the general got seated and checks were done, doors closed, and the four aircraft were made ready for flight again.

"Lee would like to say a few words to his wife. Is that possible?" asked Carlos when Pete called him back.

"As long as they speak in English so that I can understand, I'm happy to allow it. Just explain to him that we need this to succeed as much as possible and all our safety depends on you guys getting us out of here. There were a lot of lights to our north as we came in earlier, and there are a lot of good soldiers being killed down there. We think that our men have about a week here before we will have to defend the base itself."

"Pete, Lee has worked harder than I have in the last few hours and much of your safety has depended on his knowledge of their systems," Carlos replied. *"I'll get him on the phone,"* and he handed the phone to Lee.

"Harrow, Mr. Pete," Lee said on the phone.

"Good evening to you, Lee," replied the general.

"We are ready to go, sir," stated the pilot.

"Let's get out of here," Pete replied to the pilot. "Lee, here is your wife," and he called Mrs. Wang forward to speak to her husband.

They spoke in rapid English for several minutes as the aircraft taxied to the southern end of the runway for takeoff. Pete understood everything being said, and he smiled as he heard Mrs. Wang going over the map of Nanjing that Lee was reminding her about. They completed their conversation as the engines began their takeoff roar, and she handed the phone back, bowed, smiled, and nimbly ran back to her seat.

Within five minutes, the four aircraft were in the air and flying level at 900 feet above ground. They were able to do this with the infra-red systems aboard the three gunships tracking their altitude, and the tanker cruised along behind them watching their directional changes with her radar on short-range mode. A direct route to Nanjing was fixed and they were in a loose formation with several hundred yards between each aircraft.

The general knew that with all the world's satellite directional systems out of commission, the only real way left to find other aircraft in the night's sky was by radar and heat scanners. They were far too close to a country that might have fully operational aircraft, but the radar screens were empty in all directions. Their flight to the coast of China over the Yellow Sea would take two hours, and many of the crew got more than an hour's sleep, including General Allen himself.

He was awakened when the pilot told him that the radar screen showed them to be 100 miles off the China coast. The snow was gone and the stars could be seen peeking through intermittent clouds. There was a sliver of a moon that made the water sparkle beneath them.

They were coming into the mainland 50 miles north of Shanghai in case there were Chinese fighters in the urban areas. They were very low, still skimming the waves at 500 feet. The four aircraft planned to intersect the coast, rise up to 1,000 feet just like allied bombers did over Europe during the Second World War, and meet up with the river that would take them directly into downtown Nanjing. Once they reached the second of three bridges across the river, the idea was to be at 2,000 feet, and hopefully flares would light up the area and give Mrs. Wang a chance to guide the gunships towards the headquarters building.

The flares would last for seven to eight minutes, and the general wanted them dropped directly over the building. The three gunships would still be in the dark sky several hundred yards away from the building, flying in circles at 3,000 feet.

General Allen gave orders to test the guns, and all the weapons aboard the three gunships were fired to make sure everything was ready. The general asked the co-pilot to surrender his seat to him and asked Mrs. Wang to come forward and sit just behind and in between the pilots.

They reached the river and only had 60 miles to go. The city in front of them blazing over the horizon looked weird. It was still all lit up as the pilots lowered the air speed to 200 miles an hour, which wouldn't throw out so much noise from the engines, and the dozen crew members in each gunship got down to their tasks of readying the aircraft for battle stations.

The air around them glowed as they flew over the lightened city of Nanjing. Mrs. Wang pointed out the faintly lit silhouette of the first bridge a few miles ahead.

"We need to go through the dead center of the bridge," the crew member on the infra-red scanner said. "Pilots, climb to 2,500 feet to be safe."

They flew over the bridge and the river began a long turn to the southwest. The aircraft followed the turn and a second bridge appeared out of the blackness several seconds later. Mrs. Wang tapped the general on the shoulder and made a motion for them to fly over the bridge and then turn south.

"Fly over the bridge and then turn 40 degrees south over the southern river bank. I want 130 knots, pilots. I don't want to miss this building," the general ordered over the radio.

Mrs. Wang tapped him on the shoulder again and pointed to a small river inlet going south, just past the bridge.

"Follow that smaller river inlet going south," he ordered.

She then tapped him on the shoulder and pointed to two large buildings, a taller building next to a smaller building on the right side of the inlet only 100 yards in front of them.

"Drop flares now! Our target is the largest building right underneath us. Turn slowly to starboard. Howitzer gunners, I want the armor-piercing missiles to go right into the middle of the roof structure and then the HE right after them. Fire now!"

As the flares lit up the sky, the two 105mm guns opened up together and began pouring heavy projectiles into the building at the rate of ten rounds per minute. "*Easy Girl* and all 20mm cannon gunners, use all you have on the taller building. I think the second building is also part of the complex, I can see a sky bridge linking both buildings. Rake it up and down and then transfer backwards and forwards between the taller and shorter buildings!"

"Fire!" shouted the crew each time a round was fired out of each howitzer, and they shouted it ten times a minute for the next three minutes. The flares were not necessary anymore, as the building lit up the sky and several cars and vehicles exploded around the perimeter of the building.

"Howitzers, fire 20 rounds each into the shorter building's roof and work your way down the walls," ordered the general, flying slowly in *Ghost Rider* only 600 feet above and several hundred yards away from the building.

"Fire!" went the gunners as projectiles from the two howitzers and bursts of tracer from the four Gatling guns sprayed several thousand rounds per minute.

The building was dancing like a person whose feet were on hot coals, and suddenly the smaller building collapsed within itself. The larger building, now a third lower, again became the target of the two big guns.

"Howitzers, pour your remaining rounds into the last building! I don't want to see pieces bigger than a quarter. All 20mm guns, hold your fire and give me an ammo report."

"Fire!... fire!... fire!... fire!... fire!" continued the gunners as projectile after projectile went into the building, reducing its size by three or four floors per minute. One gunship could have flattened the building, but two just decimated it.

Within 12 minutes, the buildings' remains were strewn over a wide area and there was just thick smoke where the tall 30-story building had once stood.

"Gunners, pour another 60 seconds' worth into whatever you see remaining around the building, and then we are out of here. All 20mm cannons, fire into the smoke to make sure nothing has survived," and everything opened up, literally flattening the smoke and everything in it.

"All gunners, hold your fire! Pilots, set a course for Beijing at 3,000 feet. Scanners, give me any information you see down there."

It was hard to get any scans. The flames were so intense that nobody could look at the area without having to shield their eyes. The scanners showed intense heat and nothing standing, and then the lights in the entire city and surrounding area suddenly went dark. Apart from the massive fire, the area below them was as black as night.

"Ammo report, gunners," the general reminded them. After several minutes the reports came in—two thousand rounds of 20mm ammo, full magazines of 40mm ammo, and only 18 rounds of 105mm ammo left between the two gunships. One team had been a fraction quicker than the other and had fired off two more projectiles.

Now it was time to see if they would survive getting out of China. General Allen looked at his watch. It was exactly midnight China time, and the sky was still clear. The general looked back to see tears in Mrs. Wang's eyes.

"Why are you crying?" he asked her.

"Because those people killed so many, many others, and that makes me sad," she replied.

* * *

The chairman and his 15 comrades had watched the lone 747-400ER aircraft take off from Shanghai Pudong International Airport with much fanfare several hours earlier at 9:00 am that morning. There was a military band playing, the Red Guards stood at attention and faced the departing aircraft, and at the moment the chairman felt like it was all coming together. There was nothing that could stop him now.

Comrade Feng, back on the 29th floor of the Zedong Electronics building, was not too sure. He was the most senior man in the building now, his superiors were at sea and he was now in charge of relaying all information.

He had tried Comrade Wang's phone, and twice now, Wang hadn't answered it. He also had the chairman's satellite phone number, but if he called the chairman, and the man was in a bad mood, the chances were that he would be in extremely deep trouble. Nobody phoned the chairman for just any insignificant reason.

It was 4:00 in the afternoon when he saw several transponder reports over the sea around Japan and Korea for the second time. He had been scanning the screens since he had seen three transponders in the middle of the vast ocean, miles from anywhere several hours earlier. Where were they were coming from? He could only surmise that they were Chinese or North Korean aircraft checking out something. There was no other air force that could fly aircraft into that area. The first transponder distance had even been too far for Chinese aircraft to reach without in-flight refueling. They had to be North Korean.

The second one confirmed his thoughts, because this time they flew close to South Korea and were only 50 or so miles offshore. His orders were to tell Comrade Wang about any transponder movements anywhere, and for the third time he called Wang's number.

* * *

Comrade Mo Wang was sitting in the bus after a leisurely lunch in downtown Shanghai, about to arrive at the docks for the second time that day to board the ships. The flotilla of ten ships was due to leave Shanghai Harbor at 6:00, an hour from then.

His cell phone buzzed for a second and then stopped. It had done this a couple of times that afternoon, and this time he had a chance to take it out of his pocket. He looked at the weirdly lit up screen and was surprised to see that it had nothing but dashes across it—not what he had expected. *It must have been damaged when I dropped it,* he thought to himself as the bus pulled up to the wharf next to the aircraft carrier towering up above them and blocking out the sun. He would have to wait until he got to his room before he could get the spare phone out of his luggage.

He didn't have time, however, because just then the chairman told all the men that there would be drinks and celebration as the ships left Shanghai and he expected all of them to be with him as they began their journey to invade and capture the other half of the world.

They entered the carrier through a large cargo door in its side, and the captain of the ship escorted them up several flights of stairs to the flight deck. They followed the uniformed men, impeccably dressed in Navy white, as they walked across the outside flight deck where several fighters were standing. They walked past them across the wide runway and over to the port side of the ship. It was so high that they felt as if they were on the roof of a massive building.

The view of Shanghai and the harbor was fantastic once the group reached the port side. They could hear orders being shouted and the grinding of steel chains, as well as new rumblings beneath their feet. It was an hour yet before darkness would creep into the area, and the sun was just getting low over the buildings of the city.

"Isn't it a wonderful feeling to be so high and know that the whole world is at your feet, Comrade Wang?" the chairman asked, standing next to him. Wang hadn't noticed that the chairman had sidled up to him, as he had been so deep in thought. "I get the sense that something is troubling you, Comrade."

"Something does not feel right, you are correct in sensing my feelings, Comrade Chairman," replied Wang. "I've had this knot in my stomach for a day or two now that something out there is not as it seems. I should have had more phone calls from my men telling me of great victories, but I get somebody different on the phone every time I call. I know this young man Bo Lee Tang, he is a good man and dependable, but I cannot get over the sound of his voice. It didn't sound like him, yet he could prove everything I asked him to make sure it actually was him and not an imposter. Comrade Deng should have called twice today, but I haven't heard from him. The squads clearing the runway in New York were meant to contact me directly, as well as Comrade Fung back at Headquarters. Yet I do not receive a phone call but Comrade Feng does. Comrade Chairman, these are our elite troops. It is part of their training to do as ordered."

"I understand your need for discipline and information at all times. That is the making of a great leader," replied Chairman Chunqiao. "But today is a day of glory. This is the only aircraft carrier in the world. Look at her magnificence. Look at her power, Comrade Wang. We are invincible only because we defeated our enemy before we even attacked. The rules of war are to defeat your enemy before you go into battle, and we have done that, Comrade. Yes, there will be problems arising out of the fires and the ashes of the enemy's defeat, but without their Army, their Navy, and their Air Force, America is a small mouse and we are a large cat. Who is going to win, Comrade? Who is going to win?"

The ship slowly grumbled and vibrated underneath them. Several tugs slowly moved and guided her to the large entrance to the docks, and beyond that, the open river and then the ocean. A dozen or so sailors began to distribute glasses of champagne to the 16 dignitaries, and they could faintly hear the band still playing across the harbor. The whole mass of shipping began an orderly move towards open water.

Alarms sounded and dozens of soldiers in dress uniform ran out of doors everywhere, and within two minutes thousands of them lined the complete flight deck of the aircraft carrier, one arm length apart except for where the Politburo was standing. Fanfares sounded out of horns on the ships as they glided by thousands of soldiers waving their goodbyes.

As the sun set, the Shi Lang left the protection of the harbor, the tugs disengaged, and she and the four smaller warships left for open water to allow the massive container ships enough room to get out of the harbor behind them.

Once they reached the sea, and at ten knots, the naval ships aimed for Panama and sailed at reduced speed so that the container ships could catch up with them and get into formation.

By the time night covered the area, the five container ships had left the river and were only a couple of miles behind. Within three hours, the flotilla was only a mile apart and the coast of Shanghai disappeared off the short-range radar screens in the dark night behind them.

Once the VIPs had gone back inside the aircraft carrier's tower, they moved to the bridge to watch the whole flotilla coming together. Night lights began flashing from the others around them as the sea worsened, and the radar screen showed the ten ships getting into formation for their pass 200 miles south of the Hawaiian Islands in two days' time.

Dinner for the Politburo was served at 9:00 pm in the main dining room on a large table. By this time, several bottles of champagne had been drunk and the group was in a festive mood. They had still not been allowed to visit their rooms, and Wang was desperate to get his replacement phone and call Feng to get updates.

The chairman's control console with the five red buttons had been placed in the middle of the table, directly in front of the chairman's place at the head, and the first course of the meal was served to the rowdy group. The chairman had placed his own satellite phone next to the display, and none of the men had ever heard it go off, ever.

It was three hours later, and after the main course, that Wang managed to leave the room and, with an escort who knew the ship, retrieve the extra phone from his stateroom. It took five minutes to turn on, and he watched in horror as several messages arrived on the screen, all from Comrade Feng, the latest only an hour ago.

Comrade Wang climbed back up to the flight deck with his escort to get perfect communications and dialed Feng's number—the red number written on all the phones. A new phone, it took several seconds to patch itself through. Finally, at 11:15 pm he finally got a hold of Comrade Feng, who was in his office on the 18th floor of the smaller headquarters building.

"Feng, I apologize that I have not been in contact with you," said Wang into the mouthpiece, "but I dropped my old phone earlier this afternoon and it took me several hours to realize that it was broken."

"Comrade Wang, I don't know where to start. We have had battles everywhere," replied Feng, totally stressed and frustrated.

"Did the aircraft land, Feng?"

"Yes, Comrade, they are on the ground. They landed in America an hour ago. Twelve hours ago, I tried to call the termination squads at JFK, and the man who spoke was totally drunk. He shouted at me and told me not to disturb him, and I couldn't understand why they had been drinking. That's why I wanted to call you."

"The men clearing the runway were drunk?" asked Wang, his mouth open, and again his face was white with worry.

"The men were totally drunk! Next, Comrade, Comrade Deng was attacked by two old World War II military aircraft. They were hit with machine guns and rockets in Alabama," continued Comrade Feng.

"How could that happen?" asked Wang. "How could somebody know first of all that Deng was an enemy, and second, that Deng was in the middle of a state like Alabama? Are they continuing, Feng?"

"I lost contact with them. I've tried to contact them as well as Bo Lee Tang, but with no luck," continued Feng.

"How could the Americans know that Deng was traveling towards North Carolina? Could Bo Lee Tang be captured? Has he told the Americans about Deng?" And then realization hit him so hard that the knot that had sat in his stomach for a couple of days rose upwards, and he swallowed hard, trying to keep the bile down. He suddenly remembered that voice. It wasn't Bo Lee Tang! It wasn't Bo Lee Tang's voice, because his was deeper. It was a voice from the past—the voice of his nephew Lee Wang. Lee Wang wasn't dead. He must have survived the termination attempt in Salt Lake City. Lee Wang was alive and dangerous. Wang felt sick and moved to the side of the ship, hearing Feng ask him if he was still there. "Give me a second, Feng, I need to figure this out," he replied, his face sickly white. He knew his life had somehow suddenly lost its remaining usefulness to the cause.

"I have more problems, Comrade," Feng continued unabated. "I have seen transponders off the coast of Japan and

Korea. Someone is flying aircraft in the middle of the ocean."

"North Korea," replied Wang, still reeling over the first news.

"Of course, the North Koreans are flying raids into American bases. They must be. I'm sure they are destroying everything American they can find. There are at least five or six American

Air Force bases within bombing range of North Korea."

"I agree, Comrade," answered Feng, "but the last transponders were over the China Sea coming from South Korea to here in China—directly towards Nanjing and Shanghai. There were four transponders traveling at 300 miles an hour."

"How long ago was this?" asked Wang.

"About thirty minutes ago, Comrade," Feng replied. "I have also received the most puzzling news from JFK Airport in New York. It seems that the chairman himself is overseeing the disembarkation of troops at the American airport. One of our pilots called in on their phone to tell me that the chairman had arrived in his private jet and was controlling the refueling and unloading of the cargo from the transporter. How can he be there? Isn't he with you?"

"Of course he is here with us. I saw him just 30 minutes ago," replied Wang, disbelieving what he was hearing. It was all too much to take in at one time. His mind was becoming blank. He was getting a brain freeze and was unable to give orders. "Where are you now?" Wang asked Feng.

"I'm in my office in the new building looking at my screen. I have a full team of 20 men on the 29th floor control center watching every screen and answering any calls to back me up," Feng answered.

"Hang up," Wang ordered. "Feng, give me five minutes to get back to the chairman. Then call him on his phone and tell him that he is in New York. I want you to find out where he really is, and then I want you to get back to the control center and tell all the pilots and soldiers at the American airport that they have been infiltrated and to shoot everybody, even our drunken termination squads—everybody who did not fly in with the aircraft to New York. I want that airport secure, understand?"

He hung up, wanting to be sick over the side. He did not have time, however, as he quickly made his way back to the party.

It was in full swing when he got there. It didn't look like anybody had missed him. The chairman was looking over some maps with the admiral when the chairman's satellite phone suddenly rang. It was set on a very shrill and loud tone—a tone only the chairman had so it would be clear whose phone was being called. The room quieted instantly as the chairman, rather shocked that his phone was actually ringing, put his hand up for silence. He answered the phone and put the phone on speaker and back down on the dining table so that the room could listen.

"Comrade Feng, this is Chairman Chunqiao. You are on speaker phone and talking to the whole Politburo. What is your problem?"

"*Comrade Chairman, I need to speak with you privately, please,*" Feng begged.

"There is nothing that can't be told to all of our members," the chairman replied. "We are all one now, and our destiny cannot be changed. Where are you calling from, Feng?"

"*I'm in my office in Building Two, Comrade Chairman.*"

"Why are you calling me from your office and not your station on the 29th floor of the control center, Comrade Feng?" the chairman asked.

"*We are getting so many reports coming in, Comrade Chairman. I have a full staff of 20 operators manning every computer terminal, and I'm using the one in my office that oversees everything.*"

"And Comrade Wang was worried that there were no communications," smirked the chairman, looking over at Wang, who was motionless in his chair and sporting a sickly-looking face. "So Feng, what is so important that you call me in the middle of the night?"

"*Aircraft transponders and a second problem in New York, Comrade Chairman,*" continued Feng. "*For the last several hours, there has been a lot of aircraft activity over Japan and South Korea.*"

"Of course there is," laughed the chairman. "North Koreans are killing Americans for us. They will destroy over 500 useless aircraft and 10,000 American soldiers around the American bases in Japan and South Korea. I'm sure that the North Korean pilots are enjoying themselves, having the upper hand on two world powers at the same time."

"I agree, but the latest four transponders are coming towards our mainland and directly towards Nanjing. We saw them 50 miles off our coast 20 minutes ago, and they were heading away from Korea and into China."

"They can only be Chinese fighters or bombers returning to the mainland," answered the chairman, beginning to get angry. "Why would North Korean aircraft be coming towards Nanjing, except...." And then he thought for a second. "It is not possible that North Korea would attack Zedong Electronics, Feng. That is ridiculous! What was the other problem about New York?"

"The other problem was you, yourself, Comrade Chairman," continued Feng. *"Comrade Chairman, you were..."* and the listeners heard a massive explosion come through the line—so loud that everyone in the room could hear it.

"Feng! Feng! What is happening?" shouted the chairman into the phone, picking it up and taking it off speaker so he alone could hear.

"We are being attacked!" shouted Feng. *"I can see the large building out of my window! It is exploding like I've never seen before! It sounds like rockets are going off inside the building! I'm by the window and I saw an aircraft light up a second ago. It was a big one—a bomber, I think,"* he managed to say before there was another massive explosion and then a third one, and the men could still hear the noise even though the phone wasn't on speaker anymore. Comrade Wang sank into his seat.

"Comrade Feng, who is attacking us?" demanded Chairman Chunqiao, shouting into the phone, extremely angry and perplexed. He needed to know immediately.

"I don't know, Comrade Chairman!" Feng shouted back, the explosions continuing in the background. *"I think it can only be North Korean bombers, or the Chinese bombers you said were returning, Comrade Chairman."* Feng's voice suddenly rose to a high-pitched shout. *"They are starting to bomb this building; they are now shooting at my building. I can see*

a bomber, I can see a bomber, it is… Aaaaaagh!" There was the sound of a massive explosion before the phone went dead in the chairman's hand—the beep, beep sound of the other end losing telephone contact.

"How dare they attack us!" the chairman yelled, putting down the phone and looking at the people around him. "We give our allies the best opportunity to join us and destroy their enemy and they turn on us like a pack of dogs!"

"Who is turning on us, Comrade Chairman?" asked Wang, deeply skeptical that the chairman knew the correct answer.

"It must be the North Koreans," he replied, reaching for the fourth red button and pushing it without hesitation.

This button shut down every electronic system in Zedong Electronics' allied countries. Just like the rest of the world, every civilian, military, and government machine using an electronic-control system went off the air within 30 seconds. The termination frequency was relayed to the parts, or whole electrical units in the millions of electronic parts especially made and sold to these countries.

In North Korea, the lights went out; the highly sophisticated electronics aboard its newest guns, tanks, and the dozens of aircraft bombing the northern areas of South Korea went silent and hundreds of new explosions rocked the area as many of their aircraft hit the earth. Even the young North Korean Premier's plane with him aboard on its way to the front to inspect the damage they had done to the dying South Korean troops defending their territory went down.

The same happened in Iran. Their entire air force was airborne, bombing and fighting American and NATO military bases in Iraq and the surrounding countries. They all dropped like flies as their lights went off and machines of all types stopped working. It was the same in Pakistan, Afghanistan, and the Sudan. The rapid shutdown of the rest of the developed world very quickly came and went.

"Does anybody think that our own government could not be behind suggesting to the North Koreans that attacking us was in their best interest?" asked Chairman Chunqiao to the group of shocked men. Wang, still wanting to be sick, could not move.

"Why would North Korea attack us? We have given them a share of world domination with us. Why would they attack us, without somebody suggesting it to them or offering them a better deal?"

"Why would North Korea attack us, Comrade Chairman?" asked Mo Wang, looking straight at Chairman Chunqiao. "Why would our own government attack us? They are already on their knees due to us cutting off their military strength. They are already like a vassal state to us and would do anything we asked of them. I believe somehow the Americans are behind this. I believe that with all the uprising in America against our termination squads, Comrade Chairman, I can't even communicate with over 50% of our teams. I believe America has somehow attacked us."

The chairman pondered Comrade Wang's answer for several moments, and then looked up and around at every table. "Wang, give me the phone number of the pilots of the aircraft leaving New York. If they do not respond, then I might believe that you are on the right track. If they do respond, then I want to hear that both aircraft are in the air and on their way back to China. What are the phone numbers for both aircraft?"

Comrade Wang looked at a long list of numbers he kept in a red pocketbook in his shirt pocket and gave the numbers to the chairman. The first number he stated aloud was the one for the transporter 747—the more important aircraft. Chairman Chunqiao got a quick answer from the pilot. "Are you on your way back to Shanghai?"

"*Yes, Comrade Chairman,*" replied the pilot, suddenly sitting up straight in his seat. "*We are an hour out of New York and bound directly north for our secret landing location. No, there are no problems with our 747,*" he added, puzzled why the chairman was phoning him so quickly after they had seen him in New York just an hour earlier. "*Unfortunately, the other aircraft is having a minor fuel problem,*" the pilot reported. "*The pilot said that he was having fuel starvation at high altitude a few minutes ago and he has descended his aircraft down to 20,000 feet. We can* see him on radar about five miles behind us and he is still with us. *The pilot believes that the problem is sorting itself out the lower he goes. He will stay at 20,000 feet until the problem clears itself, Comrade Chairman. We think it is just dirty fuel from New York and that he will ascend and join me in an hour or two. There is no need for concern and I will update you if you wish, Comrade Chairman."*

"Don't call me, call Comrade Wang. Do you have his number?" asked the chairman. Wang also nodded to the chairman that he did and the chairman terminated the call and put the phone down. He explained to the whole group what the pilot had said to him and then looked at each member.

"Comrade Wang," he stated as his eyes fixed on the man he was beginning to blame for all his problems. "I understand your concern. The aircraft are fine and there were no problems in New York. That means our termination squads cleared the runway, our troops landed, and nothing was out of place. I honestly believe you are beating the wrong horse, Comrade. How are Americans coming halfway across the world to bomb our headquarters? How could they even know we exist? It's absolutely impossible. You disappoint me, Comrade Wang. The Americans get panicked, the shutdown closes down the whole country—everything. They don't even know who formulated the attack. The Americans and the Europeans can only think it's the Russian or Chinese governments, or maybe North Korea or Iran. They could never think it was a conglomerate of private electrical companies here in China. And you want to tell me that with all their satellites destroyed, they fly like angels across the world and accurately destroy our headquarters, a building that they don't even know exists? Wang, this is real life, not an

American Hollywood film production." "But…" started Comrade Wang.

"I don't want to hear any more. I think we should vote on this issue immediately," continued the chairman. "We have sixteen votes on this table. Gentlemen, who here believes the Americans are to blame for the destruction of our headquarters?" Only Comrade Wang put his hand up.

"Who believes it was a country we have just terminated by me pushing the fourth button two minutes ago?" the chairman asked. Ten members put up their hands. "Who believes that our headquarters was destroyed by Chinese fighters, or bombers belonging to either of the two Chinese governments?" Three people put up their hands. "Who believes that foreign aircraft were used, but they were assisted or ordered to by people in our own Chinese government?" Twelve members put up their hands. "Good, I believe that I agree with the 12 members of this Politburo and blame our own allies and our own government for this attack on our world sovereignty."

Comrade Wang's phone went off again, and the chairman, tired of this man's continuing interference, asked him to either turn it or leave the room. Wang knew what was going to happen and, much to the dismay of his Politburo colleagues, got up, bowed, stated his apologies to the chairman, and left the room.

"I have a bad feeling about Comrade Wang," the chairman confessed to the group after the door closed behind Wang. "I do not think he can take the pressure of his position, and I think we should bring the number in here down to 15. Gentlemen, how many of you believe that it is time to conquer the whole world and take everybody out of the picture? If I press the fifth button, nothing except our 35 aircraft, our five naval ships, our three satellites, our 500 cell phones—of which 250 are already in America and Europe—our ten container ships, and an unnamed area north of here will still be operational in the whole world.

"Gentlemen, if I press the fifth button, we are either going to control the world, or we will die trying. There is no going back, except to pick up the Chinese pieces in a year or so and turn the billions of humans worldwide who have survived into workers for our new world. How many of you vote to press the fifth button?" Everybody put up their hand.

The chairman took a key out from his right trouser pocket, opened the lock to the fifth button and, again without hesitation, pushed it once and closed the lid. It was done. The rest of China shut down. Everything still powered up around Shanghai and Nanjing and the surrounding areas where the hundreds of companies had produced the products for Zedong Electronics shut down. The Zedong Electronics universities, their training facilities on the island, the production plants, everything apart from Shanghai Pudong Airport and the Shanghai docks shut down and went dark.

"And our final decision before we open some fresh, cold bottles of champagne, gentlemen," continued the chairman. "I understand Comrade Wang has been a good, hard-working member of our organization. He has done well and should always be remembered for his dedication to our cause. I would like a vote on this matter. How many believe that he is not strong enough for his position and should be relieved of duty?"

Eight men put up their hands—the ones who always agreed with the chairman and the ones the chairman could always count on. "Last, do we terminate Comrade Wang and his knowledge about our operation immediately, or shall we simply demote Comrade Wang into a lower position and maybe have the man fill ex-Comrade Feng's old communications position and allow him to continue to be an asset to us? Raise your left hand for immediate termination, or your right hand for demotion out of the Politburo. Please vote now."

This time, nine men voted with their right hands and five with their left hands. The chairman jotted notes about who raised which hand, and then got up and walked over to the wall to personally open a bottle of champagne in an ice bucket. "Good. I like the vote. Comrade Wang is a good man and I have always treated him as a friend. I will personally tell him the news in the morning. Let's enjoy our newfound freedom. Gentlemen, we now own the whole world, and nobody can stop us."

All 15 men began opening the rest of the dozen cold bottles together. Wang was forgotten, and for the next several hours they toasted themselves and their newfound dominance. It was a joyous occasion as the ships steamed away from a dark and cold Asia, and the humans aboard the ships didn't care. They were going south, down to the warmth of the equator.

* * *

Comrade Wang was unhappy. He knew that they were going to push the fifth button, and he was already on the phone trying to find Lee Wang.

Chapter 14

Z-Day +7 – The Beginning of the Second Week

EXACTLY ONE WEEK AFTER THE beginning of the year, North America was racked by the coldest weather seen in many in a long time. Frozen wind gusts blew snow into piles, covering everything in its path. Temperatures hovered between zero and -35 in places for days on end. Roads that were normally cleared and passable disappeared. Even small buildings were totally covered, especially where lake effect snow was in abundance.

For many who were still alive, the drifting snow kept away the wind chill, and people huddled in groups, covering themselves with everything warm they could find. In many places, they went out to chop more wood for the fireplaces, now the most important place in people's homes. Here, people stayed warm and cooked coffee and food pulled out of freezers in the other parts of the house. They slept around the fire, which burned continuously day and night. Fuel was abundant, since many American houses were built with wood, and it was plentiful from other houses where people didn't have a fireplace and were either long gone or frozen.

Many millions had died, mostly due to the freezing conditions, but many also had fallen to thugs and gangs stealing and killing anyone who had stockpiles of food. The cities were the worst hit. The only place for warmth was in basements where fires were started with wood from the local parks or furniture that was chopped up from various apartments in the buildings. Others died asphyxiated from carbon dioxide poisoning, not understanding the mechanics of survival.

The laws of survival were a forgotten art for many Americans who had depended wholly on the "system" to supply them with everything they needed—even information seemingly unimportant in a situation like this. In the cities, this lack of survival instinct was worse than in the country, where stockpiles of supplies were more abundant and anybody with a little creativity could keep themselves alive.

Gang violence in the north was curtailed for the time being by the weather, wind chill, and snowdrifts, making it difficult to move about. People became reclusive, staying in one place and living off what they had. Once that ran out, there was nothing else to eat, except the frozen bodies outside.

In more southern areas, life was a bit warmer, but the incidence of violence and the killing of innocent people climbed drastically as folks became more aware of what they had to do to survive.

It was either kill or be killed, in a country where gang-related violence was the norm before the beginning of the end. Many of the stores, now with doors missing or hanging open, were empty or full of products unnecessary for human survival. Many people still had a store of food—the hoarders, the conspiracy theorists, and the rich. Freezers were still cold in the southern areas, but the produce was beginning to thaw and many were cooking the thawing food to halt the decaying process for a week or two. Many had looted cans of food, which would keep them going for a while, and rural communities had animals to kill and eat if marauding gangs didn't steal them first.

As Chairman Chunqiao had correctly predicted, humans became their most feared enemy in terms of their own survival, and there was nothing hungry and cold people would not do to ensure their continued habitation on Earth, even if it was only for one more day.

After the first week, the longest week modern civilization had ever known ended; over 100 million people in North America alone had perished.

***

The 100 engineers under guard in the terminal at JFK were given two opportunities—either work for the American people or be left to the wrath of the American people. They decided to work. All their satellite phones were bagged and taken to McGuire Air Force Base, the new command center, and then each Chinese engineer with their Air Force engineer chaperone started going through the equipment unloaded out of the 747 transporter. Most of the parts were designed to repair the movement of electricity. It seemed to be a major flaw in the Zedong Electronics plan. It was fine to send in new parts that actually worked, but they were not much use without the electrical power grid, and billions of parts would be needed to get the North American power grid working again.

Generators were sought after, and small mobile electricity makers were needed by the millions. The only engines of any sorts still working were old carburetor-fed combustion engines. Any engines with carburetors and no management systems—from a small push lawnmower to an old truck engine—would run for a long time. All the engine needed was fuel, and there was tons of that around. With 90% of all North American vehicles sitting useless somewhere, there was a lot of fuel to go around for the rest.

Once again, the problem was electricity. Most gas stations needed electricity to pump the fuel out from their underground storage tanks. Therefore, it took an engineering degree to figure out how to produce the electricity to pump out the fuel needed to feed the electricity, and so on. It was a vicious circle, but easily done with the use of a combustion engine, or large deep-cycle battery, or solar and wind powered electrical systems that most governments had thought unimportant until now. Civilization would take 20 or even 30 years—a whole generation—to get human life on the planet back to the safe and comfortable lifestyle everyone was used to.

Major Patterson and his crew were airlifted back to McGuire to rest, or so they thought. They had done their job well, and fresh troops were airlifted into all four New York airports by helicopter, with the two large helicopters bringing in small bulldozers hanging from the strong underbelly hooks. They were destined to clear the snow off the runways so that the aircraft could come in and deliver more troops.

Once the bulldozers were in, the area was checked for any vehicles in the many parking garages around the airports. Airport parking garages were usually full of motor vehicles, and they searched for anything that would start. The ones that worked were driven out to the areas of the airport where engineers went about using all the power inverters they could find to turn the engines into mobile generators to light and heat critical areas. Over 70 vehicles were found in the JFK garages alone—mostly old American cars with large gas guzzling engines perfect for generating electricity.

It took two car engines to power up the landing-light system on the already cleared runway. The system was fed from the motor vehicles into a large inverter they brought in from McGuire which fed raw energy to the lights themselves and cut out all malfunctioning electronic-control systems. It took several hours of modernizing the electronics, but the lights came on when someone started the cars stationed at each end of the long runway. Now equipment could be carried into JFK at night.

One large car engine could run several small electrical heating units, blowers, and electrical bar heaters found in stores. The Air Force flew these in by the hundreds. A second car engine could run the terminal lighting systems, and any available propane tanks could get the stoves working in the terminal's restaurants and feed the workers.

By the end of Day Eight, JFK was lit and semi-heated so people could work and sleep. Military camp beds had been brought in and porta-potties dotted the outside areas next to the walls of the terminals, inconspicuous and hidden from anyone landing.

The aircraft themselves changed inside. Several teams pulled out the seats and made them into living quarters where less lighting and heating were needed to make them warm and comfortable. A beautifully painted Qantas 747 became a warm, cozy home with fully stocked kitchens and bars for 100 people, once the unnecessary seats had been placed in warehouses out of the view of anyone flying in unannounced.

The five bulldozers worked 24 hours a day. Snow hadn't fallen for a day now, and JFK's runways were still clear, but the other three airports could hardly be seen under the snowdrifts. Only white shapes in the snow, aircraft wrapped in heavy layers of frozen precipitation and the snowbound terminals showed the outline where runways hid under feet of winter weather. The large lifting helicopters moved the bulldozers into La Guardia and soldiers began clearing its main runway.

Once the bulldozers had been moved, men again went in search of old vehicles in the parking garages, got inside, and hotwired them. They were driven outside the garage towers where the helicopters picked them up and carried them over snowdrifts and placed them where the engineers needed them. It would take 24 hours to clean the runway, and the same would be necessary for Teterboro Airport, which was next. Newark would be last. Teterboro would be the deployment airport for troops into the other three airports when needed, and all seven of the operational troop-carrying C-130s could ferry in 100 troops each at a time to wherever they were needed.

The third job of the always-working helicopters was then to bring in food and supplies for the troops and an ever-growing number of locals who had seen or heard the action. Once the runways were cleared, the C-130s flew in from Air Force bases that had warehouses full of stored meals for the overseas troops, and they were flying in 5,000 meals at a time on pallets. There were only five C-130s available for this work since the other two were down in North Carolina doing the same thing, but they started hauling 25,000 meals per day into the four airports and the supplies were stored in the empty hangars.

By the third day of work, the bulldozers were working on Newark's runway. With the increased activity at the airports, children began to venture out foraging for food and pushing their faces up to the high security fences to beg the armed soldiers stationed around the perimeter for anything edible. It would take an entire week to get the airports ready for the incoming attack before they could even start on the harbor area. Between that work and distributing food, the troops were working 24-hour shifts.

Carlos and Lee were exhausted. They had worked nearly 20 hours a day for several days in a row, and in a few days there would be renewed satellite phone communications around the world. The stolen 747 had flown into McGuire Air Force Base at 9:00 am that morning, as had all the important electrical equipment being airlifted in from JFK.

Once the small pallet of remaining new phones had been off-loaded and opened, Carlos and Lee started a phone directory file on the computer, listing the numbers for distribution to all the phone users to ensure that nobody spoke to the enemy by mistake.

Both Carlos and Lee had an operational Commodore computer linked up to be able to log in all the numbers, and a really old black and white printer that could print copies, and they issued the first phone number list for transfer with the HC-130 tanker being refueled for its world trip. Each phone—all 25 of them that now had an international delivery destination, as well as another 50 for the Air Force bases around the country—were recorded on the list. Each phone was numbered, and its projected destination was typed onto the sheet. Another 20 phones were added as extras, and blanks were added where the new owners' names could be written in. The list would be updated once the aircraft returned from deliveries.

Carlos had prepared ten phones for the 747's first flight over to Europe. Six were for the Air Force bases in Europe. The first two phones were for the commanders at Ramstein and Spangdahlem Air Bases in Germany, and a third for Aviano in Italy. The two Air Force bases in Britain, Mildenhall and Lakenheath were to be issued one each, and the sixth one was for Incirlik Air Base in Turkey. Another four were reserved for front-line battle commanders in Iraq.

The first HC-130 fuel tanker, the one General Allen had loaned to Preston, flew in from the North Carolina airfield and was being refueled to take a satellite phone over to Lajes Air Base in the Azores. From the Azores, and with its extended range, the plan was to fly her directly into Turkey or Baghdad and help ferry a platoon of troops at a time from the front lines into one of the safer bases.

Very few items were needed overseas, but several 5,000-watt military generators, a complete field hospital, and 1,000 gallons of gasoline in five-gallon canisters were loaded aboard the 747, as well as blankets, beds, and anything else anybody thought might be needed over there. Carlos, studying the world's weather two hours after receiving the phones, printed out three copies of the world's weather on a flat printed map of the earth—exactly what was being transmitted onto his simple screen—and then gathered the phones for the 747.

Each phone and a charger had already been packed up into a plastic Ziploc bag with the new owner's name on it, and Carlos headed out to the giant Air China 747 sitting on the runway and saw that the fuel tankers were already clearing themselves away from the aircraft. He climbed up the steel stairway to the front of the aircraft and went in.

A guard of six fully armed men would stay with the aircraft throughout its journey. They had already gotten comfortable in the first class area. Seats had already been made into beds and it was weird to see a machine gun, rocket launchers, and cases of ammo ready for use in the aisle of the very luxurious aircraft.

The Air Force pilots were waiting for him. They were handed their own satellite phone, and Carlos could guide them if weather was going to be an issue. Right now, the only weather issue was in Germany, where it looked like a snowstorm was blanketing the area north of the Alps. Carlos had several timed prints of satellite photos for them showing the last 24 hours of the storm's movement.

Since they were heading straight into Ramstein, the runways were expected to be clear, but they had more than enough fuel to fly into Aviano, Italy, if the weather closed the two central German bases. From there, the jumbo jet was to hand over the satellite phones for further distribution with the HC-130 which would arrive 12 hours later. Once the phones were distributed, more accurate weather conditions could be relayed to pilots from the bases they were flying into.

In the last 12 hours, Lee had worked on getting a dozen old-fashioned military mobile radio beacons working again and had been waiting for parts to be brought in on the transporter. Many of the old military mobile beacons were in metal containers about three feet square and two feet high and could be moved around on a forklift with a small generator inside the unit as its power source. Much like a normal radio frequency, an aircraft's radio could look for the beacon's transmitting noise and then home in on the location where the beacon originated. These units were sent mostly into forward areas with dirt airstrips to bring in supplies. Due to the electrical outage, these simple and antiquated directional systems were the only choice available, and the 747 was about to be loaded with six of these units in her cargo hold.

The HC-130 bound for Hawaii, and Japan would have another six aboard in an hour or two, and once these were distributed, any aircraft would be able to direct its autopilot onto the homing beacon from up to 1,000 miles out.

Carlos and Lee were happy to finally see the 747 take off at midday on the eighth day, fully fueled but still very empty for such a large aircraft. She turned eastwards and headed out over the Atlantic for Europe and the Middle East. They had realized that the massive aircraft, light on luggage, could bring back more than 750 troops at a time, and it would take at least 24 hours for every round trip.

It was 1 a.m. in China, and an hour after the attack in Nanjing, when General Allen called Carlos, giving him the good news: the attack had gone well. Mrs. Wang had showed them the right buildings, and thanks to her, the Zedong Electronics headquarters was now a pile of broken rubble. He had also seen the lights in Nanjing go out.

Carlos told him that the whole of the rest of the world had gone dark, including North Korea, Iran, and even the entire area the general was flying out of several minutes after the actual attack time.

There were several small areas of lights to his south, around a Shanghai airport and the city's harbor area, he believed. He had seen a faint light of the fires in Nanjing on the screen a few minutes earlier, but had left to deliver the radios to the 747, which had just taken off for Ramstein.

"*Carlos, ask Lee to use one of the satellite phones and call the red number. I want to see if that number is still operating,*" instructed the general. Lee did, and after several seconds an engaged tone was heard by Carlos and he relayed the information. "*I've been thinking about our upcoming attack,*" continued the general. "*Carlos, please hand Lee the phone.*"

"Harrow, Mr. Allen Key," said Lee into the phone.

"*Hallo, Lee. Your wife is okay and asleep at the rear of the aircraft. I'm heading into Beijing and should be in the area in about an hour. I was thinking about these 747 aircraft. Where do you think Zedong Electronics has them stationed?*"

"It can only be Shanghai Pudong International Airport, Mr. Allen Key. There are two airports in Shanghai, but Pudong is further out of the city and I would think that they have them all at this airport ready to carry the Red Guards into New York. There are two very faint lights in that area—the only ones left in the whole world."

"*How many aircraft does Air China own, Lee?*" asked the general.

"*Civilian aircraft are not my specialty.*"

"I don't know for sure, but they must have a lot of the 747s like the Air China one that left a few minutes ago. Also, they have purchased some of the big new European ones in the last couple of years, Mr. Allen Key," Lee replied.

"*Thank you, Lee. Please hand me back to Carlos.*" Lee did.

"*Carlos, I want you to cancel that flight—the HC-130 flight into the Azores and then Turkey,*" stated the general. "*You still have the marines at McGuire? The ones who arrived from North Carolina an hour or so ago? Also, are there two Chinese-speaking pilots, Captains Wong and Chong? They were with Joe Patterson in JFK. I need to speak to the chief of the Marine detachment, Patterson, the two Chinese-speaking pilots, and the crew of the HC-130 immediately.*"

"I'll call you back in ten minutes, Pete," replied Carlos.

Carlos gave orders to three men standing by, ready to help him at any point, and they ran off to go and get the personnel the general wanted. This gave the general, a pretty fast thinker in his old age, a few minutes to work out a beauty of a plan. Joe Patterson's brave actions at JFK had given him a fantastic idea. They were still waiting for Major Patterson and the two Chinese pilots when a soldier returned and told them that they would be several more minutes. Carlos told the soldier to go out to the aircraft and stand by. He also phoned General Allen back and told him about Lee repairing the 12 mobile beacon units, and that six were already on their way to Europe and the Middle East. General Allen was ecstatic, and thanked Lee profusely for the idea. It made his day to know that a real plan was coming together in his absence and that also, within a couple of days, international flying could be made safer and easier for the pilots. Carlos then told him that a radio beacon was already operating at McGuire as of 20 minutes ago, gave him the frequency, and told him that there were still another three they were working on. The general reckoned that there must be dozens of them in Europe, and told Lee to get several of the necessary parts loaded with the Air Force engineers going to Hawaii and Japan. Lee told him that he could have another two ready within the hour, and the general ordered him to get them placed into the HC-130 he was about to have the meeting about.

"Good day, gentlemen," the general started as Carlos put the phone on speaker 10 minutes later once everybody had arrived from different places on the large base. *"First of all, Marine Lieutenant Smith, well done down in North Carolina! You guys did a fantastic job, and I have an even more exciting mission for you. Major Patterson, well done again. Captains Wong and Chong, you are to be commended. Actually, all of you will be recommended for a promotion once we have won this thing. A luncheon with the president is certainly in the cards in the not-too-distant future. Lieutenant Smith, can you get 24 parachutes from your base in North Carolina, and are you all parachute trained for low-level insertion?"*

"My entire platoon is well-trained, sir, and yes, we can get chutes at Camp Lejeune," the lieutenant replied.

"Good. Captains Wong and Chong, have you completed parachute training?" the general asked.

"Yes, but just basic training and the minimum amount of jumps needed," Captain Wong replied.

"The crew of the HC-130, are you there?" the general asked.

"Yes sir, Captain Pierce here," the commander of the aircraft answered.

"Captain Pierce, what is the range of your 130 if you take her up fully fueled with a payload of 5,000 pounds, bleed all the tanker fuel into your tanks and instead of refueling another aircraft you refuel yourself? If I'm right, you can increase your range to 6,800 miles?"

"In that configuration, and depending on cruise speed and altitude, I think we could do more than that. I reckon on closer to 7,000 miles, sir. Maximum range is 4,500 miles, plus 2,000 miles of tanker fuel, plus a reduced cruise of 330 miles an hour at maximum altitude; 32,000 feet," Captain Pierce replied.

"The 747 flights into JFK came in from the east, but I bet they went over the polar route to get here. Am I right, Captain Wong? You flew the 747 back here to McGuire, right?" asked the general.

"Yes, sir. We had already turned north 30 minutes out of U.S. international airspace at 32,000 feet to head over the polar route and in the direction of China when we left the transporter and 'crashed' due to fuel starvation," Captain Wong replied.

"This is crazy, but listen to my plan," continued the general. "I believe that the 130 can get you over the polar icecap to Osan, South Korea. The flight will be about 6,800 miles. If necessary, you can go in early at Misawa, Japan, which will be around 200 to 300 miles shorter. Carlos can help you navigate. Take the two repaired mobile beacons Lee has repaired with you, and I will give you instructions as to where to leave them once I get to where I'm going. I want as many pilots and co-pilots who can fly 747s or Airbus 380s as you can fill into the back of the 130.

"All the new and modern aircraft are the same to fly in the long run. Captain Pierce, you will have enough pilots in your back seat to help you get there. Refuel in Osan or Misawa and go low into Shanghai Pudong International Airport. I hope to be there to fly in with you. It's imperative that all the men who can fit in the back of the C-130 are able to parachute out. They will do so at low level a mile or so away from the airport. You can take all the old satellite photos and maps of the area around Pudong in our classified files that you need to finalize your attack plan while in the air. Under the command of Lieutenant Smith, I want you to infiltrate the airport. You should find dozens of beautiful aircraft, and I'm sure they will be fully fueled and ready to go. Beware; there could be thousands of soldiers in the area ready for deployment into New York in a week or two. I want you to fly out as many aircraft as you can. If they are not refueled, fly them into Osan. Even an unrefueled 747 could fly as far as South Korea on reserves. If they are full of fuel, then fly them straight to our base in Turkey.

"Now, the mission will be dangerous and will take as many pilots as you can fit to help fly the aircraft out of there. I reckon there are up to 30 aircraft waiting for us. Even a set of Chinese pilots flying the aircraft with three marines itching to shoot their nuts off should want them to get airborne and give us another few planes. Captain Pierce, you will drop them in at less than 1,000 feet and then you are out of there if I'm not around, understood?"

Everybody agreed to a plan that would be finalized in the air.

"You guys need to get going, because I'm going to hang around this area, and I hope to be over Pudong with our three rearmed gunships in case you need help. One more thing, guys. I don't believe the Red Army, or the Red Guards, or whatever they call themselves, will shoot at the 747s while they are taxiing for takeoff. Shooting their own aircraft will piss off their boss and destroy their only way to get to New York. Major Patterson, Captain Wong, we'll need you to do your 'Supreme Commander' thing again."

"Yes, sir," both men replied, smiling broadly.

"You guys prepare. Patterson, get an aircraft immediately down to North Carolina to pick up the parachutes and get them back to McGuire. Actually, Carlos, call up Preston and get Buck in the DC-3 to pick up 30 parachutes and reserves from Camp Lejeune and fly them up to you at McGuire. That will save you an hour. You should be on the ground in China in 24 hours, which gives me enough time to see Beijing and hopefully Moscow before flying back to Osan and meeting up with you. Now go!" The men left.

"Carlos, I'm going to put on transponders and leave them on. I don't want to go into a foreign country's capital without warning them, if they can see me."

Carlos watched as four transponders began blinking on the screen a second later. The general was 100 miles south of the capital of China, and he still hadn't seen one aircraft other than the three around him.

* * *

General Allen flew into Beijing Capital International Airport an hour later. It was three in the morning, and the airport was dark and quiet. They had found the main runway through infra-red scanners, and they did a sweep over the runway surface with landing lights, noticing thin patches of ice here and there, but mostly dry asphalt. They did not have much information on the airport. It wasn't one the Air Force frequented, and Google was not available, so they couldn't just pull up what they wanted.

The three gunships went into a wide arc flying low over the main city, hoping to attract attention, and then flew out a couple of miles and turned into long finals. With the main runway far ahead of them in the dark, the general turned on all their lights, again trying to grab attention, and the fourth aircraft with its lights on was circling above the runway guiding them in. They landed without a problem. One gunship reversed back to the beginning of the runway, and the other two taxied to the other end so that there were lights on either end for the tanker to land.

Once they were all on the ground, they formed up behind *Ghost Rider* and looked for a place to park. The nearest terminal, full of Air China aircraft, looked the best. It was weird to see a terminal with every one of its bays full with aircraft. The Chinese had certainly known about the pending event, and Pete wondered if any of the aircraft were flyable.

They parked in a line behind a couple of older Air China 747s and brought their engines to a stop. There was no welcoming committee, and the general donned a winter coat. With two pilots carrying carbines, they stretched their legs and walked across to the empty terminal with flashlights. It was totally shut down and there were no lights anywhere. The general climbed the ladder up a moveable walkway to the terminal and opened the door. It was unlocked, as was the door to an Air China 747.

He walked in with his flashlight and found his way to the flight deck. He pushed several buttons, which in normal operation would have given him a response, but this aircraft was as dead as the rest around the world. He walked out and down the ladder in time to see an old army jeep with its lights on pull up to the aircraft, guns pointing from both sides. The 20mm Gatling guns in *Easy Girl* had already swiveled and were pointing directly at the jeep, which was several yards away from *Ghost Rider,* and its four occupants.

General Allen, with his general's star shining brightly, walked up to the jeep and stated "American Air Force" to the four men, who turned their rifles onto him. "Does anybody speak English?" he asked to non-comprehending stares. Two men got out of the jeep. He stared directly at the highest-ranking man, who looked like a lieutenant or a captain. General Allen shouted out to anyone in *Ghost Rider* to bring out Mrs. Wang. The Chinese soldier didn't really know what to do, but he saw the insignia on the general's coat and snapped to attention. The rest followed suit. Rank was, after all, rank.

Mrs. Wang timidly came out of the aircraft and walked over to stand next to General Allen.

"Mrs. Wang, please tell them that we are on a peaceful mission around the world to find out if everybody is in this unfortunate condition, and that we want to find out who is to blame for this madness. Tell them that I come directly from the President of the United States and have a message for their Head of State," explained the general.

Mrs. Wang translated and waited for a response. The soldiers discussed the situation among themselves and the two still seated in the jeep prepared to drive off.

"Before they leave, Mrs. Wang, I need permission to refuel my four aircraft. I can do it myself, I only need their permission and the closest outlet pipe or a fuel tanker."

Again she rapidly spoke to the men. They pointed to an old fuel tanker, gave her a rapid reply, the two men got back in and then they all drove off.

"They said to wait and that they would give your message to the government in Beijing 20 kilometers away. It will take them one or two hours to get back, and by that time, it should be dawn," Mrs. Wang told him. "They said that all of Beijing was dark and they thought it was the Americans who had turned off the lights. You can help yourselves to any fuel you can find. He stated that he thought that the fuel pumps don't work."

General Allen shouted orders for the lights of the aircraft to be turned on, and the nearest cover underneath the dark wing of the 747 in front of them was opened to connect them to the underground fuel pipes. The HC-130 tanker, with two of her engines running again, started her transfer pump and got in as close to the rear of the 747 as possible and then pipes were run from her to the underground system. If the storage tanks were close by, then she could suck the fuel out of them, but if the storage tanks were far away, she had no chance. Much of the piping and fuel worked on a gravity-feed system assisted by electric pumps, and hopefully nobody had closed the tanks. It had only been a week since the problems had started and the underground tanks, and pipes were all one-inch-thick steel.

Her main pump was connected, and slowly the fuel began to flow. Her incoming pump did not have as much power as the larger pump generators airports often used to fill large aircraft, but she managed drawing 100 gallons a minute into her half-full tanks. At this rate, it would take two hours to fill the three gunships and another full hour to refill the tanker.

The three gunships taxied in close to her, and again pipes were brought out. She could pump fuel out at a much faster rate with her second pump into one of the three waiting for fuel. They were not empty. The flight from South Korea had left them with third-full tanks, but they still needed to get to Moscow, which would be another 3,600 miles, or 12 hours of flying time non-stop, and the tanker would need to refuel the other three aircraft. Fortunately, they still had the soft bladders to help with range, and another hour of fueling would have those full as well.

Nearly three hours later, they had just started filling the extra bladders when three vehicles drove into the airport. They were old, black Russian-looking cars, like something out of the 1960s. They had flags waving above the headlights, and the sun, now rising just above the horizon, made the scene of the old war birds and black cars look like something out of an old movie, if one didn't turn around and look at the modern 747 behind them.

Three men in black coats and hats got out of the cars. Each one had a younger man with him—*interpreters*, Pete thought to himself—and they walked up to him. One of his men went back into *Ghost Rider* and brought out Mrs. Wang.

"Good morning," greeted General Allen. "Do you take Amex for fuel?"

One of the younger men started translating to the three men, and they smiled.

"I have just flown in from South Korea, via Japan. I'm here on a peaceful mission from the President of the United States to find out who caused this catastrophe worldwide and tell China and Russia that the United States did not do this horrible deed." The same translator did his job, and the three older men listened.

"I am the interior minister," the translator began after listening to the man in the middle. "My colleague on my right is the minister of foreign affairs, and the colleague on my left is from the Ministry of the Environment. By the age of your aircraft and the danger you have placed yourself in to fly these aircraft around the world, we understand that the United States of America is not to blame for this catastrophe. We do not think that Russia is to blame either, but of course we would like verification of that. Unfortunately, we have had no communications outside of Beijing since the first day of this year."

"Do you know that there is a Chinese invasion force at this moment sailing across the Pacific?" asked General Allen. "It is an invasion force of soldiers, Chinese soldiers, and they are intent on invading the United States in a week or so."

"My apologies," replied the interior minister. "Unfortunately, this invasion force you speak of has nothing to do with the current government of China. Taiwan, of course, is another matter, but we know nothing of any Chinese army or invasion force. We have no information at all."

"So, Mr. Minister, your government does not mind if we blow this invasion force out of the water?" asked General Allen, looking at Mrs. Wang to translate it for him. She did so. The three men looked at each other, shrugged their shoulders, and the minister of foreign affairs responded in rapid Chinese.

"We do not know of any invasion force, General," Mrs. Wang translated for him. "If you believe there is one, then you must do what you have to do to defend your country. We are still on friendly terms with the United States of America and do not wish to invade your country. We do not want our country invaded either and I'm sure the perpetrators of this horrendous crime will come up against the wrath of your United States of America, and many other countries. We would like to be included in any form of international communications you may have, so that we can at least communicate between our two countries, since it looks like this problem will not be solved overnight."

"I agree, and thank you for your diplomacy," replied General Allen. "I will be able to get a communications device to you if you allow us temporary landing rights at this civilian airport, and we could also bring a homing beacon on our next flight to allow our aircraft to guide themselves in after that. As you see, we do not have very modern aircraft anymore. Just like your pilots, our pilots do not have satellite navigation." Mrs. Wang translated.

"We would appreciate a communications device and will allow you landing and refueling rights at this airport. We will also make sure that we have equipment and power available to keep our runway clear and make our landing lights operational. It will still take us a few days. You may have our fuel in exchange for any communications devices you can give us. We need to set up engineering establishments in our country to begin manufacturing new parts for new telephones," the minister responded, smiling.

"I expect to have an aircraft here in a few days, and the pilots would appreciate good landing conditions. I am leaving now for Moscow and will hopefully have the same meeting with members of their government," ended the General, shaking hands with the three older men, who, along with their translators, solemnly got back into their old limousines and drove off.

The Chinese army still hung around—hoping for American chocolate and cigarettes, General Allen believed—the same they had been given an hour earlier. This time, they received a case of each. They thanked the Americans by smiling and then drove off, leaving the general and his men totally alone in the middle of China.

The sun was well up by the time they had finished refueling. The general had called Carlos as soon as the Chinese dignitaries left and asked him to place four more phones into the second polar-route HC-130. Carlos told him that the first of the two HC-130 tankers was already 30 minutes into its flight to Hill and then was aiming for California, Hawaii, and Japan as ordered. He had placed two extra phones in the aircraft just in case. The general asked how the polar-route flight was progressing and was told that the parachutes had arrived and were being loaded, and that the aircraft was fully fueled and would be out of McGuire within 20 minutes. General Allen asked Carlos to put six more phones in that aircraft.

"*I just want to point out, General,*" answered Carlos, "*we have 241 phones in total. Ninety-seven are, or will be, operational here, with another 80 heading out to other establishments. We don't know how much feed the satellites can take, but for the next couple of years, I reckon that around 500 phone numbers will be the maximum, since Lee has guessed that Zedong Electronics has somewhere between 300 and 500 of these phones set up, of which we already have 241.*"

"Roger that," replied General Allen. "Three of these phones are for future communications with the Chinese government and the other three I will offer the Russian government. The Chinese government has already paid for the phones."

"*You said PAID for them?*" asked Carlos, puzzled.

"Yep! They paid for them," laughed the general. "They paid 21,000 gallons of gas for them."

"*Okay,*" replied Carlos. "*I'll put the phone numbers down as Chinese governmental phones.*"

"And leave the red numbers on, in case the Zedong officials reappear and our friends here can contact them. Bye for now," finished General Allen.

They took off directly for Moscow, 12 hours ahead of them, and they felt better after Carlos told them that even though there was a bad storm over northern Europe, and the whole of Britain and Scandinavia was clouded over, the area around Moscow was clear and it shouldn't change for the next 12 hours. After 12 hours of sleeping and snoozing by all the men, except for the pilots on duty, they landed in icy conditions on Moscow Central Airport's runway. The lights were on, the runway cleared, and three camouflaged single-seat, piston-engine trainer aircraft had come on their radar screens two hours earlier, just before dark. The three other 130s joined General Allen's aircraft in formation, *Ghost Rider* guiding them into the capital of Russia.

* * *

Oliver was doing his usual rounds in the early morning on the tenth day. This time he had company—a lot of company. Three men walked with him around the runway and checked the aircraft, stopping at each one and making mental notes while they chatted. Preston was on the left of the president, who was enjoying the morning walks and the freedom the White House couldn't offer, and Mike Mallory walked on his right. The Secret Service men had been asked to keep watch but stay close to the house and nearer to the first family, who now had the use of the whole house.

Grandpa Roebels and Michael were itching to get back to California to check on the farm and their small engineering laboratory in their farm hangar and start working on repairing the damage done to the aircraft equipment they had taken out of the general's private ride.

They had left shortly afterwards in the Pilatus with two fully armed men as guards and an Air Force colonel—an ex-F-16 pilot who was to fly the aircraft back to the farm. Their flight plan was to land and refuel at McConnell Air Force Base in Wichita, Kansas, deliver a satellite phone and orders from General Allen to form a civilian Air Force, and distribute any available military and civilian food to the people of Kansas.

From McConnell, they were to fly into Holloman AFB in New Mexico and give base leadership a phone as well as the same orders. From Holloman, they were flying up to Beale in northern California and then down to Travis Air Force Base to give them the same package. The two engineers would be dropped at their private airstrip, and the two Air Force soldiers would first make sure that the farm was safe and then remain with the two older men as protection.

The colonel would then make his way back across the states, visiting another five or six bases and handing out more packages and a Presidential letter giving the base commanders the complete six phases of the food distribution plan copied on Presidential letterhead and with the Commander-in-Chief's signature at the bottom. It was a one-page description for setting up the distribution system in their immediate areas. The president had received a packet of Presidential letterhead paper from the White House, and Martie typed and printed the letters out for him as needed.

Over the last two days, the entire group, with the whole first family involved, had worked on the plan when they had all been together at the farm. Preston had explained the latest developments of the plan to the general, and he had gotten permission from the general to use all available Air Force personnel as long as their neighbor Army, Marine, Coast Guard, National Guard and Navy bases were included. The plan was pretty simple, and there was not much more that could be done for the people until the war was over.

Since there were so many Air Force bases around the country, they were perfect staging points for supplying food. Most of them had adequate food supplies to feed their personnel living on base, as well as thousands of civilians around the base, until the war was over. With the last news from the general, people were hopeful that it would only last another two weeks or so.

If they won the next battle, the enemy's head would be cut off, and after the capture or destruction of the aircraft or ships they were using to enter the New York Harbor, the enemy would be at a disadvantage transporting fewer fighting soldiers over the ocean and into the United States.

Once the last battle was fought, only then could the whole new plan go into maximum effect with what was left of the country's infrastructure. America needed all the C-130s to go to work feeding the people. The plan was to supply airports that had long enough runways to handle the C-130s with food in bulk that could then be distributed up to 200 miles in all directions by local aircraft. Each of the airports could be controlled by a platoon of soldiers, once there were enough soldiers and aircraft to fly them in, and they would guard the mission and the food.

The soldiers were to go out with each aircraft, distributing the cases of rations to make sure that the food was handed out in a fair and orderly fashion. People would have to show their ID to get a week's supply of food. The air bases would get their personnel working and count the millions of cases of military MREs (Meals Ready-to-Eat) that had their own flameless ration heater included, and FSRs (First Strike Rations) that were much lighter rations with a shorter shelf life and were eaten cold. Pilots flying out to distribute the food would need fuel. Luckily, many smaller airports still had supplies that could last several weeks, even into spring.

Phase One of the project was to get copies of the letter explaining the president's plan on White House letterhead out to all the Air Force bases in the country. Their first task was to communicate with any other Army, Navy, Coast Guard, National Guard, or Marine bases around the area and hand them a copy of the direct order from the president. Each Air Force base would receive a satellite phone, and a command center was set up at Andrews to begin work on the supply system after the war was over.

Phase Two had the Air Force bases locating and communicating with all local private airfields within 200 miles of their bases where aircraft could be commandeered for communications, as well as getting the airports ready to receive food supplies. This phase was to run from the war's end to mid-spring, when most of the military food stores were expected to be exhausted.

Phase Three would then come into play. The farmers would be expected to grow fast, ready-to-eat food as soon as they could plant and grow. Then the whole distribution system would be reversed. Supplies from the farms would be then transported back to the Air Force bases for consumption and further redistribution. By this time, all the mobile Army or civilian vehicles would be commandeered to collect and redistribute produce from the farms.

Phase Four would be new canning and bottling plants set up at all the airports to allow food storage to begin for the next winter. Once that happened, the system would be self-sustaining and should grow to where the survivors were fed and would be able to give back by working in the production system. Only then could a dollar or a whole new currency be worth something again.

Preston had even gone ahead and designed Phases Five and Six, the retooling of all the engineering in the country to try and get the natural gas supplies up and running, since they had only enough fuel to maybe last the country until the end of the summer. This is when the two older men became excited and flew back to California. Hopefully one day, every electrical company in the country would be activated, given electricity, and retooled to replace the billions of defunct parts that read "Made in China."

Grandpa Roebels and Michael were excited to start work on that plan back in California. Luckily their farm was untouched, and their first job was collecting several electrical engineers they knew who lived around them. Their idea was to get Silicon Valley up and running again within the next 12 months.

The meeting of the day on Preston's farm was coming to an end by late that morning. The team—the first family, the Smarts, Mike Mallory, John, Pam, Joe, David, Buck, Barbara, Ling, Martie, and

Preston—was very happy with their accomplishments. The plan was in draft form, and Martie was printing off copies of the Presidential order to be sent out.

The team was ready to fly into Seymour Johnson in every available aircraft to get the first load of food when the call came in from Carlos to Buck.

"Good morning to the farming community," Carlos greeted them over the old radio, now in the hangar so it wouldn't wake the first family at all hours.

"Are you still alive up there, Carlos?" Preston stated into the radio mic.

"I would be more alive if I could get some sleep and see Sally for more than five minutes at a time! We are all working 20-hour shifts up here and are allowed to use our radios again. Anyway, orders from Pete are for Buck to go down to Camp Lejeune and pick up 30 complete parachute sets. We need them up here at Mr. McGuire's place ASAP, and I mean ASAP. We have an aircraft waiting for them. Martie, please ask the Commander-in-Chief to give you the order on letterhead. And guys, they are urgently needed, so don't dilly-dally getting up here. Full cruise power, please." Martie's letters from the president were almost all printed out, so Buck and Barbara got up, stretched, and headed out to start pre-flight checks.

"Are you winning the war for us?" Preston asked Carlos.

"Boy! It's moving fast up here. The only time anybody gets any rest is if you are lucky enough to go out on a flight as a passenger," replied Carlos. *"But we have a fantastic plan, and you guys are going to love it. Unfortunately, it's hush-hush at the moment."*

"Even hush-hush for me?" asked the president himself, smiling as he asked the question.

"Only because I can't say anything over the radio, sir, but the plan, if it works, will help us get our troops back quicker," responded Carlos.

"Any plan to help our guys get back automatically has my approval," replied the president.

"That's what Pete said you would say, sir," replied Carlos. *"Anyway, all the big mama's will be up here working hard until further notice. You guys down there must do the best you can. And, by the way, you only have a week. Pete*

wants every available aircraft up here in seven days' time—everything with guns that is."

"We have the Presidential letters for the food distribution, Carlos. Can you see that they are distributed when aircraft go out to any Alpha Foxtrot bases in the country? We have 50 copies for you," said Preston, changing the topic.

"*Send them up with Buck and I'll get them out on every available flight,*" replied Carlos.

Martie ran out to *Lady Dandy*, her engines starting up, and delivered all the necessary papers. Buck and Barbara quickly headed out for the Marine base in a southern direction. That left only four usable aircraft on the apron for transporting food—the FedEx Cargomaster, the 210, and the two Cessna 172s. *Baby Huey* was up at McGuire working her butt off, and the tanker had already left for McGuire earlier that morning, again on Pete Allen's orders. Preston had quickly made sure that his underground fuel tanks were topped up from the local airport, since he had been given three hours advance notice.

Will Smart was happy to be in control of all the communications at the farm. Everyone had a job to do, but due to his fear of flying, he was still excused from flight duties. His wife wasn't afraid, however, and she was planning to fly down to Seymour Johnson with the pilot team. The four kids were happy as a group, and their job was to make sure the guards around the airfield all had food and fruit juice.

With the farm and the Presidential family under the protection of the Secret Service and Air Force, the four aircraft took off for their first day of food distribution with Will and the first lady sitting next to the radio with the use of a satellite phone. The flight team would be joined at the air base by *Lady Dandy* when she got back in a couple of hours.

The plan for the day was to get food out to four airports, find a suitable hangar, begin storage, and speak to the locals. If they could reach four airports a day, a small amount of people in the southern United States could be fed before they had to travel north. They flew into Seymour Johnson, where the base commander had pallets of the military meals waiting to be packed inside the small aircraft.

"We are still checking our stocks," said Colonel Mondale as he shook everyone's hand and invited them in for a special FSR cold lunch while the supplies they were going to distribute were packed up and they waited for *Lady Dandy*. "We have two warehouses full of all types of field supplies, and so far we have 1,850,000 cases of food rations in stock. I know that Fort Bragg will have much the same, and the Marines should have even more. I'm thinking that we have around 6 million cases of food here in North Carolina. Each case is between nine and twelve meals. The FSRs are lighter for your smaller aircraft. A case holds nine meals for an adult, weighs 23 pounds, and does not have the unnecessary extras like the food heaters. These have a shorter shelf life and I suggest you get them out first. The MREs are heavier and should be left here until you can use the C-130s to transport them into the civilian airfields."

"How many cases of food do you think are in the whole country?" asked Preston, realizing the mammoth task ahead of them.

"Well, we always hold enough stock for at least 90 days for our troops in the field. I don't know that exact number—only a couple of brass at the Pentagon know, or did know—but since we have more than one million men and women over there, I'd say we have around 100 million cases of food."

Preston looked at the group and thought for a few moments. "So, if spring is 12 weeks away, and we need to give farmers at least the same amount of time to produce fresh food, that means we have enough food to last about 30 million people, one tenth of the country's population."

Suddenly, the enormity of the situation hit all of them right between the eyes for the first time. How could such an enormous mass of people survive without electrical power? The whole system was so weak and useless. The people themselves had been molded, due to the luxuries of modern civilization, into weak and brittle beings. Mother Nature could destroy everything we built at any time, and the world's population could destroy themselves just as quickly, it seemed. It looked to the group like only a small percentage of the American population could survive, and they knew the extent of the catastrophe was worldwide. What would happen to the billions of already starving people the people with food were already feeding, now that those with resources had joined the ranks of those without?

"We have around 100 large field electrical generators in our warehouses, and we are looking through our inventory for more items of use. I've checked the generators, and they do work," added Colonel Mondale, breaking Preston's train of thought. "I'm sure that Camps Bragg and Lejeune have just as many. That will at least give some electrical power to necessary facilities."

"Thank you, Colonel," replied Preston. "You know, guys," he continued, "if I have anything to say about the next world order, I'm going to make sure that civilization is organized correctly this time. I'm going to work on Phase Seven of my plan—to make sure that this horrible destruction of humanity can never happen again, at least not by man himself. And I have the two perfect men to sell my idea to—the president and the general. Now let's do a hard day's work and feed as many people as we can before we have to go north. I hear *Lady Dandy* coming in."

Mike Mallory and John his trusty co-pilot had decided to take the FedEx Cargomaster to the airfield where the Southwest passengers had stayed overnight to test out the distribution plan. He could carry 120 cases of FSRs at a time, and their allotted area was D.C., Maryland, and Delaware. He knew these states well.

Preston, flying the 210 with Maggie as his co-pilot, had picked both the Carolinas. He knew the area well because of the crop duster business, and he was carrying 50 cases per flight.

Martie and Pam had wanted Virginia, and headed up there with both 172s in formation, as they could only take 30 cases per aircraft with the back seats pulled out and the co-pilot's seat free.

Buck and Barbara had decided on Tennessee, since *Lady Dandy* could carry much, much more and fly further with 350 cases. It wasn't much, but at least they could get something done, and two to four flights a day would mean a few less people starving.

Even though each case was nine days of meals for one person, the team had decided that they would give one case to each civilian and tell them that they had to make it last for two weeks.

The hangar was still empty when John and Mike got there, the ground covered in a few fresh inches of snow that made landing a little dicey, and it wasn't long before the same three tractors appeared.

Mike explained to the farmers, who looked happy to see him return, that they would have to keep the runway clear at all times, and that the whole airfield as well as the nice warm hangar would commandeered by the U.S. Air Force. From now on, it would be a food distribution and local pantry for needy people in the area.

Mike asked the farmers, still sitting on their tractors, how many aircraft had been in and out since he had left nearly a week ago. "None," was the reply. He then asked how many aircraft in the hangers were flyable. Nobody knew, but one of the tractors drove off to bring the owner of one of the aircraft back. Mike then asked the farmers to go back to their farms and bring as much wood as they could, build a guard post, and barricade the front gate to make sure the airfield was secure.

From now on, he told them, the population in any area had two choices—either assist with the food distribution effort and work to turn local airports into future military-guarded warehouses, or not receive any food supplies at all. He explained to the farmers that once the enemy attacks were over in a couple of weeks, only then could larger C-130s with hundreds of cases come in and really get a truly worthwhile food distribution system going, and that there was only enough food until spring. Then it was up to the farmers, once again, to feed America, or what was left of it.

The farmers responded that they had enough food, but that the local townsfolk were pestering them for something to eat, and they would be more than happy to dole out the military food in an orderly manner until guards arrived. It saved them giving out their own supplies, which were limited.

Once Mike had explained things to the farmers, they were more than happy to do as he asked. Mike then went around to each hangar and opened the doors. Since most pilots kept the keys somewhere in the hangar, it was possible to see which aircraft would start and which had the bad electronics. It was a small hobby airstrip in the middle of nowhere, which meant that most of the aircraft were at least 20 years old or older.

He counted 22 possible aircraft in the hangars around the airport. Ten hangars were empty and he presumed that the aircraft would make it back sometime in the future. Of the 12 aircraft, ten started on the first try, but most of them were small and would not carry many supplies. The number of aircraft would help make up for their small size. Only six of the aircraft— two high-wing Cessna 172s and four four-seat, low-wing Cherokee 140s were powerful enough to fly out at least 100 miles in any direction, and the rear seats of each could be hauled out to carry one pilot, one guard, and 20-odd cases per flight.

If all six aircraft flew out to the same distribution point, like a smaller airfield, at least 120 people could receive two weeks' worth of rations, and they could do that four times a day. The idea Mike and Preston had formulated was to feed at least 1,000 people from every small rural airport in the United States, and there were at least 15,000 airports around the country, they reckoned.

From this larger airfield, once food could be airlifted into it with a C-130 and then military trucks, at least 5,000 people could receive basic rations to keep them alive every couple of weeks. It wasn't much, but if many of those 5,000 people could be fed and help the farmers with planting, then the new spring crops would feed a lot more people. The initial distribution building blocks were small, but better than nothing, and nobody knew what the population count would be by the time the country got through the next two months of bitterly cold weather.

* * *

The mood aboard the Chinese aircraft carrier was subdued. After the news of the air strike at the headquarters building in Nanjing, and all suffering from hangovers the next morning, the ship was quiet. The flotilla was 300 miles off the coast of China and on a direct heading for Panama at 20 knots.

Mo Wang had been up all night phoning all his termination squads in the United States. He was only able to communicate with 20 of them out of the 100 he tried. The rest either did not answer their phones, or could not answer their phones, he assumed. He had had many phone calls go through, but with no one talking on the other end. He had tried to communicate, but the person on the other end had always just hung up.

He had also thought about things until close to 2:00 am when the chairman had personally knocked on the door of his stateroom, quite drunk, and told him that he had been demoted. He was now to fill Comrade Feng's old position of chief communications officer. "Comrade Wang, please hand me back your lapel badges. I expect a full report at our morning meeting, and it better not be only bad news, or your demotion could be extended, understood?"

Comrade Wang had no choice but to nod his agreement.

Maybe the chairman has forgotten that we are on a communication-challenged ship in the middle of the ocean, he thought to himself. "Yes, Comrade Chairman," he responded.

Once the chairman had left, Mo continued to try all the satellite phone numbers he had on the list Feng had given him before they left. He had answers from the 20 squads who reported in that they were all on their way to New York, that the weather was pretty bad, and they had had to shoot many people who were beginning to get in their way begging for food. Mo had over 50 phones hang up on him when he tried to call them, and then he reached the phone numbers on the list that had arrived in the transporter and gave up. They would still be in their packing. He would try those in a few days.

It was time to write his report.

* * *

General Allen and the four thirsty C-130s were escorted into

Moscow's Domodedovo International Airport by the three old, armed, single-engine turboprop fighter aircraft about the size of the Pilatus. It had taken ten minutes of searching the radio bands to find the radio frequency the Russians were using. Luckily, all three of the Russian pilots could speak limited English. Pete had explained his rank over the radio, saying he was on a peaceful mission ordered by the U.S. President, and that they wanted to see if Russia needed help or was in better shape than the rest of the world. The Russians had asked that the three gunships' gun crews stand back from their weapons and they would escort them into the international airport in downtown Moscow.

It was totally dark as they neared the city, and the general ordered all aircraft lights normally used in civilian flight patterns to be turned on. He explained to the Russian pilots that they had flown in from Beijing and had important news for the Russian government. They had just enough fuel to reach the airport, so they needed to go in as fast as possible. The airport's landing lights were the only lights that appeared over the horizon. The rest of the city was black, and this observation allowed the general to relax a little.

Russia was in the same situation as America. The old fighter aircraft had already made that obvious, but the lack of lights in Moscow made him feel even better. He was not going to die just yet!

Ten minutes later, they followed one of the fighters down on final approach, several hundred yards between each aircraft, and they felt very relieved when the wheels touched down and they followed the Russian aircraft to a secure area of the airport, away from the civilian terminals. Here there were a couple of hundred troops, all with weapons pointed at the aircraft—far different from the welcoming committee in Beijing. The engines stopped, and with *Ghost Rider* ahead of the others, the general once again got his hat and coat and left the aircraft, alone this time. He had ordered the guns manned again just in case.

Three soldiers, colonels by the look of their insignia, saluted him as he exited the aircraft. He saluted them back and was escorted to five black cars, this time, standing 100 yards away from the stationary

C-130s—very similar to the three black limousines in China.

There were a dozen older men in long black coats and fur hats waiting by the vehicles, guarded by at least 100 men. General Allen walked straight up to them, stopped, saluted, and said, "General Pete Allen, United States Air Force, on a mission directed by the President of the United States."

In perfect English, the man in the middle stated that he was a member of the government and so were five of his associates. The others were members of other organizations.

"I would like to report to you on what is happening in my country and what I've seen so far around the world," General Allen continued. "I would also like my four aircraft refueled, because I must head back to the U.S. air base in South Korea via Beijing. I believe that my report will take half an hour, and I would like a reasonable report on your country's devastation so that I can give a report back to my president. I have a crew of 48 men and one lady aboard who could do with a cold or hot meal and some water or liquid other than vodka, if you have some. We have been flying non-stop now for two days."

The men smiled slightly at the mention of vodka, and he was asked to follow them. They walked into a fully lit terminal. The building had been blacked out from the inside, and all the curtains were drawn. It was a small military terminal in a warehouse building, extremely luxurious, with thick leather chairs and a bar and food counter to one side. The member of the Russian government who seemed to be in charge explained to the general that the visitors could use this facility and that they should use it during refueling. All the men and the lady could sit in the warmth and eat what they wanted. The man spoke orders to one of the soldiers, who marched off to tell the American crew. The general halted him for a second, asking the soldier to allow his own men to refuel the four aircraft. The man nodded.

General Allen was served a warm and tasty meal and the choice of a Coke, coffee, and bottled water as they all sat down in a private lounge and waited for his report.

He asked three questions before starting. Was the whole of Russia without power? Was the country's communications affected internally as well as externally? And had this catastrophe had anything to do with the Russian government, or any Russian electrical companies inside or outside Russia?

"To answer your first question, General Allen," responded the man who looked like the most influential person in the crowd, "more of Russia is having electricity problems than we would like. The answer to your second question is that we have very little communications internally and no communications externally—that is, until you arrived out of nowhere on our radar screens five hours ago. Thirdly, we do not believe that any Russian electrical companies are involved with this crisis. Also, I personally do not believe that any departments of the Russian government are involved, as many of the department heads are here in this building tonight. Now, please tell us what is going on."

General Allen did, not relaying any secure information that wasn't necessary, just as his Russian counterpart was doing. He told the story of Zedong Electronics as told to him by Lee Wang. He explained the power outages around the world and the blackness of the entire planet from space.

The general also explained how they had got an old project satellite back into operation and found the three Chinese satellites which did not belong to the Chinese government. He explained the cell phones, and that a dozen were useable and he could offer them three phones on the next flight. This would give Russia communications with the United States and China.

It took an hour, and the food was good, especially the caviar. A case of good French champagne was opened and glasses passed around to the 20-odd men in attendance. General Allen fielded dozens of questions and answered in a way that would preserve world peace as well as secure his interests in getting U.S. military troops back home. The Boeing aircraft were not mentioned, but the attack on the buildings in Nanjing was.

The champagne went to his head slightly and made him realize how tired and old he was. At 60 years old, he wasn't meant to be running around the world like a teenager. Three hours after landing, however, snow began to fall lightly outside and they were ready to go.

His four aircraft would be escorted to Omsk in southern Siberia—Russia's second-largest city 1,400 miles southeast of Moscow and 2,200 miles from Beijing. Here the three Russian fighters would be at their furthest range and the American aircraft could land and refuel at a Russian Air Force base. He had told the group that if his aircraft could use that same base as a stop between China and Russia, he would put a radio beacon there for future trips.

They laughed and told him that Russia had a lot of old working electrical devices of all types. Nothing was ever thrown away in Russia, and all Russian aircraft already had a full system of radio beacons and their frequencies went all the way in and out of Russia in all directions. All that was needed were the several military AM radio frequencies. As long as aircraft were entering Russia on peaceful missions, they now had the "right" to fly through or into any major city any time they wanted. He was told to tell the Chinese that they would be offered the same opportunities.

Everyone shook hands with General Allen, the most senior man telling him the President of the United States was welcome to visit at any time, by special order from the Prime Minister of Russia himself. The three satellite phones were also welcomed and would be used wisely since they did not have a satellite communication system anymore either.

The benefits of flying with an escort, as well as the new radio beacon frequencies coming out of the military base in Omsk, gave all the crew, except the eight pilots flying the aircraft, four hours of hard-earned sleep. Even the responsibility of monitoring the only satellite phone on board was given to them, and General Allen slept as well as the other crew members until touchdown in a snowy Omsk four hours and twenty minutes later.

The weather was headed south, and the general was escorted out of Russian airspace, saying goodbye to their escort, who reported back that they had orders to wait for the Americans' return. The freshly refueled C-130s headed on a direct course to the base in Osan, 2,800 miles east of them.

His current *Ghost Rider* pilot told the general that the phone had rung twice while he was sleeping and a Chinese voice had tried to communicate. The pilot had done what everybody had been told to do when answering a call—listen for the Allen Key password from the caller before uttering any communication. The general checked in with Carlos and found out that his phone had also rung once from this unknown caller, and he told Carlos to get someone to call up all the numbers on the American list and remind the ones answering the phones to keep quiet until the password was given.

Carlos relayed the information to the general that *Mother Goose* was inbound to Osan, heading over the northern route, and that her estimated time of arrival was six hours and forty-five minutes. They had hit bad weather and were having to make a 30-minute detour flight around a large storm. It was beginning to blanket most of Russia, and the general should expect to have the same problem in three or four hours. Osan was still open and should continue to be long enough to get both flights in and then out to Shanghai.

"How many people did we get aboard, Carlos?" General Allen asked.

"*Twelve pilots. The engineering crew was replaced by all pilots, Pete,*" Carlos replied. "*There isn't a non-pilot aboard except the ten guys from south of the border. In total, we have 22 people on the flight manifest, with full fuel and full gear for 30. You will have to pick up more men on your next stop. I'm sure you can find one or two of them who are able to drive.*"

General Allen agreed, saying there should be enough to choose from in Osan, and he wanted the flight's phone number so that he could talk. He immediately called *Mother Goose* and found them flying in pretty lousy weather, but now actually thinking they had a decent tailwind and that they could get back on schedule. The commander, a sleepy Major Patterson, who was a pilot himself, told him that they were supposed to check in with Carlos in an hour. *Ghost Rider* was still working on the several radio frequencies they had received from the Russian military. These frequencies were expected to work well into China. He gave all the frequencies to the pilots of the tanker, and after several minutes, they told him that they had new fixes on three very faint radio beacons—enough to plot their exact position by intersecting the three beacon locations to their aircraft's position. They came back, thanking him and telling him that they did have a tailwind, were 110 miles off course but still 160 miles closer to Osan, and that they could make it in with 40 minutes of fuel to spare.

General Allen called Carlos back. "Carlos, did you know that you could be out of a job as the world's only air traffic controller pretty soon?" he laughed into the phone.

"*Thank God for that!*" Carlos replied. "*Being out of a job will give me a chance to fly instead of watching the world's weather for you all.*"

All the flight personnel who were not flying managed to get three to four hours more sleep before the bad weather and turbulence made it almost impossible. The general was pretty refreshed after seven good hours of sleep, however, and decided to shave, with a bowl and a bottle of water serving as his shaving equipment.

The C-130s were strong aircraft, and the elements battering the aircraft outside were not much of a concern. The luxury of very faint radio beacons still obtainable at 29,000 feet were also helping them stay on course, and three hours after the general shaved, they landed in snowy conditions on a freshly cleared white runway—one hour after *Mother Goose* had arrived direct from McGuire AFB. It was the morning of the ninth day—cold, blustery, and snowy.

All of the men on the mission who had done nothing but sleep in some cozy bit of space on the airplane were rested and ready for action. Major Patterson had already rounded up ten experienced pilots at Osan, and 30 men were going over the parachute gear, preparing it for use and familiarizing themselves with the best the Marines had. One of the radio beacons was already being set up close to the southern end of Osan's longest runway, and it would be operational by takeoff, several hours later.

General Allen immediately held a meeting with all soldiers, pilots, and crew. "Ok, guys, I want to hear your plan," said the general, "but first I want *Mother Goose* to head up to Misawa in Japan ASAP and get the second radio beacon operational. I will personally deliver the third one to Beijing once our operation at Shanghai Pudong International Airport is over. I want the 30 parachutes dropped in low by *Blue Moon* and *Easy Girl*, with fifteen to an aircraft plus a pallet of arms. They will go in just before dawn, and the final decision on your landing site is perfect. The open land between the ocean and the west side of the airport should be far enough away for the snow to blanket the sound. Captain Wong, well done at JFK. This one is going to be just as easy, as long as we don't end up with troops blocking the runways with trucks, or whatever they have that can stop the aircraft from taking off. We cannot win against the larger numbers of troops they must have stationed there, but remember, complete surprise is on our side. Now, tell me exactly how you did it at JFK, and what is your plan for getting into the aircraft here?"

Major Patterson and Captain Wong spent an hour telling General Allen what had happened at JFK, as well as the plan they had formulated on this trip over the North Pole at 31,000 feet. It was very risky, but with the element of surprise and the way the Chinese engineers and soldiers had reacted to hearing of the Supreme Commander's surprise visit, it certainly could be done again. Hopefully nobody knew where the real Supreme Commander was at the moment, but it didn't matter, and to the men they were going to encounter, he was most probably God!

Mother Goose left two hours later, refueled, and headed on her way to Japan, then over to Hawaii, and back to McGuire. She had done her job. Now it was up to the men she had brought in to increase the size of the U.S. Air Force commercially.

* * *

The snow came and went, winds moving it around, and toward nightfall it began to fall in earnest. The bulldozers worked to keep the runway clear.

Only an inch or two had fallen when *Blue Moon*, *Easy Girl*, and the second HC-130 tanker were fully fueled, and the two gunships, each carrying 15 men, took off two hours before dawn.

The flight was 90 minutes into Shanghai, and the general would only take off in *Ghost Rider* once the men were on the ground, to conserve fuel. He didn't have a tanker anymore, but Beijing was a lot closer this time with the Russian radio beacons.

Once again, the satellite phones were the main communication tool—smaller and lighter than radios—and the men were dressed in the same clothing taken off the termination squads in New York.

Both gunships were able to guide themselves into the area accurately with their infra-red scanners. Mrs. Wang had been transferred into *Blue Moon,* and once the men were down, they were to refuel from the tanker to get them into Omsk, 2,850 miles away.

From Omsk, they headed into Moscow and delivered the three promised cell phones, and then headed for Turkey, which was the meeting point for all the U.S. aircraft heading back to the States. General Allen would be the last in, once he had delivered the radio beacon into Beijing, refueled, and then flown into Omsk for more refueling. He would then head south into Turkey.

The pilots reported reasonable snowfall over the area, and it didn't take them long to find the LZ (landing zone) several hundred yards southwest of the airport. The snow had stopped falling and the clouds were scattered. The dark of night just before dawn was not a problem for the scanners aboard the gunship. Both aircraft reduced speed as much as possible to reduce engine noise. The pilots reduced altitude down to 900 feet and the jumpers only had seconds before they landed.

All marines were experienced at this, and they had gone over the drills several times with the less-experienced pilots—teaching them low-level static-line parachute tactics. The tanker stayed aloft at 20,000 feet. She couldn't help in any way, so she waited patiently for the two gunships to rejoin her. The rear door of the AC-130s opened, and the jump lights turned from red to green. Fifteen men ran out the back two at a time on each side of both aircraft in three second intervals. Their parachutes' ripcords were pulled by the static line inside the aircraft as they jumped. The last parachuter ran out on one side, and a large case of carefully packed AK47s and ammunition was pushed out on the other side by two men. Its larger parachute's ripcord was also pulled as it left the aircraft.

The two aircraft turned right and glided out to sea as silently as possible and gently gained altitude to meet up with the tanker. Together they turned far out to sea to the east of Shanghai into a northwesterly direction and got on course for Omsk.

Several minutes later, the first group joined up and reported to Major Patterson. Everybody was okay, despite one slightly sprained ankle, and the second group headed by Captains Wong and Chong arrived ten minutes later with no injuries.

Major Patterson's men searched for and found the slightly banged-up pallet of their equipment stuck inside a now roofless and broken chicken coop. After a little trouble, two of the men handed out the arms and ammunition to the rest of their squad. They wrapped their 15 parachutes onto the now-empty pallet with a timer and explosive device that would go off in three hours' time, hopefully destroying all evidence, as well as a dozen or so chickens, if they didn't go out to peck around the field before the explosion went off. They then found and joined the other group with the two Chinese-speaking pilots.

Major Patterson phoned General Allen, telling him that they were on the ground and unhurt. Already, from this distance, they could see a dozen or more aircraft standing in a long line facing away from the terminal and towards the runway that rested between the men and the aircraft.

If all the aircraft had been parked head in at the terminals with the walkways attached, it could have presented a problem.

It would have been difficult to get them moved back from the gates and onto the runway for takeoff. They couldn't see all the aircraft, because a short snow squall blotted out the terminal halfway down, but that was fine—they had seen as much as they wanted.

The first terminal facing the west at Shanghai International was extremely long, and older satellite photos studied in the aircraft on the way over had shown that around 24 aircraft could be parked by the west-side gates.

A couple of men cut holes in the high fence surrounding the airport, noticing that several lights were on in and around the buildings, as well as at the aircraft control tower. There were no guards to be seen. They certainly weren't expecting any form of attack.

Once inside, they kept to the perimeter of the fence, carefully moving in the blackness around the south end of the runway. It took the group 20 minutes to get closer to the aircraft. By that time, the faint dawn light was beginning to show more and more of the airport stretching out in front of them.

Major Patterson and all the men were dressed in the same confiscated Chinese clothing he had worn at JFK. He moved toward the main apron of the airport. He was ready for his mission and blatantly walked out to the middle of the apron with Captain Chong to make sure that they would be seen and started looking at the first airplane.

Captain Wong ran to the tower and climbed the stairs as fast as he could with two marines, their faces totally hidden behind veils. He reached the airport's command center, or tower, and found it unguarded with the door unlocked. He walked in and started shouting orders, pointing down at the tiny figure of the "Supreme Commander" just barely visible checking aircraft.

"The Supreme Commander has arrived to do an inspection of the airfield," ordered Captain Wong in Mandarin as the men sat straight up, suddenly at attention. He quickly looked outside and counted fifteen 747s facing outward toward the runway. At the end he could just make out the same transporter he had seen at JFK two days earlier. It must have refueled somewhere on its return journey, because it didn't have the range to get from New York to Shanghai non-stop like the passenger version.

"The Supreme Commander has been given an army of elite troops from the government in Beijing as a gift, and he needs 12 aircraft to collect them. Are those aircraft refueled and ready to fly? Where are the pilots?" he shouted at the man who looked to be most senior.

"The aircraft are fueled and ready to fly. I will wake the pilots immediately. They are in their quarters, Comrade," the man replied, stammering nervously.

"General Wong to you! I am the Supreme Commander's bodyguard commander. Is there an alarm to warn the soldiers about aircraft movements?" the captain demanded.

"The soldiers are controlled from the security detachment on the floor below. I can send a man to tell them that the Supreme Commander is giving orders to move aircraft," the man replied, still standing at attention.

"Do that immediately!" ordered Captain Wong. "The aircraft will be flying into Beijing and will return in 12 hours. I need space and quarters for another 5,000 men. Tell the commander of the soldiers to find them space to sleep until we leave for

America, understood?"

"Yes, sir!" The man stuttered and shouted orders to one of the five men in the tower, who bowed and ran off.

"Does the front line of aircraft have mobile stairs so that the Supreme Commander can inspect the aircraft?" was Captain's Wong's next question.

"We only have three flights of mobile stairs, and I can get them out there from below the tower, General," the nervous man answered. Captain Wong nodded, noticing that the American squad of men was in formation behind the first aircraft. The man in charge of the tower immediately picked up a microphone and spoke to what Captain Wong assumed was the ground crew.

"The Supreme Commander doesn't want any troops out there. He has his own elite troops under my command, but the pilots have three minutes to get dressed. He wants 11 aircraft to transport the troops. Is the transporter loaded and ready to go?" Captain Wong asked.

"Yes, sir," the man replied. "It is ready for its flight to America and fully loaded. It is being kept warm inside so that the parts do not freeze."

"Good, because that is what the Supreme Commander is giving our Chinese government minions in Beijing for the men. We will need to get it reloaded once it returns in three days' time," added the captain.

"But there are no more parts here at the airport," replied the tower controller.

"We have a new load coming in from Nanjing," replied Captain Wong sarcastically.

He watched as three sets of stairs were being pushed hard by hand out to the furthest three 747s, and he then noticed five Airbus 380s on the opposite side of the terminal at specially built gates. "Are the European aircraft ready to go?" he asked.

"No, sir, they are still having their seats removed and are not yet refueled."

"The Supreme Commander wants that work completed by the time he gets back from Beijing, in case he must go back. Wake up your workforce and get all those aircraft ready. The aircraft we are taking tonight will be arriving back here and I'll need a welcoming committee ready when the Supreme Commander returns from Beijing. I'm flying with him, and so are my elite troops. I will go down and wait for the pilots. Understood?" The man nodded.

Captain Wong and his two heavily armed guards ran back down the stairs, making as much noise as possible. On the floor below was an Army colonel by the looks of him, and he saluted as the three men nodded at him and continued down the stairs. He looked rather confused.

Three of the first-in-line, beautiful Boeing 747's front doors were already open, and two men could be seen through the cockpit windows going through ground checks as the aircraft doors were already being closed.

The stairs were already on their way to the second group of aircraft as the pilots—30 of them—ran out from the terminal, still dressing and trying to put their uniforms together. Captain Wong issued orders as they arrived, getting a crew aboard each of the next three aircraft as the doors opened. He shouted at the pilots that the first three aircraft had pilots from the Supreme Commander's own private group and they were to get into the fourth, fifth, and sixth as spare teams.

The stairs were placed close to the next three aircraft, the doors opened, and three Chinese pilots entered each of the front doors with two of the Supreme Commander's pilots and a marine. The stairs were being pulled away as the first engines started up, and the panting ground crew moved the stairs towards the next three in the row. Everybody was working as fast as they could, with Major Patterson, still in the middle of the apron, moving his arms around in gestures nobody could understand, but which sure looked good!

By the time the third set of large Boeing 747-400ER aircraft had their front doors open, the Chinese crews and American pilots with a marine per aircraft were climbing the stairs.

Now there were three left—two normal 747s and the 747 transporter at the end. The ground crew, now hot and breathing hard, pushed the stairs to the next two aircraft, but they had to push a lot further to the third, the 747 transporter, which was a hundred yards further along and standing on its own. The "Supreme Commander" followed the ground crew that marched over to the transporter, looked up to the tower and waved at them, and entered the last aircraft.

By this time, Chinese soldiers were appearing from areas behind the terminal and were forming up into squads.

Captain Wong decided that it would take at least ten minutes to get the checks done and the last aircraft's engines started. The first three planes were already on the move, so he suggested to the "Supreme Commander" to waste some time walking over to the men before they had a war on their hands.

The two men went down the stairs after watching a marine knock four Chinese crew members out cold and allow the last of the American pilots to get into the co-pilot seat to begin start-up checks. They walked down the stairs with Captain Wong a few steps behind telling the ground crew to wait for them to return. They moved directly towards the several hundred troops, now dangerous and ready for action at a moment's notice.

The "Supreme Commander", his face still covered, stopped several yards in front of the men and bowed to them.

"Our Supreme Commander is traveling to Beijing to pick up more great soldiers," Captain Wong shouted at the top of his lungs. "He will return in a few hours to give you a personal speech on the success we are expecting in America. He has a surprise for all of you! For every man who does his job well in New York, he will receive a thousand acres of land and a large

American house. He will explain the plan once we return from Beijing. He is proud of all of you and looks forward to giving you your own part of America when we have won the final battle."

With that he bowed to the troops, then to his "Supreme Commander", and then whispered to him to get back on the aircraft as the guard stood to attention and presented arms. They seemed excited at the news, many smiling and looking joyous.

As they got to the steps, the first three 747s were already taxiing down to the southern end of the runway half a mile away, with the second group of three just leaving the apron in a line.

Wong and Patterson walked up the stairs. The "Supreme Commander" reached the top step and, as he had seen several presidents do, waved to the whole airport in front of him. As the first engine of the transporter began its whine, the door was closed, and the ground crew quickly moved the stairs out of the way.

They had now set the plan in motion, and all they could do was hope that everybody believed them for a little while longer.

"You should get a bloody Oscar for your chit-chat out there, Wong," praised Major Patterson, dialing the phone to call the general and give him an update. "What did you shout out to those guys?"

"I just gave away a thousand acres of farmland and a big house to each man when they get there," Wong replied as he got into the left-hand cockpit seat and they heard their aircraft's engines begin to scream. The heavy transporter began to move. Their aircraft was the last in the queue, and they trundled over the apron to follow the other 11 massive aircraft many yards apart.

"Comrade Chong, are you flying?" asked Wong in Chinese over the radio as he took control of the heavy transporter since it had only been handled by the co-pilot in the right seat up to then.

"Affirmative, Comrade Wong. I'm in the aircraft two in front of you," Captain Chong replied, making it sound like it was two Chinese pilots talking over the radio.

"Comrade Chong, cut out right and head over to the eastern side of the airport. Hopefully the guy in front of me will follow you. We can all get out of here quicker if we use the western runway as well. The Supreme Commander is in a hurry."

"Roger, Comrade Wong. The feeder road is coming up, and I'm turning to the right." As planned, the two aircraft in front of Captain Wong both turned onto the feeder road 200 yards apart in front of him.

They were all taxiing at a rapid rate, but big jets like these had to wait at least two minutes before takeoff between each aircraft to subdue the air turbulence from the one taking off in front. The last of the twelve aircraft moved rapidly towards the western side at a fast pace and turned left to taxi to the end of runway as they saw and heard the first 747's engines pushing the aircraft down the other runway. It took Captain Chong another four minutes to get to the runway end, turn, and begin his takeoff. By that time, there were a lot of orders in Chinese being shouted over the radio.

"They have somehow found a hole in our plan, Major. Their troops are mobilizing," shouted one of the pilots over the radio in English as the fourth aircraft on the eastern side began its long takeoff. They were still taxiing in the wrong direction and turning right to head to the runway when Captain Wong turned the heavy transporter onto a second, smaller stretch of asphalt runway 50 feet before the main runway and told all the pilots in English to get out of there as fast as possible—the troops were coming.

Major Patterson immediately got on the satellite phone to *Ghost Rider*, who was still a few minutes out, and told him to come in hot and come in quickly—they needed covering fire.

The second 747 began its slow trundle down the runway several yards in front and fifty feet to the left of Captain Wong's aircraft. Captain Chong's aircraft was already climbing into the air nearly a mile in front, but Captain Wong had to wait, at least a minute or two, and it was the longest and slowest-moving time of his life. It was so long that he only waited 50 seconds before he saw trucks moving out from the terminal and slowly pushed the four 747 throttles to maximum.

They couldn't see what was happening on the eastern side anymore, as the weather was coming in, but his job with the fully loaded 747 transporter was to get it off the ground. Explosions started happening to his right as his jumbo jet, on full power, began to gather speed, and he could just see another 747—*the seventh*, he thought to himself—on the other side begin its slow climb into the sky and into the lowering cloud base at the end of the eastern runway, over a mile away.

Suddenly, there was a massive blast of light by the terminal several hundred yards to his right as a fireball flew into the air. The explosion was so big that his jumbo vibrated as the shock of it hit the aircraft. He watched as *Ghost Rider* flew directly over him at a couple hundred feet, lines of tracers from the gunship firing into anything around the terminals that was moving.

A truck exploded a couple hundred yards in front and to the right of the strip of tarmac on which he was taking off, halfway between the feeder runway he was on and the western side of the terminal. Then, the tower itself disappeared as a second massive blast directly underneath it literally enveloped the tower and disintegrated it.

There was only one thing that powerful. An aftershock hit his aircraft hard again, and this time he was accelerating at 95 knots and it vibrated the whole aircraft. The gunship was blowing up fully fueled 747s.

Another 747 climbed away on the other side of the airport as he came abreast of the burning truck and saw two jeeps trying to cut him off a couple of hundred yards ahead of him and speeding abreast of his runway.

One suddenly exploded, and the second one blew up less than a second later.

The transporter was now approaching takeoff speed and needed another several seconds to get airborne. The engines were screaming, not used to taking off at absolute maximum power, when he felt another massive explosion way behind him, and a missile passed pretty close by, several feet above his aircraft. *"Thank God it wasn't a ground-to-air missile,"* he thought as he pulled back on the controls, felt the front wheel lift, and watched the computers aboard begin to work the heavy aircraft off the ground.

He was a little under takeoff speed as he pulled back on the stick, and he switched over to manual override and hauled back on the controls as he pulled the aircraft off the ground, climbing at an attitude that would have made any passengers sick if it were a passenger model.

"We have nine in the air so far," reported Major Patterson to Captain Wong as he wrestled with the aircraft for height. "We are number ten, and I've lost visual. The 11th one was halfway down the eastern side and the last one is a couple of hundred yards behind it—a little too close for survival. He's going to get into dangerous turbulence. Meanwhile, *Ghost Rider* is breaking up the airport buildings, and it looks like two or three 747s are burning fireballs down there."

Captain Wong brought the aircraft engines down to normal takeoff power and cleaned up the aircraft's wings, bringing in the flaps. He slowed the high climb rate slightly, watching the ten aircraft on the radar screen as the 11th one left the eastern runway behind him and climbed hard to get out of the area. The airport was long out of visual range, and the 747s which had taken off before him began to form a line in front of his, climbing up to cruise altitude and slowly turning into the direction for the U.S. air base in Turkey. Captain Wong didn't have orders, and he circled above Shanghai, gaining height. He was expecting the general to send them somewhere else once he was done down below.

It took a couple of minutes before General Allen came back on the radio.

"How did you get that last aircraft got off the ground, pilot? I just don't know, the turbulence must have been darn crazy!" Everyone heard the general communicate with the last aircraft.

"I didn't think we were going to get off the ground, so I let her run another 200 yards to the end of the runway and took her off underneath the dirty air the aircraft in front was making. She's okay, sir—a little beaten up, and the galleys must be a mess, but we are joining the end of the line for our destination," replied one of the Air Force pilots.

"Well done, pilot," said General Allen. *"I'll buy you a drink when we get home. Guys, head to our designated destination. I'm heading on and will be several hours behind you. I'll call you with more details on the phone. Our cover is blown and they are listening to us on this radio frequency. Radio silence from now on. Out."*

"Good job, Wong. Remind me to give you and Chong a promotion to major once this is all over. Wong, you alone will set a course for McGuire. You are on your own, I'm afraid," the general continued, now using the secure satellite phone. *"Go the Bering Sea route. Refuel at Elmendorf, and that will give you at least an hour of reserve fuel into McGuire. Well done, Colonel Patterson. Your promotion is also done. Just remind me when you get back to McGuire. I'll call you back in a few minutes,"* the general continued with the crew in the transporter listening on speaker phone.

Captain, soon-to-be major, Wong had been given his orders and went to work setting a course with the several new radio beacons at his disposal for a lengthy flight over the Bering Sea.

"We have diluted their fleet by 12 aircraft. Unfortunately, we also destroyed a couple beautiful birds down there. I counted 29 747s and five Airbus 380s before we helped ourselves, is that correct?" asked General Allen, calling the transporter back on the satellite phone.

"That's what I counted," replied the now Colonel Patterson. "I assume they had 30 passenger 747s, but we already have one, and now they have only 15 or 16 of the passenger 747s left plus the five Airbuses. I know the Israelis filled one up with over a thousand passengers at one time, but they were women and children. I think that they could get at least 500 fully armed troops into each one and over 600 in the Airbuses. If they are going to send in troops to JFK, then now they can only fly in a maximum of 12,000 troops at any one flight instead of 20,000."

"I hope they still come over," replied the general. "I want the remainder of those aircraft. But I'll call the president and let him know that we can start transferring a minimum of 6,000-plus troops back to the States per day now, until we acquire some more aircraft. At least we can get all our men back within eight months.

"Colonel Patterson, you and Majors Wong and Chong will now set up a trap at JFK and the other airports around New York after Major Chong flies you guys into McGuire in about 15 hours. You will have to refuel in at Elmendorf in Alaska. I believe that we have 11 days left to set up a plan to capture their troops and get the rest of their aircraft. Remember, guys, this is our whole American air transportation for many years to come. I felt really bad blowing up those aircraft, but I needed to create a diversion. I just hope the fire did not spread to any of the other aircraft, but we will see in a few weeks.

"I'm off to Beijing and then Turkey and Iraq to work on getting our troops home. If anything happens to me, Patterson, I want to give you the rest of my battle plan and will do so on my flight into Beijing. I'm going into Beijing in Ghost Rider *alone*. I have set the others on a course for Omsk and then Turkey, and I don't want to take any other aircraft with me. For some reason, I have a weird feeling that there could be something wrong in Beijing. If there isn't, then I'll see you in Turkey. I'm sure tired of traveling. I'll call you in a few minutes, but I need to chat with Carlos first. Out."

Chapter 15

The Beginning of the End

OVER A PERIOD OF DAYS, and with another few inches of snow and negative temperatures, the three airports were made ready for normal use. The C-130s worked non-stop out of McGuire, Andrews, Seymour Johnson, and Pope Field, bringing in troops, supplies, electrical equipment, and necessary food for storage, as well as for the ever-growing number of civilians collecting food each day around the airport perimeters.

Six radio-transmitting beacons had been modified so far, transported, and activated, and the large incoming Air China 747 was the first to have modern directional technology available again—descending from 37,000 feet and using the frequencies located on the radios from as far as 900 miles out over the North Atlantic.

Three of the beacons were now working at JFK, La Guardia and Newark. The next three were slightly south at McGuire, Andrews, and Seymour Johnson, and another radio beacon was being installed at Preston's airfield.

The first captured 747 landed back at JFK 24 hours after leaving for Incirlik Air Force Base, and with 650 tired and dirty American soldiers aboard.

They were immediately moved into one of the three modified JFK terminals ready with beds to house 1,000 troops per terminal, and the turnaround on the jumbo jet was six hours before she was refueled, prepared, and left empty for her second trip—this time non-stop into

Baghdad over 3,600 miles away. She could complete a return trip in a 24-hour window and refuel in Germany if there was no fuel available in Iraq, or she could make the entire trip without refueling at all.

Beds, bedding, generators, porta-potties, rations, and clothing were being flown into the three New York airports on a 24-hour basis. Unfortunately, the rations would not be enough to feed the military soldiers and the rapidly growing civilian population around the fences, but the transporter with Captain Wong arrived at McGuire on the ninth day, flown in by an extremely tired crew, and was off-loaded, refueled, and reloaded with 100,000 meals. The aircraft, with a fresh crew on board, was flown the short flight into JFK. The 747 could take as much as all the C-130s together, and the 130s were diverted into other bases once the food supplies became low at McGuire.

Nobody knew the exact date of the attack on New York Harbor—Zedong Electronics hadn't made it official yet—but Carlos and his 30-year-old computer could see any attacking sea force as soon as the ships came into view. The Chinese satellites were much higher up. They did not have telephoto or zoom camera lenses, and he tried as hard as he could but could not see any ships on the screens from their digital footage. The view from Navistar P was far better, and he believed that he could see a large ship sail into the 175-mile view around the United States that he currently had on visual.

Carlos had brought the satellite 100 miles lower over the United States to get a better view, and he tried hard to see the incoming 747, but it was still too small for such an old screen.

None of the American aircraft used their transponders in case they could still be seen from wherever the Zedong Electronics personnel were viewing the screens. He did not know that the blowing up of the building in Nanjing had made the enemy virtually blind. Nobody on that side had thought to upgrade any of the satellite-receiving equipment on the ships, and the pictures they were seeing were about the same quality Carlos was viewing.

The Chinese electricians had always expected to have a direct HD feed in from Headquarters, but now they relied on the lesser-quality equipment aboard the naval ships by pointing their dishes at the nearest satellite location. They had also lost control of the three satellites. Lee Wang and Carlos now controlled them after cracking the communication codes imbedded in them.

Once the main communication from the headquarters buildings had been terminated as a result of General Allen's bombardment, the three-satellite system in space had asked for continued control directions. And, after two days of work, Carlos and Lee had finally cracked the codes to take over control of the satellites.

New York Harbor hadn't been repaired yet. The 200 engineers were still working on getting the airports ready, but there was a growing operation to the south. Dozens of old bulldozers from all the naval bases between Norfolk, Virginia and New York were beginning to clear the scrap metal of broken trucks and cars off I-95.

General Allen had met with Vice Admiral Rogers twice since the beginning of the year, and just before the general's trip around the world. The vice admiral, a little embarrassed about how few ships the U.S. Navy could get operational, had offered up his Navy Seals and any naval motorized vehicles he could get mobile. The Norfolk Naval Station had started work immediately, and they had already cleared 20 miles of the northbound strip of I-95 highway, beginning on the southern Virginia border. He had also communicated with several of the naval bases further north, and a dozen northbound clearance operations had started on the 8th day of the year to open the vehicle supply route from the south.

This was going to help the convoys like Colonel Grady's, now leaving Fort Bragg and stopping next in Apex, North Carolina. Preston was in for a shock—he had a couple of visitors coming to pay him a call.

* * *

The President of the United States was helping out as much as he was allowed to by his bodyguards in the business of distributing food in the neighboring states. The only aircraft he was allowed to catch a ride in was *Lady Dandy*, currently on her third flight into a small town of 2,000 people just across the North Carolina border in Tennessee.

All six of the aircraft had worked hard for the last two days—*Lady Dandy*, Sally's Pilatus, the FedEx Cargomaster, the 210, and the two Cessna 172s. It was on the evening of the ninth day when everybody met up again at Preston's airport.

They all flew in just before dusk after each completing three flights out of Pope and Seymour Johnson. That day alone, over 2,900 more people had been delivered a two weeks' supply of food, and it was time for a cold Yuengling for everybody. Cold brown bottles were being popped everywhere. Even the president had a couple in his hand, one for him and one for his tired wife, when Preston got a radio call from the guard at his gate. A Colonel Grady from Alabama was there at the gate wanting to visit, and hundreds of military vehicles were waiting in a line for a mile down the road behind him.

"Let him in," replied Preston. "Nobody is flying in tonight. I'll disconnect the lights. Tell them to drive in and park next to each other along the length of the runway. It will be easy for them to get out in the morning."

One by one, the large trucks towing the howitzers drove in and were directed by Air Force personnel. They drove along the runway towards the south end, turned in, and parked across the width of the tarmac.

It took 30 minutes, but finally the whole length of the 2,700-foot runway was full of vehicles facing the house and hangar. It was a powerful sight as the sun was going down.

The aircraft in the hangar were being pulled outside with the tractor so that as many as possible of the 800 men who had arrived could sleep on their field mattresses on the cement in the warmer building. It wasn't that warm in the hangar. The doors had been opened several times that day, but 50 degrees was better than the 30-degree temperature outside, the beer was reasonably cold, and the hangar would soon heat up with all the bodies arriving.

The three dozen porta-potties were still at the airfield and would now come in handy. They were in a line behind the old red barn, now full to the brim with ammo and other military supplies that hadn't been needed yet. Many of the Air Force troops had already shipped out with the C-130s to several locations, and there was now only the minimum guard of 30 airmen and Captain Pierce protecting the farm.

Colonel Grady came over to shake Preston's hand and got the shock of his life when the U.S. President and his whole family came out of the hangar to wonder at the massive amount of Army vehicles which had just arrived.

"Is he…the real…?" Colonel Grady asked, his hand frozen in Preston's and his mouth open as the president walked up to the growing group as if he owned the place.

"Attention!" shouted the colonel, and every single man who was moving stood to attention and saluted in the direction of the president.

"At ease, gentlemen," the president responded, smiling as he and the first family came over to greet the colonel. "It's good to see that the U.S. Army still has some firepower," the president said to the colonel, shaking his hand.

"It's not much yet, Mr. President, sir, but we are growing in size with every army barracks we visit. Your official letter sure helps the commanders get their act together," the colonel drawled in his very southern accent. "This is just the vanguard of our total forces. I didn't want to wait for the colonel at Bragg. He's 24 hours behind us and I left 400 men to help him prepare for travel. He has the same amount of older troop carriers we have here. We have also cleared the road up to here from Fayetteville, and he'll catch up with us once he gets on I-95."

"Good news, Colonel," said Preston. "The Navy has dozens of bulldozers on the northbound side of I-95 and they are clearing a lot of highway miles per day. You are going to have to use your bulldozers to clear up to the North Carolina-Virginia border, and then it should be plain driving from there. They have squads all the way north to New York. Over a dozen naval stations are clearing a path for you."

"That will help us get there a little quicker. I thought the Navy used boats, not bulldozers?" laughed the colonel. "Preston, we all have MREs with us and the men can sleep next to the vehicles tonight."

"How many do you have here tonight, Colonel?" Preston asked.

"Just shy of 800 men," Colonel Grady replied.

"If you set up your guard positions," continued Preston, "I'm sure most of the men can sleep in the warmer hangar tonight. There should be enough room if they bed down in lines, and the best part is that we have enough beer to go around—at least two per man, as long as you allow them to have a couple of drinks, Colonel."

"I'm sure the men will appreciate that, Preston, Mr. President, but we don't want to take all your stocks," Colonel Grady replied.

"We already had enough here and then the Air Force brought in a pallet of beers. Actually, you guys are drinking on the hospitality of the U.S. Air Force tonight, Colonel," replied Preston.

"Well, if that's the case, I'm sure my men could stomach a few beers."

"What do we have here, Colonel Grady?" the president asked, looking over the long line of vehicles and still holding his first beer in his hand.

"Oh yes, Mr. President, let's give you a tour." The colonel ordered the men to form up and continued talking to the president while his soldiers got into formation in front of their vehicles. "Preston, we have grown since you and I first met in Alabama two days ago. This group is the vanguard, or the lead group. You told me to get up there as fast as possible, and that's why we are here. We have twenty-two 155mm howitzers and twenty-eight 105mm howitzers, all pulled by these trucks here." The colonel showed the group the first 50 large trucks with the large howitzers towed behind them.

They had now been joined by everybody on the farm, including Joe and David, who had heard the racket. Introductions were again made, and the colonel continued walking down the long line with men in formation saluting the president as he came up to each group of men.

The first family was excited to meet as many of the troops as they could, and Preston was handed the president's beer so that he could give a return salute to the troops.

"Colonel Smith at Bragg is getting another six 155mm howitzers behind six of his trucks—all museum pieces and as bad as mine—and he has two old M103 heavy tanks still on their original tractor-trailers. They are beauties, Mr. President. They have the bigger 120mm guns, and seventy of their projectiles are armor-piercing. He also has two still-operational older M1 Abrams with the smaller 105mm guns. Unfortunately, their tractor-trailers don't work and the Abrams are going to have to get up there under their own steam.

So far, we have a total of 89 troop carriers, nine fuel tankers, and 15 old jeeps, of which eight are Mutts."

"The Mutts have TOW missiles, with anti-tank and armor penetration to about 15 inches with 'normal' armor. 'Hardened armor' is another matter, but the TOWs don't mind if they hit tanks or ships—they will just go where they are aimed. Then we have 27 old trucks, of which several used to be garbage trucks and are now carrying ammunition. Then we have 15 ammunition-filled trucks pulling large 88mm mortars, one rocket launcher vehicle (post-Vietnam War), and a hospital tractor-trailer. That's 130 trucks standing in front of you, and another 120 getting mobile. There are another 2,200 men ready to move in from Fort Bragg, but they are still searching for enough vehicles to transport them. The Fort Bragg commander is filling another five 10-ton dump trucks with all types of guns, ammo, mortars, flares, and all sorts of nasty surprises for anybody wanting to attack us. He has another couple of fuel tankers he will need refueled every 100 highway miles or so. Mr. President, we have built a small army, and we have enough firepower to sink anything that gets within three miles of the U.S. shoreline."

"I believe you, Colonel," laughed the president, impressed at the 30-year-old vintage trucks with the extremely modern-looking soldiers standing in front of them. The picture just didn't look right, but at this stage who cared.

The night grew cold, but the hangar was warm. Much of the snacks from Preston's large stocks had already been handed out to the soldiers—chocolate bars, packs of jerky, several bags of peanuts and potato chips, as well as 200 cases of all types of beer, much from the gas station's supplies Joe had bought. A line was formed, and each soldier received three cold beers each, enough to have a party.

* * *

Mo Wang was still baffled as to why the plan was not going according to what the Politburo had expected. The chairman, he had realized, had been blinded by his own sense of power and could not handle a disruption in his power breakdown. Mo was quite shocked that the man who had designed this plan could not accept that things could, or would, go wrong. Mo knew little about the unwinding of the master plan, but he tried to work out the possibilities.

First, the termination squads in North Carolina disappeared. The same little airport which had seemed to be in the middle of the turmoil was attacked for the second time, and 200 of his best troops suddenly stopped communicating with their satellite phones. Then, this voice was heard, the voice of Lee Wang, who said he was Bo Lee Tang, from the past, which led him into a false sense of security. Then the headquarters building in Nanjing was bombed, with aircraft coming out of nowhere.

Mo thought about the situation for a long time, but he could not piece the little airport in North Carolina together with the bombing in Nanjing. There was no way a little airplane out of a little airport in America could suddenly fly across the world and bomb a building several thousand miles away, with no method of communication and no directional satellites to lead it precisely into an attack. Then it hit him hard.

"Somehow they were using Zedong Electronics' satellite system to direct some special type of aircraft across the planet. That's why nobody speaks to me," he suddenly realized. "They are using code to speak on our captured satellite phones to each other. Lee Wang pops up from nowhere, the squad sent in has not terminated him, and he joined forces with somebody who can fly aircraft across the world."

It was the only explanation Mo Wang could come up with.

"Somehow they have cut into the continuous feed coming from the three satellites…" and then the big one hit him.

"If they are seeing everything the satellites can see, they could be tracking our ships and our attack force. They know we are coming and will be ready for us with a far bigger force than we expect!"

For the rest of the day and well into the night on the second full day aboard the aircraft carrier he pondered the situation and what he could do about it. He slowly pieced together parts of what had actually happened, in the same way Carlos and Lee Wang had done days earlier. Mo managed to get through to 15 of the termination squads, now in convoy and still on their way across America from the West Coast. He warned them about a possible surprise attack against them, and that they should be careful when they entered New York. He wanted them to get into position and survey the airports, reporting back to him what they found at the three airports, and then check out the harbor.

It was dawn on the third day aboard the aircraft carrier, and now they were in the middle of the Pacific—1,000 miles from China and halfway to reaching the Panama Canal where resupply ships were waiting to refuel and restock the ships and men on board. From there, they would set sail for the final part of the journey into New York Harbor, now only 11 days away. Something had to be done, and he bravely went up on deck as the sun climbed into the empty horizon. There was nothing visible apart from the ships around them sailing at 18 knots, and he knew what he had to do.

The sun was fully over the horizon 20 minutes later when he went in search of the chairman's rooms. He had wanted to view the sunrise, an hour ahead of Shanghai, since it could be his last.

He knocked and was surprised to find the chairman dressed and having a breakfast of tea, noodles, and strips of fried pork.

"Come in, Wang, I'll get some breakfast and tea ordered for you," the chairman stated when he saw who was at the door. "It looks like you have been up all night."

"Yes, Comrade Chairman. I have been trying to work out what

has happened around the world in the last couple of days," Wang replied, bowing and entering the large set of rooms behind the portly chairman.

"Well, I suppose I'd better hear your results of a full night of thinking," the chairman replied, showing Wang a chair at the table and ordering his man-servant to get breakfast for his guest. "It is so nice to get up one hour earlier, thinking that one is refreshed and fully awake while others in Shanghai are still asleep or trying to get the drowsiness out of their systems."

While he ate, Wang told the chairman his worst fears, everything he believed could have happened in America—Lee Wang, the satellite phones, and the satellites they had lost control of, which he believed were now being controlled by the Americans. He had been speaking for 20 minutes when the chairman's satellite phone rang. He picked it up off the dining table and answered it.

He listened for several seconds and then Wang saw the chairman's face go red as he replied angrily into the phone.

"What do you mean that I should have a nice flight into Beijing, Colonel Dong? Have you lost your marbles or something? I'm not at Pudong Airport. I'm here on our aircraft carrier 1,000 miles away from Shanghai. What do you mean that a man like me is dressed and entering an aircraft! That's not me! That's an imposter! Send out the guard and stop any aircraft from taking off. Go upstairs to the control tower and find out who the men are that spoke to the traffic controllers! Do it now, Colonel Dong, or you will be reverted to a private, you stupid man!" he shouted into the phone.

"Somebody is trying to steal our aircraft in Shanghai," the chairman stated to Wang. "Do you hear that? Imbeciles are trying to steal our troop aircraft!"

"It must be the same Americans who have been causing our problems," answered Wang. "I have all the termination squads heading for New York to find out the truth at the Kennedy airport, what happened there, and what happened to our passenger aircraft that supposedly went down with engine failure."

"You and those damn Americans!" replied the chairman angrily.

"Those stupid Americans are not worth worrying about. They have always been the most stupid people on this planet, and I promise you, Comrade Wang, they are not clever enough to beat an attack from me that has been thirty years in the making. They couldn't even win their wars in Vietnam…Iraq…Somalia…Afghanistan and how many more. They have actually never won a war, unless you consider their Civil War a war. Wang, I'm sick of your stories about Americans. America is the most useless nation I have ever met! They always push their beliefs and views into every other country's daily life and blend reality with their Hollywood-film rubbish. America, its politics, and its people are nothing more than a massive wave of insecurity, totally destroying themselves with fake beliefs and their fake lives of plenty. I'm doing the survivors of America a favor by taking them over. First, I'm going to turn every American into a hard-working slave—a slave who will wish for nothing more than to have died when we turned out their lights."

The chairman stopped. He was trying to catch his breath. His anger was getting away from him and he sat down and wiped his brow. *Nothing in my whole life has ever gone wrong. Why would it go wrong now?* he thought.

"I bet that when Colonel Dong returns, he will tell me who the real antagonists against Zedong Electronics are and that they are going to pay for their atrocities against me and my powerful new order. Believe me, Comrade Wang, they are going to pay."

The phone rang again, and the chairman answered, listening for several seconds. Wang heard an explosion come from the phone's speaker and a voice shouting at the other end—something about the men being Chinese infiltrators. They had spoken fluent Chinese and whoever the voice belonged to had even seen the eyes of two of them as they passed him going down the stairs, and now aircraft with propellers were attacking the airport while the big jets were taking off. Suddenly, there was a high-pitched scream and another very loud explosion and the phone must have gone dead in the chairman's hand. He threw it hard against the wall and it broke into several pieces.

Tiredly, the chairman sat down, poured himself and Comrade Wang a fresh cup of tea, and shouted several orders to the two guards standing in the room. They disappeared and returned several minutes later carrying a red console—this time with four bright red buttons under locked glass, much like the last and fifth button he had pushed a couple of days earlier on the first console, which still stood on the table.

Breakfast was important, and the chairman spent the next couple of minutes enjoying his before he spoke another word. Comrade Wang could only sit there, uncomfortable, and eat his own breakfast. A man must be allowed to think.

"You see, Comrade Wang..." the chairman continued as he finished his meal. Wang could see that the phone call had taken away his energy. "You see, Wang, the Americans are too stupid to be a force against us. It was Chinese infiltrators, not Americans. I have always been prepared for attacks against us and knew in my heart that our Chinese government would be the ones to let us down. I am prepared for every occasion."

"Chinese attackers?" asked Wang in shock.

"Yes, Wang, the only nation as intelligent as Zedong Electronics...and a nation about to die," the chairman replied, looking at the man as if he were stupid.

The chairman shouted for a new phone and continued speaking while one was found in another room. "Everything is prepared for people trying to stop me. I've spent 30 years and much money making sure that my plan doesn't fail. I'm now going to tell the rest of our aircraft to take off out of Shanghai. Our position there is compromised, and I have always had a backup airport ready for this—Harbin Airport in one of the most northern cities in China. I really wanted a second base in the city of Sanya, further south of Shanghai and our most southern city, but the flight directly into New York from Sanya Airport was too far, even for our most advanced 747 and even the Airbus aircraft. So I chose Harbin in our northwestern territory—very cold in winter but closer to America and far away from Beijing, Shanghai, Guangzhou, and Taipei in

Taiwan, where in a few hours they are going to feel my wrath. From our new airport, flying time into New York is shorter by two hours for our troops. We only need one flight of troops, because I honestly believe we don't need any more. They will fly from Harbin into New York 24 hours before we arrive. Comrade Wang, I bet you my life that we will see no Americans in New York other than women and children begging for food and ready to become Chinese citizens to get a free meal."

It only took minutes for the men to find a new phone, and it arrived quickly. The chairman made just one call. It was back to the airport, and he talked with someone new. He gave orders for all remaining aircraft to take off immediately, as full of the most elite troops as possible, and leave everyone else behind. He got angry when he was told that he had only 20 aircraft left. The Chinese pilots had stolen 12, three had been blown up, and the transporter was one of the missing aircraft. It had already been 30 minutes since the attack had begun, and he told his contact at the airport, somebody Wang didn't know, that they had three hours to get the aircraft onto the ground in Harbin, otherwise their aircraft could fall out of the sky. "Exactly three hours!" he stated into the phone, looking at his watch and explaining to the man on the other end that they had 30 minutes to get out of Shanghai because flying time to Harbin was two hours and that the deadline gave them 30 minutes to get back on the ground.

"I want three hours of time so that those thieves can fly those stolen aircraft into Beijing," he stated to Wang as he put the phone down. "They are certainly going to get a shock."

Wang thought he knew what was about to happen, and he felt sick. He felt sick, because he had spent his life helping this madman, this crazy communist, as crazy as his father before him. The Chunqiao family had spent their lives trying to destroy everything others had tried to build. The chairman's father had tried to destroy the world Mao Zedong had built 40 years earlier. Now this man, the son of Chunqiao, was doing his best to destroy the world. Not only the whole world, though, but all of Chinese history, thousands of years of advanced history—a nation who had always been in the forefront of progress.

He felt sick inside, but still smiled at the man and begged to leave. With a motion from his right arm, the chairman dismissed Wang. He had already forgotten about the story Wang had told him and from now on would only listen to his own ideas. He had never understood why he had to listen to anybody else. *Comrade Wang, what a waste of time,* Chairman Chunqiao thought to himself as Wang walked out of the room and back up on deck.

Comrade Wang did not feel well.

* * *

The general felt worried for the first time. He had achieved his main plan of not deserting the deployed American troops, especially on the front lines in the Middle East. There was not much more he could do for the civilians back home. Preston and his team would sort and help as many of the remaining population as possible.

General Pete Allen was a military man—a person who understood war and combat, not feeding millions of starving people. To date, he had achieved much and was satisfied with his team's accomplishments. They had taken the attack to the enemy. Thanks to Carlos and Lee Wang, the United States had communications with many parts of the world and the Russian and Chinese governments now knew that it wasn't America who had done this ghastly deed.

Pete Allen also realized that the world, totally dependent on its desperate need for all types of electronics to run, was literally on its knees, and millions more were going to die long before modern civilization got back on its feet. The whole of the world's civilization had been pushed back to before the Industrial Age—more than a hundred years earlier.

It was going to take time, probably decades, before all the first-world countries became first-world countries again. All the first-world countries were now third-world countries, and he realized that all the poor people in third-world countries that had existed last year, depending on free food supplies from other countries, would now die or at least drop their population numbers to those few who could survive this catastrophe—not many, but maybe enough to survive as a nation, or a nationality.

Zedong Electronics had certainly done a number on the world, certainly turning civilization back, and maybe it was a good thing. Maybe it was a good thing to learn from, to help re-write society so that it didn't depend on the stupid ideas of war and greed and electronic trinkets that had been plaguing civilization as a whole.

Now he had one more stop in Beijing to hand over the cell phones for American and international communications with China. He would refuel there, and, as a captain leaving a sinking ship, he would be the last aircraft of the flying aircraft to land in Turkey. There he would gather every aircraft and all the military personnel he could and get them to New York to repel Zedong Electronics' first and only attack on the United States. Once this attack was thwarted, he reckoned that they would run out of steam and be unable to launch another one. If they believed that America was such an easy pushover in terms of invasion, then they would be in for a shock. That could also mean that maybe their top brass were on board the ships or aircraft coming in and it would be necessary to destroy every uninvited guest trying to put their feet onto American soil. He remembered the area around the entrance to New York, and for the next two hours as they flew on to Beijing, he designed a plan of defense around New York Harbor.

He was 30 minutes out of Beijing when he called Colonel Patterson, on his way to Elmendorf in Alaska. The large group of 747s were cruising at 38,000 feet, currently 1,500 miles west of Shanghai, and would be leaving Chinese airspace in just over an hour, heading north of Pakistan and into Turkey. They were on a fast cruise and five hours away from the Incirlik Air Force Base in Turkey.

General Allen spent the next 20 minutes outlining the plan of defense he wanted set up as soon as Colonel Patterson arrived back in New York. Colonel Patterson was ordered to take the first C-130 out of McGuire and set up the defense plan in New York Harbor so that men and arms were moving before General Allen got back in an estimated two days. The general wanted to head into Baghdad and Kabul and organize the troop extractions himself. He wanted every aircraft full to the brim with troops out of Turkey, clearing the base and country of all active American personnel and, in one sweep, flying them into the three New York airports.

They would deposit their cargos and then return straight back to Baghdad on alternate days to do the same until Iraq was totally clear of troops. On the other days, the fleet would fly into Kabul and transfer all U.S. military and civilian personnel out from Afghanistan.

Then General Allen spent ten minutes describing the best way to defend New York Harbor against an air or naval attack. He had detailed such a plan decades earlier when he was a major in the Air Force. The then Major Allen had been given the task of defending New York as a scenario against a possible attack from Cuba around the Bay of Pigs timeframe.

He had just finished the plan when the pilot told the general that they were five minutes out and the weather was clear and the sun bright but cold. The landing was normal. The same runway had been cleared and the pilot had actually communicated on the radio with the airport tower ten minutes before they had arrived over the vast city.

Chapter 16

The Lull before the Storm

THE CHINESE RADIO CONTROLLER IN Beijing stated in bad English that government officials were being driven to the airport and that they would be another half an hour. A lonely *Ghost Rider* landed, and General Allen called the other aircraft to check on their progress while his crew got ready to refuel the AC-130. The temperature outside was well below freezing, but the sunlight was nice to stand in.

Blue Moon, *Easy Girl*, and the tanker were three hours out of Omsk and about to enter Mongolia. All the Russian and restored U.S. radio beacons were working well, and they were on track. The transporter was well on her way and about to enter Alaskan airspace. Now he had to have this meeting and then get back to what he wanted to do—moving the troops back home.

It was nearly 30 minutes before the same three limousines from before arrived, flags flying. They were escorted by military jeeps in front and behind the cavalcade. The same three men got out, each again with an interpreter, and they gathered in a group around the middle vehicle. Pete Allen walked up to them and gave each man a satellite phone. He also gave them the numbers of the phones, explained that the red number on each phone would dial the enemy, and gave them a short list of only five other phone numbers—the

U.S. President's, his, and the three numbers on their way to the Russian government.

The Chinese delegation thanked the general, got into their cars, and much to his relief, drove off in the same way they had come in. Once again, he was left alone at the international airport, which was desolate and empty except for a few newspapers and candy wrappers rolling by in the wind.

Refueling took another ten minutes, and the crew made sure that the tanks were as full as possible, since the next stretch to Omsk was only 50 miles shorter than *Ghost Rider*'s longest fuel range before she had to switch to reserve tanks that only gave her another 45 minutes of flight. It was going to be tight.

He looked around and went for a short walk while the crew got everything stashed away, realizing for the first time that all of the airport terminal slots were actually full of aircraft, whereas at the U.S. airports they had been mostly empty. He looked around a little closer and realized that there were hundreds of aircraft—mostly Chinese airlines at the terminals. From where he stood, he could see well over 70 aircraft, and he realized why the 747s in Shanghai had been parked in a line and easily stolen. There were hundreds of aircraft everywhere.

They hadn't lost hundreds of aircraft in the air. The Chinese aircraft were all on the ground when the lights went out. They must have been warned by Zedong Electronics. Pete suddenly he felt like he was in a trap. He immediately walked over to the nearest aircraft—the older 747 he had entered on his last visit with China Airlines on its tail. It was as dead and empty as the last time he'd been in it. He just wanted to make sure, and this time he checked all the electronic switches he could in the cockpit. It would never fly again.

He checked the galleys where the cabin attendants made drinks and food and discovered that the smell wasn't good. There were meals rotting in the galleys—meals that had been ready for passengers when they boarded. That foxed him. It looked like the aircraft had been grounded just in case there were bad parts on them, which there were, but the aircraft had been made ready for flight once it had been grounded, which meant that somebody was expecting to fly it again once the emergency was over.

Somebody had not told these airlines the complete story, or the Chinese government had been lied to, expecting their aircraft to return to the skies once the emergency was over. The galley was full of miniature bottles of whiskey—good whiskey—and he opened one, reckoning that he deserved a drink, knocked one down, and helped himself to several more before he went to check the next aircraft.

The second plane, also an older 747, was in the same condition, and he realized that China was totally in the dark about what was happening, just like America, and he hadn't meant it to be a pun. He suddenly felt cold shivers down his spine, knocked back a second whiskey, got out of the aircraft fast, and ran over to *Ghost Rider*, which was ready with her first engine already winding up.

General Allen immediately got on the phone to Carlos, who he woke up, and told him that China had nothing to do with the shutdown of the world, that they were in the same position, and that his second trip here had been to deliver the phones and make sure that it was Zedong Electronics and Zedong Electronics alone that was trying to take over the world.

He continued talking to Carlos throughout takeoff, and they climbed into the beautiful dawn sky. He opened his third whiskey, trying to sort out the heaviness in his stomach, gulped it down, and felt its warmth travel through him. He said goodbye to his friend, who was only half awake at McGuire, and sat back—the alcohol starting to take effect.

Ghost Rider, completely full of fuel, climbed through 10,000 feet and headed towards her next stop. Switching over to autopilot, Pete was asleep a couple of minutes later. Neither he, nor the radar screen, would have been fast enough to see, or monitor, the Pakistani-made, Zedong Electronics Shaheen (White Falcon) III ballistic missile 100,000 feet above them, already in a vertical dive at Mach 3 straight towards Tiananmen Square in the center of Beijing. Its powerful nuclear warhead exploded several seconds later at 1,000 feet above ground, exactly over where the famous hero of Tiananmen Square had stood in front of a tank many years earlier. Pete Allen never felt a thing.

* * *

The members of the Politburo were not present when Comrade Wang entered the boardroom on the aircraft carrier. He had been summoned by the chairman a couple of hours after he had left the stateroom earlier that morning.

"Comrade Wang, sit down. I wanted company on this important day, the day I mark our dynasty on the map by taking the life of another dynasty so that we may flourish. This is my choice as chairman of the New World, and I make this unfortunate decision alone so that I may bear the blame if it is the wrong one."

Wang noticed that he, the chairman and his two guards were the only people in the room. The new console with the four red buttons he had seen earlier was on the table, and the chairman's fingers were playing with them.

"These buttons cost me a fortune with Pakistan. Wang, do you know what these buttons are?" he asked the man sitting at the other end of the boardroom table.

"I will assume that they are buttons of mass destruction, Comrade Chairman," Comrade Wang replied, knowing that at the very least these were not buttons of peace. For a split second, he looked directly at the chairman, who had not an ounce of emotion on his face and was looking intently at Wang. It was at that moment that Wang wanted to kill him—he wanted to destroy this madman who considered himself the first ruler of the New World Dynasty.

"Guards, make sure Comrade Wang does not move from his seat. I think he wants to harm me." The guards moved towards Comrade Wang, weapons at the ready. "Cousin Wang, I dedicate this first rocket to all the Chinese dynasties that came before mine. May they live in eternal peace," and he pressed the first button. "The missile silos were built in my secret headquarters in Harbin, where all the aircraft have been flown."

The chairman then pressed the second button and then the third.

"May I ask what terror you have now unleashed on the world, Comrade Chairman?" asked Wang, knowing that he didn't really want to know.

"Of course, Comrade Wang. The first is a nuclear warhead on a Pakistani missile, one of four I purchased a couple of years ago with the promise that I wouldn't shut their country down when the time came."

"But you did shut them down, Comrade Chairman," interrupted Wang.

"Correct," replied the chairman. "But I didn't shut them down when I shut down America. And I never told them how much time I would give them. I thought that one extra day per rocket was a good deal for both sides. The first missile will wipe out all of Beijing and the surrounding area for at least 100 miles around Tiananmen Square. The second missile will completely wipe out our arch enemy Taiwan, and the third is going in between Hong Kong and our third largest city of Guangzhou, where our family has had many enemies for the last century. The fourth missile is for Shanghai, and it will not be used until we have all our troops out. I'm transferring all our troops into Harbin as of later today. Within 15 minutes, those first three areas will be totally destroyed."

"But you just sentenced 50 million people to death!" replied Wang, now shocked to the core.

"Yes, people who have turned against me and my dynasty. People who would not take orders from me, but now will come and kiss my feet for mercy. Many of them were going to die from the cold and lack of food in the coming weeks anyway. All I've done is end their misery earlier. It is also just a small part of our Great China, and the greatest people of China are the farmers and landowners who will begin to feed our people in the spring when the growing season comes. And, Wang, 50 million people is a small number compared to our overall plan and the numbers that have already died in North

America, Europe, and Russia. I don't really need more than a billion people serving me and my Politburo, and the fewer people there are, the less chance I have of people rising up against me in the century to come."

"When will all this killing of innocent people end?" asked Wang, sick to his stomach.

"When I say it does!" the chairman shouted. "When I rule America and the rest of the world! And when the world lives in accordance to the regime 'The Gang of Four' wanted in China a half century ago, as my father wished. That's when, Wang. Now go away and start preparing for the attack on America. We have ten days to get everything ready."

They were too far away to see or hear the explosions, but ocean swells larger than normal brushed against the ships several hours later. Wang did not know what to do. He was powerless to try anything brash, and he looked down at the water trying to figure out how everybody had been so enthusiastic at the beginning, and whether all in the Politburo would still be as enthusiastic as they were in the beginning if they had witnessed what he had just witnessed. Humans were obviously not as civilized as they thought they were, and if death and destruction was the only thing consuming mankind, then this world was not fit for humans to survive.

* * *

Carlos, wakened by the general, was watching his simple screen half-awake when he heard electronic chatter coming in from the satellite feed. Something was going on. The satellites were directing something. They seemed to have a new line of input data coming from this new location, and he was powerless to do anything. He looked at the information coming in. The three satellites were directing more than one object out of North China, and suddenly he knew what they were.

"Oh, my God!" he said to Sally, still in bed sleeping.

She came to life groggily. "What is it, Carlos?" she asked, watching as his face went white in front of the screen.

"I think the satellites are directing in missiles," he replied.

"Where?" she asked, sitting up and suddenly wide awake.

"They could be anywhere. I can't see them, and the only thing I can see is the transponders from the 130s going into Russia and General Allen's leaving Beijing."

"Oh, my God!" he said again. This time Sally wrapped the blanket around her and went to stand next to Carlos. His face lit up slightly several minutes later as the screen showed a brilliant blast of light larger than the size of a pinhead. "Some sort of missile has detonated in Beijing, right on top of *Ghost Rider*. It must be a nuclear warhead with a light that strong!"

"Somebody is blowing up Beijing with a nuclear bomb?" asked Sally.

"Not just one," replied Carlos, the satellite feed showing multiple missiles. "They could be coming straight here for all we know, if they are intercontinental or ICBMs."

"The general was in Beijing?" asked Sally.

"Yes, he had just taken off from there. He would have been 40 to 50 miles from the blast. Enough to blow him out of the sky, and the shock wave would have turned *Ghost Rider* into confetti."

"*Ghost Rider*…General Allen…is gone?" she asked.

"Looks like it," Carlos replied. "Try and call his number. Oh! There's a second blast, right on top of Taipei in Taiwan. Somebody is bombing China, Sally. And there's a third one, just north of Hong Kong. That's three nuclear explosions in three minutes!"

Sally phoned the general's number and all she got was a busy signal. She tried again and again, until after the fifth time, she stopped and put the phone down. Carlos picked up the phone and called the President of the United States, who was still asleep down at Preston's farm.

"*Did you see where the missiles came from?*" was the first question the president asked Carlos.

"I could tell by the feed that the missiles had come out of north China. It will take me a day or so to get the exact longitude and latitude from the directional computations that have been recorded on the computer. We set that up yesterday. If it's in code, Lee might be able to decipher it. If he can't, then the closest I can tell will be within a couple hundred miles. There's nothing much up there in northwestern China apart from a few small cities, but we could set up a secondary code telling the computer to deactivate the directional information from its original source as soon as it begins, and we can naturalize any more missiles."

"*So what you are saying is that Zedong Electronics, or somebody else in China, is sending nuclear missiles into other areas of their own country?*" asked the president.

"Yes, sir," Carlos replied.

"*And they could have dozens more?*"

"Yes, sir."

"*Can we direct our nuclear missiles into this area using the same system they are using?*" was the president's next question.

"Not yet, sir," replied Carlos, still stunned at what he had just witnessed—potentially the beginning of the world's first nuclear war. He asked Sally to get dressed and fetch Lee using the jeep they had for their use from the house he was using on base at McGuire. "I will need to write a program, Mr. President. It could take up to a week, and even if Lee and I achieve that, it won't do any good if we don't know the approximate location of the missile silos, plus they could have different silos in other areas. We only have less than half a dozen missiles in our armory."

The president asked Carlos to keep him posted on any new developments and went to fetch the first family. He wanted to move to McGuire.

Lee arrived several minutes later and nodded when Carlos brought him up to date. He was saddened by the death of General Allen and asked Carlos if his wife was also on the aircraft. Nobody knew, and it took Carlos two phone calls to find out that Mrs. Wang was in Russian airspace and about to land in Omsk. He was comforted by the fact that *Ghost Rider* was the only fatality.

"The general must have known that something was about to

happen," said Carlos to Lee and Sally. "Pete always had a good sixth sense, and I feel really sad for the loss this country is going to feel—Pete's friends and so many respected colleagues—when they hear about his death. The country must not forget him. By out-thinking the opposition, General Allen has almost singlehandedly beaten back a massive attack against the world and the United States of America that was 30 years in the making by clever and educated opponents. We still need the general's luck for the next couple of weeks."

An hour later, Carlos and Lee were working on a new code to send up to the Chinese satellites when Carlos' satellite phone rang. As everyone usually did, he answered and waited for the caller to say Allen Key. This time, the caller didn't say the code words, but asked in English to speak to Lee Wang. Carlos put his hand over the receiver.

"Lee, someone who sounds like a Chinese man wants to speak to you," Carlos whispered. Lee froze and looked at Carlos for advice. There was no Chinese person who knew where he was, and he shrugged his shoulders and said nothing.

"My name is Mo Wang," said the voice on the other side. *"I am an old friend of Lee Wang and I need to speak with him. My number is..."* and he gave his number and hung up.

"What should we do?" Lee asked Carlos after hearing what the man had said. "He is the man—you know, the one who recruited me and then tried to kill me and my family. He is an old friend, but I won't ever trust him again."

"Well, maybe he wants to discuss the upcoming attack, and we could find out some information if we play our cards right," replied Carlos. "Even though they have nuclear weapons, they don't know that we have some, and, like a game of chess, we could overplay our game and tell him we are ready to blow up the rest of their world. It will shock them to hear about our made-up strengths, and maybe they will all go home and dig holes to bury themselves in."

"You mean bluff them into not attacking us?" asked Lee Wang.

"Why not? We have lost our commander, and I don't think we have much more to lose right now. Our element of surprise is running out, I reckon. I know it's a secret right now, but it's time I told you that we also have nuclear weapons and the president wants you and me to set up an attack similar to what they have done in China. Maybe it's necessary to attack them with nuclear warheads, but I personally don't want the war to go that far."

It took another several minutes before Carlos phoned the number back and immediately heard the same person's voice on the other end. "Good morning, Mr. Mo Wang," Carlos spoke into the phone. "My name is Carlos Rodriquez. My uncle is the Colombian Ambassador to the United States and you called me on my phone. I am putting it on speaker phone."

"You mean one of our phones, Mr. Rodriquez," the person on the other end replied in perfect English.

"No, actually this has always been my own personal phone since I purchased it a year ago. I don't believe this phone ever belonged to you or your organization, Mr. Wang. Maybe the new parts did, which I had to pirate from one of phones we captured when your troops attacked ours last week."

"So you are in North Carolina, Mr. Rodriquez?" Mo Wang asked.

"No, I'm not, but I was there when we completely wiped out your men, Mr. Wang. And I believe we will do so again and again until you and your company are dead—in about ten days, I believe?" He heard the sound of a grunt of shock on the other end of the line.

"You know where we are?" asked Wang, not believing what he was hearing.

"Of course we do, Mr. Wang. We have our own dozen satellites monitoring your movements right now." Carlos embellished the truth a bit. "We destroyed your headquarters, most if not all of your troops here on the ground, and we are about to destroy what you have left. Oh, and thank you for your aircraft. They are going to really help us get all our troops back home to await your arrival."

"You stole our aircraft?" asked Mo Wang, trying to fathom that he had actually been correct all along. *"And Lee Wang has helped you find out about us?"*

"Yes, we stole your aircraft in reparation for the aircraft you destroyed. And yes to your second question. Mr. Wang works for me now. His wife is currently in Russia giving their government some of your captured satellite phones and telling the authorities there who is to blame for the destruction of their country. They are free to use our satellites and send over as many nuclear missiles as they wish to destroy your country, as we are about to, and, I believe, as your group has already started to do a couple of hours ago. It's going to be a big turkey shoot over there. By the way, Mr. Wang, we asked the Russians not to destroy you. We want that pleasure for ourselves. I just don't understand why you are destroying your own country."

"You know about the missile attacks?" Mo Wang then asked, knowing that his chances of a long and fruitful life were now most likely in the hands of the Americans rather than those of the chairman.

"Our satellite feed showed Beijing, Taiwan, and Hong Kong being destroyed by your own missiles coming out of northwestern China—not the United States or Russia—so don't try and bullshit me, Wang. Your headquarters were destroyed, your satellites can be erased at any time, and if you think you can attack us with your modern weapons with no satellites to guide them, you are very much mistaken. Mr. Wang, we can take you out at a push of a button. If we had known that your organization had nuclear missiles, we would have taken out your three little satellites sooner. A small mistake on our part that cost over 40 million lives, unfortunately—innocent Chinese lives."

"I am not in control of what is happening," replied Wang. *"The chairman is giving the orders."*

"Should I know his name?" asked Carlos. "Is he important enough for me to know his name? Don't tell me it is Mao Zee Tung. I won't believe you, Mr. Wang."

"His name is Chairman Wang Chunqiao, son of Comrade Chunqiao from the Zedong days of 'The Gang of Four.' Chairman Chunqiao is president and CEO of Zedong Electronics, and my boss," replied Wang, now not knowing what to do.

"I'm sorry, but his name doesn't ring a bell. I suggest you hand him your phone when we are finished and tell him to call me when he's ready to be terminated." Carlos was having way too much fun.

"By the way, this conversation is being recorded and will be sent to the President of the United States, who will decide when to end your attack once and for all," Carlos continued, winking at Lee. He now had control of the man at the other end, if he didn't hang up. "Or we could play back this recording to your Comrade Chairman when we meet with him in a few days. I'm sure looking forward to the introduction. We have been moving hundreds of thousands of troops into your arrival area for days now."

"What can I do to help you get rid of this madman?" asked Mo Wang honestly.

"Not much," replied Carlos, smiling for the first time that day. "Your friend Lee Wang is sitting right next to me and he said not to trust you."

Suddenly the communication turned into rapid Chinese, Mo Wang talking excitedly to Lee Wang, since he realized the phone was on speaker phone.

"I'm very sorry, Mr. Wang, but I don't speak Chinese anymore," replied Lee sincerely. "I'm an American citizen and you have attacked my country. Not only that, but you tried to kill my family. I am looking forward to being there when the president, a very nice man actually and far better than you and your organization, presses the button to end your life. If you wish to speak with me, you had better continue in English—my Chinese is very bad."

"Wang, call off your hit squads," added Carlos angrily. "We are ready for them in New York, Washington, Los Angeles and every city you care to mention. Tell them to disappear and never be heard from or seen again. Tell your chairman that we are ready for him. My buddies are excited about getting into battle with their aircraft, tanks, guns, submarines, ships, helicopters, and believe you me, Mr. Wang, they are all itching to get into the action first. Just send the 20 remaining aircraft you have over to us. We want to get our troops back, and if it wasn't for those aircraft, you would all be dead by now. Oh! By the way, I look forward to meeting you personally in a few days. Look for me. I'll be one of hundreds of flying fighters, and when we meet, you will hang by the neck until dead, right next to your chairman. Bon voyage, Mr. Wang!" And he hung up.

Carlos put the phone down, his anger dissipating now. At least if the chairman was told of the conversation, or if he was actually listening in and it was a ploy, they wouldn't be so certain of their survival.

"I don't think you made Mr. Wang very happy," suggested Lee, smiling.

"I hope not," replied Carlos.

* * *

It was a fantastic sight, and it certainly raised the morale of everybody there, when on the 11th day, four fully laden 747s flew into each airport, disgorging 500 fully armed troops, fresh in from Turkey with their gear.

Newark's cleared runway was ready as the four jumbo jets lined up for their final approaches, coming in from Incirlik Air Base. Two thousand troops per airport was the goal General Allen had hoped would be realized. Now they had an even better chance of winning the war, and 11 more flights, or nearly 80,000 troops, could arrive before attack day.

The 747 transporter had arrived several hours earlier, flying in from Alaska. Her electrical component cargo had already been unloaded at McGuire, and she had been refueled to get to Seymour Johnson and back to carry a full load of food into JFK. Using the airport's fuel generators as backup and running with new parts, and with the central fuel-pumping terminal using the largest airport generator and several smaller military ones all tied together, fuel was once again retrievable from the central fuel location in New Jersey. Now all three airports could fill the 12 thirsty jets with 64,000 gallons of fuel each and get them airborne with fresh crews five hours after landing. The transporter would need five hours just to unload, and the refueling queue would be back in the air by the time she needed fuel—this time at JFK.

Two thousand new soldiers to feed per airport per day was a big deal, and all three of the airports had brought in cooks and field kitchens so that supplies of any fresh food could be served instead of MREs, at least until it was used up.

Colonel Patterson had received his new insignia, as had Major Wong, who had flown the transporter most of the way from Elmendorf in Alaska after getting some sleep during the 7-hour flight from Shanghai to Alaska. Patterson got a shock that his promotion had already been phoned through to the base commander at McGuire, as well as orders from the general that he was to lead the attack in New York.

Everyone had heard about the death of the general. After the call to Wang, Carlos had phoned all the numbers necessary to tell them the news about his death. The president had ordered that the nuclear explosions in China be kept from everyone else for the time being.

The remaining incoming troops would now be flown into Teterboro, now the busiest airport with C-130s and helicopters going in every few minutes. Once the airlifting began into Teterboro, the C-130 transporters were to go out to the bases and move in troops and any vehicles or guns that could fit into their holds.

Here at Teterboro, General Allen had planned to house 60,000 troops within the first ten days, with the 747s bringing in 6,000 new troops per day. The other three airports were ramping up for another round of 2,000 troops during the second week, and then Newark was to be supplied with as many troops as possible who could walk into the harbor area around New York once they were airlifted into Newark, which was the closet airport. The airports were up and running, and the 200 Chinese and 200 American engineers were being trucked into New York Harbor daily to repair all electrical machines or lines for whatever was needed. The Chinese electricians had a master plan, and the American engineers just went along with it.

The two remaining gunships and HC-130 tankers arrived back a day later, minus *Ghost Rider*. They were all refueled, and would wait for the funeral to be held later that afternoon at McGuire for the 14 lost aircrew, including General Allen, who had been aboard the lost aircraft. Carlos had gotten a lift back to Preston's farm to pick up his P-51, and all the people at Preston's farm had flown up in *Baby Huey* and *Lady Dandy* to attend the funeral.

There weren't many people left at the farm. Even Will Smart had risked his life, choosing the helicopter over *Lady Dandy*. He sat on the floor of the helicopter, holding both his kids' hands as they and the president's kids sat with him. The president and first lady were comfortable in the upholstered chairs that had been reinstalled to make *Baby Huey* into Air Force One again. With Will's eyes tightly shut, *Baby Huey* took off in a northerly direction towards McGuire under Buck's steady hand.

Lady Dandy had flown directly into McGuire with Barbara in the left seat and an excited Maggie as her co-pilot in the right seat. Joe and David had wanted to attend as well, and they arrived with Captain Pierce and 20 of his troops in the DC-3. Mike, John, and Pam had offered to stay behind to feed the dogs and as many people as they could get to with the Cargomaster, Pilatus, and Cessna 210 working most of the daylight hours. Preston had flown up in the 38 in formation with Martie's and Carlos' P-51s on either side of him.

Everyone had wanted a flyover for the funeral, so Preston organized one, and the 11 C-130s the general had carefully looked after and returned to perfect condition were all brought in for the short ceremony. Time, unfortunately, was running out.

It was a somber funeral, with 14 coffins laid out in a row. They were all empty, but it wouldn't have been a funeral without something to remember the lost crew by. Carlos had arranged for his uncle and father to be picked up from the Colombian Embassy in another Huey, and Vice Admiral Rogers and several of his naval personnel arrived in an old Coast Guard C-130 they had just refurbished and gotten flying the day before.

Michael and Grandpa Roebels, as well as the base commanders of Edwards and Hill AFBs arrived from Edwards aboard a C-130 with Captain Jennifer Watkins in the pilot's seat.

In the last four days, Jennifer had visited 30 Air Force bases in the United States and had given out satellite phones. It was the first time since that busy day at Preston's farm that so many aircraft were in one place. Even the three refurbished F-4s had been flown in by pilots of the general's direct command. Just to spite the enemy, something General Allen would have done, every aircraft flew in with their transponders on. First, the president said a few words about the man he had only really gotten to know several days earlier. "Pete was an American who put his country first. I don't even know if he was married or had any children. He did his job for his country, not allowing anything or anybody to distract him from saving this land. Thanks to him, the United States of America now has the opportunity to continue to be a free and democratic society for the long term."

He explained that this funeral was also a tribute to all the

American people, military or civilian, who had died since

January 1st. "Don't let us forget the millions of innocent people around the world who have died for nothing more than someone's thirst for power and greed." He silently took his seat.

The Colombian Ambassador stood at the podium and said that Pete Allen was one of the finest men he had ever met. He had helped Colombia overcome the drug war in the early years by providing U.S. aid and Air Force aircraft and helicopters to help with curtailing the war against the gangs and drug lords taking over Colombia. Thanks to Pete Allen, his country of Colombia was still also a free country.

Vice Admiral Rogers said a eulogy for his fallen friend. "I grew up with Pete Allen. We were at a high school military academy together. Nobody could out-think Pete. He was a tactician. He lived for planning battles. Unfortunately, Pete was a straight-talking man and had been passed by for promotion by Air Force generals now long forgotten, when he wouldn't stand down from verbal confrontation. He was not one to beat about the bush, and he called a spade a spade and pissed off many. I knew Pete's family well. He and I had both courted the woman who became his wife at different times, and he definitely won the prize with Marge Allen. Unfortunately, she died of cancer in 1995, and he was pretty lost without her for a while. Marge and Pete Allen had two sons—Captain Peter Junior and Lieutenant

Joe Allen. One died in combat in Iraq and the other in a civilian car crash here in the United States. Both had been active-duty military and were single when they died. His elder son Peter was shot down in an Apache helicopter in Iraq in 1996, and Joe had been a marine for ten years when he was killed in a car accident driving from Washington to North Carolina in 1998. In three years, this proud man lost his entire family, but he never shirked his duty to his country. He got through the turmoil in his life and moved on to the kind of greatness we saw in him over the past week. Hopefully, he is now reunited with his loved ones in Heaven. General Pete Allen, as well as the entire Allen family, should always be remembered for their support of their beloved country, the United States of America."

The jets had been separated from the piston aircraft, and all the aircraft radios had been tuned in to the funeral, which they broadcast through their radio microphones. A band played as the captured 747 transporter came in very low in formation with the three F-4s, one in front and one on each side. Then the second wave came over as a 21-gun salute was given to the general and his crew by Air Force troops commanded by Captain Pierce. Then the piston-engine aircraft came over low and slow at 500 feet. It was led by Preston in the P-38 with Martie and Carlos in the two P-51 Mustangs, followed by all 12 of the flying C-130s in an arrow-shaped formation. The formation had a hole in it right behind the lead aircraft flown by Sally and Jennifer, with the two gunships next in line. Between them was a hole where *Ghost Rider* should have been. Behind the hole was the latest addition to the fleet of aircraft—the Coast Guard C-130 of Vice Admiral Rogers.

The band played and the soldiers stood to attention as the aircraft passed overhead.

Chapter 17

Preparation for Invasion USA

MO WANG DIDN'T KNOW WHAT to do. It had been an hour since he had spoken on the phone to America. Even his worst fears about what the Americans actually knew had been surpassed. Carlos Rodriquez had been upfront about everything they had done, how much they knew, and even that they knew where he, Mo Wang, was—in the middle of the Pacific with ten ships.

Of course they wanted the aircraft. It was the only way to transfer their troops back to American soil. They wanted all the aircraft, but did they know where they were now, in the chairman's secret military base in Harbin? That must have been where the missiles had come from. Now, Harbin was the most dangerous place to store an army and all the aircraft Zedong Electronics currently had in their arsenal.

Mo certainly wanted to get off the ship, but the middle of the Pacific was not a good place to do that. He also realized that he should not talk to the chairman anymore, or it could become deadly for him.

Comrade Mo Wang knew that he did not want to be a part of this madness any longer and decided that Panama could be a good place to start a new life. He had a small suitcase full of American $100 bills. All the Politburo members had received the same suitcase a year earlier as a joke from the chairman, who said that they should spend it as soon as possible since it would be worthless after Z-Day. Maybe it would be worth something in Panama.

If he could become friendly with this Carlos Rodriquez, he would still have the cell phone and he could still be in contact with the New World after the chairman was destroyed in New York. Mo Wang felt dirty and used. Mo Wang hadn't killed anybody of his own free will. His termination squads had been trained at a secret location—most probably Harbin—by the chairman, and then placed under his control to destroy all the operatives he had found and trained. He was not a killer, and did not like the eagerness his first cousin Comrade Chairman Chunqiao exhibited when terminating people.

Yes, Mo Wang was part of the Chunqiao family. His father was the chairman's youngest uncle. The chairman knew this well, and that was why Mo Wang had got away with so much. And it was time to tell Lee Wang that he was also part of the Wang family—a first cousin to Mo Wang by marriage. Mo Wang had always known this. The chairman didn't, nor did Lee. He had watched as the young Lee, always at the top of his class, had flown through his schooling, always getting the highest grades.

Even in university, Lee Wang—fifteen years younger than he—had excelled, so much so that Mo Wang had made sure that young Lee had been given a chance with Zedong Electronics. In those days, it was the only company to work for before all this crap about taking over the world had become the reality.

Mo Wang reckoned that they could have taken over the world peacefully by just doing what they were doing—building every single electrical piece of equipment in the world. He had had a drink with the chairman a year or so before Z-Day and had suggested to him that the more peaceful route was just as good. It would only take another decade before the world was totally dependent on the products their 400 manufacturing companies produced, and then the sky was the limit for asking top dollar.

The chairman had laughed at him—yes, laughed in his face—and asked him what enjoyment was there in taking over the world peacefully? China had always been a powerful nation. Enemies were brought before Chinese leaders and dealt with, not chatted to like stupid politicians chat to each other. Kings and queens of enemy factions and countries were beheaded, and the people enslaved as worker bees for the most powerful dynasties. China had been slaves to the rest of the world for too long, and it was time to show its power and bring the whole world to their knees to beg the most powerful dynasty in the world for mercy. And he was about to do that, starting with the most powerful country in the world—the United States of America.

From that day on, Mo Wang hadn't slept much, and now he just really wanted to jump ship. It took him many hours, but finally he gathered up the courage to pick up the phone. It was midnight, and he was about to sink his first cousin Chairman Chunqiao. He hoped that if he did, then maybe he could die peacefully in a place like Panama. "I would like to speak to Carlos Rodriquez, please," Mo asked as the phone was picked up.

"Comrade Wang, I presume?" replied Carlos.

"Am I calling at an inopportune moment, Mr. Rodriquez?"

"Not really," replied Carlos, sipping a beer. *"Lee Wang and his family and I and a few others have been burying our dead this afternoon. I'm just hanging out with Lee and a few friends of mine, like the President of the United States, and having a drink to remember our fallen. I'm putting you on speaker phone so that the 30-odd people around me can hear what you have to say to us, Mr. Wang."*

"You mean that the American President is there with you right now?" asked Mo. This Carlos person always backed him into a corner so quickly.

"Yep! He's one of the boys, and we are deliberating whether to take you out today, tomorrow, or the next day. We haven't decided yet."

"Today would be better, Mr. Rodriquez. Then I could also finally rest easy," replied Mo Wang. "I have decided that I will be leaving Zedong Electronics in Panama in three days' time. Lee Wang, are you there?"

"Yes, I am here," replied Lee, bending toward the speaker phone. He didn't really need to. The room full of people had gone so quiet that there wasn't a sound. There were the president, five Air Force base commanders, Vice Admiral Rogers and three of his men, the

Colombian Ambassador and Manuel, Colonel Patterson and the two new majors, Wong and Chong, Preston, Martie, Joe, David, Buck and Barbara, Will and Maggie, and Lin and Ling Wang. All the other pilots had gone back to duty, and every transport aircraft was back in the air ferrying in equipment from all over the eastern part of the country.

"Did you know, Lee, that you and I are related?" Mo, in English, explained to Lee that he was family after all. Lee was shocked, but did not react visibly to the news.

"Carlos, I'm going to tell you everything I know. I have not been responsible for any deaths, but I am part of the overall picture, so I will consider myself guilty. But this madman, my cousin, needs to be stopped before he destroys the whole world." For another several minutes, Mo gave his new audience the rundown on the leader of Zedong Electronics.

"As you already know, we are two days out from the Panama Canal. Zedong Electronics has many troops in Panama, and has taken over the country so that we can pass through the canal without hindrance. We will spend the last day before we pass through the canal getting our naval ships refueled and supplied from tankers and supply ships. I believe that they will return to the coastal area around Harbin to refuel so they can return to resupply the ships coming back into the Pacific and then going into Los Angeles. I only learned about his secret base in Harbin this morning. Harbin is where the missiles originated. He has one left. He purchased four White Falcon missiles from Pakistan a year ago. He told me himself that the fourth missile is destined for Shanghai once he has all his 60,000 troops out of there. It is not meant to fly to the United States. He wants your country untouched because it will be his new base of operations."

"What are your naval ships?" asked Carlos after receiving a written note from Vice Admiral Rogers.

"We have the aircraft carrier from which I am speaking to you, two modern destroyers, and the last two modern frigates made in China only last year. I don't know much about ships, but their numbers are 85, 170, 171, 572, and 573. Your Navy will be able to tell you about them since Google no longer exists. I'm sure you will know more about them than I do. But, Mr. Rodriquez, much more important are your people. We are the escort for five of the world's largest container ships. These five ships are full of billions of pounds of food that the chairman is expecting to use to bribe the women and children in America into accepting a red Communist passport. I'm sure that your people are now desperate for food, and there is enough for millions of meals. They will go in first to New York Harbor, 24 hours after the aircraft you have not yet stolen fly into the three airports and drop in 12,000 troops. Those troops will walk to the harbor and fortify it. The number was meant to be 20,000, but you brought the numbers down when you stole the planes. Then those aircraft will take off and return the next day with another 12,000 troops to land in Washington, D.C. Two weeks later, they return again and land with another 12,000 troops in Los Angeles. By then, all your West Coast troops are expected to be traveling by road to New York to fight the East Coast battle, if there is one. I believe that there are 30 of China's most modern and powerful fighter aircraft on this ship. Again, speak to your Air Force so they are ready for battle. You need the food, but I'm sure you don't need the naval ships. If you do, then you will form a plan.

"The chairman expects to take over New York, fight any Americans that resist, take over Washington D.C., and then work on the West Coast. He has 60,000 well-trained troops. I'm hoping that the chairman doesn't hear that I have spoken with you, because he will terminate me for sure. As you asked, I have told the rest of the termination squads to lie low and not get close to New York, or they will surely die. There are about 200 men left, and once I get off the ship, I will tell them to disappear and wait to see who wins the war. These ships are fully armed and they will use our three satellites to work their armament systems."

"*Not anymore,*" replied Carlos. "*We control them now. We have controlled them since an hour ago. Your cousin Lee is the best you could have ever given us. I just don't know why you employed him as a floor cleaner?*"

"Sometimes a floor cleaner can get promoted into better

positions," replied Mo Wang. "Now, I've told you and Lee Wang the story, come and find me in Panama. They say that the weather is warm this time of year. Carlos Rodriquez, good luck." And with that, Mo Wang hung up, his job done and his destiny sealed.

"What do you think, Lee?" asked the president after Mo Wang had hung up. "Do you think your cousin is setting a trap for us?"

"I don't think so," interrupted Mrs. Wang. "We know him well and were all surprised to realize that he was part of such a ruthless bunch of men. Remember, we also joined Zedong Electronics, much like he did, and at that time, in our part of China there was not much more to look forward to."

"I agree," added Lee. "I think he has been in a frustrating position. If he didn't do as they expected, he would not be alive. But I still do not trust anything anymore at face value. I think we must back up and prove that this attack will actually happen like he says it will. We can find the ships on the satellite before they reach New York, and I'm sure our aircraft can search for them. Without satellite communications, their ships cannot fire their very new and fancy missiles with any accuracy, and I believe that we can still win the battle for New York. And I just might check out those Panama weather reports once the war is over."

"General Allen knew a great deal about their plan already," added Colonel Patterson. "Before he died, he gave me implicit instructions on how to defend New York. He didn't know about the food ships, and I'm sure we can tweak the plan he gave me to make sure that the valuable food gets to those who need it most." He then went about telling the group what the general had planned for the arrival of the invasion force.

* * *

Colonel Grady was slowly making his way up I-95 as the group at McGuire discussed battle plans. The second convoy had caught up with him within a day of leaving Preston's farm. The first convoy had reached the southern Virginia border when the second convoy reported that they could see the tail end of the convoy up ahead. They were getting low on fuel, and the colonel got on the phone to Preston. "Good evening, Preston. Grady here. I'm going to need one of your tankers to fly in and refuel our tanks down here in Virginia. We will need about 6,000 gallons per day and the second convoy now just behind us will need about the same. Plain old regular gas will do—none of your fancy flying fuels now, just 50% unleaded and 50% diesel."

"Hi, Colonel Grady," replied Preston. "How are the roads? Can a 130 get down on the cleared highway?"

"Oh, sure. The Navy has done a good job. We can increase our speed from 20 miles an hour to 30. We could go faster, but the old tanks have a maximum speed of 30 miles an hour. We have enough fuel for about three hours at 30 miles per hour, and I thought that I could send our tanker trucks up forward several miles and then the Air Force could come in and fill them up. We now have eight tankers, all old M-49s from the 1960s. They hold 1,200 gallons each and I'm sure your 130 could fill up a couple of them at a time. I could send four of them forward 100 miles and they could be refueled and ready for us when we get there. Leapfrog the tankers, if you know what I mean. I can refuel eight vehicles at a time, so we could have both convoys refueled in four hours. I think that we can stagger the vehicles every couple hundred yards to head up to the next refueling spot as they are filled, which will give us a 100-mile convoy, but at least we won't have hundreds of vehicles hanging around waiting for fuel."

"Send your tankers up front," replied Preston, "and I'll get the Air Force to stage a refueling point every 100 miles until you get into New York—the quicker the better. Call me when you get your tankers forward and we will have our two 130 tankers refueled and ready to transfer your unleaded and diesel, Colonel."

The HC-130 tanker aircrews were called, and Preston quickly explained to the base commander what Colonel Grady wanted. The Air Force set about flying in the two tankers to land on the cleared northbound I-95 highway, 100 miles into Virginia from the border. It would take the aircraft two hours to get there, and they could easily fill two of the trucks each. Another four road tankers would be positioned another 100 miles nearer, and the time the 130s took to unload their fuel, fly back for more and then return, the tanker trucks would be moved to a new forward location by the time the 130s arrived. They reckoned that the Army convoys would be in New York within 72 hours.

Back in North Carolina, the supplies were going out as fast as possible. The crew of the Southwest flight worked hard on the empty farm with most of its aircraft gone. The Air Force guards were down to a dozen, and the hangar was quiet and empty now that the battle had moved north. With the smaller aircraft Mike, John, and Pam were using, they would never run out of food supplies from Seymour Johnson. The 747 transporter was now also flying into Seymour Johnson every day, often parking next to the smaller aircraft and also packing in food. The three little aircraft looked like flies compared to the massive 747, which loaded more in one flight than they could load in a year, but people were being fed and America needed to hang on for another week to ten days before all the aircraft could get involved with feeding the population.

On January 13th, the Chinese engineers were gathered into a JFK terminal meeting room. Most of the engineers still had bumps on their heads from when they were captured.

Preston, Colonel Patterson, Carlos, Lee and Majors Wang and Chong flew in to meet with them. They had worked hard with their American counterparts and needed a little time off. The president was flying into JFK in *Baby Huey* an hour later once the terminal was secure and the engineers seated.

He did so, and Buck brought Air Force One down gently where the first 747 had been captured. Guards had been posted all the way down the Van Wyck Expressway and around the entire terminal area. Fresh snow covered the ground, and the wind was blowing a negative wind chill factor as the Huey lowered herself onto the recently cleared terminal apron. The president and his Secret Service agents walked into the warm terminal building and each was handed a cup of steaming coffee as they arrived.

Colonel Patterson brought the meeting to order as Lee strode up to the platform. In Chinese, he began: "Does every person here speak decent English? If you cannot understand English, please stand up." Nobody did. "So, we will now continue this meeting in English." He promptly switched languages. "The United States of America considers all of you prisoners of war. Does anybody not understand that?" Nobody moved. "The President of the United States has come here today to offer you amnesty if you would like to be a new citizen of the United States. You are not soldiers, you are engineers, and this country now needs your knowledge to repair what has been destroyed. We know that your job here was to get the airports and harbor operational for the invasion of the United States by the CEO and president of Zedong Electronics, Chairman Wang Chunqiao, and the company you and I used to work for. We were all employed because we were the best in our fields. You are all expert engineers, and what are you going to do after the invasion is beaten back by the armies of the United States? I believe, as one of you but also as an American citizen, that you can either stay here or go home. Before you make that decision, I need to update you on China."

Lee paused to formulate his words carefully. "Chairman Wang Chunqiao dropped three nuclear weapons on China yesterday. One destroyed Beijing, the second destroyed Taiwan, and the third destroyed both Hong Kong and Guangzhou."

There was a loud murmur among all the engineers as they questioned the truth of that statement and spoke amongst each other. Lee allowed them a few moments to do so.

"Why would he do such a thing, and how do we know you are telling the truth?" asked one engineer.

"I have family in Beijing," stated another, and Lee put his hand up for silence.

"We control the three satellites owned by Zedong Electronics," continued Lee. "I'm sure some of you worked on them, or knew somebody who worked on them. Our commander, who was running our defense against Chairman Chunqiao's attacks, was killed in

Beijing. He had flown in to deliver satellite phones to the Chinese government so that they could communicate with America as well as Russia. He had just left Beijing International Airport when the first missile exploded. We could see the explosions on the satellite feed, and we had not mastered the satellite control codes at the time. There is a fourth nuclear missile in Harbin, and Comrade Mo Wang told me yesterday that it is aimed at Shanghai and is meant to destroy Shanghai once the chairman has flown all his troops out of Shanghai Pudong Airport. As you have seen, the American Air Force went into Pudong a couple of days ago and stole some of the chairman's Air China aircraft so that America can begin to fly its troops back from all the wars they were involved with before this crisis. Many of you saw these aircraft fly into the three New York airports yesterday, and they are due in here again today with another 6,000 American troops out of Iraq. We know all about the attack here in New York next week, and we are preparing to destroy the leaders of Zedong Electronics before they destroy the rest of the world. How many of you come from the Shanghai area?"

Most of the engineers raised their hands.

"You may thank the United States Air Force, my friend Carlos Rodriquez," he added, pointing to Carlos, "and me, because that fourth atomic bomb destined for Shanghai next week will not reach Shanghai. It will be redirected out to sea and destroy itself. For the rest of you who had family in the destroyed areas, I'm sorry for your loss and you may thank the chairman yourself when he arrives in America. You have two choices, and if you decide to become Americans, the president will forgive you. I will now let him explain." Lee returned to his seat, and the room was silent as the president came forward.

"Good day. I know that you are the best in your fields," the president started. "What Mr. Wang has told you is the truth. We have our own nuclear weapons ready to fire on my command, and we have the satellite, or shall I say satellites, to guide them anywhere in the world we want. America has not unleashed a weapon of mass destruction to kill civilians since the Second World War, but the chairman of your country unleashed three of them minutes apart to kill his own people. This man needs to be stopped. Look what he has done to the world! He has taken humanity back 100 years, and you could say that the world has gone back into a new form of the dark ages. Now you must each make a choice. You can either stay under guard or continue to be a prisoner of war, or you can help us fight this monster and begin to get the world working again. So far, we believe that it's possible that two billion people have died worldwide and certainly another billion or two are going to die before we can get our planet back on track. I promise you that once we have secured the destruction of Chairman Wang Chunqiao and his accomplices, we will fly you back to China to look for your families and bring them back to the United States. He cannot explode his fourth nuclear missile over Shanghai anymore. If you would like to stay there, you will have that choice, but the United States of America blames China and its people for this catastrophe and we will not look at China as a friend for many generations to come. We will probably never do business with China again. Now, make your choices and come and help us design and develop a new country and a new world. Hopefully we can learn to live in peace again, and I hope that this destruction of our civilization is a turning point toward a better world."

The president left a totally silent room.

Now it was time for Colonel Patterson to complete General Allen's plan for fending off the invasion force. Lee Wang was put in charge of discussing the engineers' options with each of them, helped by his wife and daughter as well as Majors Wong and Chong. *Baby Huey* took off to fly north with the president on board, as well as one Secret Service agent, Colonel Patterson, Preston, Carlos, Vice Admiral Rogers, and the McGuire base commander. The weather was clear but cold, and several thermoses of coffee and snacks had been put on board for the flight over the harbor.

Colonel Grady and his long convoy were doing well and would arrive within 36 hours. The biggest problem was the massive increase of starving people around the four airports. Over 100 troops were doling out a week's supply of rations per person at each airport, and the 747 transporter was working non-stop to empty Seymour Johnson of supplies. They managed a flight into each airport every 24 hours, and 10,000 people per airport were receiving two weeks' worth of rations every day and told not to come back because there was going to be a massive battle around the airports, on the highways, and in the harbor.

Each person was given a printout telling them that this was all they would receive until February, and not to come back or they could find themselves in the middle of a war zone. The note stated emphatically that they were not to go anywhere near the ground around New York Harbor, or they could be shot on sight by either side.

"I'm wondering if the men could be flown into Newark only, now that there are fewer aircraft to fly in," Preston mentioned to Colonel Patterson as they flew over Newark, which was the closest airport to the harbor area.

"I wouldn't disregard JFK," replied the colonel. "They flew into JFK before, and if you look at a map it's only about a 20-mile hike to the Verrazano Narrows Bridge, which is the only entrance and a strategic defensive location. The general wanted the area around the bridge to be packed full of howitzers and troops on either side, but not on top of the bridge."

"Why?" asked the president. "We have several trucks of explosives about to head to the bridge. If all else fails, we can blow it up and topple it onto the aircraft carrier and hopefully a few more of the military vessels—either to destroy them or stop them from escaping out to sea."

"Destroy the Verrazano Narrows Bridge?" reacted Preston.

"The weight of the bridge should just about cut through the aircraft carrier, or at least sink it," Colonel Patterson replied. "General Allen thought that it was a small price to pay for the destruction of the ships that are really going to be a problem. Carlos and I talked a little earlier. We do not have a GPS system good enough to launch our sophisticated missiles at these ships. They have massive amounts of hard armor and their defense systems, even without using their GPS missile directional systems, are still a force to be reckoned with. Some of their fast-action big guns and 50mm cannons can wreak havoc on our normal troops. Most of our old battle guns will be wiped out in seconds by dozens of their rapid-fire guns.

"Why don't we take them out with a nuclear missile before they get here?" asked the president.

"You just say the word, sir, and it will be done—just as soon as Carlos can pinpoint them on his computer screen," the colonel said enthusiastically. "However, that also destroys the food ships and could be the death sentence for a million or more Americans who will starve to death without them. We don't have enough food right now, and maybe those five container ships will only feed New York and maybe Washington for a couple of weeks, but the general's main dilemma was whether to destroy the food ships and lose food for a million people, or lose a couple thousand troops and hopefully obtain control of the attack. Also, the long-distance benefit of having these ships is that they may be the only large ships left in the world. If Los Angeles is to get another five of these container ships full of food in two weeks' time, then these five ships heading for New York would not get back in time to reload. That means that there must be more ships sitting in Shanghai Harbor. That's why he hasn't blown up his main airport and harbor. I have thought about Shanghai for much of the day. If he is now moving his troops into Harbin, we can assume that the troop numbers at the airport and harbor in Shanghai are being depleted, which gives us the chance to go in and capture anything he has there. I bet they are also full of unprotected fuel ready to supply Los Angeles with food."

"I could have a dozen naval officers ready to go in at a moment's notice," chimed in Vice Admiral Rogers. "With ten of those massive ships under our control, we could move mountains of men and equipment across the ocean. It could be the means for the survival of mankind in other areas if that amount of food could be transported, say, into England or France, or even Japan in the future."

"Well said, sir. General Allen knew that you would be on the same wavelength. His idea was to fly two of the 747s back into Shanghai full of troops with protection from the two remaining gunships and the fuel tankers to get the gunships there. Unfortunately, we have no operational helicopters with rapid flight deployment capability. It would take too long to disassemble and reassemble them on the other side, but several jeeps and some smaller armored vehicles could be transported to Shanghai with the transporter, refueling in Alaska. One point that really got to General Allen was how did they fly the transporter here with the other 747s in the first place? It doesn't have the range from anywhere in China and must have been refueled and joined the incoming troop carriers from a different location."

"Could it fly into Panama?" asked Preston. "They control Panama."

"No way! It's even further to Panama, Preston. General Allen believes that the chairman, or whatever he is called, has another base somewhere, but we might never find out its location. At least we can halt his missiles from anywhere."

"We have some Rat Patrol jeeps and two armored cars in North Carolina," added Preston.

"They would be perfect, plus one or two other vehicles—maybe mortars and rapid-movement vehicles. We can see what Colonel Grady brings up with him. I'm sure he said he had an old multiple missile launcher that would be useless against hardened ship armor but great against a base of troops." "So what is your idea, Colonel?" asked the president.

"In a nutshell, sir, I believe we should attack them in Shanghai at the same time they are attacking us here. Land our aircraft in Shanghai Pudong, unload the mobile equipment, and drive the ten or so miles into the harbor. Then we take over the ships, drive back to the airport, reload our valuable equipment, and fly back. Stupid and simple, just the way I like it. Hopefully our old trucks and jeeps will shock the Chinese troops into immediate surrender." Everyone laughed.

"What about your plans for New York?" the president asked, now that they were flying over the Verrazano Narrows Bridge at 2,000 feet. Not a ship or boat could be seen anywhere. The sea was completely empty of shipping.

"First, we have somewhere between 12,000 and 20,000 of their troops getting off aircraft at our three airports. They may reduce that number now, but we can't take that chance. By the time they land, we will have 25,000 troops in and around each airport. I'm hoping that they will unload and start marching towards the harbors using the freeways. It should take them between 2 to 6 hours to get to the harbor area. But they will never arrive."

The colonel looked at the group for approval. "The plan is to sneak a couple of men aboard each aircraft as they are refueling, if we can. There are a couple of places underneath the aircraft where they can get in through the main undercarriage doors, or through the cargo hatches, of which there are several. I'm sure the men are coming in armed to the teeth, and they will have supplies underneath in the cargo areas. Our men will gladly give them a hand with the unpacking and hopefully put a little present into whatever they are carrying. We are putting together several very small exploding devices, mainly a grenade surrounded by a fingernail-size piece of C4 with an electronic detonation device in it. The blast should be strong enough to ignite the grenade, and that, with the C4, should kill or maim the men standing around the poor guy carrying it. We have about 300 of the detonation devices from the two transporter loads. We can make miniature bombs to be ignited by a satellite phone call. Hundreds of special computerized numbers can be dialed into the phones and we can make up the phone numbers. I'm thinking of only using three numbers, one for each location, and we have about 90 engineers from the Marines, Navy, Army and Air Force working on them right now. We expect the aircraft to be refueled by our new Chinese-American engineers, and they will have American marines and pilots dressed the same as last time. All we want is for them to lie low until the aircraft are out to sea. Then we conk them on the head and bring the aircraft into McGuire and Andrews—the whole bloody lot of them. As a backup, we will have our trusty pilots in the air in their World War II machines, and they can persuade the enemy pilots to turn around, or threaten to shoot them down, until the 747s with higher air speeds quickly pull away from them. At that point, if they have not turned around by then, we will have no choice but to shoot them down. We have the frequencies they are using and we will just invite the Chinese pilots to choose life or death."

"We will only have minutes before they speed away from us?" asked Preston.

"Not if you are 20 miles in front of them and at maximum altitude," replied Colonel Patterson, an Air Force pilot himself. "Your four aircraft's dive speeds are as fast as a 747 and you can warn them, even shoot one down. They won't know what you're flying until they see you and then they may go to maximum power and laugh at you, but they won't laugh at the three F-4s that they will meet next. The Phantoms will be our last resort to catch our sitting ducks.

"The next phase of the master plan I discussed with the general was attacking the men who get off the aircraft. As you see below us, the New York harbor area has major highways, and they will have to use them to get such a large number of troops over land to the harbor area. We will place ambush zones all the way down the highways and attack them from buildings, bridges, overpasses, and wherever we can shoot at them. We will have another 10,000 troops stationed at all the entrance points to the harbor. I'm sure some will get clever and move through side roads, buildings, and alleyways to get to their main rendezvous point, somewhere in the harbor. Phase Three is the sea battle. Vice Admiral Rogers already has his three submarines in the area, and we will place them with their propellers facing the shoreline and their torpedo tubes open and ready."

Colonel Patterson went on for another hour pointing out the areas around New York Harbor and the best places to position the available hardware.

"What are we going to do about their aircraft?" Preston asked about their top-of-the-line fighters. "We will have no chance against them."

"They can shoot you down before you even see them, but General Allen's idea was to get rid of their runway, the aircraft carrier. Once that happens, they will have no choice but to land somewhere in the United States. It would be nice to get a few of those, and we'll be ready for them. None of you guys will be in the air when they arrive. We will pound their runway, and they will have a maximum of about three hours flying time, maybe four. We are going to hit them so hard that their fancy Chinese computers will not know what to defend themselves against first," exclaimed Colonel Patterson. "But, it all depends on three scenarios—whether they all come in together unafraid, whether the naval ships come in first, or whether the food ships are sent in first."

Chapter 18

Invasion USA

COLONEL GRADY ARRIVED TWO DAYS later, on January 15th. Two of the trucks had broken down only 20 miles from the harbor area, and he sent two trucks back to get the 155mm howitzers they had been pulling. Every big gun was needed.

The second convoy, organized by Colonel Grady, was scheduled to arrive out of the combined Army bases around Texas on January 17th and they had a dozen more 155mm guns, which seemed to be the biggest guns towable that still worked. Most of the more recent Army artillery had been built with forms of computerized systems since the 1990s.

The airports now had 24,000 troops—8,000 stationed at each—and the fourth flight of 6,000 troops flew into Newark direct from Baghdad and were transported over the water into the main New York harbor by two destroyers the Navy now had operational, as well as any old tugboats and barges that were still working.

Bulldozers from the airports were clearing the highways to the harbor area so that the incoming enemy would not have broken down cars and trucks to use as cover. All of the major highways were fenced on both sides of the road, and Colonel Patterson hoped that the enemy wouldn't have wire cutters with them.

The Air Force wanted the incoming aircraft badly, and the airports would be cleared of American military personnel before the arrival, except for the pilots and marines now being flown out of Quantico instead of Camp Lejeune. The C-130s had already pulled 5,000 marines out of Camp Lejeune, and the rest of the marines were still overseas, apart from 3,500 men that were being deployed out of the closer Marine base. The idea was to collect men from more remote bases first, which took more time, and then bring them from bases closer and closer to New York.

The U.S. Marines would be the major attack force along the highways, and the invading soldiers would be left alone until they had exited the airports, so that the aircraft would not be in the middle of a firefight.

Within 24 hours, and after much discussion, the Chinese engineers had all decided to become Americans. They had seen the forces grouping around the zones of invasion and realized that the chairman could be on the losing side and there was a chance of survival if they stayed where they were. The engineers were civilians, not soldiers, and if they would be allowed to go back to China and collect family, then why not.

Over the second week, the numbers of soldiers grew by the day. Colonel Patterson worked non-stop to get General Allen's plan into place, and by the end of the second week, it was time to get started on the harbor area containment plan.

The Texas convoy arrived a day late, but it had grown in size traveling from Army base to Army base, collecting a couple more trucks, howitzers, and tanks as it headed across the eastern United States. By the time it trundled into New York and aimed for the harbor, the highways were clear and desolate, with faces of American soldiers looking out of every building as the hundred-mile-long convoy entered 440 south toward the New York harbor area.

They had traveled up I-70 and then I-78 into New York. The journey had taken six days, and several vehicles had broken down. Mechanics from the Army bases they arrived at returned in other trucks to collect any howitzers or important vehicles left behind.

Finally, the convoy arrived in New York and reached the checkpoint at the I-78/440 intersection, and set up to guide vehicles to their positions around the large harbor area. Two hundred and seventy-three trucks, tanks, and jeeps, exactly the same types and models Colonel Grady had arrived with three days earlier at Preston's farm, were told to go south to 278, turn left onto the Staten Island Expressway, and aim for Fort Wadsworth and Fort Hamilton either side of the outer bridge into New York Harbor.

With a grand total of 50 155mm howitzers and dozens of truckloads of projectiles, 25 of the big guns were deployed in a line just off the water from the old but still stable walls of Battery Weed to under the trees of the Arthur Von Briesen Park. The old dock area was too weak to have big guns firing on it, but several large mortar placements under camouflage netting were placed on the breaking concrete. The old Catlin Battery, last used during World War II, was also overgrown, so the guns were placed just off the rocky shoreline and under the first line of trees, giving them natural camouflage.

On the north shoreline, the second line of 25 guns were placed on the grassy areas on the north side along the Leif Ericson Highway, and again placed under camouflage so that nobody from the water could see the gun placements until the very last minute. Each gun had well over 100 projectiles, mostly armor-piercing, followed by high-explosive heads. Several of the 70 smaller 105mm howitzers were placed in between the larger guns on both sides, as well as on both ends of the bridge.

Over a ton of explosives were set under each strut right underneath the two main struts of the bridge. The main cables were also prepared with explosives, and the whole main center was designed by the Air Force and Army Engineers to explode and drop into the water. The Army Corps of Engineers in charge of the explosive work didn't want to destroy the whole bridge, but just the center part, which could be rebuilt at a later stage. The engineers figured that the two concrete pillars would not be affected by the demolition of the middle part and dozens of mortars and rocket launchers were carried up by helicopter and placed on the highest positions in the area.

The colonel was not going to take any chances. Nobody had really done this type of warfare for 100 years or more—artillery cannons against ships—but the main idea was to fire so much at one time into the ships that their defense systems would become overloaded and not be able to repel all the projectiles going in. Aircraft would not be used in the initial battle, since they would just be cannon fodder for the superior Chinese fighter jets, and anti-aircraft guns were brought in from everywhere to give the bigger howitzer placements cover from the air.

It was assumed that the large container ships would be sent in first to test the waters, and that they would aim for and berth at the Global Terminal—the only docking facility big enough for these massive container vessels. There would be room for all five to berth at the terminal, and several container cranes could unload one ship at a time. Colonel Patterson assumed that the unloading of one ship at a time was their plan, since the Chinese engineers had been given a schedule and repair jobs for every piece of the Global Terminal only. The colonel thought that if he was the chairman, he would make sure the overall area was made safe before the engineers worked on getting the other dock areas repaired.

It was surprising how many old trucks the Army actually had, a miniscule percentage compared to the more modern vehicles of all types that were now useless metal junk until somebody got the electronics of the vehicles working again. But that could take years, or a decade, or even longer.

The president flew back to the White House for the first time in two weeks. It was as he had left it, but at least more communications were available and there were now both radio and satellite phone communications. The old Hughes satellite dishes were cropping up everywhere, and the president realized that a very limited Internet communication system could be in the pipeline in a year or so.

* * *

The cities of the United States and most of the countries in the northern hemisphere were not nice places to be. With very little law and order, except in and around certain parts of New York, it was horribly cold. It was the middle of winter, and snow was building up so high that two-story houses were now underneath the snowline and people walked and gathered whatever they could above the ground level.

Crime was still on the increase. Every store was empty and often burnt to the ground, but underneath the snow, people lived away from the wind chill factor that was present on a daily basis, and many dug tunnels from one house to the other and became scavengers, eating whatever they could find.

Luckily, the temperatures had been near or below freezing for most of the time since January 1st, because it kept the millions of dead bodies frozen, but once it warmed up, most people who were still alive had plans to evacuate the high population areas. These places would become cesspools of rotting corpses and diseases once spring arrived.

Many had already tried and found places as far south as they could go in the States, but winter was long and it would take months to walk to the warmer areas of Florida, Texas, and even Mexico.

Here, gangs had begun to get very powerful, had daily battles for territory control, and killed indiscriminately. Thousands died on a daily basis. Unfortunately, there really was no better place to go. Most people shot first before asking who was there, and nobody was safe.

On the other hand, Panama was much warmer than the northern states, and gang violence was non-existent due to the 10,000 Chinese soldiers who were in control of the area around the canal. It was probably one of the safer places to be at the moment.

Mo Wang, holding a suitcase in each hand and dressed in local attire, including a Panama hat, walked down a street in Puerto De Balboa, a couple of hundred yards from the massive naval ships being supplied, looking very much like a tourist. It had been a long journey to get off the ships.

Once they had dropped anchor to take on fuel and supplies from the military supply ships already there, he had carefully packed his two suitcases, the first with a few clothes and three satellite radios, and his smaller suitcase with money and all the valuables he had. He placed the suitcases and himself aboard a large weaved supply basket, about the size of a basket found underneath a hot air balloon.

It was hanging from two thick ropes that transferred food stuffs across the water from one ship to another. It was impossible to get down to sea level from the aircraft carrier, and he waited for dark. The crew was still hard at work transferring supplies from the smaller ship to the aircraft carrier's supply doors three floors higher than the supply ship itself. He waited carefully until the basket arrived and was unloaded before he made his move. Mo Wang walked up to the now-empty basket, threw in his cases, told the sailors manning the basket that he was going to have a meeting with the supply ship's captain, got in the empty basket, and was transferred to the supply ship within five minutes.

Nobody had expected him or questioned him. It wasn't their duty. He gave a few sailors on the other side a shock when his head suddenly appeared and he climbed over the side with his two suitcases and demanded where the captain was.

He was escorted halfway there when he told the sailors that their services weren't needed anymore and asked if smaller boats from the Panama shore had made any appearances selling goods. He was told that they had, during the daylight hours and on the shore side of the ship and opposite the side of where the aircraft carrier towered over the smaller supply ship.

He slept through the rest of the warm night in a lifeboat, out of the way and under a tarp, and awoke to much noise early the next morning. There were at least 30 boats of all types close to the ship's side several floors below, and he arrogantly walked down the stairs to the small boats selling their wares.

Nobody seemed interested in him, and since most of the sailors were busy with the supplies, he reached a crane-looking winch where most of the small boats congregated. Two armed guards were there making sure that nobody used the crane to lift themselves into the boat. Mo Wang asked the men if they knew who knew how to work the winch because he needed to hitch a ride to shore to look for some girls for the officials on the aircraft carrier.

They automatically asked what was in the suitcases, and Mo Wang looked at them as if they were stupid and replied that they were full of money—useless money to entice the girls aboard. Not thinking that they had any control over what the officials wanted, they allowed Mo Wang to get into the smaller weaved basket and he was winched down the three levels to the boats below.

The vendors tried to sell him fruit and clothing, but he finally motioned with his hands and in bad English stated that he wanted to go to shore. One boat captain, bigger than the others, pushed his way through and asked in English what he was prepared to pay for the 300-yard boat ride to terra firma. He had already pulled three $100 American bills out of the thousands in his suitcase and that, plus his old Rolex wristwatch, was a fair deal for his 10-minute ride. Expensive, but at least he would be free, and his Rolex was 20 years old anyway. He was sure that he could find a replacement if he needed to know the time in his new world, which seemed unimportant at this precise moment.

He walked along the road in Puerto De Balboa and realized that even though little had changed here, it was still a port and a far more dangerous place than he was used to. He searched and located two Chinese soldiers walking around, he presumed to keep order, and he ordered them to escort him to a hotel or place of safety since he had important orders from his comrades on board the military ships.

His Chinese identification made them come to attention and salute him, and together they walked for an hour towards the better part of town where they found a decent hotel on the outskirts of Panama City and opposite a large bus depot where it seemed that old and colorful buses were still running.

Mo Wang thanked his two guards, gave them an American $100 bill each, and they seemed extremely happy, telling him the American money still worked well in Panama.

He then paid a $100 American Ben Franklin, got several local notes in return as change for two nights, and checked into the hotel under his real name. He went up to his room and changed into clothing that he had bartered for with the boat owner while he was bringing Mo into the harbor. He left his Chinese-made clothes in his room, pulled out a couple more Ben Franklins just in case, and walked out of the back door, the money suitcase in his right hand, the large Panama-style hat covering his head, and Mo Wang took the first bus out of town an hour later.

Being a man of means, he already had three passports, one Chinese, one American, and one British, all with his photo in them beside different Chinese names. The first bus out of town was going north. It wasn't that he really wanted to go north, but it was the first bus out of town and it was heading into San Jose, Costa Rica, and could hitch him up with points even further north.

Mo Wang didn't really know where to go, but he had heard nice things about Honduras, and an island called Roatan just off the coast of Honduras, where one of his nieces had moved years earlier. It sounded better living on a small island than on the more dangerous mainland. He had enough money to last him the rest of his life, and he could start all over again, maybe becoming a fisherman, or a chicken farmer—something simple.

The chairman hadn't thought or cared about Mo Wang for a couple of days. He had more urgent things to do, like go over the battle plans with his ship's captains and the several colonels on board the ships to make sure that the attack was successful.

The Chinese fighters had completed several takeoffs and landings on the carrier deck and only one aircraft had been destroyed so far. The pilot had missed the arresting cable across the deck and the aircraft had fallen over the end of the ship, taking a couple of soldiers manning an anti-aircraft gun with him.

The attack team rarely left the meeting room during the two days of restocking and the 24 hours it took all ten large ships to travel through all the Panama Canal locks one by one. Being extremely large ships, it took far longer than usual, and the aircraft carrier—a pretty small one compared to the more modern carriers—fit through with inches to spare.

Once they were done and Mo Wang was many miles away from

them, they set a course for the western edge of the island of Puerto Rico, and from there they cruised due north, 200 miles off the American shore, and aimed straight for New York Harbor seven days sailing in front of them.

* * *

Preston and his team spent a couple of days flying and practiced firing their guns at a firing range they could use at Quantico, the only place around that had an area big enough for them to be able to use their guns and rockets. Several trucks and other useless modern military vehicles had been placed around the open-ground firing range, and slowly they got better at precise aiming.

They had to be good, because they would be the fighter cover for the troops on the highways fighting the Chinese soldiers once they got out of the airports. They practiced flying very close to each other in case they needed to give a few fingers to the Chinese pilots in the 747s, telling them where to go and escorting them in to land.

The weather turned very cold and snow fell for three days, grounding just about everybody except the daily incoming flight from the Middle East going into Newark's cleared runways. The 747s had to land on clean runways, and the engineers, with more and more electrical generators coming online now, had Newark's directional systems and landing systems working as well as before the catastrophe.

They had already used many of the new Chinese electrical parts, and the engineering teams realized that even though they had tons of electrical parts, many would not work until some sort of electrical power station came online. The first thing they would do once the attack was over was see if they could get the closest nuclear reactors up and running again and a simple power grid established—at least around areas of New York. But until then, they would be using over 1,000 military field generators, getting only the necessary electrical equipment powered up.

The snowstorm dropped three feet of snow into the area, and

only the three runways and disembarkation areas around the aprons were cleared to continuously allow the aircraft in. The enemy soldiers could fight their way through the snowdrifts, as far as the American forces were concerned. Why make it easy for them?

Colonel Patterson was hoping that they did not come in with snow camouflage, but it didn't really matter with 30,000 troops now filling every window, rooftop, or any other place they could see the highways, as well as dozens of minor and side roads from the three airports into the harbor area.

The harbor area and coastline around New York Harbor looked untouched. The heavy snow helped to hide the 53 155mm howitzers. Three more had arrived from a New York Army base, and the 40 105mm howitzers placed on either side of the entranceway were camouflaged and, with the fresh snow, now invisible to any shipping arriving under the Verrazano Narrows Bridge.

Another 40 105mm howitzers had been placed on five large river barges, pulled by two working tugboats into the area a mile in from the bridge, tied together and placed horizontally to look like an island.

Every gun had been camouflaged, and two of the now three destroyers had entered New York Harbor sailing under the bridge, and their lookouts with powerful binoculars could not see one gun placement.

In addition to the howitzers, there were well over 100 large mortar teams in placements around the area—several on and around the area of the bridge that was not expected to fall if it was detonated. Several of the Mutts, jeeps, and even other vehicles had been placed on the roofs of buildings nearby, loaded with armor-piercing rockets that hopefully would be accurate enough to knock out any smaller guns aboard the ships.

Colonel Patterson was told by Colonel Grady that even if the biggest guns could not get through the modern hardened armor of the ships, they certainly could destroy the upper superstructure of the warships if they concentrated on those areas. Fifty anti-aircraft cannons had been placed slightly further out from the shorelines, and their main task was to protect the bigger guns from the air. The Chinese fighters would have to go through a wall of flying steel to destroy the bigger guns, as the satellite-guided munitions under their wings would be useless in this fight. They had lost all of their guidance systems, since Lee and Carlos now controlled the satellites.

Vice Admiral Rogers had his three submarines tied up at the old wharf by Battery Weed, less than 1,000 feet inside the harbor from the Verrazano Narrows Bridge. They were to dive and sit close to the harbor floor at about 50 feet, literally send as many torpedoes as possible in the direction of the aircraft carrier once it entered the kill zone and then aim for the rest of the military ships.

The three submarines had simple wire-guided torpedoes that were 30 years old, but they could still pack a punch and sink a ship, especially an aircraft carrier built in the Ukraine. The vice admiral reckoned that at least 18 to 24 torpedoes could be launched before the submarines were taken out and hopefully only by the fighters, but at 50 feet in murky waters, they would be totally invisible from the air. The Navy had worked out a system of aiming the torpedoes from a command center above the submarines on the battery, since the submarines would be firing blind.

Two of the destroyers were hidden from view at the Staten Island ferry terminal, and they would be positioned behind larger ships where they could sneak out and attack anything coming deeper into the harbor.

The older destroyers didn't stand a chance against the more modern Chinese ships, but they could get off several shots if they fired first, and the closeness of the battle would guarantee hits on the foreign vessels. The third destroyer was hidden behind the back end of Manhattan Beach Park, and once the attacking ships entered under the bridge it would sail at full speed behind them to close off the entrance and take up her battle stations from outside the harbor bridge.

Carlos wasn't working with Lee much anymore. Both Maggie and Buck had joined Lee in his place, both as good and knowledgeable as Carlos in the software field of electronics. Maggie was now Lee's assistant, and Buck was helping most of the time since he wasn't flying Air Force One around. The president had been told to stay home, away from the war. This arena was for soldiers, not politicians.

Barbara worked long hours flying *Lady Dandy*, often with the help of Martie or Preston when they had spare time at night, and she helped ferry in soldiers, ammo, projectiles, and mortars from the surrounding Army and Marine bases as the bases received phones for communication and the commanders could give a list of what their armories had.

The snowstorm had given everybody a good two days of rest, something they were all desperate for, and now they were a little behind in setting up the circus of all circuses—the Invasion of the USA.

"I see them! I have found the ships!" Lee Wang ran out on the 19th day of January, three days before the assumed day of attack. Carlos, Preston and several others ran into the communications building at McGuire to see what Lee was so excited about. There they were, the minute dots that could barely be seen by the naked eye, 500 miles offshore just south of Jacksonville, Florida. The ten specks were steaming in a direction which would bring them straight into New York Harbor.

Lee, with Carlos' permission, had moved Navistar P's orbit from the central USA and had positioned the satellite directly above Birmingham, Alabama. He had also brought the satellite's orbit above Earth down by 100 miles to get a wider and closer viewing range, and now they could see the ten dots with small wakes behind them as they sailed into the Atlantic area.

The ships couldn't be seen on the Chinese satellite feed and the satellites hadn't been touched in case the enemy might be alerted by the movement. Lee didn't think that the enemy actually knew they didn't have control of the satellites anymore. Maybe the only satellite control center had been at Zedong Headquarters.

"It looks like they are doing about 20 knots," observed Vice Admiral Rogers once he had studied the computer screen for a couple of minutes. "That gives us two days. I think we need to bring our plan forward by 24 hours."

"Are we ready with our plan of defense?" Preston asked Colonel Patterson, who had just walked in and was quickly briefed by Carlos. He had arrived late the night before and had gotten several hours of sleep for the first time in days.

"Yes, I think so," he replied. "There's not much more to do. The next flights in from Kabul are due in another four hours. I think that we should unload, refuel, and fly ten of the 747s into Seymour Johnson to have their seats removed and get our larger food distribution plan started a day early. Seven of the bigger, more southern cities in the Pacific Time zone have clear runways. Five of the passenger aircraft can go straight into Edwards and begin distributing supplies into Las Vegas, Phoenix, San Diego, Los Angeles, and San Francisco. The others can go into our supply bases in Texas and cover Dallas, Houston, Santa Fe, Denver, and Salt Lake, if their runways are clear. The 747 transporter is going to deliver food into Chicago, Washington D.C., and Philadelphia for the next three days, but it will take another ten hours to clear Chicago's runway. They only have three bulldozers working. Once we have more aircraft, we can get them onto the Baghdad and Kabul routes and have another couple left over for supply runs out of Texas. We received word a couple of days ago about a very large Army food-storage warehouse at one of the bases in Texas, from the colonel who arrived with the Texas convoy, and he made me promise to distribute the food supplies in and around Texas. I want to fly three new 747s into that base as soon as we have them."

"What about the defense perimeter?" asked Vice Admiral Rogers.

"All ready, and a day early is even better," continued Colonel Patterson. "It will save the troops from getting cold and bored. We will be short one flight of 6,000 troops, but we now have close to 85,000 soldiers on the ground in and around the airports, the harbor, and on every street and window overlooking possible escape routes from the highways. We are ready to delay the arriving troops. Over 190 mobile-command radios are now operational, every gun team is patched in, and every platoon or company of men, guns or ships can be given firing orders. Or they can just stay tuned to the running commentary from our spotters around the highways, or be ready in the harbor area for Phase Two. We even have a radio on top of the Statue of Liberty, wired directly into my Harbor Command Center on top of the south tower of the Verrazano Narrows Bridge. The bridge explosives are in place. Gentlemen, we are as ready as we could ever be."

"That means we could expect visitors any time after dawn tomorrow," added the vice admiral.

"Correct," replied the colonel. "I want all fighter aircraft in the air from here to McGuire as soon as the first incoming 747 aircraft touches down. The aircraft with the least range will take off last. The F-4s will only take off once the first empty 747 aircraft are back in the air. The incoming troops will see nobody, apart from the expected Chinese engineers refueling the aircraft and smuggling themselves on board each one. Can we trust the Chinese engineers to play their parts, Lee?"

"Yes, I believe so," replied Lee, who, with his wife and daughter, had spoken to each man one at a time and had offered whatever the man wanted to get him on their side. Only seven of the 100 engineers had not sounded happy about defecting, and another ten had been suspect. The others had welcomed the opportunity as long as they could go back and bring out as many family members as they wished once the contest had been decided. The 17 engineers that were still suspect had been placed under guard at JFK, and Majors Wong and Chong were already in place to assist with the refueling and become the new pilots of two of the incoming aircraft.

Lee was to be flown into La Guardia to help with Chinese communications at the third airport. There were only ten Chinese engineers there due to Colonel Patterson's belief that with their reduced flight size, the chairman might only use the two closest airports instead of all three.

Colonel Patterson was right. Twenty-three hours later, and two hours before dawn on a cloudy but cold morning, several aircraft entered the edge of the old, most powerful radar screen on *Blue Moon*, which was circling over McGuire at 5,000 feet to get the maximum information out of her radar capabilities.

The aircraft, in a long line, were arriving from the north and were over Prince Edward Island, 1,000 miles from New York. It would still take the aircraft two hours to reach New York, but radio messages went out over the vast mobile communication system and hundreds of truck and car engines started and landing lights and the three airports' repaired electronics and aircraft-directional systems came alive to guide the aircraft in. It took only one radio message from *Blue Moon*, who immediately prepared to land, to warn everybody. America got ready for its invasion.

Colonel Patterson had decided to monitor proceedings from Newark's control tower, and he had two other Marine majors who would be in command of the battles, if there were any, at the other two airports. Newark Liberty International Airport was far closer to the harbor area, and these incoming troops had to be taken out quicker than those from the other two airports. Twenty-five thousand troops were in hiding around Newark airport alone, all the way from the airport to the Bayonne side of the Newark Bay Bridge, which was the major ambush site for this section of the attack.

The Newark Bay Bridge was nearly 10,000 feet long. The invading troops, or the majority of them, would have to walk across it. Once they were trapped on the long bridge, they could be attacked from the air at both ends, and hopefully made to surrender if they wanted to survive.

Dozens of heavy machine guns were hidden in the buildings nearest to the Bayonne end of the bridge, and teams were ready to carry them into place and cut off the two empty stretches of highway on the bridge. With more heavy machine guns camouflaged on the other end, the only hope for the Chinese soldiers would be to jump into the freezing water, which would mean certain death.

Everyone got into their positions and waited. Preston climbed into his P-38 because at the last minute Colonel Patterson had asked him to be air cover for the Newark Bridge and be airborne to strafe the bridge, hopefully to help scare the invaders into surrendering quickly.

Another Air Force pilot was to fly his P-51, and with Martie and Carlos. They were ready to help guide the refueled and airborne 747s into McGuire if they couldn't get the American pilots aboard.

Blue Moon quickly landed and got off the radar screen. The incoming 747 pilots might have seen him. All the fighter aircraft waited. They didn't want to show up on the incoming aircraft's radar and scare them into landing somewhere else. Even after such a long flight in from China, they still had reserves of fuel to land somewhere else in the United States, even as far south as the Caribbean islands.

It took over an hour before the lead aircraft showed up on the less-powerful radar screens in the airports, and the air traffic towers from different airports watched as the 23 blips on the screen slowly came closer and began to merge into two different lines. Thirty minutes later they were just over 100 miles out and the aircraft slowly turned into a long final approach to both JFK and Newark, just as Colonel Patterson had hoped for.

Just in case some of the aircraft could peel off and still go into La Guardia, he waited until they were 20 miles out before telling all the troops at La Guardia who had access to motorized transport to get aboard and head over to JFK. It would take them an hour, but at least 1,000 more men driving in to assist the 20,000 troops already in place on the roads out of JFK would help if need be.

As the sun rose over the horizon, a small slither of light between the ocean and the lower cloud layers, the silhouetted shapes of aircraft could be seen by nearly everybody as they glided in, a mile apart, into the two airports—ten coming in from the northeast into JFK and 11 from the southeast into Newark.

It didn't look like any would change direction towards La Guardia, and the waiting became long and slow for the airport soldiers. It was still very cold and the air around them was totally silent of noise.

Everybody who had a part to play at the airports got ready, and the aircraft came swooping in to the coast of the United States from the orange-colored eastern horizon one after the other. The engineers, both Chinese and American—the Americans all wearing the well-used clothes of the termination squads long since dead—waited patiently on the runway.

At JFK, they had set up ten refueling generators, each able to pump in fuel through one pipe only. Two were normally used, one under each wing to refuel a 747-400 with 63,000 gallons, or an Airbus with over 70,000 gallons. At least 45 minutes to an hour would be needed for each plane. Since nobody expected the aircraft to fly further than McGuire or Andrews, one pipe would pump in enough for the short trip and only 20 minutes of fuel was needed to be pumped into each wing.

The colonel had reckoned on 20 minutes for the incoming pilots to be disabled and hidden somewhere in the aircraft. He also prayed that apart from the pilots who would stay aboard, none of the Chinese troops on the ground would know anything about refueling aircraft and how long it should take.

Newark only had eight generators ready to pump fuel into the 11 incoming and thirsty aircraft. It wasn't enough, and nobody had been told where the aircraft were going to land. Lee Wang had monitored satellite calls and only two calls in the last two days had been received from the enemy. One was to ask if everything was going according to plan, from a voice he didn't know. He had told them that the three airports were secure and that they would be ready within 24 hours of the phone call. He had been asked about refueling, with the other end of the call not giving away any information, and he had stated that the pumping systems were operational and ready.

The second call was from the incoming pilots telling them that they expected to be refueled and out of America within the hour. Lee had replied that they would do as good a job as possible and that there was food and drinks in the terminals for the pilots. The pilot responded that they were not allowed to leave the aircraft, but they would appreciate food and refreshments being carried aboard. The plan was set, and the American pilots got ready with trays of food and tea urns and even wore the captured engineer white coats to look as official as possible.

One by one the aircraft gently came in and landed at the two airports. It was a beautiful sight for anybody who loved flying to see the long final approach of lines of majestic aircraft as far as the eye could see. A group of 30 Chinese engineers headed by Major Wong at Newark, and a second group under Major Chong at JFK, got ready in the termination squad uniforms to welcome the troops and make it look like they were ready for their arrival.

Over 300 snipers covered the apron area on the rooftops of the terminals, dressed in white camouflage and invisible to the incoming aircraft with white sheets pulled over their rifles and bodies, which blended with the deep snow perfectly.

Men with batons directed the first aircraft into their refueling positions, and mobile stairs were towed by old cars and trucks into position by the left side doors facing the terminal, three to an aircraft. As the first engines began to die down, the fuel lines were connected to the empty wings and jet fuel began to flow. Immediately, Chinese troops dressed in green camouflage descended down the stairs and a commander walked up to the majors, who waited for them at both airports.

The Chinese commander at Newark spoke rapidly to Major Wong, bringing out a map to discuss the movement of his troops. The major responded, showing him the way out of the airport, then pointed at the map and showed him the direction of the bridge as the first aircraft slowly emptied hundreds of armed men. Wong gave several orders to his squad in Chinese, and they ran forward to assist the American Air Force technicians with the refueling underneath the first eight large aircraft.

Much the same happened at JFK. As soon as the first aircraft stopped disgorging heavily armed troops, the men in white coats were ready to climb the stairs to "feed" the pilots. Once the new pilots were aboard, the stairs were immediately pulled away to be towed to the next aircraft waiting to disembark. This move was planned to stop any of the Chinese troops from getting back into the aircraft.

The strategy went according to plan at both airports. Once the incoming troops realized that the airports were secure and that there would be no fight there, they relaxed a little as they stretched and slowly got into formation for their march to the harbor. Many had run out to surround the aircraft with a defense perimeter, and that had been expected, but no American troops were anywhere close to the apron area. Jokes were made by Wong and Chong with the incoming commanders about their ability to secure the airport, and slowly the troops were brought back to line up with the rest in front of the large refueling 747s and Airbuses.

At Newark, and only with 747s to refuel, Major Wong recognized the colonel he had run past in Shanghai's tower, but with the cold weather, they all had their faces covered, apart from their eyes, and all the people waiting for the aircraft on the aprons were mostly the Chinese engineers and heavily bundled up with winter clothing.

It didn't take long for the first companies of hundreds of men to move off towards the airport exits and out of the way. The soldiers in formation, sticking out like sore thumbs in green camouflage, started marching to the cleared roadways to get them out of the airport and in the direction of the harbor. By the time all the aircraft were empty 30 minutes later, the first troops were already a quarter of a mile away and still marching in ranks, moving down the allotted and cleared highways, unaware that they were being watched by thousands.

The first refueled 747s, already under the control of the new pilots, were beginning to start up their aircraft and move the rears of their engines around so they faced the exits, and this made the last of the troops move even faster to get out of the noise and wind blowing behind the massive engines.

Much like the operation at Shanghai Pudong Airport, as the first aircraft began moving, all the refueling stopped. The equipment was pulled away and the remaining aircraft began a rapid deployment to the end of the runway for takeoff as fast as possible.

At Newark, it took 30 more minutes for the larger number of troops to get out of the apron area. The most forward troops were already yards from the middle of the Newark Bay Bridge as the jet engines started. Shots and muffles could be heard by Major Wong in a couple of the aircraft, and the stairs were quickly pulled back from the last aircraft where it sounded like a firefight was taking place inside.

The refueling hoses were immediately hauled away, and somehow a small puddle of fuel ignited underneath one of the aircraft. The men refueling the aircraft must have lost some as they hurriedly dragged the equipment away, and suddenly the whole undercarriage area broke into flames.

"Get the other aircraft out of here," shouted Colonel Patterson in the control tower over his radio. "Fuel fire on the apron!"

Three other aircraft were still pretty close to the one on fire, and several men ran forward with fire extinguishers. A couple of dead men fell down the stairs, and now heavy rifle fire could be heard from inside the aircraft. Slowly, the other aircraft got moving, and the sound of rifle fire was drowned out as jet engines screamed everywhere moving fast to get onto the taxiway. The first 747 was already trundling down the runway at takeoff speed and about to get into the air when there was an almighty explosion and the whole 747 in front of the terminal, with dozens of men aboard, suddenly blew up. It had taken on very little fuel, but the thousand or more gallons of exploding jet fuel in her wings was enough to create a shock wave that broke all the windows in the terminals several hundred feet away. The first 747 was far enough away down the long runway to not be in harm's way, but the closest 747 less than 100 yards away was sprayed with flying debris.

Colonel Patterson shouted at the pilots to check their controls as the aircraft still trundled away from the blazing inferno. What was left of the last large aircraft and the massive cloud of smoke from the fire blinded the whole area above the apron.

"All troops in the areas around the roads, our surprise is over," shouted Colonel Patterson into his radio. "You may fire at will if you feel it necessary. November Bravo Bridge area, how many Charlies do you have on the bridge ambush area? Men manning the return roads back into the airports, make sure no Charlies get back onto the runways to the aircraft. We still have the majority of the aircraft on the ground and need 15 minutes to clear the runways. Over."

"This is Rear Command on the November Bravo Bridge, we have about 1,000 on the bridge and tons more that haven't got here yet. They have seen the explosion and several officers are discussing what to do. We have not yet opened fire. Over."

"Exit Road, November Airport Command here. We still have men passing us by; most are on the road and they are still moving forward. I see a couple of men speaking into radios. Nobody has yet opened fire. Over."

"Okay, guys, wait one. I'll get back to you," continued the colonel. "All November Airport Terminal soldiers, make way to the airport exit points. Try not to be seen, and await further orders. Juliet Foxtrot Kilo Airport, what is your current situation? Over."

"Juliet Command to Pa-Pa Bear. Our Charlies must have seen the plume of smoke from your position. The airport is clear, two aircraft in the air and six to go. We need ten minutes, and we are closing down the Van Wyck Expressway *from the terminal area and will move forward. Over."*

"Roger that. Everybody hear that? Try and stay hidden until—" Suddenly the area between the airport and the bridge erupted as thousands of guns all began firing.

"All groups! Fire at will! The war is started. All fighter aircraft get in here, hit the largest most open groups and keep your hits on the highways only. Remember, we have friendlies everywhere!" Colonel Patterson had to shout into the radio mic since he could hardly hear himself speak.

Preston had already taken off ten minutes earlier and was approaching the New York area. He could see a couple of the 747s already airborne and heard Major Wong now checking with each aircraft to see if they had control of it. Over his two radios, he also heard the F-4s taking off from McGuire 20 miles behind him as well as the three P-51s already heading out to sea just in front of the two AC-130 gunships. Everybody was in the air, and Preston was still climbing through 10,000 feet when he saw plumes of smoke already coming from the Newark Bay Bridge area.

"Air Cover to Ground Control. Where do you need me first? Over."

"Rear Bridge Command to Air Cover. We have a large bunch of Charlies who haven't reached the bridge yet and have set up a defensive perimeter. They are on the north side of the road leading up to the bridge area. I suggest you come in over the main steel skeleton atop the bridge and fire down the highway. Over."

"Confirm you have no friendlies on the actual roadway. Over."

"Roger that. We have no friendlies on asphalt. Over."

"Coming in," replied Preston, testing his guns. This time he would not be an amateur. He dove in near vertical over the dock area, and the P-38 rapidly gained speed. He aimed for the bridge and the steel skeleton structure over the center area. Preston wanted to use the four .50-caliber machine guns first, since they would do the most damage, and he noticed blackened areas of the actual roadway where there could only be masses of people lying down on the asphalt. They were hiding the white center lines of the traffic lanes from view.

At 400 miles an hour, he pulled out of his dive and for several seconds poured a thousand rounds into an area about a mile long on the north side of the road. He pulled up and went vertical, his stomach feeling like he was on a roller coaster, and then he let the right wing drop down and again went into a steep dive, taking the Hispano cannon off safety as he neared the bridge, this time coming in from the Jersey side. He aimed for the southern side and blew bits and pieces of roadway up all the way to the skeleton structure where he released the trigger. He couldn't have much ammo left.

"We are coming to join you," shouted Martie into her mic as she saw Preston rise in front of them three or four miles ahead. All but three of the 747 aircraft had already turned towards McGuire, and the F-4s were harassing the last three of the Airbuses to turn back. Something had gone wrong, and the Chinese pilots were heading out of the area with little fuel and at maximum power.

"Go in two by two," answered Preston. "Each of you pick a side of the road and strafe the area south of the bridge skeleton for about a mile."

"Roger that," replied Carlos. "Come on, Martie, let's go and get some retaliation for all the people these bastards have killed!" The two P-51s went in.

Preston came up to join the Air Force pilot in his P-51 and circled, waiting for further instructions.

"Air Cover, this is Turnpike Command. We have a retreat of Charlies trying to get back to the airport. We are not holding them. Can you come in from the south and help clear the road for us? You can't miss them; it is like a crowd coming out of a ball game."

"Air Cover, this is US1 Jersey Command. We have hundreds of Charlies still heading towards the fight. They are getting onto the highway from the main exit roads out of the airport and we would like you guys to go in before we start a ground assault. Over."

"Roger that," replied Preston. He and the pilot in his P-51 went straight into the turnpike area and strafed a mile of both sides of the road with machine guns until Preston heard the tell-tale clicks that he was out of ammo. He told Carlos and Martie to head over to US1 with their aircraft and hit the area between the entrance to the airport and the roads leading onto I-78.

"November Bravo Bridge Ground Control to Air Cover. Thanks, guys! There are bodies piled up everywhere! We are closing off the bridge and starting our ground assault. Confirm that you know there are friendlies now on the bridge. Over."

"Roger that, there are friendlies on the Bay Bridge!" stated the four pilots into their mics as they continued to pound US1 with machine guns and rocket fire. There were large masses of enemy soldiers pinned down by ground fire and now sitting ducks from the air. Over the course of ten minutes, the four old World War II fighter aircraft threw everything they had at the last stretch of road before they had to go back to refuel and rearm.

"We are out, guys. Let's go and refuel," Preston called to the three Mustangs, and for the first time, he saw smoke coming out of his Mustang's engine exhausts. He told the pilot he had damage and the pilot reported that his oil pressure was dropping and he would nurse her into McGuire. Preston put a mayday call out for assistance at McGuire and they escorted the damaged aircraft back, interrupting the landing pattern of the larger 747 commercial aircraft that were immediately diverted to Andrews further south.

They could still hear the two busy gunship crews over the radios, blasting the enemy forces outside JFK until the gunships were called into Newark to help on a side road teeming with Chinese troops— over 1,000 of them who were heading into the completely burned-out harbor area where Mike Mallory and his crew had spent their first couple of days.

Preston's Mustang, with its engine now silent, and Air Force pilot flew in and landed safely on the runway, followed by one fire truck that looked like something out of a 1930s movie. Preston was sure it had somebody ringing its bell.

The other Mustangs followed it in, landed on a second runway, and taxied up to the fuel tankers where Air Force technicians were waiting to supply the aircraft. It would take 30 minutes to get them back into the air, and the pilots stayed in their aircraft listening to the battle on the ground.

Twice more that day they went up and fired at pockets of Chinese troops hiding in locations that were hard to get at by ground troops between the harbor and both airports. Most of the action was now centered in the Newark harbor area, and the battle had gone from mass termination to pockets of troops firing at each other, along with hundreds of snipers on the roofs taking out the enemy when they saw them. By the time the three tired fighter pilots landed for the third time, the gunships were already down, the newly captured aircraft were gone and already on their way to Baghdad to pick up troops, and Preston wondered how many they had captured, and whether his Mustang's engine was destroyed.

By nightfall, over 3,000 of the Chinese troops were being held in the terminals at the two airports. The ten C-130s were taking out the wounded 60 to 100 stretchers at a time to McGuire where a hospital area in a large warehouse had been made available to process the wounded.

There were now only pockets of Chinese troops in and around the harbor area, fighting against American marines with night sights on their rifles. Since a new and final battle would commence the next day, the thousands of dead enemy bodies were checked for vital signs and satellite phones along the roads, their numbers counted and hundreds of bodies left to freeze where they lay.

A post-battle meeting was scheduled for 2200 hours that night at McGuire, and several tired commanders were flown in from the airports with the wounded to give their reports to a central command desk of personnel, who wrote down the events and losses on both sides. By ten, the meeting had gathered at McGuire. The C-130s were still bringing in wounded American soldiers and commanders who would report to the meeting and then return to move their troops closer in towards the harbor to kill any pockets as their circles tightened, and hopefully take up their new harbor positions by 3:00 am and get some sleep.

A tired and dirty group of over 50 Army, Air Force, and Marine commanders, the three airport commanders, and the dozens of pilots sat down in the 100 chairs set up for the meeting.

"Good evening, ladies and gentlemen," stated a grubby and tired Colonel Patterson. "I believe that today has been a great victory for the forces and civilians of the United States and that we have won the first day. Thanks to a combined effort, we believe that very few enemy soldiers got through to the harbor area and they will certainly be found during our battle tomorrow. At Newark Airport, we managed to capture ten of the eleven aircraft, with one being destroyed by a fuel explosion. We lost a dozen good men on that aircraft, as well as four ground crew members, two Chinese engineers, and two American engineers. At JFK, we somehow managed to lose control of three aircraft, all Airbuses. We believe that our squads of men were overwhelmed by troops stationed in certain aircraft as a precautionary measure by the enemy. The rest were overpowered. One lieutenant reported that there were a dozen enemy soldiers on the aircraft he had boarded. His troops killed all of them. They lost three men but managed to capture the aircraft and forced the pilots to land at Andrews. Several others reported that there were only pilots aboard, so either they were meant to be there, or we boarded them before all the troops had exited. Unfortunate, but with the loss of 54 brave men in total, of which seven were Air

Force pilots, we managed to increase our growing fleet by sixteen usable aircraft, which are already halfway to Baghdad to pick up troops. By the way, we have the initial group of aircraft scheduled for arrival in Newark at 2300 hours tonight—another 6,000 troops coming in to help with tomorrow's battle.

"To recap, we lost one 747 at Newark and the only Airbus destroyed was fired on by our F-4s after the pilots refused to change course. The two other Airbuses following the lead aircraft quickly turned around. It was a total waste, because the Chinese crew only had enough fuel for an hour's flight time, but our pilots could see armed troops with guns at the heads of both the pilots in the Airbus cockpit. The onboard soldiers must have unfortunately overpowered our guys again. One 747 and a second Airbus 380 have damage from bullet holes through windows and through several of the cockpit flight controls, but they landed safely and are being checked out as we speak. If they can't fly, we can at least use their working electronics in the dozens of dead 747-400s sitting around here in the United States. Thanks to you, our million troops overseas can be returned to the United States within three months now instead of eight."

The colonel paused briefly for the applause from the crowd. "I believe that they have lost the ability to fly in more troops, which makes it easier for us from now on. As far as the ground battle is concerned, we got all their men out of the airports, which are safe again. We had our soldiers go in behind them and create havoc once the air cover had done their job.

"We believe that 12,000 troops landed in 21 aircraft. So far, we have 3,450 wounded and non-wounded enemy prisoners under guard in the two airports, and we are still flying their wounded to our military hospital setups here and at Andrews. We have not counted all the bodies, since there are still hundreds around side roads and in alleyways, but a search is going on right now.

"Enemy deaths so far are close to 6,200. We have collected only seven satellite phones and 103 backpack radios. The commanders believe that at least another 1,500 to 2,000 bodies are not yet counted, which means that we could have between 500 and 1,000 enemy troops wandering around our streets, and I'm sure several of them can communicate with each other. Hopefully they will all be accounted for by dawn.

"Ladies and gentlemen, our losses are substantial. At the airports, as I said, we lost 54 good Air Force men. Newark highways area lost 147 Army soldiers, Newark dock area lost 45 marines, Van Wyck Expressway is short 41 Army soldiers and ten marines, Nassau Expressway lost 59 Army soldiers, and the Belt Parkway lost 87 marines. The total of American fatalities so far is up to 443 with another 296 wounded and 17 critical. We have one aircraft with several rounds through its engine that cannot be repaired before tomorrow's battle.

"Twenty-four hours from now we should be victorious. We are expecting ten ships—five container ships and five military vessels. I'm certain that many of the enemy soldiers walking our streets don't know the whole story, and hopefully the sketchy details from these commanders will not affect the main battle. I'm looking forward to tomorrow. We have reliable information that all the enemy commanders except one are aboard the aircraft carrier, and it all depends on how they enter under the Narrows Bridge tomorrow.

"Folks, our American civilians need that massive amount of food coming in. It could feed cities for months, so we must not harm any of those container ships. We will have over a thousand snipers placed around the docks that will pick off anybody who shows their head once the five container ships have docked.

"After that, it's open hunting season on the military vessels, and we have so much ammunition around here that I think we could put the earth out of alignment!"

Everyone laughed. "We have 20 squads of Navy Seals ready to climb aboard the container ships, and the snipers will back off once they go aboard.

"Their supreme aircraft carrier fighters can only stay airborne for three to four hours at the most, and when their runway sinks, they either die in freezing water, or land at one of our airports and introduce themselves to one of our welcoming committees. None of our aircraft, except the three F-4s, have any defense against what I believe is approximately 30 of their heavily armed fighters. I'm sure that they will have helicopters somewhere on their ships, and those can easily be taken out by heat-seeking missiles, of which we have hundreds. Once their fighters have used up their rockets and guns, then can our aircraft take to the skies, but they are fast and you will have to shoot well to hit them. At that time, the best we can manage to defend ourselves is to prevent the howitzers on the ground from getting pelted by these fighters."

For another ten minutes the colonel went on about the three different scenarios possible in New York Harbor. Several questions were asked about ground troops, and he replied that all American ground troops would be converging into the harbor area, making sure that the thousands of troops aboard the ships didn't reach dry land. A second meeting would be held in two hours' time, with the artillery, rocket, and mortar sections to coordinate fire missions. With American submarines and warships in the harbor, they did not need friendly fire.

* * *

The last meeting of the Politburo was held at the same time in the meeting room of the aircraft carrier, now only 300 miles out of New York Harbor. The room was full with the 14 men, minus Mo Wang, whom nobody had seen for a couple of days, and several of the Red Guard commanders. The captains of the nine other vessels were on video screens piped in from their ships and the fighter aircraft commander was also in attendance. The chairman was on his satellite phone listening in to his panicked commanders on the ground in New York.

"What do you mean that you don't know where you are!?" he shouted to some poor guy on the other end. "Ask an American how to get to the docks! Of course we expected some form of fight, that's why you are there, you stupid man! I already know that all the aircraft took off and are on their way back to China. Several others have confirmed seeing them leave. Yes, we lost a couple, but that's war, Major Fu. Now get your men to the harbor area and I'm sure you will find thousands of other men waiting for you who will laugh at you for getting lost. How many men did you say you have with you? 23? How many did you have to start with? 500!? Major Fu, may I suggest that they are not dead, just lost like you, and are waiting with the others.

"I have been told by several commanders that the fighting was sporadic and there were not more than a thousand American soldiers and several old propeller aircraft. I don't want to listen to any more of your problems, Major Fu. Go and find the harbor and secure it for our arrival tomorrow. Remember, we still have another 4,000 men aboard these ships that will certainly pitch the battle in our favor."

The chairman angrily hung up on the poor man, lost somewhere without lights in a dock area he didn't know and surrounded by snipers with night sights. Major Fu wouldn't see another dawn.

"And we call these troops our finest?" snapped the angry chairman at the crowd listening to his conversation. "What has happened to our youth? Wait until our real crack troops get on American soil tomorrow! I want all American males terminated within 20 city blocks of the harbor area. I don't need any more problems when I step ashore—just female Americans, happy to see their new leader's arrival."

For the rest of the day, the Politburo went over the plans for the invasion of their new country. Several times, the chairman asked one of his aides to get one of the pilots of the 747 aircraft on the phone, but he couldn't get through. The chairman wanted to get the next load of backup troops in as fast as possible. For the first time in his career, he was slightly worried about his master plan.

The sailors on board the ships prepared for their arrival in New York just after dawn the next morning.

It's weird that weather often doesn't play its part in well thought-out plans. It is also likely that bad weather for one person is good weather for another.

At dawn on the morning of January 20th, and after an inch of fresh snow in the New York area overnight, the sun rose behind the thick clouds that had formed along the northern coast of the United States. A light snow was still falling, and thousands of men huddled for warmth in their thick white winter fatigues, brewed warm energy drinks from their ration packs, and cleaned and prepared their weapons.

The incoming ships couldn't be seen by most of the American forces, but radar from the Coast Guard C-130 circling ten miles offshore and to the west of New York could see the blips on their screens perfectly. The ten ships were now stationary, three miles offshore, and Colonel Patterson—receiving a continuous feed in his cold command center on top of the right tower of the Verrazano Narrows Bridge and underneath white tents—was totally blinded by the clouds hanging well below his vantage point.

He now depended totally on the C-130's continuous information, flying at 5,000 feet. If her radar screen could see the ships, the ship's radar screens could see her. The colonel had placed her ten miles back from shore to make it look like she was just patrolling, and a second and third C-130 were also visible on the ship's radar over Washington D.C. and Philadelphia, making it look like New York wasn't the only area with air patrol. He didn't want the invading forces to think that the United States was totally useless. It wouldn't look right.

The C-130 bait aircraft was 20 miles west of the harbor area and directly over Morrisville Airport in New Jersey. She could easily be attacked with sea-to-air missiles. Colonel Patterson was hoping that she would get their fighters airborne, and in either scenario, the attack would take time to reach her and she could sink down and disappear into ground cover within seconds of a missile or aircraft being launched. Also, the first missiles would be satellite-guided, and Lee Wang was ready to scramble the satellite feeds to disrupt any incoming missiles and make them useless.

The vacant ground in and around Morrisville Municipal Airport where the C-130 would land once attacked from the aircraft carrier was filled with all sorts of anti-aircraft weapons pulled in from dozens and dozens of military bases from New Jersey and the surrounding states.

Forty M-163 Vulcan anti-aircraft vehicles were ready, placed under trees and next to hangars on the airfield. Even though they were old and many had been pulled out of museums, their 3,000 rounds per minute were deadly for any aircraft if they found their mark.

Several old Bradley fighting vehicles with cannons and TOW missiles had arrived from the Ohio area, 35 Mutts (jeeps) with TOW missiles and dozens more vehicles—mostly old jeeps with all types of cannons made to be temporary anti-aircraft defense vehicles—waited for targets, any targets, and Colonel Patterson hoped that the one lame duck could be the beginning of an ambush for the more advanced hawks—the hawks that would have to fly in close under the low cloud base to see what was so important below the single aircraft.

Another hundred antiquated units, mostly with TOW missiles, had been positioned between the Verrazano Narrows Bridge and around the New York harbor area and could open up on the aircraft if needed. The destroyers and frigates could also fire at the C-130, but that would give their complete element of surprise away to the enemy, and as the slow sun rose and the dark skies became a lighter grey, nothing happened.

Sporadic shooting had been heard throughout the night as snipers around the harbor shot at anything that moved on the streets below. There were few civilians in the area—any people the military had met the day before had been given a case of military rations per person and told to get out of the area. Dozens of city blocks in New York and New Jersey were covered with snipers on the roofs of every building, and it was two hours before dawn before everything went quiet as the snow began to fall and the snipers moved lower and lower to street level to make sure nobody was missed.

Nobody was in a great hurry on the enemy ships out at sea. Their powerful engines kept them still in the calm water and thousands of men waited for the chairman to give his command to start the day's action. He was on deck sniffing the air and looking towards the dark grey shoreline three miles away. The American coastline could just be seen through the tapering snow and, drinking from a large china cup of steaming green tea, he held off the attack, hoping that the clouds would lift with the sun's rays warming the area and giving them more sight. He wanted to watch the action unfold.

For another ten minutes, he drank from his cup, leaning on the balcony of the ship, just looking towards his new country. Several camouflaged military personnel around him waited with their aides wearing backpack radios to communicate his orders. He had been told about the three aircraft on the radar screens and had asked his Air Force commander why the closest American airplane was so far from shore. The commander had replied that either it was air support for ground troops coming into New York to fight or it was the Americans' early-warning system using its radar to search for incoming aircraft or shipping.

"So they already know that we are here, three miles offshore?" the chairman asked, and the man confirmed that. "They still have guided missiles that can destroy our aircraft?" he then asked. Again the commander nodded to confirm this.

"But our aircraft's satellite-guided missiles can attack their aircraft from a much further distance. Also, their aircraft can take off once ours take off, as they will see our aircraft taking off on their radar screens, yes?" was the chairman's next question as he drank the last sip of tea. He looked around and noticed that the snow had stopped, and even though the temperature was slightly below freezing, the clouds had risen slightly and he could just make out the towers of the Verrazano Narrows Bridge, which in an hour or two he would officially rename as the aircraft carrier passed under. The Air Force commander confirmed the chairman's last question, and then it got serious. "How long can our fighters stay in the air?" he asked.

"Three to four hours depending on fuel usage. Less than one hour if they are in battle conditions," replied the commander.

"Let's take our new country, gentlemen," the chairman ordered. "Admiral, send in the five food ships. I want to know what or who is going to attack us, and I want to make sure our engineers and our troops are in the harbor area and not American soldiers like our commander said yesterday. I hear no shooting or loud explosions, and I believe everything is quiet and ready. I want 12 fighters to take off and go and destroy that pesky fly out there and destroy everything below where that American plane is flying. Get ready to refuel and rearm those aircraft when they return, and then get the remainder of the aircraft off the carrier once any enemy contact has been made. I want as much ammunition on deck to resupply the aircraft as quickly as possible. It will be safe on deck once we have the second flight of aircraft in the air to protect us. Tell the first wave to go in low, and as soon as they get halfway to that American aircraft, the first fighter will release their missiles to blow it out of the sky. That will be the start of the battle. Get the container ships into the off-loading facilities as quickly as possible. Our ground troops should be ready and our engineers will be there to welcome the container ships. Admiral, since we don't have tugs to help the ships berth, tell them to be careful and to follow the simple berthing plan we have given them. Make sure that the container ship with the 1,500 Red Guards ready to scale down her sides goes in first, just in case."

Orders were communicated, and ships began to creep forward again inch by inch as the massive engines powered them. The whine of jet engines could be heard several flights below as the chairman looked down to survey the action on the flight deck. He was extremely excited for the first time in his life.

* * *

"We see heat spots increasing on the carrier deck, and we are descending to 2,500 feet," stated the radar engineers in *Blue Moon* as she hung in the air above Morrisville Airport, the 400 men below ready to fire on any incoming aircraft once the enemy opened fire.

"Roger that," replied Colonel Patterson. "Immediately after the last fighter takes off, get her down onto the ground, into the prepared snow-walled area, get her propellers stopped, and get the white tarps over her. Gentlemen, I believe you will have five minutes once their missiles are scrambled by us and go into space before they come in with guns blazing. All anti-aircraft commanders around Morrisville only—open fire once the first missile is released.

"All harbor troops, I've been told of ship movement, and the five container ships are edging forward. Do not fire on them until ordered. I repeat, no harbor gunfire until my direct order. Please confirm that!" Hundreds of radios replied with their confirmation. "I believe that all five ships will dock on either side of that one Global Terminal area. The snipers will be ordered to fire once the first ships are secure and our guys are safely out of harm's way. Wong—if the war out here hasn't started and it's safe for you to do so, go out and wave to our official welcoming party at the terminal. Get dozens of the large welcoming silver helium balloons into the air and look happy. We want to entice the other ships in ASAP and the balloons will help screw up their aiming systems."

"We have the first aircraft off the carrier," reported *Blue Moon*. *"We are going into final approach and will land once they form up and come towards us. Have fun, guys, enjoy it! Out."*

The aircraft dropped down to 1,500 feet, turned onto very short finals, less than a mile out, and literally dropped out of the sky towards the runway. Once down, she would shoot straight into her little hideaway surrounded by snow walls ten feet high and large white tarpaulins would be draped over her. She was no match for the incoming fighters.

One by one the fighters took off. The first aircraft turned right, out to sea, and then came over the aircraft carrier at 500 feet as the 12th one left the steel runway and rose up to join them. The rest, 17 aircraft, were already being lifted up to the flight deck from below and being prepared for takeoff, as were three helicopters that would go in and survey the harbor for any form of shipping or a surprise ground attack.

"The American aircraft is landing," stated the first Chinese fighter pilot on their secret radio frequency as he noticed the C-130 getting lower and lower on his modern radar screen.

"Permission to destroy the aircraft?"

"Permission granted," was the reply, and he toggled the switch and two of the world's most modern Russian missiles left his aircraft and sped towards *Blue Moon*, 15 miles ahead.

"Missiles hot," the forward radar position on the other tower of the Verrazano Narrows Bridge reported to the colonel and Lee Wang. Still at McGuire with all the other pilots and aircraft ready to go, Lee activated the scrambling software he and Carlos had designed a couple of days earlier.

The Chinese fighter pilot was surprised to see his rockets suddenly turn skywards and begin to go vertical, not something he had expected. He ordered his next two aircraft to fire their missiles at the C-130, who was now only 500 feet above the ground. They locked their missiles onto her and four new missiles sped forward, yet also went vertical following the heat ejections of the first rocket motors towards space.

"Missile malfunction," reported the pilot over the radio. "Changing to heat-seeking missiles, two locked and launched," he said calmly as his next two shot forward and the C-130 landed. Three seconds later the missiles lost their target as dozens of silver balloons were released from the airfield ten miles ahead and hundreds of already warm military engines started to mess up the missiles' telemetry. One of the missiles went into an old truck driving down the road a couple of miles in front, and the other headed into an empty burned-out strip mall where some form of fire must have been smoldering.

"Missile failure," reported the lead aircraft. "It looks like an airfield where the American aircraft went in, and we are starting to get return fire from units on the ground," he added as a couple of aircraft easily dodged the sidewinders aimed at them.

"Go in and destroy the airfield with the rest of your missiles at close range," was the reply from the Air Force commander as he looked towards the container ships cruising a mile in front of the rest of the stationary naval flotilla. They would be under the bridge in about ten minutes. All was still quiet as he watched his three helicopters take off from below him and turn towards the bridge.

"We have three helos incoming. Keep your heads down—no movement, no firing—and make sure they can't see you. Look like snow, guys, and bury deep," ordered the colonel as he saw the helicopters coming towards him.

Now only five miles from the airport, the wing commander in the lead aircraft ordered his fighters to lock onto targets as suddenly a wall of tracer bullets erupted from the airfield in front and came towards them, blowing up the aircraft to his left just as he ordered the aircraft to split up and fire at anything that moved on the airfield. Missiles were locked onto the hangars, which had been emptied for the occasion and had coal stoves inside each of them omitting heat. The buildings were like saunas inside. Several missiles left their launchers as dozens of lines of cannon tracer came up to meet them. A couple of the missiles flew straight into the wall of incoming fire and exploded, which rocked the lead aircraft.

The fighters banked to the left and right, some going higher, some diving to get closer to the ground, when everybody on the airfields began firing as fast as possible. Two aircraft erupted into balls of flame as they were hit and several of the empty hangars blew up as the missiles reached them.

"Take out anything hot you can find," ordered the wing commander as his aircraft suddenly shuddered underneath his seat, and he watched as his right wing began to fall apart and separate itself from the rest of the aircraft. His ejection seat worked fast and he was out of the aircraft seconds before it began its death dive, exploding just before it hit the ground. His parachute opened several seconds before he hit the roof of a flat building, breaking his right leg on impact and knocking him out.

At the same time, the helicopters came in low over the bridge, and Colonel Patterson ordered two groups of five Mutt units armed with a TOW missile on each to be uncovered on the road several hundred yards south and north of the bridge to take out the three helicopters only half a mile away flying just above his height above the right tower of the bridge. The helicopter pilots would be able to see their deployments pretty soon, as well as the men on the towers from this close a range.

All three of the helicopters immediately tried to dodge the incoming missiles, but this was close-range shooting and the TOW missiles followed their movements. Colonel Patterson felt the shock waves of the exploding helicopters as all three blew up less than 300 yards from him.

"Well done, Mutts. Run! Get out of there. I'm sure the ships immediately located your jeep positions, run!" the colonel shouted. He saw dots of light as several of the ship's guns fired, and seconds later both areas where the old jeeps had stood exploded into orange balls of flame. "Hold your fire around the harbor!" he ordered, as he trained his binoculars onto the firefight going on 20 miles away at the Morrisville airport.

* * *

"Why did our helicopters explode?" shouted the chairman to his Air Force commander as the two frigates 300 hundred yards away began firing at the shoreline.

"They were hit with missiles from either side of the bridge, but the Americans are now history," the man replied, as they all saw large fireballs climb skyward on both sides of the bridge.

"Don't hit my bridge, Admiral," warned the chairman.

They watched as the first container ship reached the bridge, was not attacked, and carried on into New York Harbor.

* * *

The fighting at the airport was in full force. Most of the hangars were burning, and the remaining seven fighters were spending much of their time dodging tracers and incoming missiles from every direction. Another aircraft exploded and several vehicles on the ground did the same as they were hit by cannon fire.

The men on the ground had fared reasonably well. They went into the empty hangars as planned, destroying one to two guns that were too close. But now that the airfield was on fire, the enemy fighters began to take out the ground fire with what they had left. The cannons on the ground were red hot as rounds were fed into them as fast as was possible, and the men behind the sights followed the aircraft a couple of miles out as they turned and came in firing cannons in return. Another two were hit as several more ground units exploded. There were just too many vehicles to aim at.

Suddenly the fighters pulled away and the gunners followed them as they retreated back to their ship, hitting one more aircraft before the area went silent.

"Morrisville, your kills and losses, please?" asked Colonel Patterson as he saw several dots getting closer from the smoky area that was the other battle zone.

"Morrisville reporting," stated someone whose voice Patterson didn't recognize. *"Commander took a direct hit. I counted seven aircraft down and the last one left with oil pouring out of its ass."*

"Roger, I have it visual. It just went into the ground," replied the colonel. "I count four returning to the mother ship. Harbor area, do not—I say do not—fire at the returning aircraft until I give direct orders. Morrisville, continue. Over."

"I've seen about 15 direct hits down here. The C-130 is okay and we have the two medic trucks driving through the airport gates. Every airport building is destroyed. Over."

"Well done, guys! You did a good job," commended the colonel to whomever he was speaking. "Get your wounded sorted out fast, you only have ten minutes max. *Blue Moon*, get airborne. Morrisville airfield, prepare for a second round of incoming as she gets airborne. Out. Bridge spotters, a sitrep please?"

"All five container ships have passed under the bridge and are currently two miles from the Global Terminal. There are hundreds of soldiers on board. We see four aircraft returning to the carrier, which is still about two miles out, and we believe that others are about to take off. Without our airborne eyes, we can't tell precisely. Over."

As he said that, another fighter took off from the carrier and headed out to sea. It would take *Blue Moon* another five minutes to get airborne, and this time they didn't know where the aircraft would be heading, but at least eight were history.

"*The two destroyers are moving this way,*" added the observation post on the other tower. "*It looks like they are all slowly turning to head in.*"

"Okay, guys, we are about to warm up around here. Harbor troops, you heard that the container ships are swarming with Charlies. Snipers, you will be ready to fire once I give the order. You should be well in range in about ten minutes. Make each round count."

On the buildings around the Global Terminal, 300 snipers had regrouped from the roadways around the harbor and airport areas. Now each one was ready for the incoming ships with mountains of ammo and each one was within 1,000 yards of the terminal depot.

* * *

"What happened to our fighters?" demanded an angry chairman as he saw four fighters line up to land. Another 12 had taken off and were now circling over the ships as they turned towards the bridge to follow the container ships into New York Harbor.

"I don't know," replied the Air Force commander. "I assume that we hit their main Air Force airport, as it was extremely well defended."

"We will go back once we have taken their harbor and destroy everything around there. Can those defenses attack our aircraft over the harbor?" asked the chairman.

"No, Comrade Chairman," was the reply. "The air base is at least 20 miles away and too far to be of any trouble."

"Get those fighters over the harbor bridge. I want air cover as we go in. You can get the remaining fighters off the ship as soon as these others come in," he ordered.

There were only five more fighters that were ready, and the Air Force commander wanted to wait to get all nine off together. By that time, he reckoned he would know all the strengths of the opposition forces and could then take them out. He had missed the information that the other naval ships were now heading for the harbor. He felt that they were moving, but the aircraft carrier had to wait, pointing north to get the last two aircraft aboard still flying in from the south.

The two Chinese frigates quickly entered the harbor under the bridge, their guns bristling in all directions as they arrogantly swept in under the bridge at 20 knots, keeping to the main shipping lane in the middle of the river.

* * *

"Everybody keep down. I want the carrier in if we can. Snipers, hold your fire. How far out are the container ships from docking? Over."

"The first one is entering the enclosed water now," reported the command center by the cargo terminal. They were stationed in one of the massive cranes that the engineers had spent three days getting to work again. *"They have formed a line and seem to know where they are going. The third ship is about 700 yards directly behind the first one, and the second one is aiming herself towards the south wharf to her left. The fourth one is beginning to follow her. Over."*

The waiting was becoming tense. Slowly, the fighters landed back on the carrier's deck as the second dozen circled at a couple of thousand feet above her. The destroyers were already halfway to the bridge, and it had looked like they had slowed slightly to give the much larger ship time to catch up.

Colonel Patterson looked through a powerful telescope he had brought for the occasion—far more powerful than his binoculars—and he saw pallets of what looked like missiles and boxes of cannon rounds being brought up to her flight deck via several elevators. He counted nine aircraft on her deck area and three more helicopters. One had its rotor running and it took off as he watched.

Several minutes later, the carrier was moving slowly towards the bridge and the helicopter came directly towards him only a mile away. "Do we have any more Mutts with TOWS?" he asked into his radio. "I have another helo coming in over the sea."

"We have two Mutts with TOWS 100 yards further north of the last ones, but no more on the south side," somebody replied.

"Take out the helo in 30 seconds and run for cover. Anti-aircraft weapons on the north side only open fire on any incoming aircraft once the Mutts fire, but not before, and make your first shots count. The aircraft will turn your area into a disaster zone if you are slow. Over."

"Roger that," said several voices.

Thirty seconds later, everybody saw the stripes of light head towards the helicopter, and it turned into a white blaze of fire as it disappeared from all radar screens. The ships were waiting this time, and several seconds later the whole area around the two old Mutts erupted into flames and their metal lives quickly came to an end.

Colonel Patterson knew that he had at least another 40 of these vehicles around the harbor, but very few that could shoot at the seaward side of the bridge.

The fighters peeled away from the carrier and came into the area in a single line, throwing missiles into every building surrounding the latest cloud. Over 50 guns and missiles immediately returned fire, and three of the first fighters exploded, only a couple hundred yards from shore. A fourth went straight into a ten-story building and blew up inside, and slowly the whole structure collapsed onto itself.

The remaining eight fighters turned in all directions to escape the enemy ground fire, and another was hit at a low altitude as it turned sharply to the north and directly over the shoreline.

* * *

"Get the ships to terminate that whole area," screamed the chairman, as he watched the destruction of his valuable aircraft. "Get those others into the air! Kill the Americans!" he screamed at the Air Force commander.

"They can't take off until we turn north to south—the wind is too strong for a side wind takeoff," replied the Air Force commander.

"I don't want to hear excuses—get those last fresh aircraft off now," ordered the chairman.

"I can't, Comrade Chairman! They will be destroyed!"

"Must I do everything myself, you stupid man?" replied the commander as another aircraft exploded going into the area north of the bridge and all four warships opened up their large guns. He grabbed the handset out of the shocked commander's hand and ordered every aircraft off his aircraft carrier, or they would be fired at by the guns aboard the ship. Engines immediately began to whine as he threw the handset down and again surveyed the scene.

* * *

"Submarine command center, fire full torpedoes towards the frigates. They are coming about and will pass in front of you about 400 yards out in 50 seconds. At that range, they should be sitting ducks with all their attention on the north side. I believe that you will only have one chance to take out both ships, sailors, because our boys are taking one hell of a pounding up there.

"Snipers, commence firing! The cat is out of the bag."

"Artillery, I want you to wait for the more powerful destroyers and keep your sights on them as they enter under the bridge. They are only a mile away and are at full steam coming in with their guns blazing hot.

"Shit, there are aircraft readying for takeoff from the aircraft carrier. Don't they know they can't take off in a strong side wind? It must be 20 knots out there."

The colonel watched in wonder as the first fighter left the carrier, its pilot totally inexperienced with any form of carrier takeoff other than perfect ones, and his aircraft left the forward part of the deck, flipped over and dove right into the sea.

The second pilot, a quick learner, managed to not get his wing pulled over by the breeze and slowly wobbled his aircraft in the air. He was too close to the bridge as the third one also took off and followed the second one up into the air in a wobbly ascent. The second aircraft flew between the destroyers and under the Verrazano

Narrows Bridge, where there was a Mutt waiting with a TOW. It blew up and crashed into the water.

The fourth pilot dove into the water like the first one, and the third fighter tried hard to turn before the bridge and slammed into the pylons in the middle of the bridge under full power, with exploding debris flying in all directions on the roadway, before hitting the water.

The Air Force commander stopped the final aircraft from taking off, and the chairman pulled out a pistol he had in his belt and shot the man in the forehead. He did not like his orders being interfered with.

The frigates pounded the northern area, and smoke poured forth as the destroyers reached the bridge and stopped firing at the shore. Suddenly both frigates lit up and rose out of the water like lighted candles as torpedoes hit them each from end to end, immediately blowing up their fuel bunkers and ammunition holds. Nobody aboard had even had time to sound the alarm as the torpedoes came in fast and accurate. The two most modern frigates of the Chinese Navy slumped back into the water and disappeared within seconds, only their very top towers standing out above the water level. The destroyers had already changed course and headed into the area.

"All howitzers, submarines, fire at will. South shore anti-aircraft guns and missiles, get the rest of those fighter aircraft. They are incoming from the south and looking for trouble. The carrier is a quarter of a mile from the bridge and still coming. All aircraft, get your asses off the ground—we need air cover in ten minutes."

Suddenly, the colonel couldn't hear himself speak as every gun around the harbor threw whatever it had at the two destroyers, both at full speed at about 30 knots and blowing holes into anything they thought deadly. He watched as dozens of white tarpaulins were pulled away from the howitzers. As in a ballet, they all turned together to face the destroyers that were broadside to many of them and the air below him completely filled with lead.

There were dozens of guns on each ship, and everything they had lit up to fight back. The 155mm rounds began hitting the sides of the ships, and some were so close that they went into the hardened armor. One of the destroyers lit up like both of the frigates had done and literally rose into the air, her bow leaving the water for a split second and then crashing down. It kept going, explosions erupting from every part of her, and she went straight down and keeled over, showing her hull.

Colonel Patterson directed the fire onto the second destroyer as the aircraft came over for a second sweep, and several big guns blew up on the south side in the park—two of the aircraft never made it out of their dives and went straight in, killing many Americans.

He could only see three remaining aircraft, and they were heading south and coming in for a third run when he looked over towards the aircraft carrier. She must have had her engines in reverse, as mountains of water was rising up her rear end, but she was still coming forward at about 15 knots, now only 200 yards from the bridge.

The colonel looked back into the harbor area, telling the engineers with the explosives on the bridge to get ready. The second destroyer was plastering the south shore as he saw three torpedoes head in her direction. They were aimed towards her aft, and she nimbly turned to face the area and the torpedoes passed her by.

The next two torpedoes were side by side, 100 yards behind the first three. She sprayed the water area around the shoreline with fast anti-submarine guns. There was a large balloon of water as one of the submarines took what the colonel thought was a direct hit before the destroyer leaned horribly over as the two torpedoes hit her on her starboard bow area. Both torpedoes had come from the submarine she had just hit, and they opened up her bow like a can of sardines. This time, there was no explosion. She just slowed and began sinking from the bow, her tail lifting out of the water. She slid most of the way into the water before she stopped—her bow must have touched bottom.

The aircraft carrier's bow then slipped under the bridge several hundred feet below, still moving forward at three to four knots, her engines still in reverse. Slowly she was being brought to a halt.

The last fighter, desperate to remain alive, tried to come in from the east onto her aft deck, and the sprays of water literally lifted the aircraft up and threw it onto the high deck where it exploded into a ball of flame. This set off a massive explosion where the supplies had been placed on the deck, and a second, even larger explosion sent shock waves all the way up to where Colonel Patterson calmly watched.

There wasn't much left to do, apart from looking at the aircraft carrier trying its best to get into reverse, but even though the engines were working at full power, it took a lot of time for a ship of that size to change direction. The smoke from the area was everywhere, and all of the firing from the big guns had stopped.

Colonel Patterson asked about aircraft. Their own F-4s were now overhead, and two of the pilots stated that they were already forcing one of the enemy aircraft down into Newark and there were two more, empty of weapons that needed guidance, and they wanted to collect. Preston came on the air stating that he, Carlos and Martie had one aircraft between them and were working on forcing it down into JFK, and the third gunship came online a few seconds later also saying that it was being helped by *Blue Moon,* who had arrived to show a third pilot the way into Newark. The F-4 pilots stated that theirs was now down—one of the F-4s was flying on top of it so that it couldn't take off again, and the other two screamed up to search for the last two remaining aircraft.

This was all happening while Colonel Patterson kept his eyes on the aircraft carrier and his ears glued to the radio announcements. Suddenly the aircraft carrier's smaller guns started blasting away at the aircraft in the sky, tracers going up from the forward area inside the harbor and its rear guns outside the harbor mouth. It took another three seconds before the massive tower of the aircraft carrier towered directly under the middle of the bridge. Its forward movement stopped, and it slowly, inch by inch, started moving backwards, back out to sea.

* * *

With the dead body of his Air Force commander slumped on the floor of the bridge, the chairman took over the battle. He had ordered the frigates to fire into every building around the harbor area and destroy every visible building. Again, it was under his orders that the two destroyers went in under full power a few seconds before both frigates erupted into massive explosions.

Then he ordered the aircraft carrier to full steam ahead to catch up with the destroyers. The admiral tried to intervene and suggest that the carrier stay outside until the battle was over, but he was told to shut up. Then the first destroyer blew up and a couple of his fighters dropped into the harbor a mile or so away. It was then that the chairman realized that he might not be competent to fight a battle such as this one, and he ordered the admiral to take over.

The admiral immediately ordered the carrier's engines into full reverse, and the chairman shouted into his radio for all the troops on the container ships to get off and kill everybody they saw. They did that, and hundreds of Red Guards came down the sides of the ships on ropes, only to be mowed down by the waiting American troops. Their falling bodies turned the water red around the first four ships.

The two American destroyers approached the second Chinese destroyer, whose captain hadn't even seen the two old World War destroyers firing shells into her as fast as their nine 105mm guns on each ship could. It wasn't only the two torpedoes that blew his modern destroyer apart, but well over 70 rounds from the rapidly firing guns on the old destroyers that went into her before she sank.

The last container ship was not yet docked, and she had her engines in full reverse when the nearest destroyer fired a round into her bridge, killing everybody there. The engineers below deck closed down her engines as they felt the vibrations of the explosions vibrate badly through the whole vessel.

The vessel was still moving and now out of control. Ropes were shot over her bow and stern by the destroyers. The few soldiers on board who tried to shoot back were mowed down by several heavy machine guns on both American ships. Once the crew realized that they had no chance, they waved white flags and secured the ropes as the destroyers, acting as tugs, slowly stilled the massive ship 20 times bigger than they were.

The chairman was in shock. Minutes earlier he had ordered his Politburo up on deck to be with him as they went under the bridge. He was excited about renaming the bridge, but then as the men arrived, everything seemed to go wrong.

The 14 men looked on in disbelief as one ship after the other exploded, and they all held on as the vibrations of the engines in reverse tried to still the large ship. Slowly, they inched under the bridge, and the chairman put his hands up for silence. He shouted out as loud as he could, "This bridge will now be renamed the…." Suddenly hundreds of massive explosions filled the air from the bridge directly above them, shutting him up once and for all.

Hundreds of blinding explosions hurt their eyes and deafened their ears from the noise as the bridge span above them was ripped away from the two towers. Very slowly the whole structure above the aircraft carrier began to descend, gathering speed as it fell right on top of them.

The chairman of Zedong Electronics—the most powerful man in the world, the man who had already killed one third of the world's population—still had his arms outstretched as tons of steel and cement came down, crushing the whole tower of the aircraft carrier and imploding the steel structure into the flight deck as if it were paper. It turned everything underneath it into hamburger meat, and the whole bridge hit and then sliced and diced the dying ship in two. Within seconds, there was nothing left apart from rolling water and explosions, as hundreds of pockets of air boiled back up to the surface.

The whole bridge, the Politburo, the chairman of the New World, and the entire aircraft carrier were gone—gone forever.

To Be Continued in…

INVASION USA III
The Battle for Survival

INVASION USA IV
The Battle for Houston
The Aftermath

Please visit our Facebook page:

Facebook.com/TIWadeAuthor

to become a friend of the INVASION USA Series, get updates on new releases, read interesting blogs and connect with the author.

About the Author

T I WADE was born in Bromley, Kent, England, in 1954.

His father, a banker, was promoted with his international bank to Africa, and the young family moved to Africa in 1956.

The author grew up in Southern Rhodesia (now Zimbabwe) and his life there is humorously described in his novel, EASY COME EASY GO, Volume II of the Book of Tolan series. Once he had completed his mandatory military commitments, at 21 he left Africa to mature in Europe.

He enjoyed Europe and lived in three countries, England, Germany and Portugal, for 15 years before returning to Africa, Cape Town, in 1989.

Here the author owned and ran a restaurant, a coffee manufacturing and retail business, flew a Cessna 210 around desolate southern Africa and finally got married in 1992.

Due to the upheavals of the political turmoil in South Africa, the Wade family of three moved to the United States in 1996. Park City, Utah, was where his writing career began.

To date, T I Wade has written fifteen novels.

The author, his wife and two teenage children currently live 20 miles south of Raleigh, North Carolina.

Printed in Great Britain
by Amazon.co.uk, Ltd.,
Marston Gate.